DIARY OF A
SOUL DOCTOR

from the *Ashington Casebooks*

compiled by Dr. Jack Rivers

Other Books by Caitlín Matthews:

The Barefoot Book of Princesses
The Blessing Seed: A Creation Story for a New Millennium
The Celtic Book of Days,
The Celtic Book of the Dead
The Celtic Devotional
Celtic Love: Ten Enchanted Tales
Celtic Memories
The Celtic Tradition
The Celtic Spirit: Daily Meditations For the Turning Year
Celtic Visions
Celtic Wisdom
Celtic Wisdom Sticks: An Ogam Oracle
The Celtic Wisdom Tarot
The Complete Lenormand Handbook
Da Vinci Enigma Tarot
The Elements of the Goddess
Fireside Stories,
How To Be A Princess
In Search of Women's Passionate Soul:
      Revealing the Daimon Lover Within
King Arthur and the Goddess of the Land
King Arthur's Raid on the Underworld
The Little Book of Celtic Lore
Mabon and the Guardians of Celtic Britain
Psychic Protection Handbook
Singing the Soul Back Home: Shamanic Wisdom for Every Day
Sophia, Goddess of Wisdom: Bride of God
Tales of the Celtic Lands
This Ancient Heart
Voices of the Goddess: A Chorus of Sibyls
While the Bear Sleeps: Midwinter Tales

Written With John Matthews:

Animal Tales
The Arthurian Book of Days
The Complete Arthurian Tarot
Celtic Myths
Christmas Tales
The Complete King Arthur: Many Faces, One Hero
Elemental Encyclopaedia of Magical Animals
Encyclopedia of Celtic Myth and Legend
Encyclopedia of Celtic Wisdom: A Celtic Shaman's Sourcebook
Faery Magic
The Faery-Tale Reader
The Fourth Gwenevere (with John James)
Ladies of the Lake
The Little Book of Celtic Blessings
The Little Book of Celtic Wisdom
Mad Professor's Laboratory
Magic Toy Box Sea Stories
Storyworld
Tales from the Haunted House
The Trick in the Tale
Walkers Between the Worlds:
      The Western Mysteries from Shaman to Magus

DIARY OF A
SOUL DOCTOR

from the *Ashington Casebooks*

compiled by Dr. Jack Rivers

by

Caitlín Matthews

Diary Of A Soul Doctor:
from the *Ashington Casebooks* compiled by Dr. Jack Rivers

Book Design by Jeremy Berg
Back cover image by Caitlín Matthews
Cover Photo by Sandra Cunningham/www.dreamstime.com

Published by Starseed Books
6592 Peninsula Dr
Traverse City MI 49686

ISBN: 978-1-939790-16-3

Matthews, Caitlín
Diary Of A Soul Doctor/Caitlín Matthews

First Print Edition: November 2016

Printed in the United States of America,
the United Kingdom and other countries

www.lorian.org

DEDICATION

Diary of a Soul Doctor is dedicated to those who tend the soul, but especially to all students who have trained on the *Walkers Between Worlds* shamanic programme, and those colleagues who continue to research and explore the soul in the Spirits of Institution Group.

ACKNOWLEDGEMENTS

I am grateful to all the friends who read some of the earlier stories over the years and encouraged me to continue, especially David Spangler, Felicity Wombwell, and Penny Billington. As will be evident, my chief debt is to the writings of Dion Fortune, particularly to her *The Secrets of Dr Taverner* (1926). Although she inspired the notion of this book, these cases are largely drawn from elements of my own shamanic practice which, over the last 26 years, has given me more ideas and challenges than Jack or Ash might possibly deal with. My special thanks to Lorian Press for publishing these stories, and to John Matthews for his kind editorial services. The song, *Sacred Companions* on pp.201 is by myself and can be heard on *Deep Well in the Wild Wood*, available from me at www.hallowquest.org.uk

CONTENTS

DIARY OF A SOUL DOCTOR
An Introduction by David Spangler

A few years ago, the English author and spiritual teacher, John Matthews, and I were having a conversation about writing fiction. As old friends, John and I often talked about the books we'd like to write and the stories we'd like to tell. I said that I loved the series of short stories about a master of the occult in Dion Fortune's book, *The Secrets of Dr. Tavener* and wished there'd been more of them. "Well," John replied, "my wife Caitlín is already writing her version of those stories."

This was like holding out a handful of candy to a baby. I immediately implored John to ask Caitlín to send me what she had written thus far. So it was that a couple of days later, an email arrived with a PDF containing two of the tales about Dr. Richard Ashington and his Watson-like sidekick, Dr. Jack Rivers. I was delighted and enthralled. Then I was downcast when John told me that Caitlin wouldn't be producing any more of these stories for awhile as other writing assignments had a higher priority and would be keeping her busy for some time to come. If I wanted more tales about Ash and his specialized clinic, The Beacon, I would have to wait. So, I waited. I'm a patient man, but it was hard!

Now that wait is over. You hold in your hands the *Diary of a Soul Doctor*, and you are about to enter the magical and exciting world of Ash, Jack, and their occult adventures in treating those who medical science has abandoned and who need the specialized services of a true physician of the soul. You will not be disappointed.

You might think that writing stories about the occult would be easy. Come up with a plot, throw in some magical mumbo-jumbo and some special effects, maybe a ghost or a demon or two, and presto! There you have it. But occultism is not fantasy where anything goes. The occult is not really about the supernatural but about the hidden side of the natural world, unrecognized by most of us simply because we don't pay attention to it. Science and medicine have been throwing light on the unseen forces of the earth for some time now, giving us germ theory, electromagnetism, quantum theory, and the like, all outside the realm of our five senses. Occultism is simply a form of science that pushes the boundaries a bit further into the phenomena underlying the natural world, revealing knowledge that ordinary science has not quite caught up to yet. For all its mystery, though, this esoteric knowledge and the abilities it can convey remain grounded in the natural world and in the innate capacities of the human being.

i

Therefore, someone who is going to write about the occult would do well to be grounded themselves in understanding and appreciation of the natural world and human psychology. The realms and powers that the occultist works with are not simply "made up," any more than the quantum realm of physicists and mathematicians or the microscopic world of bacteria with which doctors deal is "made up" simply because we cannot see them with our unaided eyes. These subtle realms obey natural laws just as the flow of electricity or the chemical reactions in the body obeys natural principles. Utilizing these laws may be called "magic," but in the end, it is no more "magical" or supernatural than building and programming a computer.

When Dion Fortune wrote her Doctor Tavener stories nearly a hundred years ago, she drew on years of study and practice of the psychological sciences of her day as well as on a deep appreciation of nature and its laws. This is what gave her stories, fantastic as they might seem, their feeling of authenticity and verisimilitude. She wrote about what she had herself lived and experienced.

This is equally true for Caitlín Matthews. She has been an occultist, a healer, a counselor, and an explorer of the unseen dimensions of nature for many years. This gives her stories of Dr. Ashington and his healing center their ring of authenticity. Caitlín writes of what she knows, and the stories are grounded in this knowledge.

But understanding the esoteric side of life is only half of what is needed; the other half is to tell a good story well in ways that bring characters to life and fill their adventures with excitement. Caitlín does this in spades. More than just an occultist, she is an excellent writer. Her characters live and breathe, carrying the reader unhesitatingly into what may be unfamiliar terrain and making it seem so real that when you look up from the book, you can be surprised that you are not sitting in the Beacon yourself.

I have no doubt these stories are destined to become classics in the genre of occult mysteries and fiction, taking their place as equals with the best that Dion Fortune, one of the finest occult storytellers of the last century or of any century, wrote. If you're like me, you will finish the last story with reluctance, not wanting the association with Ash and Jack Rivers to end. We can only hope that Caitlín will discover more diaries of the soul doctor with more stories to tell. If so, we will have to wait for her to write them, but I hope it won't be too long. I hate waiting.

About *Diary Of A Soul Doctor*

The Soul Doctor of this series of ten interlinked stories is Richard Ashington. Known to everyone as Ash, he is a healer and psychologist with a magical background. Calling upon a wide range of esoteric skills to track down and heal the cause of baffling conditions and mysterious situations, with his dependable, and sometimes skeptical assistant, Jack Rivers, Ash investigates cases that have baffled doctors, defying diagnosis or detection. His cases, annotated and compiled in the diaries of Rivers, explore how the ancient past stirs once again to disrupt the present, how re-incarnational bonds defy modern conventions, how supernatural happenings create fear and disquiet, and why unchecked evils spread their miasma into ordinary lives.

Ash and Jack pursue the clues to the epicenter of each case, from the celebrity newswoman who finds herself stalking a man, to a dangerous beauty-spot where an ancient evil still claims lives; from the possessed rock star of a heavy metal band, to a teenage girl who lies in a coma after an ill-starred attempt to initiate herself as a witch, Ash's casebooks reveal the spectrum of spiritual pitfalls with which our world is ill-equipped to deal.

Just as the cases of Sherlock Holmes are presented through the pen of Dr. Watson, so too, the cases of the Soul Doctor come to us through the diaries of Jack Rivers, Ash's assistant. Set in Southern England in the recent past, come to the sanctuary of the Beacon, and discover how the lost art of soul-healing is applied.

Diary of a Soul Doctor opens up a new genre of mystery fiction in which the soul is the battlefield and metaphysics the weapon of choice.

'I don't care if you call him a shaman, exorcist, ghost-buster, magician or priest without portfolio, I only know that Ash was grounded in the science of metaphysics and that he could bring healing, peace and resolution to cases that have confounded medical science.'

– From Jack Rivers' Diary.

TO THE READER:
FROM THE DIARY OF JACK RIVERS

It is a good, noble and a fair thing for a man or a woman to see and behold himself in the mirror of stories, those which have been written by our ancestors, for they give us good examples of what they did, how to live and to avoid evil.
– Geoffrey de la Tour Landry: From *The Book of the Knight in the Tower*, written for the instruction of his daughters. 1372 trans. Caitlín Matthews

Reading back over the diaries of my career in mental health and healing has proved a fascinating and illuminating process, especially the years that I spent as the assistant of Dr. Richard Ashington. Since I retired, I've found myself thinking often of those times. I realise now that I was never so involved with the care of my patients as when I worked with him. There is a luminous quality to my memories of that time that is more highly coloured than the rest of my career. Of course, that is because Ash was like no other person of my acquaintance. My wife tells me that I can be quite a bore when it comes to after-dinner anecdotes about him, but he stands alone as a remarkable human being whose unique insights and ways of working remain unequalled in my experience.

People have never been able to decide about Ash. They divide into two camps, one lot insisting that he was merely a charlatan, while the others can find no higher praise for him than as the wisest and most knowledgeable doctor of souls. You see already how his reputation is likely to be remembered? But how to describe what he did so that the world will remember him in ways worthy of his skills?

When your health is dodgy, you visit the doctor. When your mind is traumatized, you see the psychologist. But when your soul is troubled to whom do you go? I mean, how many priests of your acquaintance would you trust to put you right? There are few clergymen of my acquaintance who truly know their way around the world of the spirit and can handle the dangers you're likely to encounter there. — No, I don't care if you call him a shaman, exorcist, ghost-buster, magician or priest without portfolio, I only know that Ash was grounded in the science of metaphysics and that he could bring healing, peace and resolution to cases that would have confounded medical science.

Ash goes to the epicentre of disquiet, working to shift its causes rather than applying splints, plasters and potions. He is one of a kind. His soul-doctoring would have the General Medical Council in fits if it ever came to their attention. But though his area of expertise borders on the extremes of the pathological, his work is nearer to that of a priest than to that of any medical practitioner. He says that he is answerable to a higher authority than the G.M.C. Based on the evidence, I am inclined to believe him and so keep my own counsel after all I have seen.

No one knows quite how Ash came to have the skills that he had. From remarks he dropped over the years, it is clear that he was an eminent member of a very respectable magical order, for his abilities and methods had an authority that you don't find in the mere dabbler in the occult. It is certainly on record that he was the chief protégé of Melanie Rydale, a near-mythical woman to Jungians in this age, for she was one of Jung's early trainees and thus had drunken from the *fons et origo*. Her abiding reputation in the Jungian field is based squarely on the school of psychology that she attempted to develop. But it is fair to say that her reputation was in no way decreased by the rumour that she was also an alchemist. It wouldn't surprise me to know that she had been a member of the same magical order, for there are hints enough in her published writings, some of which I read while in residence at the Beacon, Ash's establishment, which was left to him by Melanie.

He certainly knew many influential people who confided and trusted in him, for many of them consulted him over the years. Though I am not at liberty to reveal who they were, let's say that some professional fields would not be so well regulated now had it not been for Ash's treatment of some of their protagonists. His array of colleagues was drawn from across the full spectrum of human life. Fellow psychologists and doctors probably made up the lower percentage of his acquaintance that included abbots of both Christian and Buddhist establishments, artists, performers, writers, an exorcist, several notable archaeologists and many musicians. He also played the piano well enough, in my opinion, to have been a professional concert pianist had he so chosen.

So many years have flowed under the bridge since we worked together, I've felt recently that it would be prudent to document some of the adventures that we had, if only to understand and explain them to myself. Perhaps they might be published after my death, for surely everyone in these cases would be dead and gone also? But, just in case, I will change the names of all the principles so that none of my children will face a law-suit. My recollections of these cases come from different times and stages of our acquaintance and did not happen necessarily sequentially. I have remembered them as best I can, as some of the most extraordinary cases I have ever dealt with, always with Ash guiding me to the source of truth and healing. His ways of healing tell their own tale and, to rephrase the old lager advert of my youth, they certainly reached the parts that other methods could not reach.

The only real problem I can foresee is the nature of the cases and how they are likely to be received by any reader. After all, reading over my diaries I note how often my own reason revolted, how often I discounted what seemed to me some trivial detail, how often I challenged Ash as to his methods. My own narrow view of life constantly got in the way of seeing the bigger picture, so how can I expect anyone else to believe what I write?

I suppose I could insist, in the best tradition of film-makers and journalists the world over, that all these stories were true, based on real-life events, but would anyone believe me? They say that life is stranger than fiction, after all — in my experience, people tend to believe the fiction more readily. It has been unkindly suggested by some that my memory is not as accurate as it might have been, and that my extreme age casts in doubt my faculties in general, but I hold to what I have recorded here.

Truly, the suspension of disbelief necessary to read these cases is quite demanding, especially in a world where people increasingly believe only in the reality that they can see, feel, hear and touch, and who hold that this world is all that there is, and that this life-time is all that we get. But, as I myself move towards my latter end, my mind returns to many of these cases in search of soul-comfort. For if this world and this life were all I had, I would indeed be sorry for it.

Ash opened up a wider universe to me, giving me the sense of being held in a much greater context than just my everyday routines. That sense of surety has remained with me and, while I would not grace it with the title of belief, nor swear that I had a continuous awareness of that surety, it nevertheless remains with me in my old age. For that, I will ever be grateful to him.

I am hopelessly beyond the pale, I realize, re-reading this. I daresay that, in most people's estimation, I have joined the ranks of the gullible fools who will believe in anything, who consult tarot-readers and mediums in search of some spiritual crutch with which to stomp about the world and so justify their weirdness.

But I have only to bring Ash to mind to know that this is not true. It is fair to say that his belief in the evidence of symptoms led him back not only to the causes of some prime deviations from normal life but also to the sources of great spiritual illumination. It is to the world's loss that psychology did not see fit to examine these evidences for itself, for it is possible that there would now be fewer people under medication or in mental institutions. His greatest cause of sadness was people's inability to perceive what was actually present for, by ignoring such evidence, he felt that souls went astray and the vulnerable became unsupported.

If there is any further service I can do for him now, these many years on, then it is to record as faithfully as I can, his many cases so that the world can judge for itself. So then, Ash, this is for you......

Case 1: THE TROUBLE WITH DAPHNE WEIR

I have never known whether it was coincidence or what Ash calls 'a moment of truth' that led me to the medical employment agency that afternoon. It certainly marked the point when my career passed beyond the strictly orthodox into a region beyond what is inadequately called 'alternative.'

Flipping through the vacancies in the over-heated foyer of the agency, I saw nothing to inflame my heart. My last residential contract had been summarily terminated when the small hospital where I'd been employed for the last six years closed, due to lack of funding. Now I was nearly out of funds myself, as the severance pay cheque dwindled in my account. For the last week I had been camping out on my sister's unforgiving futon in Islington, while following up dead-end jobs. I had seriously had it with the National Health service and was desperate for something more fulfilling, but soon it would be a case of beggars not being choosers.

'Has anything new come in?' I asked, giving back the folder with its uninviting posts to the receptionist.

She entered my criteria of expertise again and scrolled down her screen, obviously not expecting anything new. 'Oh, there's this one. Shall I print it out?' She pressed print, without asking, and extended the page with a well-manicured hand.

I can't even remember the wording of the post now, only that it was residential, private and mercifully out of the city. Hope leapt. What I recall most vividly was a sense of quickening excitement that perhaps my life was flowing towards something more purposeful. After a failed marriage and six years of dedication to the care of the mentally ill, at a professional level, I yearned for the recognition of my peers and some career fulfilment that extended beyond the statutory increment payable to my grade.

Noticing that the salary seemed suspiciously generous, I cautiously asked, 'Has this been advertised long?' That week I had criss-crossed the streets of London in quest of too many posts whose promise and availability had vanished like a mirage. Better qualified people than myself were being turned away from such choice posts.

The receptionist parried my question with a degree of wariness that put me on my guard, 'Oh, it's a perfectly legitimate post, I assure you. It's been advertised a couple of times before—a few weeks ago now... It's just come back up ....It might not suit everyone, but you said on your file that you didn't mind being in the country....'

So others had applied and turned it down! Was the owner of the practice some kind of freak at the extremes of the medical fringe? Or was just that it was located on some God-forsaken island somewhere with a boat every second Tuesday?

'When are the interviews?'

The receptionist glanced at the screen. 'I'm authorized to send applicants over to the London practice anytime between 9am and 11am this week.' She phoned to confirm my arrival and scribbled down the address for me. 'They will see you as soon as you can get over there. Don't worry, I'll send over your CV to them.'

It was quarter to eleven as I leapt into a taxi I couldn't really justify. It was just striking the hour from the nearby church when I was finally decanted onto a pavement off Harley Street. The brass plate screwed to the wall read 'Dr. Richard Ashington.'

The name was familiar in some way I couldn't fathom. From the basement reception, I was shown in, despite my late arrival. Ashington himself was a thin, clean-shaven, dark-haired man in his fifties, I judged, though he had that timeless kind of face you see in certain kinds of hippies who seem to have stretched the sixties to inordinate lengths. However, there was nothing of the hippy about him, even though he was dressed unconventionally for a Harley Street consultant, in a cream open-necked linen shirt and dark jeans. His grey eyes were the most striking feature you noticed. They seemed unusually penetrative, the grey of the pupils rimmed with black. I felt myself — not judged — but rather witnessed. A sense of rightness buoyed me up, even though this was the ninth interview of that weary week.

The consulting room had a subtle quality that set it apart from the usual Harley Street office. Everything in it was arranged in a very harmonious and pleasing way, from the creamy wooden furniture and pale golden couch to the bronze Buddhist statue of Manjusri with his severing sword. I noticed that the usual family photo was absent from Dr. Ashington's desk and that, instead, there was a small modern icon of a Black Madonna set on a stand. The only other item on the desk was my speedily-downloaded *curriculum vitae* which lay before him, naked and appealing.

His handshake was firm, 'Dr. Rivers, I will be frank with you. I need a residential warden for the Beacon, my country nursing home. The work is not arduous, for we usually have only a handful of cases staying with us at any one time. There are two permanent nursing assistants to see to the daily running of the home, and we also hire night and relief nursing when required, but I need a colleague upon whose care and judgement I can absolutely rely when I am absent here in London.'

'Others have applied?' I could have bitten off my tongue, for this was a post that I really needed.

He looked at me evenly and without rancour, 'Others have indeed applied but the position did not suit their needs.' He glanced at my C.V. 'I see that you are not married? Do you have any commitments in that department?'

I was so astounded at the impertinence of the question that I failed to answer him.

He was perfectly frank with me, 'I only ask because the self-contained unit situated on the premises is suitable only for a single person, and the post of warden is strictly offered as a residential position. The area is fairly remote from local amenities and entertainments. If you were a family man, it might prove to be difficult for your wife and children, or for your partner.'

After wondering whether Ashington had ever heard of equal opportunities, I found myself refreshed by his lack of political correctness, for these conditions suited me perfectly. The drawbacks of a medical post are not always revealed so searchingly upfront. After qualifying, I took my share of positions that glowed on paper only to be groaned over in reality. Nothing stood in my way except a record of mediocrity, so I had little belief in my powers to impress him. Having established my credentials in the failed romance department – Amy and I had long since parted and there was no-one else on the horizon – I lapsed into awkward silence.

Ashington then said, 'Tell me, have you any questions you wish to ask me?'

This was the strangest interview I'd ever had. 'What is the scope of your practice?' I asked.

He leaned back in the black leather chair, 'I see the rejects, the discards from the pack that my Harley Street colleagues have given over, the persistent malingerers, the unclassifiable and the hopeless, the mystery cases and the just plain baffling. My methods are unconventional and go beyond the textbooks. If you chose to work with me, you will doubtless witness some things that our profession would discount as pathologically impossible.'

Again that unaccountable sense of rightness ran through me. He had said 'work with me' not 'for me.' Heartened that he was already regarding me as a colleague and not an employee, I said, 'Provided we can bring help to those who most need it, I am satisfied. To be honest, I am less than happy with some of the methods that are meted out, for they seem to seal over or compound the issue rather than deal with the problem.'

Pleased with my answer, he added, 'The kind of cases we will be dealing with often stretch beyond the usual boundaries of professional practice, Dr.

Rivers — though not in any unprofessional way, I think you will find. For my part, I only ask that you will give me your trust and utmost discretion.'

'You have it,' I said, really meaning it. Though afterwards I wondered how I could have been so certain I could trust a man on such brief acquaintance.

He extended his hand, 'I would like you to call me Ash — it's how I'm known by everyone at the Beacon. How do you like to be known?

'Jack.' I took his hand and shook it firmly to seal my promise.

A bare week later, my belongings had been cracked out of storage and installed in my new accommodation. I finally bade a thankful farewell to London and to my sister and her hard futon — to our mutual relief, since she'd been unable to invite any friends over during my occupation — and drove down with Ash to the Beacon. Leaving behind that car park known to motorists as the M25 orbital, we drove south to the line of the South Downs where we turned off into the network of B roads that lead deeper into the country. The tang of the sea was in the air, though the line of the Downs hid us from sight of it. Beyond dense woodland, rose the Iron Age fortification known as Hartsworth Beacon with its crown of beeches, part of the chain of beacons once used to signal along the South Coast from the Armada onwards.

The land's welcome was palpable, especially to me on that autumn morning. I had the impression that this rich, fertile countryside had been host to many peoples over the centuries. Ash informed me that archaeologists had found evidence from every level of occupation in the acres surrounding his private nursing home. As we drove, I gave my homage to the majestic line of the chalk hills that we were shadowing, promising that I would make many long walks along its broad shoulders.

I began to hope that Ash's place was not one of those residential care centres which essentially caters for the leisured, well-heeled addict in rehab, with tennis court, swimming pool, and indulgent facilities that would trivialize this lovely location. But I need not have worried.

The Beacon was a flint-faced house that had had two modest but tasteful extension wings added over the last century. It had been owned by an old woman, the last of her family, with whom Ash had studied. On her death, she bequeathed the premises to him on the understanding that it was used as a sanctuary for unquiet souls who could find no other healing. It was set in its own south-facing grounds surrounded by flint and brick walls which had, I was relieved to see, no security spikes to keep the inmates inside as is often the case in residential mental establishments. As you drove up, you had the impression that this was just a charming private house that nestled in the protective shadow of Hartsworth Beacon. Once under the arch of the gate, and leaving the drive behind you, you entered an enclosed garden bordered by fruit trees and fragrant with flowers. House martins were permitted to nest under the eaves of the roof and raise their young every summer. It was the house in which every exile from sanity could find their soul.

'Ah! The house of the perfect eaves!' I breathed, to Ash's amusement and pleasure.

The entrance hall was large and welcoming. Set in a niche on the left was a picture I recognized: none other than Melanie Rydale. A copper lustre vase of autumn anemones beside it sent waves of delicate fragrance from their boughs of fluted golden blooms. As soon as I saw the picture, I was able to place Ash immediately.

Melanie Rydale was one of Jung's women, a scholar in her own right and, some said, an alchemist. So this rather arcane and secretive woman was Ash's mentor! I learned later that he was the best-known pupil of her school of psychology, and considered to be her chief continuator. I regarded my new employer and colleague with new eyes, wondering why on earth he had chosen a no-body like me to assist him in this lovely location.

When Ash said it was remote, I had been unable to picture anywhere this near the south coast as very far removed from habitation. But apart from hikers and Sunday tourists headed for Hartsworth Beacon, the lane led only to the nursing home. Our nearest neighbour was a farmer down the lane; farm-workers and a part-time forestry commission officer who lived in a caravan three miles away, while the nearest shops and post office were in a village six miles distant. For company I should have only the two nursing assistants, a charming married couple some years older than myself, Gillespie and Wendy McLain, who lived over the west wing, and Cinnamon, a disdainful ginger feline who regarded Ash as her person and everyone else as her servant. My delightful self-contained apartment was over the east wing, while Ash himself curiously occupied the rather dark rooms immediately facing north to the Iron Age hill-fort.

Over the next month I settled into my new post. The work was not just interesting but engrossingly absorbing. At first it seemed to me that Dr. Ashington's methods were little short of witchcraft or shamanism, for he dealt with the soul as a sacred entity, not just as a damaged psyche that needed fixing, and in such ways that awakened first wonder and then respect in me. While he would see clients at his London practice, he preferred that some cases be dealt with at the Beacon which received, not inmates nor patients, but guests. Rather than prescribing strong anti-depressive drugs or administering sedations that tamed and lowered the system, he was for the old-fashioned and much neglected restorative of rest and nature, unless there was no other option. Guests could roam the surrounding countryside, sit in the gardens, listen or make music in the music room or use the materials in the well-stocked art studio.

I can testify to the therapeutic effect of the house itself. After battling with the rush-hour traffic to reach the Beacon, I would find myself slowing down to enjoy the last stage of my journey so as to savour my return. Once inside the gates, I would let the beauty of the house fold its healing mantle around me. My spirits rose when considering the safety of its three hundred year old walls and the well-balanced proportions of its rooms that were simply and unpretentiously furnished. For, while Ash's London consulting rooms were fresh and modern in design, everything at the Beacon had its own patina of age and comfort. It was here in this blessed place that I began the diaries that have been the basis for these chronicles.

Ash's insight into our guests' needs might be summed up in something he said the week after I arrived, when I questioned the lack of a television in the house. One of our guests had complained that Beacons was too quiet and that there was 'nothing to do.'

'Television disorders the house rhythms and upsets the guests,' he said. From my experience in residential mental institutions, I appreciated what he meant. I had seen too many wards of semi-comatose people hypnotized by the pervasive eye of the flickering screen. 'There's too much competing for our attention in this society. People neglect the most basic sacred duties when they are continually distracted. Here they have space and quietness to focus on what they have most neglected.' Later during my time there, when mobile phones became ubiquitous, they were also forbidden. If people needed to make calls, they did so from a cosy, sound-proofed area converted from the old boot-room. The lack of distraction helped many come to the heart of their disturbance much quicker than if they had been constantly over-stimulated.

After a couple of weeks, Ash and I drove up to London together. 'I want you to sit in on my new cases, so that you can understand how I work,' he said as we left the Downs behind.

I had had more time to evaluate Ash as a person, finding him cultured, musical and intelligent. He was delighted that I shared his love of classical music. About his personal life, I knew little. He did not seem to have ever been married. Indeed there was something of the loner about him that I associated with the religious vocation, for he had a mixture of detachment and compassion in his make-up. He certainly wasn't gay, as my sister rather pruriently suggested when I phoned to thank her for her hospitality. He was simply complete in himself.

In the library, I found a series of articles he had written in *Future Psychology* that demonstrated he was still very much continuing the rather metaphysical trajectory of Melanie Rydale. But where most Jungian clones cooed and speculated in a wide-eyed manner about magic and the supernatural, Ash seemed to write about such things with an authority that seemed based more on experience rather than psychological speculation. I noticed from the biography at the foot of one of the articles that he had served on a joint committee on Possession and Exorcism with the Rev. Matthew Davidson and Rabbi Ariel Klein, for the Guild of Ecumenical Psychology.

Ash was remarkably available to his clients at unsociable times by phone and in person, and rather expected a similar flexibility from me, although he was remarkably considerate. The only times he seemed unavailable for comment was when he was meditating in his rooms, which he signalled by hanging an ancient horse-brass dug up from the garden on the doorknob of his room.

The refreshing dawn light and empty roads over the downs had given way to the stressed haze of exhaust as we made the slow crawl into the centre of London where the immensity of close conurbation battened upon us. The first client of that morning was already sitting in the reception room—a slight woman in a hat and sunglasses, who turned pointedly towards the water-dispenser as we arrived, as if not wanting to be seen. Ash's secretary, Maggie, showed her into us after a few minutes. Ash introduced me as his assistant, but after a brief nod in my direction, she entirely ignored me.

Removing the large crushed velvet hat and concealing sunglasses, the woman held up her head with accusing confrontation, 'I'm told you are discreet?' One beautifully pencilled eyebrow arched in an even higher circumflex towards my employer. Ash may have kept no television on the premises at the Beacon but I knew well enough who it was we had in the consulting room—none other than Daphne Weir, the main anchorwoman of the BBC evening news-casting team. Her capable eloquence and articulate clarity, wedded to a lovely figure and blonde beauty, had made her a national favourite. Women admired her unconventionally fashionable clothes sense—she had managed to break out of Auntie's requirement that female newscasters assume the formally suited appearance of their male colleagues—while many men suddenly found the news overwhelmingly attractive. Popular magazines like *City Male* and *Celebrity News* had both carried features on her recently, making so much of her apparently modest and unattached social life that they had succeeded in making her seem suspiciously innocent. While not explicitly stating that she might be lesbian, the features had striven to imply something deviant and un-fresh.

Both magazines had been severely censured by the press complaints bureau. In real life, Daphne Weir looked less authoritative and a lot more vulnerable. Her distinctive brown eyes were troubled, her professional direct gaze, away from the screen, strangely evasive.

Ash assured her, 'Myself and my colleague, Dr. Rivers, are bound by professional confidentiality. Please tell me your trouble....'

She stared at her handbag on the low table between us, as if drawing courage from it. Then resolutely raising her eyes, as if delivering grave news to the camera, she spoke, 'I have become ... obsessed by the image of a man — it is no-one I know. I seem to be searching for him everywhere. It's beginning to get out of hand. Several times I have woken up outside the flats where I live dressed only in my nightwear, with no idea how I came to be there. I've missed rehearsals and production meetings during the day as well. I frequently lose all sense of time and place. When I come to again, it's often miles away from Broadcasting House, sometimes over the other side of London where I must have driven, because I'm in my car, but with no memory of how I got there or why I set out.' She shuddered delicately. 'My producer told me to get sorted out. He's given me two weeks or I'll end up back in the production office. Can you cure me?'

Ash told her straight, 'These things don't have convenient schedules. Tell me how long has this been going on? And when did the lapses of memory begin?'

'In some ways, ever since I was a girl. But seriously, they started since I took this promotion from the Bristol studio and came to London last year.'

'Tell me, what is the story you've been telling yourself?'

She blushed violently, 'Do we have to have this machine on?' She stabbed a well-manicured nail at the CD recorder that quietly recorded the session. Ash nodded to me and I switched it off, though I continued to scribble notes.

'It's just a day-dream I have,' she tried to dismiss it.

'Nevertheless, please tell me about it...' Inexorably but very gently, Ash drew the tale from her.

'The image of this man has been with me since I can first remember. I've...' — she blushed again, lowering her voice '...longed for him. When I was a child, he was my invisible playmate. I day-dreamed that we lived in a hot sunny place, a kind of desert but with cities in it. It wasn't some kind of holiday paradise but rather a place where we learned music together. We had a playful rivalry, trying to out-do the other. At school, whenever I was singing in the choir, they always told me to sing quieter, but whenever I sang it was *his* voice that I was reaching out for. When I was older, I knew I would marry him.'

The rich tones suddenly became thin and hollow, 'I thought I *had* married him when I found Stephen — he looked so like the man in my dreams. But he only *looked* like him.' The emphasis in her voice was laden with disappointment and bewilderment.

Her well-publicised divorce had hit the headlines a couple of years back, I remembered. She blew into a tissue, then bravely raised her head again, acknowledging the truth, 'I knew the night before the wedding that it was wrong. It was as though my real mate had come to me that night and begged me to reconsider... but the ceremony was all arranged, the family, the marquee, everything....' She broke down.

'...so you went through with it?' Ash asked.

'Yes. It was horrible. Stephen didn't love me. He just wanted to show me off like a — possession.... Thank God we had no children!... But the worst thing was, that I couldn't hear my beloved anymore.'

'Hear?' Ash enquired, with an upturn of the head.

Now she went white. 'Am I mentally ill? I mean, hearing things... Well, I've always been aware of his voice. It sings to me.'

'What kind of songs?'

'Love songs. When I was younger, I used to think it was like the *Song of Songs* in the Bible. When I was older, it was more like love songs off the radio.'

'And the singing began again when?'

I looked hard at Ash, for she hadn't said the singing *had* begun again. But Daphne hadn't noticed. The story just came tumbling out.

'It was nine months after the divorce. Only the voice was more like a moan of agony. I just associated it with my own pain and tried not to dwell on it, but it just got worse. I wanted to find him so as to stop the pain. Some days it's so bad, I wonder whether it wouldn't be easier to kill myself, because no-one can help me.' She told us of the many therapists and others she'd been to see. 'Therapy doesn't make it go away. It was only when a clairvoyant told me that you dealt with cases like mine that I made an appointment. If you can't help me, I don't know what I shall do, because it's got worse....'

Her voice was barely audible as she bent her head with shame, 'Several times recently, I know that I've been purposely following certain men in the street because I thought I picked up his trail.... Can you imagine the headlines? "Celebrity News Anchor Stalks Her Quarry!" The papers will have a field day! So, Dr. Ashington, am I some mad female stalker or what?' She pressed both palms to her face.

I noticed Ash had been looking through and beyond her at something I couldn't see while she'd been talking, but now he regarded her gravely, 'Miss Weir, you are quite right to say that your trouble won't yield to therapy, because you are not ill at all.'

Daphne flushed and opened her mouth as if to contradict him, but then let him continue, 'All that you have told me gives me cause for hope. If you will trust me, I will do my very best to help you. As you are free of your duties for the next two weeks, I would like you to come down to the Beacon where we can explore this further.'

She looked so heartened that I had to bite my lip: it seemed to me that he gave her too much hope on very little basis. After she'd gone, I tackled Ash with some warmth, for this case seemed to me to be a classic animus projection – a thing not uncommon in career women who overly identify with the masculine world.

Raising one brow, he asked, 'Do you think so? I think rather that we are dealing with a reactivated reincarnational link.'

I blinked. This was hardly sound psychological theory! I began to seriously think that the first cracks in my professional idyll had really begun to show. Ash explained, 'There is nothing pathological in the woman's make-up, I could see that from her aura. But there is a well-developed tube leading out of it, like a funnel, which shows that she is connected to something outside of her. The end of the funnel is large and open, so we are not dealing with a vampiric infestation or some other kind of invasive linkage; it's the kind of tube that connects people who are in love. I believe that woman is indeed searching for her beloved as she says. Nine times out of ten, you will find that the client is well aware of the true diagnosis.'

Now there are books two a penny on the market that deal in this sort of guff, and I daresay an equal number of gullible people ready to read them but I hardly expected to hear such theories bandied about by a professional psychologist.

Seeing my stunned expression, he turned to me kindly, and said, 'Jack, we live life after life. Some lives forge bonds so strong that the bridge of memory remains. That severely unhappy young woman is not alone in her solitary longing, I believe.'

Drawing on the technique I've often used when dealing with patients whose reality is off-beam, I chose to humour him by temporarily sharing his view of reality, 'You mean there may be someone alive who reciprocates it?'

'Indeed, but it could be messy. The problem is we don't know if her beloved is a baby or a grandfather, or already married. But I somehow think not. Whoever it is, he or she is likely to be in great pain.'

'*He or she*? My God! That could be appalling!' I tried to reason the case through, 'So, if this is a reincarnational memory, what stimulated it in her?' I asked. 'I mean, it's not as though we all remember being Cleopatra or Henry VIII. Why don't I remember past lives?'

Ash grinned, 'You mean there are enough Napoleons already committed to care?'

I fear I blushed, for this was exactly what I was thinking. But Ash didn't seem to mind my questions, indeed, he seemed quite pleased with my line of reasoning,

'Who can say what will bring us to memory? There is a greater world of which we are a part, though fewer people are aware of it today. Can you imagine what it would be like to have conscious memory of every life you've ever led? The burden of knowledge, the fear or disgust, the pain and suffering....? No, Jack, most of us do not remember, for which we should be heartily glad indeed. Even within this life, human beings don't continually remember pain. For who would wish to remember dying of the Black Death or of living as a slave? But your question is a good one... what triggered the memory? If we can get to the bottom of that, we may begin to make headway indeed. This is how I like to work, Jack — by pursuing the evidence to its source, we begin to understand how we can help.'

'Were you thinking of regressing her?' I asked with some trepidation, as I had frequently had to pick up the pieces of such ill-advised 'therapeutic' work as past-life regression. 'It seems to me that we have our work cut out dealing with this life, never mind worrying about any previous ones.'

'I agree with you,' Ash smiled, 'Sufficient unto the life is the evil thereof! The way I was trained, such matters are usually avoided until the individual is sufficiently mature to understand it, but it doesn't always work out like that. No, I shall make my own investigations. It won't place her at any risk.'

'The way you were trained......?' I echoed, unable to believe that any psychological curriculum dealt in much depth with reincarnation except as some kind of delusional fixation.

Ash had gone very quiet, regarding me with those clear, grey, penetrating eyes, 'Jack, will you trust me when I tell you that there are other well-mapped realities than the one that we experience with our senses?'

I realized then, I think, that I stood at the edge of a mountain pass in our relationship. If I was unable to go over it, then I would be left behind. But if I was able to trust my guide, despite the altitude and weather conditions, I would come over safely. I gathered my words carefully, 'I'm not an atheist — just had no real experience of anything much beyond my dreams. Even though I have no knowledge of such things, I accept that people believe they experience other realities.' After all, one of the nurses at the last hospital was a practising Buddhist and she believed in reincarnation, even though she didn't impose or apply her beliefs to her patients.

'Good! That is all that I ask of you. —But if I tell you that some people have entered those realities and mapped them, that there is a way of seeing behind the veil of appearances, and that I have learned how to do so, would you believe me?'

I remembered that photograph of Melanie Rydale in the hall at the Beacon, looking for all the world like a sibyl who knew all the answers, and knew with a certainty from whom he had learned this way of working. As delicately as I knew how, for I instinctively felt that the bond between Rydale and Ash was a precious one, 'Are you are talking of a training that is not strictly psychological?'

'I am indeed. My inheritance from Melanie was not just in bricks and mortar, nor merely in mentoring. She stood in the line of initiates who have kept open many ancient paths from long before psychology came on the scene. I also stand in that lineage and am an initiate of that line. Think of it as a family inheritance, if you like.'

As he said these words, I felt the same gathering excitement that I'd experienced in my interview with him. The thought of a lineage of people actively pursuing the aims and objectives of psychology before its beginnings in the late nineteenth century was utterly appealing to me. What must that have meant? But before I could lose myself in speculation, cold, hard reason flooded back. While Ash had spoken modestly about his involvement and not in any ego-boosting kind of way, I saw how the world would view him if anyone knew.

'Do you mean some kind of occult order?' It was hard to keep the sneer out of my intonation. God knows the bookshops were heaving with hidden treasures, masons, Templars and occult wisdom! What with various kinds of New Age clap-trap and conspiracy theory, it was hard enough to deal pragmatically with the kind of problems that loony belief fosters in the mentally ungrounded.

'Not as you mean it,' Ash replied, fluently reading my suspicions. 'The word "occult" merely means "hidden." I prefer the word "metaphysical" — that part of reality which is wound with and quite as real as the physical part. Melanie and those like her stood in the stream of influence responsible for skilful means by which metaphysical wisdom is handed down and guarded.'

'So it is hidden, then?'

Ash smiled broadly, 'Consider, Jack — you wouldn't talk about extreme psychological pathologies to people at a bus-stop — it would frighten and disgust them: for the uninitiated, you would tone it down, use familiar metaphors and so on. But you could talk about such matters to your colleagues without fear of being offensive or being misunderstood, because they are initiates of those mysteries. It is a matter of what is appropriate. In our history, consciousness has taken a long time to evolve and mature. There have been times and places when to talk about these matters — now openly accepted by science — would have brought you to imprisonment, torture or the gallows. Think of Galileo or poor Giordano Bruno! They were both men of wisdom, but they revealed their wisdom at an unwise time.'

'But all the guff on sale in the occult bookshops is always banging on about evil influences and plans of world domination that metaphysical groups are trained in.' Even as the words dropped from my lips, I was aware how stupid they were, but something stubbornly made me say them anyway.

He looked skywards for a metaphor to communicate what he believed, turning to me with, 'It is better to think of a family lineage of wisdom which attracts and trains those who are in tune with certain sacred principles — but a family made up of those with a vocation, rather than a blood connection. It is not religious, nor political, it doesn't aim to wield power or manipulate the universe. It merely holds certain truths and concepts in common. If you examine the metaphysical wisdom, you will find that it is made up of the very pragmatic truths and principles that have maintained and supported the sacred nature of life in many times and places. It is a perennial wisdom to which everyone has access, but which only a few chose to follow. I am one of those few.' It was said humbly, but authoritatively.

I considered what a difference this revelation would make to my employment. Ash clearly had loyalties and training that extended beyond anything taught by the standard psychological curriculum. I might only have his word for it now, but it seemed to me that he had been able to gain insights it would have taken years of analysis to uncover or which would perhaps never have come to light.

We talked on the way back home when he explained to me that reality, as we know it, has two sides. The side that we appreciate with our senses is the one most people understand; the other side — which we all visit in dreams — is only apprehensible by our inner senses which are not normally trained or heeded in our society today. There were ways of obtaining information, of tracking and mapping the trajectory of a problem, of finding its epicentre and then dealing with it. I later sat in on one of these fact-finding missions when, reclining on his own couch, he would lapse into a deep state of consciousness and 'send out his soul' — at least that's what I called it — while I took down notes of anything Ash reported.

What would this mean to me if his methods became public knowledge? Would I fade away, ashamed to be seen in his company, like a kind of St. Peter denying Christ? Welling up in me again was the same instinct that I was on the verge of something very special, something that would expand my experience in un-guessable ways. Despite my reservations, I was inclined to trust him.

The way that Daphne Weir had relaxed in his presence spoke powerfully for him in my book, for I have seen consultants deal with their referrals in such a manner as to compound their illnesses and raise their hackles so that any approach to healing was blocked. But I also fully realized that his professional career was to some degree in my hands, for if I made his methods a matter of public record, what would become of him? There was already a certain level of interest around his work in the psychological world that a determined troublemaker could play up.

I said finally, 'Whatever your background and training, I am happy to support you in any way that brings healing. I don't condemn or judge ways of which I have no knowledge, and I am open to learning more.'

'Thank you, Jack.' He reached his right hand over the steering wheel and we shook on it.

As we crested the line of the downs, I asked him, 'But what if she doesn't find her beloved?' The possibility seemed exceedingly remote to me.

He just smiled his maddeningly wise smile, 'Let's wait and see, shall we?'

§§

It took Daphne Weir the usual two or three days to settle into the rhythm of the Beacon. I'd noticed that guests usually mooched about a bit without any of their usual daily agendas to focus upon. Unlike others, Daphne didn't have the usual television withdrawal symptoms, but rather seemed relieved at its absence. Ash had asked me to observe her discreetly and to companion her when she required it.

She took listless walks up Hartsworth Beacon with me accompanying her like a willing dog, and had a couple of sessions with Ash, but nothing engaged her or put the sparkle back in her eyes. On the fifth day, Wendy had to go into Deddenham and asked if I needed anything. Daphne cast a longing look, so I asked her if she'd like to come along and perhaps stop for tea at The Crooked Cottage on the way back, an old-fashioned tea-shop that does mouth-watering cakes and pastries.

Wendy drew me aside as Daphne went for her coat, 'Without make-up she might not be recognized, but you will have to be responsible for her.' Daphne had dressed down considerably from her usual smart appearance, so I didn't see any problem. We sauntered about Deddenham while Wendy did the grocery shopping at the supermarket. Daphne was glad of the stimulus, I could tell, though looking in shops is not my favourite activity, it must be said. She didn't buy much, just some sandalwood incense cones from the gift shop. We later drew into the car-park of the Crooked Cottage and ordered tea in the garden, as the afternoon was fine. But I had reckoned without the tea-shop's half-timbered charm. Within ten minutes, a coach-load of foreign tourists swarmed into the shop and gardens. They were obviously on a short comfort stop and wanted instant service. The two waitresses were soon bringing out trays of tea and coffee to assuage their needs while the manageress was doing great business selling them take-away biscuits and cakes.

Daphne became tensely alert. She stopped drinking her tea.

'Are you alright?' Wendy asked her.

'I just remembered, I wanted to buy some of that lovely raspberry jam.' Daphne rose and re-entered the teashop.

After a bit, I realized that Daphne's handbag was under the table. 'She's not going to buy anything without this!'

I went back into the shop with it, but there was no sign of her. Wendy checked the toilets. Daphne wasn't there either.

We both ran out into the car-park where the coach was loading up with tourists. Trying not to panic, I checked our car and then went up and down the roadside, casting about. When I got back, the coach was turning out into the road heading north.

Wendy had spoken to the manageress but no jam had been bought. It had been a ruse to throw us off, clearly. We both made a concerted search of the area, but it was useless. Daphne had gone wandering again.

It was with a sense of shame that I reported her disappearance to Ash. 'Should we tell the police?'

'Whatever for? She's a voluntary patient, not an inmate. No, I'm sure we'll hear from her by the end of the day,' was all Ash would infuriatingly say.

I was just turning in for bed at 10.30, when the phone went. It was a reverse-charge call, which I accepted with a sinking heart.

A diminished voice spoke, 'Dr. Rivers? It's me. I don't know how, but I've ended up in a bus station in North London. I don't have any money on me.'

'Is there somewhere you can shelter, Miss Weir?'

'I don't know — maybe. The bus driver was awfully angry with me.'

I took down the details of the phone box's location and told her to stay near it. Even with the best speed in the world, it would be a two and half hour drive to rescue her.

After Daphne had a good night's sleep and a decent breakfast, I sat in on her interview with Ash.

'Tell us what happened in the tea-garden, please,' Ash asked her.

'I was eating some shortbread and then... I had that feeling again, that the man I've been seeking was calling out to me. I knew I had to get into the coach and go.'

'What brought that feeling on?'

'It was listening to the people in the garden.'

'What nationality were they, Jack?'

'From all over.' I tried to remember, 'There were Japanese, maybe some Italians — I remember some French being spoken... they were Middle Eastern folk, so probably Lebanese or Jordanian or something.'

He turned back to Daphne, 'What did you do then?'

'I must have got onto the coach, but I have no recollection of doing that,' Daphne's eyes were brimming with unshed tears of frustration, 'Why do I keep doing this?'

Ash advised her, 'Try going back to the feeling you had while you had tea. What was the trigger for those feelings or sensations, what called you?'

She stared at the carpet and then out of the window, as if seeking inspiration, 'It was something about the tea itself — I chose some tea with rose-petals in it. As the people were coming into the garden, the smell of the roses was in my mouth and nose... then I knew I had to go.'

'Which is why you boarded the coach?'

She looked down at her hands and said, 'I think so... I don't really know.'

Daphne became too upset to continue and Wendy led her back her room, while Ash and I mused.

Ash picked up the silk scarf that she had left behind, 'Do you remember the name of the coach company?'

'Bellinghams of Christminster,' I replied, 'But why do you....'

Ash was already dialling the number, 'Hello. This is Dr. Ashington speaking from the Beacon Nursing Home. One of my colleagues was at the Crooked Cottage this afternoon when your driver stopped in Deddington for tea. I think we may have found a scarf belonging to one of your party. Perhaps you could let me know if we can return it whoever it was.'

Ash listened, with the scarf wrapped round his hand. 'I see! Thank you, yes, I understand. Leaving tomorrow? I will call the hotel and see, thank you again for your trouble.'

Putting down the receiver he said, 'The party on the coach were all from a conference in Christminster. It finished the previous day and they were doing some sightseeing before going home.' He looked up the hotel's number and phoned the reception with the same story about a lost scarf. By a series of small questions, he discovered what he needed to know. 'It turns out they were an international group of musicologists attending their annual gathering, but they are all leaving tomorrow.'

'How does that help us?'

Ash picked up the local newspaper, scanning its pages until he found what he was looking for, 'The theme of this year's conference was Anatolian Music, so a majority of the delegates were Turks.' He looked very pleased about something. None of this seemed like relevant information to me.

Nothing seemed to be progressing fast. One sunny afternoon, on not finding Daphne in the garden I was drawn by the sound of plangent strings issuing from the music room.

Daphne sat wistfully drawing her fingers over the strings of a Moroccan oud – one of the many instruments in the well-stocked music room. I hadn't remembered seeing it in the music room before, this Arabic lute with its ornate inlay. It sounded out of tune to me, but then I only play the guitar rather badly myself. Seeing me at the French windows, she called out, 'Do you know how to tune it? I do want to play it so very much.'

With the help of the piano, and a quick look at a book in the library about stringed instruments, I tried to come to some close approximation of its tuning so that she could at least make a decent sound on it. No sooner had I got it to a satisfactory pitch than she seized it from me and began to play a three note tune on the open strings, and to hum a complex harmony with subtle melismas – not a Western melody at all, more like something from the Middle East. She threw back her head and sang it louder. There was an abandonment to the set of her shoulders, entirely uncharacteristic for our modest and sophisticated newswoman. I was very glad that City Male didn't have a camera trained upon her as they would have hardly recognized the asexual Miss Clean they had tried so hard to sully. She swayed the upper half of her body, eyes half-closed, becoming positively wanton.

Just as suddenly she stopped, and looked at me, as if noticing me for the first time. From the expression on her face, and the dilation of her pupils, she could have been another woman.

'Do you think we could go for a drive?' she asked me. Her voice too, had an uncharacteristically sultry timbre. I had the curious sensation of seeing someone else imposed upon her and wondered whether I was experiencing the arousal of some sub-personality.

Ash had left for London after receiving a phone call that morning. 'Emergency case,' was all he'd said as he left. But he had given me instructions to companion her, so I dutifully drove her down to the bottom of our lane, 'Where to?'

She tilted her head as if hearing music beyond my ears and pointed north. For the rest of that afternoon, we drove until she needed to stop and listen again, and so changed direction.

'Is it him?' I ventured, as we began to approach the sprawl of South London.

'Oh yes!' she breathed, with a remote smile. Had I not known her, I would have said she was intoxicated, but she was clearly in the grip of whatever was troubling her. I wished that Ash could have been with me, for I needed his guidance.

As we slowed down, her inner listening seemed to get stronger and more certain, and her commands became more urgent and peremptory. What with the increased traffic and her growing agitation, I began to be apprehensive. This was turning out to be a fool's errand. I cursed my stupidity for coming so far with a woman in such a semi-delusional condition. But we had come thus far and I had enough curiosity to want to know where this was leading.

Finally, we made two dog-leg turns into some mean back-streets, only to drive into a dead-end where the forbidding walls of a prison rose up. Daphne was breathing so quickly I thought she was in danger of hyper-ventilating. 'He's here!' she said triumphantly, about to get out of the car.

I engaged the locks and seized her arm, 'Daphne! We can't go in there just like that. It's a prison!'

A frown crossed her brows, 'But I *must* go in!' Her voice now took on the mutinous tones of a little girl's, unable to understand the hard facts. 'Can't you hear it?' She tilted her head towards the uncompromising brickwork of the prison walls.

With my hand still grasping her arm, I heard it too, the answering melody to the tune she had sung earlier on the oud. Though I tried to rationalize the experience as the sound of a CD issuing from a nearby window, I couldn't really dismiss this extraordinary experience, because both melody and tune matched the song she had sung earlier too exactly. I could understand why she was so urgently excited, because it was a thrilling, awakening song, sung by a male voice. That it was emanating from beyond these walls was without doubt. I wondered, was this what the textbooks meant by a shared hallucination, albeit an auditory one? Part of my empirical mind obliged me to try an experiment. As I let go of her arm, so the sound vanished. When I touched her again, I too could share in the audition. I pondered this phenomenon with wonder.

Inevitably, at that moment, she wrenched up the door-lock and leapt from the car, making straight for the prison gate that was the only entrance in that blind-faced wall. Hammering on the smaller inset door with both fists, she began calling loudly, 'I'm here! I'm here!'

A warder opened up the grille in the door to see who was making so free with his gate, 'What do you want then, miss? Visiting hours are not till tomorrow.'

I dragged her off the gate, apologizing for her, 'I'm sorry. She's not very well, I'm sorry to have troubled you. — Come along, dear.' It was like trying to remove a leopard from its prey. She virtually spat at me.

The warder dismissed us with, 'Well I hope she gets well soon, mate.' He chuckled, to his companion, 'That's made my day — the first time anyone's every wanted to get *into* this place since I started here. — Best take her home, mate!'

I managed her back into the car, locked the door and sucked my hand where she'd bitten me. By the time I'd thrust the keys into the ignition, I saw that a different intelligence informed her. Gone was the Middle Eastern temptress. Daphne Weir stared up in bewilderment at the prison walls, at me, at the car. 'But how....?' she began, then realizing that she was in the passenger's and not the driver's seat, she slumped with relief. Then she saw the handkerchief I'd wrapped round my hand.

'Have you hurt yourself?' she had no recollection that, minutes before, she'd bitten savagely into my restraining hand.

I told her, 'I drove you here, at your command. But I think we had better get home now, don't you?' Two passers-by were beginning to take a closer interest in us. Suddenly realizing that the potential for scandal was huge, I drew out an old baseball cap I had stashed in the glove compartment and put it hastily on Daphne's head. 'Let's get out of here.'

I swung the car round in an ill-coordinated u-turn, wildly mounting the pavement, and began the long drive back before we could attract any more attention.

Daphne wept for a while and then fell into a fitful sleep once the engine settled into its own rhythm as we hit the road south. From a service station, I phoned ahead to let Wendy know where we were, wondering whether to administer some sedation after this afternoon's excitement, but as we drew into the drive, I saw Ash's car in the space next to mine.

Wendy put Daphne to bed while I went to report to Ash. Expecting his censure, I was surprised to be greeted with a glass of whiskey instead. 'Wendy tells me you've been having adventures?'

I told him of our outing. When I reported to him how I'd heard the singing too, I suddenly knew the reticence of a mentally-challenged patient on making such an admission. A psychologist hearing voices! But Ash was unfazed by it all.

'And it was the oud that brought this on? Hmmm! Interesting. — It was definitely worth hiring it after all, then. — Jack, I think we have a Middle Eastern incarnation here, don't you?' He smiled. 'Do you know where I was today?'

'Where?'

'I received a call today from the Governor of Her Majesty's Prison, Blanehurst Rise, to attend to one of his inmates.'

'What?' I was incredulous, for this was the prison we had just come from!

'Tommy Hale, the prison doctor is a colleague of mine. One of the men on remand started developing alarming and unusual symptoms and he wanted my opinion. The man had been arrested for attempting to break into a flat last week and could give no good account of himself. Can you guess whose flat?'

'You mean — what, not Daphne's?' The coincidence was beyond the bounds of possibility. 'Who is he?'

'Cengiz Havashi, a Turkish migrant worker here on a dodgy visa. He speaks little English and grew quite violent when the police took him in. He's there on remand awaiting trial and possible extradition. Tommy's very worried about him and has him under observation.'

'You really think this is the man she's been seeking?'

'I've already given him a look-over. Would you be surprised to hear that he has a similar tube in his body-field — almost identical to that in Daphne's aura.'

So far so good, 'But Ash, if he's the man she's been looking for, what is she going to say when you bring her together with a criminal?'

'This is no criminal, Jack. Thank God we still have our innocence until proven guilty in this country. This is her beloved. It would be the same to her if he was disfigured or had one leg. She'd love him whatever.'

'Are you sure?' I was appalled, 'Ash, she's a celebrity. Her life isn't exactly a private one. The papers would have a field day, as she said.'

Ash looked into me, 'I think that the bond that is between them will help

them overcome anything.'
'What, "love strong as death?"' 'I said, quoting the scriptures.
He shook his sleek dark head, 'Yes, love strong as death.'

We stood in the lobby of the prison hospital, waiting to see Havashi. Tommy Hale told us what he knew, 'We've had to work through an interpreter as his English isn't very good. From all we can gather, he's a musician who plays in restaurants — Greek, Lebanese, Turkish. He came to England a few months ago. He adamantly swears on the Qur'an that he didn't come to burgle the flat, only to meet up with a friend. But unfortunately, he knocked a policeman down while evading capture and that's what landed him here. Is Miss Weir really a friend of his?' He asked curiously.

'Oh, she has known him for a very long time,' Ash responded, coolly stretching the truth to cover reincarnational acquaintance, while telling no lie according to his own idiosyncratic philosophy. 'How is he now?'

'The crisis seemed to come about six o'clock yesterday. Since then, he's been in a semi-conscious state. I've never seen anything like it.'

I pulled Ash's sleeve, hissing, 'That's precisely the time we were at the prison gates!' Ash nodded, unperturbed.

Tommy instructed the warder on the door of the hospital unit to let us in.

'What happened yesterday?' I asked him

'Well, I called Ash in earlier because Havashi had lapsed into a very strange state and I know Ash has some experience of this sort of thing. Apparently, the man began by singing so loudly that the other inmates in his block began to complain. Remand prisoners very often protest against their captivity and the conditions, you know. Their sense of self-worth revolts against the whole filthy system. So the warders thought nothing more about it. But then his cell-mate began to call out that Havashi was having a fit or something and so we got him out quick. It wasn't epilepsy or a stroke, that much was clear. It was almost that he was…well, in some kind of ecstasy.' He sounded embarrassed to say the word.

The prisoner lay on his bed in that comfortless place, dressed in blue regulation pyjamas. He must have been at least ten years younger than Daphne, with a full, almost Mongolian face that had an ugly speckle of pock marks. Now I have seen paintings of saints in ecstatic states of mystical communion with their god and I would have readily categorized Havashi in that bracket. We could have been looking at Rumi or one of those desert sages gripped by divine longing. For one thing there was a beatific expression on his face that I've only seen once before at the death-bed of an old nun whose dying gaze opened upon heaven. Havashi's eyes were closed, but, on examination, his pupils were rolled up. The fingers of his left hand were curled up near his left shoulder while his right hand made stroking gestures over his navel.

'Look, he's playing an instrument,' I breathed to Ash, who nodded.

Tommy monitored Havashi's vital signs and conferred with Ash who drew me to one side.

'I've already phoned Wendy to ask Gillespie to bring Daphne here quickly. Tommy doesn't think he's going to last the night. His pulse is all over the place.'

'Will they let her in?' I remembered that awful scene at the prison gates and Daphne's despair at being denied entrance. I didn't think it would be good for her to go through that again.

Tommy Hale said, 'There is no time for her to fill in a visiting order. I'll make sure the Governor is told that this is a medical emergency, if it will help this poor man. I mean, he's got no-one else in this country. His family are in Izmir, according to the records. It's her or the local imam but, to be honest, I have more faith in the power of friendship in cases like this.'

Tommy made a phone call to the governor's office to get the necessary clearance and we sat by Havashi turn and turn about, while Ash monitored his vital signs. I noticed him making certain passes over the unconscious man's body, as if monitoring other, invisible levels of vitality.

Just after nine, Daphne appeared in the lobby, escorted by a warder. She looked under-slept and frightened, appalled to be in a prison but painfully hopeful.

Ash rose to welcome her, 'Is this the man you've been seeking?'

As she took in the recumbent figure, his youth, the pock-marks, the awful lack of good dentistry in his gaping jaw, I saw him with her eyes – a poor, uneducated immigrant, entirely out of her league. I saw her draw back and look away, ashamed at herself. Then, with the same resolve that she had shown that first morning in the London consulting room, I saw her battle with her self-respect and celebrity status, and watched them lose.

Watching the feeble movements of his body to pluck an invisible instrument, her eyes filled, 'Oh, yes! Yes!' she responded at long last.

Ignoring Tommy Hale and the warder at her side, she pleaded with Ash, 'What can you do?'

'Can you remember the tune that you sang yesterday? Sing that now. Sing him back!' Ash guided her finger-tips to rest lightly on the man's chest.

Through tears, she began to sing, first the melody and then she added the words, 'My beloved, rise and come. The voice of the turtle is heard in the land. Rise and come!'

Havashi's breathing began to grow deeper, his pulse became stronger. 'Keep singing!' urged Tommy, nodding vigorously, as he felt the quickening of Havashi's pulse.

'My beloved is like a hart upon the mountains. Let him kiss me with the kisses of his mouth, for I am his,' she sang. I doubt whether the walls of this prison hospital had ever heard the *Song of Songs* before. Incongruous though it seemed, the power of her touch and her erotic singing seemed to have dramatic results.

Havashi's eyelids flickered, he ceased his tensely impassioned invisible playing, his body and its rhythms gradually relaxing into those of a sleeping man. After about a quarter of an hour, during which Daphne never ceased to sing, he woke up naturally. The first person his dark eyes fell upon was Daphne.

It needed no interpreter to read what was between them. Trust and love had found their own reward.

§§

As we walked up Hartsworth Beacon at sunset the next day, I tried to understand the story that underlay this extraordinary case. Daphne had already discharged herself from the Beacon and was back in her London flat from which she was better able to visit Blanehurst Rise. All her doubt, fear and uncertainty had vanished, as had her compulsive need to stalk strange men.

'How could you be so confident that you could help her?' I still puzzled.

Ash rested one foot on the fallen trunk that blocked the path, 'I wasn't. Only that it was obvious we were nearing a crisis. Daphne's behaviour was being more and more dictated by demands that she didn't understand, as if she was circling nearer to the epicentre. All I did was explore the nature of the compulsion.'

'How?' I was still baffled.

Ash laughed, 'Jack, I do believe you still think that I have brought together two delusional people who just happen to share the same fantasy?'

I slashed at a crop of nettles with the elder branch I had picked up lower down the hill, 'I really don't know! For a couple separated by the law's delay, who don't even speak the same language, and have never met in this life at any point, they seem infernally happy.'

'Not infernally,' he admonished, mildly, 'Try "paradisally." After all, the place of their mutual incarnations was where the first paradise was located.

"Paradise" — it's just a word for an enclosed garden. No, I merely examined the incarnational records to see where their paths had crossed before.'

My expression told him how stumped I was by this admission.

Ash pointed further up the path to the Iron-Age fort, 'It is exactly the same as with those hikers yonder. They have their compass and maps, they merely take their bearing and head for the chosen destination. I just did that for Daphne. Even though we knew nothing about Havashi, the trail led to him because we had Daphne's map.'

I asked him, 'What are the incarnational records and how do you read them — if you can tell me, that is?'

Ash looked out over the twilight landscape below us. Lights were beginning to shine in the gloom where people in cottage, farm and village were watching television and eating their suppers. In the sky above us, the vapour trails left by airplanes were beginning to break up, becoming part of the darkening atmosphere. There was just one jet etching a golden-red streak into the farthest west as it rimmed the horizon, catching the sun's reflection. 'Every life leaves a trail,' he said, pointing. 'The resonance of a life is like the vibration left in the air when a great chord is sounded. When I have the call-signature of a soul, I can track it back through many life-times, just as the air-traffic controllers could tell us from their records of where that plane has flown in the last month. A record remains. I enter into meditation and follow the vapour trail, Jack. That's the nearest I can come to explaining.'

'So what was their story then? Some royal princess and her loyal slave, was it?'

'Nothing so grandiose. The incarnational records showed that they were together in Sumer — Ur of the Chaldees — trained to be musicians in one of the temples. Both Daphne and Havashi were both men then. They were lovers, each out-doing the other in the services of love, exceeding the boundaries of discretion. It came to the attention of the chief priest who deemed their love inappropriate to their sacred profession. The musician who became Daphne was exiled south, beyond the limits of Sumer, sent to be part of the entourage of a Sumerian concubine who was being sent to a lord in what we would call Lebanon today. They've been parted ever since for several thousand years.'

'Daphne has always been aware of the loss, always seeking. From my talk with Havashi through the interpreter, I gather that he has never formed a lasting relationship in this incarnation. He always knew that his beloved was to be found somewhere. When he realized through his dreams that the old lover had married someone else in this life, he fell into a terrible depression. The fact that he was in the country at all was something of a fortuitous accident. His uncle helped him come to England in an attempt to raise his spirits and to give him something else to think about.'

'So, you're saying that his depression marked the period when Daphne stopped hearing him?'

'I believe so. When she became "available" again after the divorce, so he began to dream of her again.'

'You keep saying "her," but surely Havashi must have remembered his lover as male? So are you saying that he isn't gay now, in this life?'

He quoted solemnly, '"Love is not love that alters when it alteration finds." No, the gods have been kind, they are both of an age and inclination to fulfil their love. They have found each other and I think they will remain true to each other.'

'So how did *he* find *her*?'

'He doesn't remember how he got to her flat at all. He just remembers waking up when his hammer shattered the glass in the window-frame. It wasn't even her actual flat, just the lower-ground floor flat of the block where she lived. — That was the day that Daphne came to see us in London and checked into the Beacon. Once she stepped over the threshold here, it was the equivalent of sending out a powerful radio signal. This house is both protected and sensitive to the needs of our guests. Once she began to concentrate upon the cause of her trouble, it was only a matter of time. Havashi felt impelled to find her and subconsciously, his soul obliged by bringing him to where she had been.

'The Turkish musicologists at Crooked Cottage appeared at precisely the time when she was drinking rose-petal tea — and that put me on the scent of who her beloved might be now, which is why I hired that oud. When she started to play it, she was actively sending a signal that she was alive and nearby. His rapture was so profound, it sent him into an ecstatic trance. And ... well, you helped her find him after that.'

'Tell me, why was it she sang the *Song of Songs* to him? How did that bring him out of his trance?'

'Ah, Jack! The temple-songs of that ancient civilization were the first divine love-songs. The *Song of Songs* was the nearest thing in Daphne's education to the songs she'd sung with Havashi over four thousand years ago. The song alone wouldn't have brought him back, indeed, she could have sung any song at all, *but the fact that she was touching his body while she sang* told him that his beloved was beside him in the flesh. That guided his soul back into his body.'

Cengiz Havashi and Daphne Weir were married very quietly seven months later, after the trial. Because of the time he'd already spent on remand, he had only six months to serve for his assault on the policeman. Daphne's barrister caused the burglary charge to be dropped, as well as dealing with the irregularities in Cengiz' visa. The newspapers did indeed have a field day, but it was without the participation of the happy couple, who had stolen away to a quiet part of Turkey for their honeymoon.

When I come to think of the case in retrospect, it is quite possible that *City Male* and *Celebrity News* had been onto something after all, when their reporters tried to dish the dirt on Daphne. They were on the money that there had been something about her that didn't quite sit right with her as a news-anchor, but it was certainly not what their unsavoury minds had envisaged. But those old rumours are quite forgotten now. Since she abandoned her television career, Daphne has started recording with Cengiz. What with the story of their romance and the love-songs they've subsequently recorded, they have become one of the hottest properties on the world music scene.

Case 2: THE WEEPING MAIDEN

The Devil's Elbow is one of those landmarks you are glad to have negotiated safely in the car. It lies on one of the steep upland slopes of Maiden's Dyke where the road makes a sharp and inconvenient turn just at the tricky point where you need to go into a much lower gear. There seems to be neither rime nor reason for the angle of the bend except for a solitary black poplar tree of some antiquity that crowds the corner of the road with dark, jealous branches.

Since it's one of the only roads over the Downs that leads to the south coast from the Beacon, I found myself frequently having to go that way. On either side of the road, the land falls sharply away, and although the local council have erected black and white crash-barriers and various admonitory notices about slowing down, changing gear and generally exercising caution, the only effect of this is to make you feel even more unsafe. It's one of those stretches of road that seems strangely bare and unfrequented. Its very exposure seems the appropriate location for highwaymen or perhaps a gallows. I find that whenever I have to go that way, that it's with some reluctance, and that as I approach the Devil's Elbow, I snap into a heightened awareness of how I'm driving. Even after you've rounded the bend, it doesn't do to relax or let your attention slip, because you still have to climb the one-in-four gradient of the Maiden's Dyke where it seems as if the nose of your car bonnet is aimed directly at the sun. Just before you cross the Dyke itself, there's a momentary and uncanny sensation that you are about to launch yourself into the sky.

I would never have admitted to any of these feelings had I not been in the village shop in Chiselden one morning when our local post-woman, Janet Bagley, was collecting the parcels from the sub post-office at the back of the shop. It was a particularly large sack which she was heaving onto her back with, 'Well I hope I get over the Dyke with this lot!' The chief sorting office of the district was Frisdon on Sea and thus via the Maiden's Dyke.

Many in the usual benefit and pension queue winding out of the door nodded sympathetically, 'I'd throw a couple of 'em out when you gets to the bend, love,' said Eric Moreton, the village wag. 'The Weeping Maiden hasn't had a present in a while.'

His wife nudged him in the ribs, 'Don't you start!' she warned him.

Janet Bagley just grinned, 'I might just do that!'

A bent-over granny with a punchinello nose said, 'Just don't you throw out that one with the glitter stickers on now, Mrs. Bagley, that's for my great grandniece's birthday next Thursday. It's got a blue Brummy Bear from the cartoon series in it. Knitted it special I have.'

Janet made her way out of the crowded shop with difficulty, fielding such comments as she went. I had attached myself to the queue in order to get some stamps for the Beacon, and now I began to inure myself to a long wait.

'I wouldn't have her job for all the tea in china,' breathed the hook-nosed granny. 'Four times a day she has to go over the Dyke. I think she should be paid danger money. My Derek always drives me round by Deddenham way when we goes to the coast.' Which must have added at least thirty miles onto the coastal journey, I reckoned.

The vicar's wife behind me admitted, 'I wish Vernon would do that! He says we can get over with a wing and a prayer, but I have a hard time with the children when I drive them down into Frisdon for the skating rink. My youngest screams his head off so, you would think he was being tortured. I wish I could fit him with blinkers like Farmer Jelley's horse.'

Everyone in the queue shared their reservations about the road, so I began to feel like less of a wimp, especially after Micky Bryson, a burly farm-worker, admitted to being fearful of crossing the Dyke after dark. As an incomer to the region, I'd kept a low profile, but now I asked, 'What's the Weeping Maiden?'

After a pregnant silence in which I began to feel like a dog who'd talked, there was a buzz in the shop as several people attempted to educate me.

'She's the Devil's mistress, that one!'

''Er's the poplar at the Devil's Elbow.'

'They do say she weeps if she ain't had an offering.'

William Ford, the local verger, briskly admonished everyone, 'I'm sure that Mr. Rivers doesn't want to hear about old superstitions like that.'

I'm afraid, I disappointed him, 'Well actually, I'm very glad to hear that it's not just me who feels there's something uncanny about the place. Black poplars are quite rare, aren't they?'

The verger, who fancied himself as the local naturalist, 'It's really quite remarkable that it grows up there so high. Poplars like a good bit of moisture. What with the chalk draining down so well, it's a miracle, really. That one is a rarity and no mistake.'

But all the while he was explaining about the botanical ins and outs, I could tell that the queue was either restive to discuss the propensities of the Weeping Maiden or else anxious to avoid any more mention of it, especially the old fellow with the pipe at the front of the queue who I noticed hurried out, pocketing his pension without another word.

I thought nothing more about it until later that month, when I was to be personally drawn in to an aspect of Ash's work that was definitely beyond my statutory job-description. The call came at about 10.45 p.m. when I met Gillespie on the step, trying to put out Cinnamon for the final time that evening.

Deaf to her wheedling mews, he pushed her out the cat-flap and locked it, calling after her, 'Nae more voles on the dining table, if you please!'

Ash suddenly appeared at the kitchen door, 'Get your coat, Jack! There's been an accident on the Devil's Elbow.'

'What about the emergency services?'

'Police say that the ambulance sent to attend the accident has overturned on the Frisdon by-pass. The local doctor is attending a difficult confinement. We are the nearest help until Christminster can send out another unit.'

It had been some time since I did I stint in A & E before I specialized, but now I threw together a bag of essentials and off we sped through the night. In the search-light glare of police headlights at the Devil's Elbow, it was easy to see how it had happened. The white Nissan van had come over the Dyke from the coast and failed to negotiate the bend. The vehicle had slammed into the black poplar, ejecting the driver through the windscreen.

'He must have just rounded the top of the Dyke and ploughed straight into the Weeping Maiden,' the police sergeant said over the crackle of his radio-com. The driver lay bleeding under the tree, fortunately unconscious. We attended to him as best we could under the circumstances. Apart from multiple fractures that looked fairly straightforward, he might have serious internal injuries and had lost a lot of blood besides.

While we waited for the specialized unit that had been dispatched from Christminster General, Ash crouched very still next to the driver. He stared up at the arterial blood that had splashed up the pitted bark of the black poplar with its grotesquely whiskered bosses and burrs sticking out like facial warts. She might have been called the Weeping Maiden, but she had all the charm and beauty of an old witch to me.

'She's had libations like this before,' I heard Ash mutter to himself.

'What's that?' I asked, in some agitation, for the over-weight driver kept slipping down the slope and I was trying to wedge my knees under him as gently as possible to stop him rolling down the fearful incline behind me. Ash seemed to come out of his reverie and shook his head, 'This isn't the time nor the place. Later...'

Frankly, I was glad not to pursue the answer at that hour. This place was fearful enough during the day, never mind in pitch darkness. Since we arrived, the police had taken themselves further down the road, ostensibly to turn back traffic and to monitor the second ambulance's progress, though I think it was to avoid proximity to the tree.

It felt very lonely perched in the Devil's Elbow. I was all too aware of the steep drop behind me, unguarded now that the crash-barriers had been wrenched from their housing-posts. Part of one lay about two hundred feet below with the remains of the Nissan. The police had rigged up a rope around the Devil's Elbow by dint of passing it around the tree and attaching the ends to the tow-bars of two of their vans. While it offered scant protection as a hand-hold on that treacherous slope, I don't think I would have wanted to make much use of it, personally. I was all too aware of the power of the tree running through the twisted fibres of the rope like an electrical current.

I found myself trying to think of it as just a black poplar and to ignore its personification as the Weeping Maiden. The pendulous deltoid leaves with their arrow-like tips looked even more persuasively tear-shaped in the blue and yellow lights thrown by the police vehicles. The rotating flash of the emergency lights was beginning to have a strobe-like effect upon my retinas, for I was partially aware of something moving, with frog-like tenacity upon the trunk. I clutched Ash's arm, inarticulate with terror. He squeezed my hand back, whispering, 'Don't mind it. Just say whatever prayers you know for this poor chap!'

We did what we could, but you could feel the life draining out of him. As his respiration faltered and his pulse dropped, the menace of the tree seemed only to grow the greater. I had an eerie sense that the tree was pleased, but I kept my eyes averted from it, so as not to spy whatever it was again.

It was gone one in the morning by the time that the paramedics arrived. All we could do was help lift the stretcher into the ambulance and go home. We drove home in silence. The next morning, over a very late breakfast, Ash was called to the phone, 'That was Sergeant Hobbs from the hospital. The poor fellow died an hour ago.'

Myrtle Armitage, our young cleaning woman was in that morning. She crossed herself, 'God rest his soul! And God curse that wicked spot! That's one death too many.'

It was generally felt to be the case by the local administration. Although we lie nearer to Frisdon than anywhere else, our region is governed by Christminster District Council. In its wisdom, the council decided to remove the Weeping Maiden and to iron out the killer bend of the Dyke by dint of acquiring the requisite adjoining land for the engineers to work on.

As soon as these plans were unveiled in the local paper, all hell broke loose. The Downs Heritage Trust made formal applications to blunt the council's plans by suggesting that they just pollard the tree and widen the road, so that the Downs wouldn't utterly lose an integral and much-loved natural feature. That the Devil's Elbow was especially unloved by locals didn't count a bit. But the worst came from some group of eco-activists, styling themselves 'The Crutch,' who began a sit-in protest in and round the tree to stop it being touched. Any progress was impossible while they were in situ. The council had to allocate its budget carefully and obviously didn't want the expense of security guards to police the site.

'Why on earth are they called "the Crutch?"' asked Wendy, pouring over the paper. 'I mean, it's not exactly a title to rally behind is it?'

Gillespie crinkled his jaw into a grimace, and did a Long John Silver impersonation around the table with the upturned broom under his armpit, 'Crutch — elbow; elbow — crutch! — Get it? — Ah, lass, this lot would support the Devil hissel for a handful of lentils. What with eco-terrorists and pagan activists rushing to stop the old witch being lopped, it's a wonder they've a brain between the lot of them. Thank God political correctness is outlawed north of the Wall!'

'Well, eco-terrorism notwithstanding, you're going to have to drive via Deddenham if you want any dinner tonight. The Devil's Elbow is closed until further notice and the supermarket calls you.' Mimicking his own accent she skirled, 'Can ye no hear, you old Pict you?' and chased him out of the kitchen with the newspaper.

'Wonderful to see the ancient conflict of the Scots and English eternally replayed between those two!' I remarked to Ash.

'Oh, just ignore their Punch and Judy act. It's all for show. I blame *Braveheart*, myself!'

'So what do you think about the council's idea?'

'Well, I don't like that bend anymore than anyone else round here, but I do believe that they need to proceed cautiously or they'll end up with worse problems than they've got already,' he said, pouring boiling water onto his pot of green tea.

'How do you mean?'

'That's a place of ancient sacrifice alright, but the tree is something more than a road-hazard....It's been purposefully planted there to keep something in check, I'm sure.'

'Something *worse* than sacrifice?' Surely whatever had been anciently present must have moved on by now?

'Not worse! No, the way that the road bends just there is not an ill-considered piece of road-making. I believe that whoever laid that road knew exactly what they were doing. Perhaps it turns just there because there is an ancient boundary point which no-one now remembers. The tree was planted at that turn to remind people of something. As time has gone on, this has been nearly forgotten. Solitary horses and slow farm-wagons have given way to vehicles that drive too fast for that kind of bend. That's why there have been so many accidents there.'

'But you think that those accidents have fed into some kind of thirst for sacrifice?'

'To be honest, Jack, I don't really know. But I don't think we've heard the last of the story yet. '

I put down my coffee, reluctant to mention what we had seen the night of the accident, 'Did I really see what I thought I saw that night?' I hadn't liked to discuss it before now. The thing that had been swarming over the tree had been humanoid in shape but attached to and moving over the bark with an amphibious suction and dexterity. People don't—can't—move like that, not even ghosts of people, I reckoned.

'You did see it then?' Ash looked at me gravely. 'Why didn't you say so sooner?'

'Too scared.' I sipped some more coffee.

'It was some kind of elemental spirit associated with the site. Tell me, what were you most aware of while we sat there?'

'Ash, I'm really not sure that I want your professional services,' for he used that analyst's tone that draws out the story from reluctant clients.

'I promise not to analyse you. I would just value your collegial confirmation, Jack,' he said, diplomatically.

'Very well.' I didn't mind talking now that some time had elapsed between then and now, and in the broad daylight of the breakfast table. 'I thought the thing on the tree was pleased.... like..' I fished for an appropriate metaphor.... 'like a large predator that had been fed. You know, lions in the zoo after lunch, but nothing half so amiable.'

'Precisely! You describe it well,' he nodded affirmatively. 'I believe what we saw was either the spirit of the tree, or what lives under it.'

I choked on my coffee, 'Under it?! But Ash, they're going to fell it—what will happen then?' In that moment, I found myself seeing things from his perspective, amazing myself.

'If it's the spirit of that bit of land, then there's not a lot can be done at this stage. However, if it's something that's been tied to the site, then that's a different matter.' He regarded me over the toast, 'How is your nerve? Is it up to revisiting the site? —Strictly during daylight hours, of course!'

'Why?' I asked suspiciously. 'You don't really expect me to go back there, do you?'

'Only in the company of others. I believe the site is currently under occupation....? I'd like you to check out what's going on and how it feels today.'

'Why me?'

'Because you have a sensitivity to the land that exceeds my own. You are more a man of the earth than I. I am of the air.'

'Well, whatever that means......I'll only agree to go if you supply me with the requisite crosses and garlic.'

So that Sunday, I took a walk over to the impromptu camp that had mushroomed round the Devil's Elbow. Colourful banners snapped in the strong wind, proclaiming 'Crutch Supports the Weeping Maiden!' and 'Save Our Trees!' A line of Buddhist prayer flags had been threaded along one branch and a platform had been erected in the groins of the three main divisions of the trunk. Someone with ginger dreadlocks, a multi-striped cone hat and a set of totally atrophied nerves inhabited the platform. Quite apart from whatever spiritual danger he might be in, he must also have been freezing. A little line of benders and solitary igloo tents had been pighted along the narrow ridge, half-on and half-off the road, while the main base-camp further down the Dyke milled with supporters of varying ages and avocations.

A large blonde woman in a huge skirt, seemingly impervious to the prevailing wind, with bare-arms tattooed in Celtic bands was doling out soup from a cauldron. When she turned round to dispense a slice of bread I saw that she had a placard on her back reading, 'Dikes Against the Dyke-Wreckers.' No-one seemed to be in charge.

As it was a blowy day, I'd worn my green cagoule and had a woollen army-surplus hat to protect my ears. A thin, elegantly-mackintoshed elderly woman in a hat catching sight of my uncertainty, touched my arm and enquired in cut-glass tones, 'Another supporter come to the fold? Do have a sip, dear.' And offered me a pull on her hip-flask. Since I was cold, I didn't disabuse her of my rogue status. She was the kind of woman you'd meet in Christminster's best tea-shops and boutiques. In order to fit in with this crowd, she had attached various badges and buttons to her designer beret. I noticed that 'National Trust,' and 'Down with the Downs' Destroyers' incongruously jostled each other over one ear. The flask contained a choice single malt of some maturity, for which I was profoundly grateful. 'Very warming, thank you. How's it all going?'

'Well, Martin's organized everything very well so far, but I'm afraid the press aren't best pleased with the facilities.' She indicated a dejected cameraman pulling on his smoke in the lee of the main yurt that seemed to be the HQ.

'Have you come for the press conference? — Do forgive me, I haven't introduced myself. I am Elspeth Markham.'

I turned back the end of my right mitten and shook fingers with her, 'Jack Rivers. I didn't know there was going to be a press conference. Can I …er … stay?' I'm sure she had modestly omitted an 'honourable' at the front of her name.

She misunderstood me. With a gracious solicitude I thought only the Queen could dispense, she asked, 'Dooo you have a tent or bender of your own? Only the main yurt is becoming a little full at night. The relief team sleeps there, you understand.'

'I only wanted to see how things were progressing,' I said, warily.

She eyed me in sudden beady suspicion, 'You're not from the council are you?' You wouldn't want to be on the wrong side of the Hon. Elspeth, I concluded. She had that air of being able to summon military assistance at the fall of a finger.

'No, no! Just a local resident,' I hastily told her.

'Oh! How wonderful! – I'm sorry to have doubted your motives. We must be careful, you know. – Excuse me!' She turned away and yelled in a voice that could have cut through a disco in full heave, 'Martin! Dooo come. At last we have a resident.' She turned back and in more moderate tones, cooed, 'How very nice. We were beginning to wonder whether the residents hereabouts really cared about trees at all. We've seen none of them, you know?'

Embarrassed, I tried to explain, 'Well, I think they are mainly well disposed towards trees in general, just a little touchy about this one in particular.'

A tall, thin, white youth of great intensity dressed entirely in black, attired more like a brother from the Bronx than the more usual Gothic youth, loomed into view. Several young women swarmed about him attentively, while he frowned and shoed them back with ill-disguised impatience. Following the Hon. Elspeth's gesture, he homed in on me, 'Are you the representative of the community? Better come on in, we're starting.'

His tone didn't brook refusal, so I allowed myself to be steered into the yurt where it was certainly much warmer, being heated by a central stove. People began to settle inside its circular walls. Rather than giving a harangue, Martin held a tree branch in his hand, explaining rather belligerently, 'This is the talking stick. We at Crutch are here collectively, so we're going to each say our piece. When you finish, you hand it to the person on your left, ok? When someone's talking, you respect, clear?'

Everyone nodded, some shouted 'Respect!' in defiance of his clear instructions. That boy would have made a great Butlins red-coat if he had ever been able to summon up his sense of humour. As it turned out, he would have made a better Gestapo officer. The press were being persuaded to join the circle rather than separate themselves from our number.

Martin started, 'We're here to save this tree. It's part of our sacred heritage and no council can take that away.' He spoke for two more minutes and passed on the branch to the woman next to him. Some people shouted 'Ho!' after each speech or outburst. Being able to speak only one at a time had the effect of intensifying the passion rather than diffusing it. I feared we were in for an hour or more of dull invective and earnest, ill-considered protest. From the showing there, it would appear that the majority were druids, witches and assorted pagans, with a few hard-core eco-activists among them – of whom Martin clearly was one. The rest were do-gooders from various heritage groups, people like Hon. Elspeth who should really have been in the House of Lords, not in this gypsy band. The members of the press, mostly from the coastal papers except for a woman from the *Guardian*, each held the branch awkwardly and stated their purpose rather than their objections. The chain-smoking cameraman's joke, 'I'm from the Downs Chronicle and I'm here for the beer,' fell on exceedingly stony ground.

The talking stick circled nearer to me. While I could have crawled back through the flap behind me, it seemed cowardly. I really didn't want to touch the branch, which I was sure had come from the tree, though probably not cut off it, if the sentiments of Crutch were to be believed. Frankly, even if it had dropped off in a high wind, I wouldn't have touched it. I was trying to pull on my mittens again when the woman to my right thrust it towards me. I am too much of a gentleman or a wimpy middle Englander perhaps, but I was on the horns of a dilemma. Was it more discourteous to the democratic assembly in the yurt or more disrespectful to the Weeping Maiden?

In that split second, I made a decision and took it into my bare hand. I could feel immediately that the branch was indeed from the tree. Time seemed to slow down, my ears felt muffled or sound went dim, I can't tell which. I found myself holding the branch with the utmost respect, as if I had been given the crown jewels or the hand of a very beautiful woman. As soon as the thought of a hand crossed my consciousness, I seemed to feel a hand in mine. It caressed my hand, gripping it. Good God! Had no-one else in the circle felt this? Vitality was being pumped into me – not like the other night when that poor driver had virtually bled to death on my lap, drained of his energy. I wanted badly to pass it on, or for my lips to utter the idiotic shout of 'Ho!' like some of the inarticulate protestors had done, but I just couldn't. I had the horrible feeling that *it wanted to be in my hand.*

After that I don't remember much. I only remember coming to a resounding silence and then a round of applause. The stick passed on and was no more part of me. Afterwards, several of the pagans rushed up to me in acclaim, 'That was one powerful oracle,' said a sad-eyed young druid, with his Wellingtons showing under his muddy white robe. 'Awesome,' several of Martin's harem of young women enthused. Shaking them all off with the irritability of an Old Testament prophet, which was how they were treating me, I sought out the Hon. Elspeth who told me straight that I had burst into tears and uttered something in a language no-one understood. She seemed disquieted at my lack of *sang froid* and yet accepting of my apparent oracular powers.

'What did I say — what did it sound like?' I urged, hoping I'd not disgraced myself too thoroughly.

Elspeth thought for a bit, then said gravely, 'Very old.... As if the earth had spoken in the accents of all the men who had ever lived here.' Which sounded way too poetic for me. However, she was the only one to enquire how I felt, which was kind of her.

I made a quick examination of myself, going through all the usual routines, just to make sure I was still working properly. The major difference was that I felt much invigorated, on first inspection. The front of my shirt was indeed wet. Looking about me, I stared uphill towards the Weeping Maiden and considered it in the light of my experience. I found that I wasn't afraid of it any more. That I wanted to protect it... even lay down my life to protect it..... oh God! I had to get out of there quick!

As I turned to go, Martin stepped into my path, 'You going then?' He had a belligerent air to him that seemed to have less to do with tree-protection and a lot to do with me pulling his entourage, who even now were flocking about me in adulatory ecstasy.

'I... live locally. I don't have to camp here,' I told him, at the same time beaming silently, 'It's not my fault, mate! I didn't ask for your bleeding talking stick parliament.' I think he got the message.

One of my swan-necked maidens fell on my arm, 'But you mustn't go — it's so obvious that the Weeping Maiden speaks through you.' Nothing could have encouraged me leave quicker!

I was grateful to Elspeth, who gently unhooked my purring Nimue, and allowed me to go on my way before I got locked up like Merlin.

Back at the Beacon, I soaked out my astounding day in a deep bath, trying to keep my mind from straying tree-wards. It wasn't until I was drying myself that I remembered that the press had been present for my little outburst. Groaning and penitent I went towards Ash's study and knocked, seeking absolution.

After regarding me with interest, Ash remarked, 'You look different,' putting his book to one side.

'I've not dried my hair,' I said woodenly.

'No! Your aura looks — enhanced — like you've had floodlights put in.' He reached up to take my hand and pull me into the comfortable chair opposite him by the fire. There was a faint discharge of static between us, such as you get if you stroke a cat on a thundery day.

His eyes widened, 'My word, your walk *has* done you good!'

'Ash. Be serious! I think you need to commit me as an inmate — as of today, I think I'm no longer fit to be a member of staff.'

'Tell me.' So I told him everything I could.

'What's happening to me?' I pleaded.

'When the branch was used as a talking stick, I think that the tree picked up on the unfocused energy that was present in that yurt. It must be the first time for many hundreds of years that there's been any kind of assembly at that spot. The protesters have formed a temporary tribe and have begun to constellate a group-mindedness. They may feel that they are protecting the tree, but the tree is probably also drawing upon them. When you met together in that press conference, you were sitting in a circle. The use of the branch as a talking stick was clearly and publicly established by Martin, you tell me. — Well, I think that is precisely what it became — only not so much a stick to be talked with, as a stick that summons speech.'

I was in some agitation, 'But why did it pick on me?'

Ash smiled a slow smile, 'Tell me, doctor, how many times do you announce your profession at a party?'

No medical practitioner ever willingly vouchsafes his profession at social events for the simple reason that everyone feels it permissible to consult him about their strange aches and pains over the canapés and sherry. 'What does that have to do with anything?'

'Well, have you not sworn the Hippocratic oath?'

'Of course! But what....' The penny dropped, 'You mean the tree was trying to access me, just like a potential patient might?'

He nodded, 'Granted that all those protesters are ostensibly there to do it good and protect it, but I think that the Weeping Maiden is used to appointing her own protector. — You have sworn solemnly to protect all life from harm and to bring healing. That oath is sealed into your aura and gives you an authority not present in others at that camp, I would imagine.'

'You mean, the tree has....

'....chosen you to be her protector and mouthpiece. Yes! — In ancient times,

Jack, this would have been a great honour. Perhaps you could set up as oracle to the Weeping Maiden, stopping travellers upon their way,' he quipped.

'Don't joke about it!' I covered my eyes. 'What can I do now? Help me, Ash! It's an appalling responsibility! I didn't assent to this.' Awful visions of myself as some kind of latter-day Ancient Mariner with a tree, rather than an albatross, about my neck and 'stopping one of three,' wasn't a pretty prospect.

He nodded, 'No, of course you didn't. We live in other times when our free will is of paramount importance to us. Times have changed, but I don't think the Weeping Maiden has been informed yet. That will be our task, I think. Are you averse to me hypnotizing you?'

I've learnt the basics of hypnosis, but I can't say I've ever felt up to practising it. Its use to aid smokers quit smoking or to alter deeply unconscious embedding of behavioural characteristics seems to me to be only of limited assistance. 'I don't think you'll find me a very apt subject. I was never very good at going under when I last tried.'

Ash's smile was now like the Cheshire Cat's, 'How much do you bet me that you can resist induction?'

'I didn't think you were a betting man, and judging from your expression, I would be foolish to put down my stake. Go on then, have a go!'

It was 3.30pm by the carriage clock on the mantelpiece when Ash brought out a clear glass pendulum from his pocket and began swinging it. 'Give it over, Ash, it's clearly useless,' I said after what seemed to be a few minutes.

He had put the pendulum away and had leaned back into his deep armchair, regarding me closely with steepled hands. He flicked his eyes to the clock, with an ironic lifted eyebrow. It was 4.55pm.

'Have you moved the hands?' I demanded.

'No! The normal mechanisms of the clock did that.'

'What happened?' It was an uncanny feeling to have lost nearly an hour and half of time.

'Well, I had no idea when I sent you up the Dyke that the Weeping Maiden would take a fancy to you. I think you reminded her of the kind of priestly guardian who would have once tended that spot in the distant past. What the examination showed was that you have a rapport with the spirit of the tree and were deemed suitable. I also asked that you repeat what you said in the yurt to my dictaphone here.' He hit the rewind button and we listened to it.

My voice swam up from the magnetic tape making sounds and sentences that were definitely not English. The timbre of my voice sounded lower than normal for one thing and there was a curious shivery quality to it as if I had been talking through a sheet of baking foil. The vowel and consonantal qualities were utterly unlike anything I had heard, and I would have been incredulous had anyone else said I had uttered them. Neither of us understood a word of it.

Ash was entranced with professional interest, 'Just as the Delphic Oracle must have sounded, I daresay! — There's no need to be alarmed, Jack,' he told me as I squirmed in my chair. But the whole idea of being in rapport with a tree and becoming some kind of oracle for it was beyond bearing. 'Can't you exorcise it?'

'That depends.' He leant forward, 'Do you truly want to protect the tree from being felled? — Answer me from your deepest integrity, rather than from your human fears, if you can.'

I schooled my breath and considered in silence, trying to consider the tree from a wider perspective. This was no ordinary tree. Where I would have happily lopped an overhanging branch or taken a saw to a sucker from an existent tree in the garden, I doubted whether I could personally bring myself to fell any tree. It was a life. I summoned up the image of the black poplar, allowing myself to consider the thing I had seen crawling about on its trunk. The Weeping Maiden didn't want that amphibious thing attached to it. It wanted to be free of it.

'At present we are dealing with two different things,' I said. The words seemed to come from a far place, 'The being that has lodged in the tree is hungry for blood. It rejoices in slaughter. Many animals and people have been offered to it. The tree itself wishes to be disassociated with it since it has another purpose. We must draw the hungry spirit out and liberate the tree before other sacrifices are laid at its door. The tree is the guardian of the Maiden's Dyke, but she is not honoured in her current guise because she is viewed as a harbinger of fear and death rather than as a protector. She must come down and a new guardian be installed. — For my part, I am in the service of that guardian, not of the spirit of sacrifice.'

Ash had gone very still. He leant forward and snapped off the Dictaphone, 'Thank you for that very concise translation of the oracle, Jack. I think you've defined your job description very well.'

'What? What have I said?'

'You've just told us exactly how to proceed. Now all we have to do is put it into action.'

Ash gave me strict instructions not to go near the Devil's Elbow until further notice, for which I was heartily glad. I immersed myself in helping Gillespie with repairing the garden shed while Ash began his enquiries. I certainly had energy to spare. Even Gillespie remarked on my new-found vitality, 'You've sure been taking your porridge, laddie!'

My employer returned later the next day. 'It's no good, Jack. We can't do what's necessary while all those young people are swarming all over the site, it's far too dangerous.'

'What do you want to do?'

'To remove the intrusive spirit from the tree – to exorcise it, if you will. But we don't want it taking up residence elsewhere. I need some quietness.'

But before the week was out, another casualty was claimed. One of the young men encamped on the platform fell out of the tree, laying open his leg and breaking several bones. According to Ash, the camp was thinning out since the accident to one of its number. It looked as though the protest was officially coming to its close.

But affairs were actually coming to a head. The council could find no local man to fell the tree. We learned that they planned to bring in private contractors, Timberlads, a firm of slick operators from Borhant who specialized in the removal of inconvenient trees from city streets. Since the law changed recently, local councils have become legally liable for any damage caused by trees falling in high winds onto people or property. In the wake of a rising wave of litigation, many councils had opted for the preventative approach and had removed large well-loved trees before they could become dangerous, much to the fury of residents and nature-lovers. Timberlads was probably doing a fine trade in selling fine-grade hard-wood timber to the furniture manufacturers as well as making a tidy profit on logs for wood-burning stoves. They usually moved in before protests could be mounted, but they were known to have their own heavies to hand in case.

Ash folded the local paper in which this plan was printed with some finality, 'Time to call in back-up before we see some serious carnage. This situation has to be defused.' We drove into Chiselden and parked outside the White Hart. Sitting in the inglenook under a fine display of horse-brasses sat the old man with the pipe who had been in the post-office queue that morning I had learned about the Weeping Maiden.

Ash approached him 'Harry White? I am Richard Ashington from the Beacon and this is my colleague, Jack Rivers. I believe we both have the well-being of a local landmark at heart. Can I buy you a drink?'

Harry accepted the drink somewhat warily, 'You're not from the papers or the protest then?'

We assured him that we were not. Skilfully, Ash drew him into conversation, talking about local landmarks and customs in the area, letting it drop that he was a pupil of Melanie Rydale's. Harry took his pipe out of his mouth at that point, 'That Miss Rydale was a proper lady. We was sorry to lose her.' It wasn't long before the talk got round to the Devil's Elbow.

'My father remembers his grandfather showing him the Weeping Maiden. He was made to doff his cap and make a knee to her, out of respect. The proper thing was to leave some of your piece on one of the branches if you was working up that way. Peddlers used to put a farthing in the hole in her side for thanks. She was the guardian of the road by here.'

'When would that have been?' I asked.

Harry said, 'My great, great, great grandfer were born when daft King George was on the throne, in 1752, when they took our eleven days off of us. We're a long-lived family, the Whites. Worked the land, man and boy, these many generations.'

Ash nodded, 'It's for that very reason that I came, sir. Tell me, if the council could be persuaded to call off the contractors and the protesters subsequently went home, would your sons help fell the Weeping Maiden in a respectful way?' And he began to outline his plan.

I don't know how he did it, but somehow the council cancelled Timberlads, and modified their previous plans. Without the prospect of a public combat, some of the more hard-line activists withdrew from the camp, leaving only a few actual tree-lovers. And so it was that, just before dawn, one April morning, I went with Ash and four of Harry White's sons.

'Are you sure this will work?' I asked him again for the hundredth time, for I mis-liked the role that I would play in this.

'Just keep the thought of how many people have suffered on this spot over the centuries and how it's offended the real guardian of the site.'

Seeing the saw borne by the White brothers, the handful of protesters on duty began to gather round us, chanting, 'Save the tree.' Soon they would raise the base camp further down the hillside.

'Time for you to do your stuff, Jack,' Ash shouted over their chanting.

I stepped forward, holding up both hands. 'Listen! You've been right to defend the tree. But even you must have noticed something unpleasant about this bend. It's not coming from the tree, but from what's under it. The only way to cleanse the site and honour the guardian of the Dyke is to remove the evil that's been troubling it. That's what the tree herself is asking.'

They quieted enough to listen to me, since I had spoken for the tree before. Since not one of them was local, they saw me as the resident authority. I saw Elspeth being helped up the hill by the sad-faced druid. The sun was just rising over the Dyke and turning the greeny blue edge of the horizon a red gold.

'Come nearer to the tree!' Ash said.

I hadn't been anywhere near it since the talking stick episode, except by way of hypnosis. As soon as I came within nine yards of it, I was again stricken with that overwhelming need to protect it, but I knew I wanted to protect it in ways that transcended any political correctness, far surpassing any environmental protest. A warrior strength welled up in me.

Someone from the crowd sneered, 'Who authorized you to talk for the tree?' It was Martin, starkly white in his black clothes, looming out of the hazy light of dawn. He faced me out, cutting his way easily through the thin circle of protesters surrounding us.

'The Weeping Maiden chose me,' I heard myself state, without boasting. 'You heard me speak for her. She wants to be free of this evil that's been attached to her.' I wanted to strike him down there and then.

'Steady!' said Ash, 'Keep him talking, if you can. I'm going in.'

While everyone focussed upon us, Ash slipped through the crowd to the tree and began his ritual exorcism. Even to me, who knew what he intended, it seemed hazardous. The powers of the Weeping Maiden and the spirit of sacrifice seemed to be polarizing here and now in this crowd. The power was growing, and with the power, the paranoia that could focalize it either way. I knew I could draw upon the land, but not yet. I tried reasoning with Martin, 'You've done what you can to protect her, but it's time for her to pass. Something is lost, but something will be gained.'

I didn't even see how he launched himself at me, 'You won't have her! She's mine!' Suddenly the thin, angry youth was at my throat, and he didn't mean to fight fair. We wrestled briefly. I easily outweighed him. It should have been ludicrously easy to fend him off, but suddenly it wasn't. Martin, or whatever was in him, was fighting back like a demon. I really had to fight in earnest. Again and again he raised his nails to gouge me. I battered him in the stomach, trying to avoid his attempts to draw blood from me. The way he was moving seemed suddenly amphibious, rather like those martial arts films where they go in for slow motion footage followed by rapid, double-time attack.

In the chill dawn light, I knew that I had to draw upon powers that were ready to aid me. An ancient cry issued from my lips and the power of the Dyke filled my limbs. It was a vitality that came from the first dawn, from Mother Earth herself. She was the Maiden for whom I fought and the one who opposed me was a deceiver who wanted to subvert that power for himself. I felled him.

If it hadn't been for the White brothers, I think I might have finished him. They dragged me off of him together. But as it was, I knew that I had settled an ancient rivalry for control of this land, even as Ash was dealing with the matter on another level.

Martin's defeat only briefly cowed the protesters. They swarmed forward to pat me on the back, to touch me. I had become their leader. Now I could do what we had come to do with them on my side. 'Come with me!'

I led them to the Weeping Maiden, her dark limbs black against the golden light of the dawn spreading behind her. Ash saluted me with a curious deep gesture which I instinctively returned. I laid hand upon the poplar without fear, 'Take down that platform!' I ordered. Two of the White brothers swarmed up with the druid, who kilted up his robe. Together they untied the struts and cut through the cable that kept it up and threw down the platform to the ground.

'Maiden, you have fulfilled your task! The evil is removed. I promise that you will again guard your people. But now, it is necessary to bow down.'

The protesters around the tree took up my words and began chanting, 'Bow down! Bow down! The Maiden shall bow down!'

I nodded to the White brothers who had brought their old-fashioned double-bladed saw. No chain-saw for this ceremony. Then I touched the shoulders of four of the male protestors and had them stand ready. Reg White took one side and I the other as we cut into the Weeping Maiden. Turn and turn about, the men kept up a rota, only stopping for brief periods to wet and rest the blade. The chant helped the sawing and gave it rhythm. By the time the sun had come fully up, it was time to stand back.

The Weeping Maiden fell forward onto the road with a great crash of branches. The silence was palpable. The inspiration and power that had been upon me earlier ebbed from my limbs. Placing one hand clumsily on the fallen trunk, I wept. Soon nearly everyone was ringing the stump where she had grown, crying their eyes out.

Now that the power had left me, I was my ordinary self again, unable to command or plan. I raised my eyes to Ash, who came to my side. With both hands on my shoulders and his feet on my toes, he pushed down firmly, mouthing the words of some prayer of departing. 'Bless the place!' he urged me.

The pale exposed heartwood of the stump beckoned. It felt like sacrilege, but I stepped up onto it. 'May this place be at peace. May it be a place of honour. May it be blessed forever more.' I stepped down.

The protesters seemed to come to themselves again. Instead of a tribe, they were individuals again, appalled at what they had been a party to. Elspeth clutched at my arm, her face streaming with tears. 'It was a privilege to be part of that. I don't understand it, but it was — beyond words.'

Each of the protesters came and shook hands with me or hugged me, except Martin who stood with a pale handkerchief stained with blood pressed to his jaw. 'Are you alright?'

'I'll do! What about you?'

'Tired!' Together we sought out base camp and had a reconciliatory cup of cocoa. Something had been exorcized, that much was clear.

Later, when they had finished cutting the wood into smaller sections, the White brothers fetched some lifting gear to clear the road. One part of the tree was taken, as arranged, to the wood-carving studio of sculptor, Mark Edal, who lived a few miles away.

'Did I really lead that?' We were stretched out on the garden chairs, enjoying an unseasonably warm day. I blushed to remember how I had taken charge.

'I think the Weeping Maiden's protector was really the leader,' Ash said, 'He just happened to reside temporarily with you.'

'Thank God the *Guardian* wasn't there for that one! — That wasn't a standard exorcism that you did, was it?'

Ash wrinkled the corners of his mouth, 'No indeed! While you and Martin were wrestling it out, you certainly raised the stakes. The intrusive spirit came out to watch you and join in. When you called on the power of the Maiden's Dyke, it was easy to lay it to rest after that.'

'Is it really gone?'

'Yes! You don't need to know more.'

'But what caused it to become entangled with the black poplar in the first place?'

'As far as I can establish from my investigations of the site..' and I knew he meant he had visited it in spirit as well as looking at any records, '...the people who originally lived here venerated the spirit of the Dyke. But those who came in during the Bronze Age had another view of it — they feared and propitiated something there. They had a sacrificial custom whereby the souls of those they sacrificed were tied to the place as guardians. The descendants of the first people tried to mitigate this fear by planting a native tree that is known for keeping such horrors at bay. That's not the first poplar to have grown there, I think. But the effect of all this was to cap the power of the Dyke, making it a bottle-neck of great energy. The intrusive spirit that you saw had thoroughly colonized the tree in an opportunistic way.'

'That's why everyone fears the place but why Harry's great, great granfer venerated it, then?'

'Yes, the tree was venerated as a force that decontaminated the Dyke, if you will. That was what you tapped into. I think that there must have been a long sequence of alliances between the black poplar and a human protector until such understandings were broken down during the age of reason, and only superstition was left. You have revived an ancient tradition in a good cause, Jack.'

I bit my lip, unsure of how honoured I felt about this. 'Well, I'm glad that my protectorship is over. —I tell you, Ash, that I shall never ever again belittle or disbelieve anyone who comes to me complaining of being possessed of spirits.'

'But, Jack. What you've experienced is not possession—call it a rapport that made you act the way you did.'

'From obsessions, repressions and rapports that go bump in the night, Good Lord deliver us!' I prayed.

'Amen!'

The council finally widened the road, levelling off a little of the Dyke's dramatic ridge to the great fury of many countryside associations but to the relief of all motorists. The White brothers were appointed to take out the roots of the Weeping Maiden, a proceeding which was overseen by Ash, as I didn't feel up to it. Beneath the roots, to no-one's surprise, were found several skeletons which were swiftly assessed and lifted by the local archaeological unit. These dated from several eras, two from the early bronze age and three others from between the Iron Age and the fourteenth century. It was discovered also that there was a blind spring which had been running, unknown to everyone, through the lower roots.

The road remained closed, by general consent, until Mark Edal had finished his work. Nine weeks later, on the same point of the blind spring where the Weeping Maiden had originally stood, a seven foot statue of what was entitled the Virgin of Maiden's Dyke, was installed on a much wider bend than before. The artist had fashioned the poplar wood into the statue of a young woman with a cloak curled about her, her right hand raised in protective greeting. Her expression was calm. When Ash and I saw her in the studio, he said, 'A fitting way to end this business.' He asked me, 'How does she seem to you?'

'She looks like Our Lady of the Downs.'

'And how do you feel about her now?'

I experienced nothing of that raw earth power, nor did I feel that urge to protect. The power had run out of me when the tree was felled, 'Happy to be free of the responsibility.'

The Rev. Vernon Hallam, from St. Faith's at Chiselden, blessed the statue, bidding it guard the road for all travellers over the Dyke. Since then the accidents have stopped. Every time I drive over the Dyke, I raise my hand to greet the Virgin, no more the Weeping Maiden, but a welcome sight nevertheless. That bend has since been renamed Maiden's Corner, though there will always be a few unregenerates who insist on calling it the Devil's Elbow.

Case 3: A MATTER OF BELIEF

Round these parts, the season of Lent usually starts with pancakes and ends with Easter eggs and roast lamb, but sometimes we meet up with someone who takes his preparations for the Resurrection rather more seriously.

Being but an occasional communicant myself, I pop down to St. Faiths in Chistledon infrequently enough to be given a fulsome welcome anytime I appear — well, at least by the Rev. Hallam or his curate, Michaela Flowers, though I suspect that I am regarded with deep suspicion by members of the parish council who make up the majority of the church-goers on a weekday.

One March night, I accompanied a guest of ours who'd become ill to Christminster A & E. He needed an emergency by-pass but had not made it, and so I had had the sad task of filling in the paperwork and making the inevitable phone calls to the next of kin in the small hours. Ash had already told me to take the rest of the day off and catch up on my sleep. As I drove down the wooded back lanes, I was feeling somewhat jaded. The night's events lay so heavily upon me that even the sound of bird-song coming from the overhanging hollow ways, with their tunnel of newly budding leaves, nor even the early March sunshine could lift my mood. Evan Hooper had been doing well before his sudden crisis of the night before: there had been nothing that either I, or Ash, could have done for him.

Catching sight of the crooked tower of St. Faiths, I was suddenly aware of my own needs. I had been running on empty. With no proper sleep that night and an aching heart, I knew I couldn't go home yet without some official notification of this unexpected death. So I found myself turning off the road into the field that serves as parking for the church. Whatever else we hadn't been able to do, at least Mr. Hooper should be prayed for. He had been a rather irascible and ungracious man who had been referred to us by a friend who knew our work at the Beacon. When I'd made the call to his son, a distinct sigh of relief told me how things had stood at home. It is a very awful thing not to be loved.

Having no idea of the time, I was surprised that there were a handful of cars already parked. Then as I entered the early 14th century church, I realized that I had arrived in time for morning Eucharist. A handful of parishioners were scattered through the pews and I took a prayer book and joined them. One or two kindly nodded to me as Rev. Hallam opened his arms to welcome us in Cranmer's incomparable language. The service was said not sung, and the responses were subdued in that English way we have, both for the early hour and from the sincere nature of devotion. I peered through my fingers at the bright window of Charity in her red dress in the South aisle, and then to the dark window of Hope in her blue robes in the North aisle that only came alive in the afternoon. St. Faith herself was pictured over the chancel looking much jollier than either of her sisters, with a hand stretched upwards as if to pull down heaven and a living flame in the other that extended welcome to the viewer. Like many medieval churches, the glass was now largely Victorian. Only the vestry sported a few panes of original pre-Reformation glass that had been finally poked out by Cromwell's pike-men, and lovingly reset at the command of Sir Prosper Hartnell after the Restoration. The remaining glass mostly consisted of mixed-up arms and heads of saints, a bit of the Virgin and Child, and the shield of the local Hartnell family, now sadly died out. Their crusading forebear, Courcy de Hartnell, lay buried in the Lady Chapel, his folded hands pointing to heaven and his faithful dog still curled about his feet. That medieval window was like our work at the Beacon: hopefully putting back into order the pieces of lives that had been wrecked or shattered.

I couldn't help noticing that, right under the figure of Hope, kneeling urgently and intently, was a young man in a clerical soutane of the kind you usually find in the more spiritually-rarified echelons of the Anglo-Catholic persuasion. He faced the chapel of the Reserved Sacrament in deep colloquy with God. My professional eye, sharpened no doubt by weariness, noticed that he seemed to have positioned himself under Hope, as if he had some unruly matter on his conscience.

For myself, I prayed for the soul of our departed client and took communion. Afterwards, before I could make my getaway, the Rev. Hallam came bounding up to chat, extending an invitation to breakfast after hearing of my errand of the night before, 'I know what it's like at that emergency department: nasty tea in a plastic cup and dispensing machines that only give you chocolate or crisps. You need a good breakfast to set you up. Matty always has some splendid potato scones for me on early communion mornings.'

I really needed a bit of quiet and the thought of the rectory's tribe of children gave me pause. This doubt must have shown in my face as he added, 'You would be most welcome to join us....We do eat after the children have gone to school.'

Which is how I came to be sitting at the Hallam's vast refectory-style table in the vicarage surrounded by a flurry of children squabbling over Oaty Crunch and Rice Krispies as they got ready for school. Mrs. Hallam presided over the din with the utmost equanimity, taking my order for eggs and bacon, while loading school-lunches into satchels and backpacks, 'I'll just get these done and then Michaela will drop off the children on her way to St. Lawrence-with-Granby.' Like most priests, Rev. Hallam and his curate covered a wide area, keeping our small down-land parishes alive and functional by dint of driving between them, in order, in endless succession.

I greeted the departure of the four children with relief, nursing my coffee and feeling disposed to fritter away the rest of the day, if I could only stay awake. That feeling of an access of freedom was an unexpected bonus on such a nice day and I was already mentally planning what I might do, when the pale young man in the soutane came through the back door, presenting himself for breakfast.

Matilda introduced us, 'This is Gerald Schott who's staying with us as part of his preparation for ordination.'

I have never met anyone with a greater reserve than that young cleric, and I wondered doubtfully how his otherworldliness would work within an inner city parish. He greeted me with a self-effacing modesty, but rather as if it were I who had painfully interrupted his prayer. He seemed barely socialised enough to be out on the street, I thought.

'What kind of parish are you wanting to work in?' I asked, to make conversation.

Looking firmly at his soutaned lap, he responded in a voice as quiet as leaves falling, 'I am not sure. It is possible that I may enter an enclosed order.'

'Which one?' I countered, hardly surprised.

'I am drawn to the work of the Bernadine Brothers. They have a house in North Wales.' I had never heard of this order. His demeanour and hushed tones did not invite further questioning and an uneasy silence fell until Rev. Hallam returned from his office where he'd been dealing with some parishioner's phone call, in some exasperation, '"Could I do a wedding on Midsummer's Day?" — I mean, is it likely? — We are booked into September already!'

At sight of him, Matilda produced the potato scones from where they'd been warming in the oven, and started to pile up the plates with our breakfasts. Bless the woman! The kitchen began to fill with the smell of toasted cheese with which she'd smothered the top. I took one, and was about to fork in a mouthful of sausage as well, when Gerard Schott began one of the longest graces I've ever had to suffer. With a loud 'Amen,' Vernon and myself set to, while Gerard picked, cutting up his food into minute portions with the exactitude of a lab technician. I noticed that he ate only the scone and some mushrooms, undoubtedly eschewing the bacon and sausage because it was Lent.

Averting my gaze from his forensic consumption, I addressed myself to Vernon, who seemed quite glad of my company. I caught more than one meaningful glance between Matilda and himself, and wondered whether their austere guest was as difficult for them as their domestic ménage clearly was for him.

At the conclusion of breakfast, Gerard led another long grace and excused himself, replacing his chair under the table with the precision of a royal chamberlain, and removed himself.

Everyone in the kitchen breathed a sign of relief. I asked, 'Is he staying long?'

Matilda rolled her eyes and folded the tea towel, saying to Vernon, 'Go on, you know you want to!'

Vernon nodded sagely, 'Perhaps you would come to my study? It doesn't feel right discussing him here. Do you mind, Dr. Rivers?'

'Jack, please!'

'I know you've had a long night, but I would value your advice.'

I followed him into the tiny study that was crammed with box files and a desk covered with papers, all marked with coloured sticky notes. Vernon followed my gaze: 'Matty's filing system ensures that I get some of my many tasks done in time. Though I'm afraid the pink ones are piling up rather.'

'What did you want advice about?'

'That young man.... — What do you make of him?'

'That he would be better suited to a monastery than to a parish?'

Vernon sighed, 'You probably noticed he's already living as if he were *in* a monastery? The purpose of intent, the extreme recollection, and the custody of the eyes, yes! It's all of a piece, but I don't know at all. Matty and I are worried about him. He's so — intense. We're both sure that he's taking Lenten devotions way too far. You know, I've hardly had the church to myself for a week now? He just kneels in the coldest part of the church and — well... It's like watching an Olympic athlete in training, only he's aiming himself for Easter rather than a gold medal. Bishop Sandy sent him to us for assessment, to try and break through that impenetrable barrier by sending him to a family and a parish that has all the usual faults and failings.'

'What do they make of him at the seminary?'

'They're beginning to doubt that he's the right material for ordination at all. I know the chaplain there and many of the tutors. He made a good showing when he applied — his social skills needed honing, they thought, but he got through the initial testing. Apparently, he's gone downhill considerably over these last few months. They want him to taste what parish life is about and, I think, to be tested by the world. Matty and I feel that — well, he's a good lad, not a spot of malice in him — but there's something troubling him, that he's not confiding in me.' Vernon bit his lip, 'He doesn't trust me enough, I know, and that is my failing.'

'I don't think it's your fault. It also struck me that he had something on his conscience. But it could just be that he's on the Asperger's spectrum — has he been tested? I thought they did a psychological evaluation when choosing ordinands... Is that the kind of advice you need? Or is it a case for the Beacon, do you think?'

Rev. Hallam moved the stapler into the drawer, 'You know, I think it might. I can't put my finger on it, but that boy — there, you see how I think of him as a boy — he's so unformed, so unfinished.' His broad, pleasant face was full of anxiety. 'The world might make use of his skills in some capacity, I'm sure, but I don't think he's quite ready for the world. Even the abbot of the Bernadine Brothers is likely to reject him. "A monastery is not a dumping ground for rejects nor a retreat from the world," as my old master said.'

'What's his background?'

'Nothing special or traumatic, that I can see. He comes from a pretty ordinary family in the midlands. His people are what Christ would have called "the poor in spirit" — you know, no books or cultural pursuits. None of his people are churchgoers, either. I think his father works for a cement plant and his mother is on the checkout in a supermarket.

It struck me that Gerard might be taking the protective colouring of another social group in order to distance himself from his upbringing. Because a quiet and unremarkable life is often a greater misery than standing out from the crowd, I wondered if there wasn't a degree of playacting involved — but to what gallery he might be playing was a mystery to me. Young people often choose extremes of opposition to their family's way of life, not just in reactive ways, but sometimes out of a sense of self-survival. The few words we'd exchanged showed that he had an unaccented voice, so he'd probably worked hard at eradicating the sound of his native accent. It was already well on into becoming the classic 'voice of the vicar,' suitable for intoning on a long, following, cathedral acoustic.

'Any siblings?'

'A much older brother who's in engineering, on an oil-rig off Aberdeen, I think. — You understand, that I have gleaned none of this information from him — just from the bishop's letter? — I know I can count on your confidentiality?'

'Of course! — So, anything else?'

Vernon sighed, 'Not really! If he had been my brother, my old dad would have sent him out to strip down a bike, get really oily and then send him on a long ride uphill to work out the silliness.'

'Has he expressed any need to confide in anyone or noticed that something is wrong himself?'

Vernon shook his head, 'I think he just goes for confession once a week to Christminster — nicely anonymous, of course. He's not asked myself or Michaela for confession — well, it's not something we do that often round these parts!' St. Faiths was a traditional parish but not very interested in the High Anglo-Catholic end of things.

I stood up to go, 'Well, I'm afraid, unless and until he wants to be seen, neither myself nor Dr. Ashington can be of help. As Queen Elizabeth I said, "We don't make windows into other people's souls." Keep putting your good wife's potato scones down him and get him out in nature a bit more often.' As we stood at the back-door, I asked, 'What does he do all day?'

'Pray, mostly. Meditate in the church. Mooch in his room reading theology and apologetics. He stays out of the way unless there's a service. He doesn't seem to have any of the pursuits of a normal young man. He doesn't even watch television but goes out of the room if the children have it on, or sits there with a theological tome and an air of sufferance.'

'Does he have any friends? Or a girlfriend?'

'Not that I know of! — He's perfectly civil to Michaela, but I don't think he's a great fan of female priests in the church, either.'

Taking a sudden decision, I asked, 'Where is he likely to be now?'

'Probably in the church — there are no more services until evening prayer so he'll have it all to himself. Why?'

'Well, I wonder whether he would like to take a hike up Hartsworth Beacon with me? I think I need that more than a nap right now, especially after your wife's esteemed potato scones! — Something to blow away the sorrows of the night.'

Vernon cheered up, 'Let's go and find out! If you can get him to the Beacon, I can pick him up afterwards when I go over to St. Saviours for evensong, if you can give him some tea?'

'You're on!' I must have been mad, considering the night I'd just had, but a little conversation, some exercise, and maybe a meeting with Ash might not go amiss for this young man, who would be taken out of his usual milieu. With great good will, Vernon bounded into the church where Gerard was telling his rosary in the Lady Chapel. I stood examining the font while Vernon outlined my proposal. From their exchange I could hear reluctance from Gerard and insistence on the part of Vernon, who made it clear that a walk with a parishioner was part and parcel of his assessment and so obligatory.

§§

It was a very sulky and sweaty young ordinand who climbed to the top of the Beacon with me that morning, much impeded by the skirts of his soutane. But nature had other things in mind. The essence of Spring-time was finally upon us after a very cold month, with a froth of blossom and a frantic busyness among the bird population. Regular fluffy clouds punctuated a bright blue sky, and there were even a few bluebells beginning to show themselves at the wood shore. It was a pleasure to mount the chalky hillside and feel the soft tread of the downs underfoot. By the time we reached the summit, being able today to see as far as three counties inland and the distant outline of the English Channel southwards, we were both puffed out.

Making no attempt whatever at a bluff, manly resilience, Gerard cast himself down on the grass like a little child and drank it all in like mother's milk. The smell of the chalk soil, already dotted with the first little curling vetches, combined with the sweet grass, the prickly gorse and the vibrant lark-song made a joyous symphony. Taken away from his theology, books and cloistered routines, Gerard improved considerably, I thought. The walk had given his pale cheeks some colour and, while he lacked a sense of energy, he resembled a real human being, not a monastic cut-out.

'God has made such a beautiful world,' he breathed, like someone who had just beamed down from another planet.

'Indeed He has! — Thank you so much for coming with me this morning. It was a sad night and I welcome your company.' I was boosting the truth rather, but I know how being needed makes people feel more confident.

He peered up at me with astonishment, and some awe, 'Rev. Hallam said that you'd just attended a death. I've not yet had that privilege. Did your patient make a good death?'

'No, the poor chap was completely unprepared. His heart took him off without him making any final arrangements, I fear. His family will be shocked and at a loss, I imagine. They thought he was coming to us for rest and recuperation.'

'Then I will pray for him and them,' he replied, with utter sincerity.

I took this as encouragement because, in my book, if you can perceive and empathize with the needs of others, you have the first foundations of being a sociable being. Hauling him up, I said, 'How about a visit to the Beacon before you go home?'

We ambled down with considerably less energy than we had stridden up. I was much more weary now and really needing my bed by the time we stepped into the porch. Gerard hovered on the threshold, surveying the welcoming hallway, with its inset shrine to Melanie and the red sanctum light, and taking in the jewel-like colours in the Guardian Angel icon that stood beside it. 'But, this is a holy place!' he declared, as if he'd been expecting some kind of clinical wasteland.

When you first enter the Beacon, a sense of peace descends around your shoulders, a sense of homecoming. The smells are those of a lived- in old house, with fresh flowers, upholstery and polished wood, but with a cleanness and wholesomeness that was quite at odds with the antiseptic whiteness of a hospital. There is always a sense that, whatever your background or culture, the riches of ages lies somewhere under its roof. It is not a grand noble house, it has no such pretensions, but it imparts its cloak of sanctuary with grace and willingness. It is a place where constricted souls can expand. Over the years I've worked there, I now know that this is the real bequest of Melanie Rydale to her successors. From the drawing room came the sound of Ash playing the piano. He had obviously also been inspired by the beautiful weather and was playing a set of variations he'd been working on, based on local folk tunes sung along the Downs. He then broke off and played the Bach Prelude and Fugue in C minor that was one his favourites, and usually marked the end of his practising. I always thought he worked up to this piece, as it was so speedy.

Wendy came through with a pile of bedding from the laundry room and greeted us, 'I told Gillespie I thought that was you up the beacon! We didn't know when to expect you. You must be exhausted.' She flashed a friendly smile at Gerard, who immediately looked away. 'Is this gentleman come to see about the funeral?' Wendy lengthened her nose quizzically at his impolite reserve.

'No, this is Gerard who's staying with the Hallams—I called in there this morning. I thought he'd like to see something of the country.' She carried on upstairs, looking over the bannisters to me with a questioning tilt of the head, at the odd one I'd brought home.

I took Gerard through to meet Ash, intending to leave our guest with him, for my weary limbs were beginning to feel as if I was walking through deep water. Ash was still seated at the white Bechstein that had once belonged to Melanie, making some notations on his variations. He looked up with, 'Thank you for going to the hospital, Jack. That was a very difficult night for you! —And who is this?'

I introduced Gerard to my employer. Ash took Gerard's limp hand in his and shook it, 'Pleased to meet you.' Our ordinand looked startled both at the energy of his grip, and at the psychic scrutiny of those grey eyes that, I knew, would be perceiving both the man and what the soul held.

No question was asked, but Gerard responded readily with, 'We've just been up the hill behind your house.'

Ash nodded, as if this were a satisfactory response, 'Ah!—And how do you like your music?' Without waiting for a response, he turned back to the keyboard and played Bruckner's *Christus Factus Est*—a rather mournfully dramatic anthem that is sung in Holy Week. Ash sang along in a good baritone, '*mortem autem crucem*,' and amazingly, Gerard joined in a light tenor, '*quod est super*' with Ash using the forte pedal on this phrase for the strong chords accompanying this text, which was from *Philippians:*

'Christ was obedient under death,
Death on the cross.'

'So moving!' said Gerard, as the last pianissimo chords died away, holding both hands over his breast as if trying to stop his heart floating off.

'Very!—But not very suitable for the weather,' Ash smiled, and went into a full-blown, organ-style rendition of *Jesu, Joy of Man's Desiring*. Through the window, I caught Gillespie waltzing and weaving around with the wheelbarrow on the lawn to its joyful flow, fortunately not visible to Gerard, who had resumed his correct and austere demeanour after that brief exposure of his soul.

'I'm sorry to interrupt the music, Ash, but I really must go and lie down before I fall down. Rev. Hallam said he'd phone and let us know when he's on his way to St. Saviours to pick up Gerard. Perhaps Wendy can arrange some tea for him?'

Ash swept one of his quick scan looks over me, 'Of course. —Maybe Gerard would like to see around the grounds? I have a little time before I have to greet a new guest who's coming today.'

Finally, the young man remembered his manners, and thanked me for the walk. I left him trustfully with Ash and crashed on my bed.

§§

I slept right through our new arrival, finally surfacing at about 10.30pm to my great irritation; having turned night into day, my day would now begin in the dark and I would be on doctor's alert for a few nights before I got my body clock reoriented.

I came down from the East wing for a cup of tea and some very late supper, finding that Wendy and Gillespie had already retired, but that there was indeed a portion of dinner left over for me to reheat.

While I pottered about boiling a kettle and microwaving my macaroni cheese and veg, Ash put his head in the door. 'I thought I heard you stirring.

How are you now?'

'Severely out of kilter,' I whined.

He let me eat my very late dinner in peace, drinking his tea in a reflective silence, while Cinnamon sat—in complete contradiction to Wendy's rules—at the end of the kitchen table to receive the stroking from his spare hand.

Topping up the pot, he asked me a few pertinent questions about the late Mr. Hooper, for his records. He had already spoken to the family about arrangements for his belongings to be collected or sent on.

I came clean, 'Sorry to land you with Gerard! I was doing a favour to Vernon, really, to get the lad out from under his feet. I hope he wasn't a nuisance?'

'Not at all! He had his look round the Beacon and then sat in the library for the rest of the afternoon until Vernon showed up. Did you have an ulterior motive for leaving him with me?' he asked, mischievously.

I did a double take, 'Are you kidding me? Of course, I did!—you don't even need to ask. Just one look at him and there you are, playing the appropriate track. —Bruckner? Is that where the poor child is stuck?'

'Um! I would say that "obedient unto death" says it quite well? He has set himself a narrow furrow to plough, hasn't he?'

His words alarmed me, 'Do you mean he's in danger of death?'

'No, only that his striving for perfection, his idea of imitating Christ is leading him down a pathway that kills joy and constrains his living. It's an extremist matter of belief he's suffering from.'

'Well, I don't know what's going on in that muddled mind, but getting him to lighten up would be a start, certainly!—How is the new arrival?—Denise, was it?'

'She's in her room, in a rather sulky mood. I'm not convinced she will stay with us long.' He spoke with an equanimity that I knew from experience meant that he expected 'something to turn up,' like some kind of psychic Mr. Micawber. I found this all-seeing attitude very annoying because, of course, while I had the blinkers on, he was possessed of some kind of wide-scanning advanced radar.

The new guest was Denise Fallon, who had been brought first to the Harley St. practice by her mother. This elegant lady assured us that her daughter needed our help most urgently. Ash's attitude to such cases, where a relative or friend hails the subject to be 'looked at', was unvarying: he would always establish whether the subject wanted to be present and, if they didn't, would refuse to see the case, unless death was imminent. His view was that, 'In most instances, the instigator bringing the friend or relative may often be contributory to the trouble.' It was also true that a few were clear cases of projection, whereby the problems of the relative were simply reflected onto the subject, who wasn't ill at all. He gave such cases very short shrift, looking deeply into the eyes of the instigator with, 'Whenever you yourself feel able to come to us at the Beacon, we will be very glad to see you.' This was normally met with the numbing silence of the found-out, needless to say!

I had not yet encountered Denise, but I gathered from Ash that the mother was a coercive and controlling woman. So when I asked why he had taken the case in the first place, I was amused to hear him say, 'I thought her daughter could do with the rest, personally. Since Melanie's philosophy was that we offer sanctuary to those who can be helped, I've always tried to maintain the Beacon as a safe place. That girl certainly needs it.'

What Mrs. Fallon found wrong with her 18 year old daughter seemed to come down largely to her own inability to control or guide her. Denise had been in and out of schools since her father walked out on them years ago; then she had finally thrown over a job in some prestigious dress shop that her mother had found for her, and gone to live with a young addict who had made off with all her valuables. Abandoned and without resources, she had been forced back to the parental home where she had gone into a thunderous gloom which was threatening enough for her mother to consider having her medicated and committed. Having later met the mother, I think that, faced with the prospect of staying in her company for any length of time, I would join Denise in some professional glooming myself.

Denise was a thin waif of a thing with huge blue eyes whose innocence had been quenched by a kind of streetwise knowing you normally only see in one many years older. Her hair had been razored so close to her head that it made her look like a child—which she was not, I had to keep reminding myself. She was a young woman whose affections had been abused, but the projection of 'naughty child' that Mrs. Fallon had placed upon her daughter was clearly one that Denise could also play to her own advantage. She was inclined to treat myself and Ash as her mother's appointed keepers, and thus clearly untrustworthy underlings whom she didn't have to tolerate so, in the first few days of her stay, any sessions we attempted to have were like going to poke the caged lion with a stick. Not only was she unwilling to talk to either of us, or disclose what she was feeling, but she bit and swore. A few days in, finding no great resistance, she became rather bored with us both and began looking for handholds that served her better.

Ash declared himself very pleased that she still had the energy to be this reactive, and asked me to spend time with her and see what came out of it. I thought that she might attempt to run away, or try and find her addict lover, but Ash thought not, 'You need money to be able to keep going, and she hasn't got any. Besides, I think she is too injured by what's befallen her to seek him out. The fact that she was able to come out of that experience and not become a user herself is a mark of her innate self-respect. There is a lot of her mother in her, despite what she thinks.'

With me, Denise's spiteful and vindictive side came up first in appalling, loud asides or direct insults. The language coming out of her childlike mouth was shocking. A few of our residents gave her a wide berth, as a result. Having been severely hurt, she was exercising her need to punish as a paramount requirement. But the source of the hurt was clear enough: an over protective mother whose love crushed her out of life on one hand and, on the other, an indifferent boyfriend who had led her into degradation and then abandoned her once he had liquidized her meagre assets. We had to try and find what part of her soul could be engaged if she was not to spend the rest of her life destroying herself.

That week we had a period of near torrential rain, so none of us could go out much. Not having the grounds at our disposal meant that we all had an even harder time of it with Denise. Even normally imperturbable Wendy was heard slamming a door after a particularly aggravating morning spent with Denise in the art room. The only inhabitant with whom she formed any deep attachment was Cinnamon. I only found this out by stealth. Gillespie drew me into the alcove near the art room, whispering, 'Will you look at that!' He pointed through the glass door where Denise lay in the middle of the art room floor amid an extensive Jackson Pollock style mess of powdered paint that she had thrown about in a tantrum. Sitting on her chest was a triumphant Cinnamon, kneading and purring away, making every possible overture of love.

Now recently, Ash had been worrying about his cat because she had recently become very evasive, unlike her usual self. He could often be heard calling her in from the garden at dusk, long past the time when she'd usually come seeking food and his lap. Then she'd show up at all hours demanding to be fed and dive off somewhere, ignoring him. As for the rest of us, normally, Cinnamon would barely suffer our attempted strokes before stalking off, for she was strictly Ash's owner, demanding and requiring his slavish attention.

Gillespie's eyebrows disappeared into his grizzled hair in sheer amazement. We tiptoed off to the kitchen where, shaking his head, he said, 'Man, man, I've never seen that exclusive beastie take to another soul like that before!'

'Do you think Cinnamon's absences mean she's been up in Denise's room?' I wondered.

'Well, it's a wonder what the girl eats, because she's done gae little of that, so Wendy says.' Rather than eat with us, Denise had been taking her plate upstairs. She could well have been feeding titbits to Cinnamon.

But, whatever relationship she had with our cat, the rest of us were not feeling the love. After a particularly grievous morning when I had to go upstairs and dress my left cheek after Denise stuck her nails in my face, I roundly told Ash that I was not really helping our guest, that I had failed her by becoming riled at her provocations, and that he should take over her treatment, as I might be tempted to give a slap round the chops, else. I was furious with myself, if truth be told, because my self-esteem had been injured by her searing words, which had spurred me into giving her a retaliatory piece of home truth. — I had richly deserved her response.

At sight of my face, Ash merely said, 'Ah! I see. — I expect she will become worse up until about the 31st of the month, and then we will see.'

Exasperated by his certainty in the face of my failure, I bawled, 'How can you possibly say that? — Have you been looking into the other side again?'

'No, merely looking over her notes. I've looked at her chart.' He meant her astrological chart, but I had no time for such nonsense and must have looked both cross and hangdog, for he said, 'Jack, it's not your fault that she won't trust yet — she's not had a good experience of people loving her or letting her be. Unconditional support is the best we can offer. Give her some space. I'll ask Wendy to keep an eye, and I'll go and play the piano this afternoon and find out if anything moves her.'

I gave Denise a wide berth for the rest of the day. The next morning, we crossed on the stairs. She was taking her cereal bowl to her room, creeping past me as if I might strike her, but I just nodded in as good-natured a way as I could and wished her a good morning as I continued downstairs. Later on, having worked out that I was not going to retaliate, she drew one finger down my scratched cheek in a rueful way, then blew along her finger as if to blow away the injury, 'Sorry.' It was the smallest step forward which I was careful not to sabotage again, whatever the provocation.

I was kept so busy with Denise that when the doorbell rang on Saturday, I was astonished to find Gerard at the door. He hadn't warned us of his coming, but had just showed up. 'I was wondering if we could go for another walk?' he asked. He looked a little warm, though the day had been overcast and blustery.

I told him that I had to keep an eye on our guest, but offered him a quick cup of tea in the kitchen where Gillespie had come in to put a fresh plaster on the finger he'd caught on a rusty hook earlier in the week. I introduced them to each other.

'Did the Reverend drive ye over, then?' Gillespie asked.

'No, I walked,' came the reply.

Gillespie and I exchanged astonished glances, as it's about 5 miles to St. Faiths and there is no bus except on Wednesdays. Gerard seemed a good deal more forthcoming than previously, as he added, 'I felt so good after our last walk, that I thought I'd try another.'

Gillespie smoothed a fingerstall over his plaster, 'Well, laddie, you did fine already in the walking department, I'd say! — Since Jack here is busy, mebbe you could help bring out the seed-boxes for me? — I need to get the tomato seeds set. The hook's left a sore slicket on this hand.' Gerard meekly followed him out. I caught up with him later at supper, where he was consuming a vast spread of baked goods. Wendy herself ran him back on her way over to yoga in Borhunt.

The next day, after morning Eucharist, he was back again, making himself useful. Ash didn't seem to mind him dropping by, but I was a little perturbed. I should have seen it immediately but, once Gerard got his legs under the table, there was no getting rid of him.

Now, in many respects, the Beacon is not unlike a monastery. There is no TV except in Wendy and Gillespie's quarters, there are the rules of the establishment that we expect inmates to adhere to, there is regular meditation and so on in Ash's room, and guests are not expected to take off without advisement.

Gerard had even borrowed a bicycle from the long-suffering parish of St. Faiths to ride over every afternoon during his stay in order to imbibe our hospitality, to sit while Ash played, or else to wander in the garden and help Gillespie.

Our resident gardener had looked somewhat askance at Gerard's attire, when he first offered to do some more vigorous unskilled labour in the newly planned, raised beds that Gillespie had been working on. It involved some double digging. 'Ye'll get your skirts mucky. — I've some trews and an old shirt you can borrow.'

And that was how Denise came to meet our ordinand on loan who, stripped of his ecclesiastical costume, looked like any other young man in the garden, with ruffled hair and a healthy glow from digging. Since he was the youngest thing in trousers in our household at that time, she looked him over coolly at first. She then took a garden chair from the studio in order to sit out in the sunshine with her Walkman, settling herself in a strapless and very short dress, despite the blustery wind. However, this ancient technique of attraction had no earthly effect upon Gerard, who continued digging until lunchtime, when he came in for some of the soup and mushroom pasties that Wendy had made.

I was glad to see what a good colour he had. There had been a slight increase in weight and muscle since I first laid eyes on him. He tucked in hungrily, without the usual forensic picking at his food. Looking through the window he observed, 'Is that girl not eating with us?'

Wendy replied in a rather tight-lipped way, 'She eats when she's hungry usually, not at every meal.'

Gerard's fork hovered near his mouth as he considered this. Then he chewed his forkful slowly and asked, 'Should I take her something out on a plate?'

Gillespie looked up from his perusal of the Racing Post, 'You can always try, laddie! Mebbe you'll be successful the day?'

Without further urging, Gerard loaded a plate with food and looked around, but Wendy had the tray already in her hands with a linen napkin. Gerard poured out some juice and took a jam-jar from where it was drying on the draining board. Together, looking through the window, we tried not to make it too obvious, but eating ceased as we watched his progress across the lawn. He had put some flowers in the jam-jar and was heading right for Denise, still recumbent in the sunshine.

Of course, we couldn't hear anything from this distance, but we all waited, cringing, for the inevitable throwing of the tray. Unless Denise was left to serve herself, spilled food was usually the result, we'd learned. Astounded, we watched as he addressed her, set the tray down next to her and, with great respect, moved away to let her eat—which she did.

She even brought the tray in, without a word. I found some papers to attend to on the terrace where I could keep on eye on things. Gerard got back to his digging, but Denise was clearly unsettled. She kept throwing glances down the garden towards him, but Gerard didn't even look up, so she took to fidgeting and flouncing in her chair, finally stomping off to the music room where I could hear her running through a gamut of different instruments in a militantly un-tuneful way. Clearly, she had never met a man like Gerard before, so singularly impervious to her charms.

Our session the next morning was slightly less silent than usual. From its undertow, I gleaned that she was indeed intrigued by Gerard but still completely uncooperative when it came to opening up to me about herself. She spent most of the time twiddling and sucking the fringes on her hooded top and sighing heavily. I was reduced to asking my can-opener questions that usually begin to pry things open. But even the question—'if everything in your life were as you'd like it, what would you like to do?'—that most guests find impossible to resist, was stubbornly resisted—though I did notice that she had to yawn in order not to respond to that one. 'Right, little madam!' I thought to myself, 'Let that one stew for a few days and let's see how long we can play this game....'

Ash himself spent much less time with her but then, as the master of meditation, he could keep the silence up a lot longer than she could. He thought she was still testing the nature of the cage and getting our measure. So I reminded him that when animals do that in captivity, it's usually a preliminary to leaping over the wall of their enclosure.

§§

Despite the occasional ragging by our Denise, who found his clerical solemnity both funny and annoying, it was Gerard who finally turned the key on our difficult guest, unlocking the fact that she liked to be called 'Denni', and that her favourite food was cheese on toast. He calmly announced this to us all in the kitchen as we were having tea. Wendy promptly made cheese on toast and Gerard took it up to her. Up to this point, only our Barbadian cleaner, Myrtle, had been in Denni's room and she had made some choice remarks about uneaten platefuls of food found stuffed under the bed, causing Ash to state that a condition of being fed at all was the bringing back of spent food or used plates and cups to the kitchen. I had begun to worry about a possible food disorder, but I needn't have worried.

Gerard even stayed up there while she ate it and brought back an empty plate, saying that she would like some more. Since eating was an improvement on not eating, Wendy complied and toasted another round.

With Denni, as we now all called her, it was still a matter of one step forward and two steps backwards on some days. Any mention of her mother and she would sulk and become uncooperative, to the extent that we deterred Mrs. Fallon from visiting.

Then, just as we seemed to be getting somewhere, Cinnamon went missing. We all searched high and low but no cat could we find. Since our lane was so quiet, we didn't normally worry about speeding vehicles, but Ash was clearly fretting about her, 'We don't really know the extent of her territory. Vans tear down the road from Christminster to Chistledon.... I can normally sense her, but there is no signal.' It was this last that brought home to me that we would not see her again, since Ash's radar was uncannily accurate, in the main.

Life went on at the Beacon, but a rare sadness filled up the space that Cinnamon occupied in our hearts. While Ash's care for our guests never faltered, he was more subdued than I'd ever known him. The loss of a pet is always difficult to bear and eats into you. He went up to Harley St. for his twice-weekly clinic all alone, leaving me in charge at the Beacon. I think he was distancing himself from the loss, which was bound to be more severe at the Beacon than in London. On the first day of Cinnamon's absence, Wendy, Gillespie, Myrtle and myself had taken round lost cat notices to affix to any post, board or window in the vicinity that would agree to host it. Driving down the lane, visitors were in no doubt that we had lost a cat, as Gillespie had created such a forest of notice boards, managing to make her elegant, long-haired beauty the main campaign of the district. A couple of people responded, lured by the promise of reward, both trying to pass off perfectly ordinary ginger toms as ours, to be sent off summarily by an irate Gillespie.

Cinnamon's loss even penetrated Denni's own armour, 'Aren't you going to do a ceremony for her?' she asked urgently at our next formal session. She had noted the pet cemetery behind the sunken garden where a few generations of pets were laid to rest.

'I expect we would, if we had a body to bury. We don't really know that she is definitely dead,' I said.

'Gerry says that when there isn't a body, you can do a memorial instead.' So far, none of us had mentioned Gerard's ecclesiastical background to her, so we had no idea what she thought of this. He now turned up almost daily, without soutane, on his bike to help in the garden. If she had discovered who he was and what he was contemplating, she didn't betray it.

'I'll mention it to Ash,' I promised.

Putting her narrow head to one side she then said, 'Brody's friend, Martin, was a druid. He used to do lovely ceremonies for road kill.'

Since her boyfriend's name had never once arisen in our one-way conversations, I stepped carefully, 'Were they effective, these rituals, do you think?'

She nodded, 'They made me cry.'

Holding the silence, I forbore to comment further on the wretch who had abandoned her without a penny. Love comes in many shapes and sizes, and who was I to judge? Whatever his faults and failings, Brody's druidic mate had bequeathed a respect for dead animals to her.

All this while, Lent had been steadily advancing. The only sign of it in Gerard's behaviour seemed to be in his steadfast refusal to eat meat or have sugar and milk in his tea. Then one morning, as Myrtle, was putting on her coat to go home after cleaning, she told us that she'd noticed him down at our little summer-house. Now this rustic building, made from the planks of a felled cedar tree that used to grow at the front of the house, stood just before the ground rose up to Hartworth Beacon in what we called 'the Wilderness' — a little piece of uncultivated garden. Some of our guests liked to sit there in the summer months, but a strong March wind had started to blow, and I couldn't think there was much pleasure to be had there, as it was totally unheated.

'That's the tird time I see him from the Doctor's room,' she said. 'Must be pretty cold down dere, I reckon.'

I hadn't realised that Gerard was coming so early, 'What time was that, Myrtle?'

'Maybe 6.30am or so. I know the Doctor likes to meditate before work so I allus start there. I saw the young reverend going in. He'm some troubled, I think. He walk like he got de whole world on his back.'

If he was there that early, then it meant that Gerard was not going to morning communion, which was surely not something he would purposely miss? Something was clearly wrong. Early the next morning, I pulled on a thick jersey and went to investigate for myself, meaning only to see what he was up to. This was how I overheard Gerard praying aloud, 'Lord and Saviour, help thou my unbelief!' over and over, in some desperation. It was humbling to hear a soul in such distress. I immediately returned to the house to wait for him. After two more hours, there was still no sign of him, so I made a big mug of coffee and took it out to him, deliberately singing a few bars of a cheerful song to warn him as I approached the summer-house. He looked out somewhat sheepishly.

'Myrtle said she'd seen you down here, so I thought you'd like some coffee.' He made as if to refuse it, but I said, 'Don't worry, it's just black.' He took it gratefully and drained it down, looking thoroughly perished with the cold. 'Thank you, that was good.'

Looking past him, I saw one of the blankets from the studio laying the length of the bench with a cushion at one end, with a deep indentation in it: 'Have you been sleeping down here?'

He flinched and nodded, 'I'm sorry. I know I should have asked.'

'Neither myself nor Ash mind you coming here.... Look, Gerard, would you like to come up to the house and we can talk in a warmer environment. That wind is bitter this morning.'

I took him to my consulting room rather than to the kitchen, as it was clear that he didn't want an audience. 'Now why don't you tell me what's the trouble?'

Slowly, I got it out of him. Staring down at his hands, he confessed, 'I lied to Rev. Hallam. I told him I had to go to London for a few days. But really I didn't know what else to do.... it felt safer here....'

In the silence, I did a bit of guessing, 'Is it about your ordination?'

He treated me to the kind of astounded look that I probably gave Ash when

I first started working here. He nodded, 'I had a letter from the seminary that I had been moved off the list of ordinands to "pending review." — They're right, of course. I am not ready for such an honour.'

Trying to encourage him, I asked, 'But they haven't thrown you out or refused you?'

'No — worse luck!' he breathed in heartfelt tones.

Suddenly, the whole pattern that had been before me all the time came sharply into definition. 'You mean, you don't want to be ordained at all?' I couldn't keep the amazement from my voice.

'No! I'm not even sure I am really a Christian,' he said with a surety that rang true, with the strength of sudden realization.

'....but the Bernadine Brothers and everything.....?'

He looked right into my eyes properly for the first time, 'I tried to be the model monk, to be obedient, faithful, simple — that was my vow, that I'd spend the whole of Lent testing my vocation. It was easier at the seminary with a crowd of others, I could hide what was going on, but when I came to St. Faiths, I could see what a Christian life should be and that I didn't measure up.... Everyone was welcoming to me, but I could see what they saw...' A look of self-disgust flashed and was as quickly hidden, 'I was just play-acting; in love with the idea of being a priest — trying to kindle a flame with a damp match.... No, I don't want to be ordained at all.' Some of his original Staffordshire accent was showing through the vicar-ly voice.

'Why did you go to the seminary in the first place? What called you?'

'It was so banal at home. None of my interests were comprehensible to my parents. I wanted a spiritual life, but I'd had no exposure to any. I tried the local church and thought I'd found what I was looking for. I got baptized and confirmed and... then I just wanted to go on further and further. The old priest there — now he was a proper priest — he gave me the run of his library... and I began to fall in love with the idea of being a wise man like him... it was he who recommended me to the seminary, when he saw how keen I was... I visited the monastery as a guest and made a retreat — he said I should do that before I made up my mind about ordination, to be quiet and pray about it. But it was so easy at the monastery — like doing something I'd done before — it was so natural to me, the perfect way of life.'

'What did your parents say?'

'My family were thunderstruck, but for me it's an escape.'

'From what?'

' — from being ordinary, mostly. The mantle of a priest seemed admirably better than mediocrity, but the monastery was what I thought I wanted. — It began to go wrong in the second year of my degree. I had such spiritual enthusiasm and then I ran into problems. I began to see how misguided I'd been, and the masters at seminary saw them too—that's how I came to be at St. Faiths.'

No wonder the poor chap felt at home at the Beacon! I said, 'I know little about priesthood, but I do know that it isn't something that is learned—it's something you are born with—like Ash.'

Gerard's face flashed open, 'Oh yes, I recognized that when I first came here... that there is more than one kind of priesthood. —You have it too, you know?'

I held up my hands, 'Oh no, I am no priest, —a soul-doctor, maybe.'

'But you prescribed the best thing for me—you opened my eyes. I began to see what a sham I had built up. —Getting baptised and everything, that *did* mark my wanting to be part of a spiritual life, but I don't even know if I chose the right sort.'

Keeping my expression neutral, because this revelation was more deeply surprising, 'Has some other sort of spiritual life presented itself to you, then?'

'Well, no... oh, I don't know! It just feels as if Christianity is suddenly too small for me—am I being big-headed or what? I'm suddenly afraid that I am on the wrong path or that it is just peetering out, and I can't see the way forward now.'

'I suspect that there is more here than either of us can see, but we will get to the bottom of it. Do I have your permission to speak to Ash about this conversation?'

He hung his head, 'I haven't any money to pay to see him.'

I spoke firmly, 'Gerard, you have given the Beacon your service in the garden, don't you think it could serve *you* now?'

The session with Gerard, enlightening though it was, paled into insignificance once Ash got to work. He seemed most interested in the fact that Gerard found following a monastic lifestyle easy and natural, 'That is very helpful of you indeed, Jack. —Now let's do some preparation.... Will you kindly be my secretary for an hour or so?'

'What do you need me to do?'

He put on some incense, 'I shall be going out to discover more about the antecedents of our ex-ordinand. I just want you to take notes. Put the token on the door, please.'

Ash threw himself down on his reclining chair, cranked it back as far as it would go and covered himself with a light woollen throw, closing his eyes. Taking up the horseshoe on its length of ribbon, I put it over the doorknob outside to show we were working. After intoning a few deep-pitched tones that made my ears ring, Ash began to breathe more deeply. When he began to speak it sounded as if his words were coming from a long distance: 'The boy is to go as an offering.... *oblatus mundus mortuus*.... in perpetuity.... after the image of Samuel.' There was a lot more in Latin that I was less able to transcribe or understand. His breathing began to increase in tempo after about 20 minutes had gone by, but my notepad was largely empty. Fluttering his eyelids, Ash surfaced and drank a glass of water. When I showed him what I had got, he wasn't perturbed, 'I have a good recollection of the main points, don't worry... I have the reason why our Gerard found monastic life familiarly easy to take up — he's done it before.'

'You mean in a past life?' Once, those words would have made me blench, but I was beginning to trust the broad patterns that were often revealed when Ash made his investigations.

'Yes, he was given to a monastery as a youth, just like Samuel in the Bible. He was the youngest son of a family: as far as I could make out, he was a kind of recompense for the actions of his older brothers who had vandalized church property during the time of King Stephen. People took a dim view of that sort of behaviour then. He was given to the monastery as an oblate, or offering, on the basis of 'the world being dead to him' — taking a form of dedication that bound him, not just for life, but for perpetuity.'

I protested, 'Surely that's not possible? Even then, Christians only took vows for one lifetime!'

'Indeed! But his shame about what his brothers had done weighed so heavily upon him, that he added a rider to his vows, making it forever.'

'How do we get him out of it?'

'I've a feeling that we are about to see how very soon. Patience! — The fact that he himself feels that the path of his chosen way is peetering out is good news. We will find, I think, that there are other strands of this old story working themselves out. '

§§

So Gerard came to stay with us at the Beacon as the most sensible course of action, since it would give him space to consider things properly outside an ecclesiastical environment. When I drove him over to St. Faiths so that Vernon and Matty could be apprised of things, they were both very relieved. They made such an affectionate fuss of him that Gerard was in no doubt that, whatever his decision about his vocation or spiritual path, he would always be welcome at St. Faiths. He promised that he would speak with Vernon and together they would sort out the seminary.

Meanwhile, Denni was facing troubles of her own. A female police investigator and a police officer showed up one afternoon, demanding to speak to her. While Wendy went to fetch Denni, I asked the woman how they had tracked her here, to be informed that it was Mrs. Fallon's doing. Ash was still in London, so I requested to be in on the interview, reminding the detective that this was a nursing home and that Denni was still in a volatile and vulnerable state.

Detective Sergeant Giandeep Singh promised she would be careful, but that she needed some information. It seemed that Brody had not only used Denni's credit cards, but also used her name and details in several fraudulent transactions recently. It was merely a routine check to eliminate her from their enquiries, and to see whether she knew anything about Brody Franklin's whereabouts.

A very frightened Denni was brought down to the sitting room by Wendy. Her vehement denials that she knew anything about Brody or his plans were backed up by both Wendy and myself: she had not left the premises and, no, she had not been in contact with him.

'Just the thought of him makes me ill!' she asserted, before telling us exactly what she did think of him, in uncompromising language that I won't reproduce here.

Then, having given every impression that we were done, in that insidious way of police everywhere, Detective Sergeant Singh thanked Denni for her testimony and said, 'There is also the matter of Perrot Hale Chapel.....' The detective observed Denni's reaction, and continued, 'In the early hours of either 27th or 28th January, some person or persons broke in while it was boarded up for renovation, and did a lot of damage. Do you know anything about that?'

The Perrot Hale Chapel was a celebrated, but now run-down building, from the days of Pugin and his attempt to make Gothic architecture the pride of High Anglicanism. Once part of the Hale family estate in Kent, it was now under the care of the local authority, and about to be given a new lease of life as a concert hall, with the aid of a lottery grant. It was one of those chapels where every surface was covered by murals or panels.

Denni went instantly still, guilt written all over her. 'He was high. I tried to stop him, but he just went for it,' she said, reporting how Brody had broken in through the wooden hut that was currently masking the south door's removal. He had spray painted the murals as a gesture of pagan retaliation against Christianity, as well as breaking some furniture that had been carefully stacked out of the way of the workmen. I swallowed hard. It seemed that Ash's investigations were also bearing their own strange fruit.

The detective removed a sheaf of pictures from her bag and fanned them out before Denni, who had the grace to look ashamed. Peering through her fingers, she murmured, 'All those saints – I told him he was no better than the Taliban!'

Detective Sergeant Singh asked Denni several searching questions and the officer took her fingerprints, in order to eliminate her from accusations of contributing to any of the damage.

'What will happen now?' I asked, cursing myself for not having called our local solicitor for advice.

'We will check Denise's fingerprints. Even if she didn't contribute personally to the damage, she will still have to appear before the magistrate on a charge of aiding and abetting in trespass and criminal damage to a heritage building. It depends on the Crown Prosecution Service. As a heritage crime, it will be a matter for the Crown Court, and Denise will have to appear as a witness at the very least.'

Denni was now quivering with fear, 'And what will happen to Brody?' she asked.

'When we catch him, he will be charged with trespass and criminal damage, as well as of fraud, theft, and impersonation. There is little doubt that he will be served a custodial sentence.'

Wendy had her arm round Denni's shoulders, which now sagged in relief on hearing this, 'So he'll be in prison?'

'It will certainly carry a stiff sentence,' Detective Sergeant Singh assured her, getting up to go. To me she said, 'I am satisfied that Miss Fallon is in good hands here but, if you are considering discharging her, you must advise the local station about her new location. She is to stay within the grounds of this establishment until we have completed our investigations.'

I saw the officers out and then came back in to pick up the pieces. Gerard, having seen the police car, was waiting in the hall, 'Is everything alright?'

'Please can you get a cup of tea for Denni? She's had a bad shock.' He was about to ask me the details, but I couldn't deal with this extraordinary turn up for the book without first discussing things with Ash, so he went as bidden.

Denni was wailing, 'I thought I was safe here!' While Wendy assured her over and over that she was.

'I hate my bloody mother!' Denni cried, wrathful that the police should have found her out so easily.

Gerard hovered on the threshold. I beckoned him in with, 'Denni's ex-boyfriend has done a lot of damage and she is helping the police with their enquiries.'

'I didn't want to help them!' Denni wailed. Gerard sat beside her, holding the mug of tea, while I said, squarely, 'Look, they were bound to come calling sooner or later. We can't change what happened, but we can deal with the fallout now. — Brody isn't going to be able to hurt you any more.'

'They've not found him yet!' she sniffed.

'Well, we won't let him come anywhere near you,' Gerard said, stoutly.

I left Denni crying on Gerard's shoulder, and went off to phone Ash. I had to wait the best part of an hour before he could call back, as he'd been with a client. I filled him in as succinctly as I could, adding, 'Your prognosis about something turning up seems to have been fulfilled... but in the wrong person's story. I imagine that Brody's vandalising of the chapel isn't merely a coincidence?'

'No, but that's not the whole story yet. I think so far we've got off lightly.'

'You mean there is worse to come?'

'There's a cache of things about to be exposed, I feel. How was Denni?'

'Scared. I don't think I'd understood how frightened she'd been of Brody... she seemed very unwilling to disclose anything more.... I could kick myself for not calling the solicitor.'

'Never mind, Jack, you handled it as best you could. — Now I will tackle Mrs. Fallon and see if she will allow us to take the advice of Jimmy Stentson — he's our nearest solicitor. I don't think that the law will be too hard on Denni — she was only 17 when the damage was done, after all.'

The police visit rendered Denni more pliable but also more fragile. Although her fingerprints didn't feature in the evidence and she was clearly off the hook as a perpetrator of damage, the charge of aiding and abetting would still be to answer. Jimmy Stentson was engaged and a barrister was briefed.

Denni became less confrontational but a lot more timid, refusing to even step out into the garden unless one of us was with her. Gerard told us that she was still terrified that Brody would show up. He had chivalrously appointed himself her bodyguard, so this led to a good deal of gardening for Denni. Looking out of the window at her husband, Wendy observed to me, 'If this goes on, you'll have to write a new job description for the old tortoise, "Kitchen Garden Therapist," perhaps?'

All around us, spring had fully arrived on every bush and tree and amid glorious weather, and I prayed that we might make the breakthrough that would put Denni back together again. Her mother was beginning to nag us by phone every two to three days, asking when she might remove her daughter. She had wisely kept away when the police came, but now she became impatient, accusing us of prolonging Denise's stay. Ash kept repeating that this kind of healing wasn't something we could rush, but that she had made great strides. Of course, as to whether these strides would be to her mother's taste, we kept our own counsel. Denni was beginning to bond with Gerard and, while we didn't encourage any romance between our guests, it was a sign of healthy friendship. Gerard himself kept respectfully neutral with her, treating her more like a sister, but we weren't so sure about Denni.

The fateful 31st March arrived. We were still breakfasting around the table when Gerard came in late. 'Sorry, I forgot to set the alarm.' Then he asked, 'Has Denni had hers already then?'

None of us had seen her since last night. Gerard was the first to go and look. Taking the stairs three at a time, he went and knocked on her door and, when there was no answer, looked in. Her bed had been slept in, but she wasn't there. Wendy brought a woman's eye to the scene, 'Most of her belongings are still here, but her coat is gone.' We exchanged appalled glances and I went to tell Ash, while the others checked the rest of the house. 'I think she's finally run away,' I admitted to him, breaking in on his morning meditation.

While Gillespie and I checked our outbuildings, Gerard and Wendy looked more closely around the house. It was Wendy who found conclusive evidence, 'There are quite a few things missing from the larder—some pork pies, a large piece of cheese, a loaf of rye bread, and some other bits and pieces.'

Ash discovered that the side door had been left unlocked, 'That's where she slipped out—but where to?'

'Do we have to phone the police?' I was hoping we wouldn't have to.

'I'm afraid we do. But I'm not going to phone them until we've had at least a quick look in the vicinity. She had no money, so she'll be on foot.'

'Aye, but she could get a lift if she hitched, a bonny lassie like that,' Gillespie said. 'She's lived on the streets....'

Gerard objected, 'But she was too frightened to go out alone. Why would she suddenly leave?'

Ash asked, 'Has anything changed that we don't know about?'

'Could it be the thought of appearing in court?' asked Wendy. 'I know the case isn't even scheduled yet....'

Then I remembered that, last night, long after we were all in bed, the guest phone had rung. It was located in its own booth, created out of what was the old boot room. 'Did anyone else hear the phone last night?' I asked. I had been trying to read a novel but had fallen asleep with the light still on and the book still upright in my hands, but the sound had woken me up. 'It made three rings and stopped, so I didn't get up. — Then it rang twice more — once with two rings, and then again with a single ring. I thought it was just the usual late-night reveller trying to phone a taxi and getting the number wrong, but what if it were something more?'

Ash asked, 'Did anyone else answer it?'

'No, I'd have heard it.' The guest phone booth was under my room and I could always hear the rumble of a conversation when it was in use. We looked at each other in surmise.

Ash and I got into the car and went to search with Gerard. The lovely spring weather of the previous days had turned back to a proper March blow again. Passing the peeling posters of Cinnamon in the lashing rain as we drove down the lane, I felt the double blow of loss. Despite a long and unavailing search, there was no sign of Denni that morning. Reluctantly, Ash informed the police of her absence. They promised to send an officer to take a look.

As we drove back, Ash said, 'Now for Mrs. Fallon.'

'Oh Lord!' I covered my head. 'Was this the kind of crisis you were expecting?'

'There are other ways and means yet, Jack.'

Ash took on the loathly task of phoning Mrs. Fallon, who went into a state of angry hysteria: she had more or less expected some news of this kind and was quick to blame us. No assurances would calm her down, but on closer questioning, we learned something further. 'Well, she has good reason to be upset,' Ash reported, putting down the phone. 'Mrs. Fallon told me that her house was burgled yesterday: Denni's room has been turned over, several small valuables are missing, and someone has gone through her address book: the page with the Beacon on it is torn out.'

'Well, that can't be Denni — she knows where we are.... so... Brody?' Then I realized, 'Oh my God, Denni took off because that was him phoning her!'

Ash agreed. 'The 3-2-1 rings were a signal that she recognized, I imagine, so she ran away. Now we have to find her.' He took down a large-scale map of the county and shook it out, smoothing it over the table. He picked up a pendulum.

'Are you going to *dowse* for Denni?' I was incredulous.

He grinned, 'Let's say, we will leave no stone unturned. — It was how Melanie uncovered the spring out the back when she first bought this place. It had been covered over when the mains water was connected. She knew there must be a well of some kind. — But I would like you to do the dowsing, Jack — you have a better feel for it, I think.'

I protested, 'But I've never done such a thing in my life, unless you count bending coat hangers for rag week when I pretended to be a quack diviner at medical school.'

'Then please try again for Denni. Hold the pendulum loosely in your fingers and check which direction shows yes and no for you first.'

For me, clockwise was yes, anticlockwise was no, which I tested by asking: 'Am I female? Am I a doctor?'

Ash urged, 'Now think of Denni, and ask the pendulum to indicate. First, ask it whether she is in the immediate area.'

The pendulum swung for yes.

'Hold it over the map and ask it where.'

'How do I do that? It's a big map.'

'Start with the Beacon! Place your finger on each square at a time while you dowse, then work square by square.'

We drew blanks on all the squares I tried, except for the one to the south of us. The pendulum seemed to circle the other way at first, but I checked it twice and it kept saying yes. I frowned at the map, 'What's there? — It's only farmland, surely?'

'There will be outbuildings, shepherd's huts and other places to shelter. If she was frightened, she might have hidden in one. — But of course, she could be moving about, or even be on her way somewhere else.'

'That's going to take a bit of finding. Should we get some help?'

While Ash phoned two of the local farmers whose land was contiguous and in the square we'd searched, asking if they could check their outbuildings, I rushed downstairs and told the MacLeans, 'It's possible that Denni has run away to hide from Brody. We're going out....'

'Let me come too!' Gerard begged.

'No! It's more than possible that he may be coming here and I would like you and Gillespie to guard the house. — Wendy, will you phone the police again. Mrs. Fallon's been burgled and it's likely to have been Brody, who may be coming here — he's got our address.'

Gillespie brought two big flashlights from his workshop, handing them to me grimly, 'We'll keep a lookout for the little bugger. You get going.' And off we set once again in the car.

I drove while Ash navigated, with the map on his lap. For the rest of the afternoon, we searched. It is one thing to drive past fields in the countryside in a few minutes, but it is quite another to tramp across them, looking in hedgerows and outbuildings for hours at a time. By 6.30 it was virtually night as storm clouds rolled over us and shed their burden. Soaked, and filthy with mud, clay and chalk, we kept on until it was clear that we both needed a break and some hot liquid. I drove into Ted Jelley's farmyard, where his daughter Elaine came out to greet us.

In the shelter of her kitchen, Elaine told us that Micky Bryson their farmhand had done a tour of the most southerly fields while her father was still doing the western ones on his farm scooter. She peered up out of the window, 'But he'll have to come in soon as the light on that bike has a loose connection and only works when it thinks it will.'

We drank a mug of tea and were tucking into beans on toast when the sheep-dog curled by the roaring fire pricked up his ears and stood up, uncertainly. He whined.

'Echo? What is it? Is it Dad?'

The border collie looked up at Elaine and then at the door expectantly. Ash leapt up and opened it, on Elaine's nod. Echo stood in the yard and gave one bark. Distantly we could hear the approaching scooter. Ted Jelley turned into the yard and climbed stiffly off. He looked as bad as ourselves, his boots caked in chalky mud and the scooter like it'd been in a rally, being more mud than bike. Seeing us in the light of the kitchen, he shook his head, 'Sorry, Doctor, I've searched everywhere I know where to look, but no sign. — I think she might have been in the Three Acre field — I found a screwed up packet of crisps in a pig-arc but no-one in or near it.'

Echo, who had run up to his owner was now weaving about and whining, pointing towards the half-derelict old dairy, abandoned now that the Jelleys only kept sheep. Ted crouched down to the dog, 'What is it, Echo? — Look back, boy! Look back!'

This is normally the command given to leave the flock and look back for a trailing sheep, but Echo sped off and began scraping at the door of the old dairy. Ted lifted the latch and switched on his flashlight, training around the space. Echo ran into a corner where hay bales were stacked up, lowering his head to the ground and looking intelligently up at the farmer. In the glare of the flashlight was a wide pair of eyes and a very pale face.

Ted pushed back his cap onto the back of his head, 'Well, damn me! I looked in here earlier, but I swear it was clear then.'

Ash pushed me forward, 'Go and look, Jack. She won't be frightened of you.'

'It's all right, Denni. We know why you ran away — we're not angry with you.'

She stood up shakily and fell into my arms, sobbing with relief. Her body felt thin and cold. Then, extracting herself and fixing shining eyes upon Ash, she said, half laughing, half crying, 'Look what I found!' She turned, indicating an open bale behind her. She lifted the fold of the plastic and there, lying in splendid fettle, was Cinnamon. Five kittens were attached to her front, suckling noisily. She raised grave eyes to her owner as if to say, 'You see! I've been busy!'

I left a joyful Ash to make his obeisances to Cinnamon and her offspring while we took Denni up to the house. After giving her tea with a good slug of brandy in it, Elaine ran her a hot bath and looked out some old clothes for her, while I phoned the police to let them know that Denni was found. They were still keeping an eye out for Brody and said that, while they couldn't station an officer at the Beacon, they would keep a regular patrol.

Denni let me look her over and check that she wasn't harmed. Apart from a few bramble scratches, a sprained ankle, and a bit of exposure, she was fine.

'Have they found him?' was her first question.

'No, but the police are onto him. — They are expecting him to make for the Beacon, but we are ready for him.'

Denni drew back into her chair in some distress, so I said, looking round at Elaine, 'You don't have to go back until they've arrested him, I promise.'

Elaine nodded, 'Of course, you are welcome to stay here until it's safe to return. You can have my sister's old room.'

Ash returned, a great happiness writ large on him. Together we listened to Denni's story, 'When I heard those three rings, I knew what it meant. He used to phone my house like that as a signal that he wanted me to come. So I just slipped out—I'm sorry about the food, tell Wendy!'

'Where were you heading?' Ash asked.

'I had no idea at first. I didn't have any money, but I knew I had to go before he showed up. —I can't.... Well, I moved about a bit at first, but nowhere was very warm and I was so cold and then it rained. Over the fields, when it got dark, I could see the lights of this place and it looked much nicer than where I was—I think it was an old pig house I was in. Then I heard someone coming, so I circled round by the hedge—and that's when I caught my ankle in a hole. —I took a stick and hopped here.... But then I found Cinnamon had already discovered a good hiding place, so I stayed with her. —Is there more tea?'

Ash then phoned Mrs. Fallon who was clearly relieved and wanting Denni to come home, but he explained that she was in no state to travel yet. We then conferred together, out of Denni's earshot, in the Jelley's front parlour—an unheated room used only for best, that looked much as it must have been in old Mrs. Jelley's day. Her broad countenance beamed down from the photo frame over the best china on the sideboard. Ted's father, in another photo, hung onto her arm like a drowning man who'd found a life-raft.

'I'm so glad Cinnamon is safe,' I said to Ash. 'Will you take her back with us?'

'Not for the moment, I won't. We can collect her after this business is done. I want to get back up to the Beacon as quickly as possible.'

I frowned, 'What I can't work out is why Brody is after Denni still—what does she have or know?'

'I don't know, but I think we are going to have to find out. —He was obviously looking for something in Mrs. Fallon's house.'

'Shall I go and ask her what it is?'

'Go easy, Jack!'

Returning to the kitchen, I sat next to Denni in the broad inglenook, and took her hand, 'We're so very relieved that you're alright, but we need your help to get Brody put away.... What is it that he's come for?'

She dropped her head. Then, biting her lip, she faced it, 'When he ran out on me, I wanted to do something that made him feel as bad as me. I knew where he'd left his emergency stash. It was under a floorboard in a squat we used. So I took it.'

'Where is it now?' I asked, hoping to goodness that she'd not been using it herself.

'It's in the pig house where I sheltered. It's in a biscuit tin. I hid it under some old sacks.' She searched my face and said immediately, 'It's all there. I wouldn't use it,' she said, in a scornful voice.

'Why didn't you give it to the police when they came?' Ash asked.

A mutinous line returned to her mouth, 'Because!' is all she would say.

Just then the phone rang. Elaine answered and gave the receiver to Ash, 'It's Wendy.'

We all heard her frantic tones, 'Oh Ash, come quickly! We think he's here.' There came a shattering of breaking glass from the other end and, 'Oh, Gillespie! No!.... Gerard, quick!'

'Call the police,' Ash shouted at Elaine, as we ran to the car and raced up the narrow lane, smashing through the giant puddles where the road had nearly flooded down the brook side of the lane. In five minutes we pulled up and raced into the Beacon.

The first thing that met us as we stepped over the threshold was a bloody mallet while, just inside, Gillespie lay groaning in the hall with blood streaming from his temple. Wendy was crouched over him with wrathful, flashing eyes, 'Oh Ash! Get him! Get him!'

Before either of us could move, Gerard sprinted after Brody grabbing hold of him from behind, like a leopard leaping upon a wildebeest. Brody was rangy, lean, and savage, with a tail of long black hair and a spiral tattoo on his neck. He swung from side to side, trying to dislodge Gerard who had managed to get both legs around Brody's waist, while still clinging onto his neck.

Brody attempted to mount the stairs, swinging still to dislodge his assailant. His hand was reaching towards his pocket to produce a knife. We all shouted a warning as Brody began to jab the blade dangerously backwards towards Gerard's leg.

Gerard countered by yanking hard on Brody's ponytail, causing him to drop the knife from the pain. There was no room to manoeuvre or step in. Being the larger and stronger man, Brody finally backed Gerard into the bannisters and dropped him by ramming over and over against the wood. But though Gerard rolled down a few steps, he still managed to hold onto Brody's ankles, preventing him from making further progress.

The siren of a police-car was coming up the lane to add to the pandemonium. Ash leapt the stairs in three paces with his long legs, seizing Brody's knife-wielding wrist from behind and twisting it with an economical manoeuvre. The knife landed, quivering, in the deep-pile Axminster beside us.

Constable Davey came running in and together we got hold of Brody. While I pinioned him, the policeman snapped on handcuffs and cautioned him.

This was the point when we learned just where Denni's terrible command of invective had been learned. Brody yelled, effing and blinding, to the four winds. He was a nasty piece of work, and no mistake. Handsome enough to charm a woman but eyes that spoke of a shrivelled heart and a lost soul.

At the sound of his carry-on, and ghastly in the blue flashing lights of the police car, Gillespie sat upright, the steely light of battle in his eye as the blood began to well from his wound. Reaching for the mallet with which he'd been assaulted he cried out in a ghastly voice, 'Bàs no beatha!' The famous war-cry of the MacLeans, 'Death or Life!'

'Hold your whist, you old tortoise!' Wendy cried. 'The battle's over!' But hugged him all the same, while mopping up the blood with her cardigan.

Another squad car arrived from Christminster and took Brody away, to everyone's great relief, while Constable Davey took our statements. Then we set about the business of tidying the place up. Ash dressed Gillespie's wounds and drove him to the hospital for a scan, leaving myself, Wendy and Gerard to deal with the aftermath of our visitor. The whole household had been on alert all day, taking turns to check windows and doors. Our other two guests had already consented to go to a local hotel in Chistledon for the night, at our expense, where Wendy had driven them on her insistence. 'Thank goodness!' she said. 'This wasn't the kind of thing they needed to witness,' as she mopped up the bloodstains in the hall.

Apparently, Brody had waited until fall of dark to make his break-in, throwing one of the great white flint nodules that marked the garden path into the studio window in the West Wing. Gillespie had been onto him very quickly, but the mallet that he'd brought along as a defensive weapon – well *he* called it that – had been torn from his grasp and used against himself.

'Gerard was marvellous!' Wendy said, admiringly. 'He just poured himself all over Brody like treacle.'

Gerard blushed, 'Well, I'm no kind of fighter, but I knew enough to hang onto him. –I wasn't going to let him vandalize the Beacon like he did that chapel.'

I let them both talk on until they'd emptied themselves of the horror of it all. Ash came back a couple of hours later without Gillespie who'd been kept in 'for observation.' 'Though what they will observe about him by morning, will be anyone's guess,' Wendy said, obviously shaken that his injuries were serious enough for him to stay in overnight in hospital.

Gerard asked about Denni, and we told our side of the tale, utterly forgetting till now that we had some other good news to counter the night's events, as Ash was glad to recount, 'So Cinnamon is safe and the proud mother of five kittens.'

At this Wendy cracked up entirely and I marched her off to bed with a glass of hot milk and a sleeping tablet.

It was just myself, Ash and Gerard in the kitchen. Looking in at them, as I came down, I observed, '"So fair and foul a day I have not seen!" – God, will you look at us? It looks as if we've been a few rounds with Birnham Wood and the weird sisters!'

In a broad Staffordshire accent, Gerard declared, in the tones of a sport's announcer, 'Beacon Athletic 1: Birnham Wood 0.'

It was his very first joke in our hearing, so we laughed longer than it merited. Then, consigning our muddy clothes to the washing basket, we retired to scrape the rest of the chalk and clay from our bodies in the shower.

§§

Early the next day, Constable Davey and a member of the London drug squad took a walk across Farmer Jelley's fields to discover the corrugated iron pig arc under which Denni had sheltered, and from which a large stash of top grade heroin was conveyed safely away. It turned out later not to be Brody's emergency stash, at all, but belonged to a supplier, from whom he had stolen it.

Denni's action had not only stopped it getting on the street but had put Brody in a tight corner himself, quite apart from endangering her own life.

Later the same morning, a triumphal procession made up of Denni, Cinnamon and her kittens, made its way from Jelley's farm to the Beacon to be received by a gallant Gerard. There was great rejoicing.

After a festive lunch, though with less fanfare, Ash brought Gillespie home to the bosom of his wife, who shed happy tears. With his brows bound with the dignified tokens of combat, Gillespie milked it for all it was worth, making a noble and heroic retirement to his flat — where he was supposed to lie down — but then spoiled it all by emerging again to coo over the kittens who had been given a warm, quiet corner next to the AGA.

Mid-afternoon the glaziers came and repaired the studio window, and by early evening our two other guests had returned to the Beacon, desperate to be told the whole saga. By suppertime, we were all exhausted and went to bed early.

Denni was given the task of looking after Cinnamon and the kittens, which proved to be the best therapy of all, as Ash had surmised. She responded in kind by attending a proper, communicative session with us both, in which we learned a lot more about her needs and problems, and so we were able to help her much more efficiently.

But when the question of returning to her mother arose, she was adamant, 'I don't want to live in a town anymore. I don't think it's good for me. — I want to live in the country and look after animals. — I know Mum thought she was doing the right thing, finding me that job, but I'm no good at selling things. — I'm no good with people, like that.'

'If you start well with animals, people will become a lot easier,' Ash remarked.

'Would you consider going to college to learn how to look after animals?' I asked.

Her eyes shone with this possibility, 'If it was in the country, yes.'

Slowly and surely, the taming of Denni was effected by love, patience, and the stability of being at the Beacon. But the chief prize for civilizing her fell largely to Gerard. He was the one whom she wanted to accompany her to the ordeal of the court case. She was judged to have been not guilty of criminal damage. After a reprimand for not having come forward sooner in reporting the vandalism, she was given a referral order, under which she had to do a requisite few hours a week community service. But, because of the favourable police report of her cooperation, the recovery of the heroin, and Ash's testimony about her vulnerability and fear of Brody, as a juvenile at the time of the offence, she was otherwise exonerated. Brody himself went down for a long time.

Gerard continued as Gillespie's unofficial under-gardener but he had not been idle on his own behalf. He still went to St. Faiths every Sunday, seeing out Lent until Easter came, in a devout but much less religious way than previously. He had come clean with the seminary and finally left it, and had even made proper contact again with his parents in Lichfield. He came in one morning, while I was preparing for a session in my consulting room and said, 'I've been talking to Rev. Hallam about what I could do next. He's been helping me put things into perspective.'

I put aside my case-notes and listened, 'Tell me!'

'There's a community....' He smiled at the face I made, 'No! *Not* a monastic one—but an intentional community—Meadenham: it's run on environmental lines, in Devon. They welcome all faiths. —You see, I want to explore my spirituality before I settle to something. Christianity's given me a great gift, but it may not be all there is for me. —Vernon knows someone there and he made enquiries for me. I've read about it, and I think it's for me... but it's just....'

'What?'

'Denni—do you think she would come with me?'

A solitary blackbird was singing its heart out somewhere in the wilderness.

'What does she think about it?' I asked, carefully.

'We love each other,' he said, simply. 'I think we could find a way to make a better life than either of us had before, in a new place that doesn't judge us. —It would give us both time to consider things properly. Neither of us have a great deal of skill, but we're both young enough to learn.'

'From what Gillespie says, I gather that your gardening skills have come on—every community would welcome those!'

I asked him, 'What changed your mind?' wondering about the reincarnational dedication that Ash had learned of. Was it truly and finally cancelled?

'It was struggling with Brody. The—reality of what Denni had put up with. The intensity of the evil pouring out of him.... The courage that she'd had getting away from him.... I just knew that I couldn't hide away any more.'

Ash and I spoke with Denni who confirmed that she wouldn't go anywhere without Gerard, 'Though I shall miss Cinnamon,' she said, with meaning.

Later, looking out on the two of them walking in the garden, I asked Ash, 'Is our work done, do you think?'

'Our part is done. Their part is continuing,' he agreed. 'Her experience of the world of men and his experience of the world of spirit weren't of the best, but together they seem to fulfill Plato's myth of the divided parts of a soul that have met up finally.'

'He will hold her up when she is down, and she will try his patience, I imagine. But I agree, they fit together.... But are we sending out the Babes in the Wood, I wonder?'

'They will do well enough, 'Ash smiled. 'I think it is indeed time to ask Mrs. Fallon to visit.'

As expected, Denni was apprehensive about this. She had only had one rather constrained visit from her mother just after the arrest of Brody. This had had the effect of confirming Denni's plans for her future, that they didn't lie in that direction.

In the confines of Ash's office, Mrs. Fallon's reaction to this new turn of events was predictably outraged, 'I bring my daughter to your establishment and this is how you repay my trust?' Two bright red dots of sheer pique painted either cheek as she pulled herself up to an authoritative five foot five, 'Well, I can assure you that not a penny piece will I pay for this appalling breach of professional care.... letting her go off with that... that... nine stone weakling.' It was true that Gerard's physique wasn't yet very impressive, but he had started to put on quite a little muscle from working in the garden.

Pulling on her cotton gloves — Mrs. Fallon was a hat and gloves kind of woman — she stalked off to find her daughter and get her to come away with her. She found them together, Denni resting in Gerard's arms on the swing seat in the back garden.

Gerard faced Denni's mother with great politeness but firmness. 'We are both over 18, Mrs. Fallon. I promise that I will take the very best care of her.' The *fait accompli* was sealed by Denni's exhibition of the engagement ring that Gerard had made for her out of some copper wire. Mrs. Fallon, knowing when she was beaten, swept out.

Gerard and Denni were accepted at Meadenham where they continue to live today. Ash didn't pursue Mrs. Fallon for the fees he was due, saying merely, 'Her daughter and her son-in-law did most of the healing for each other, after all.'

As a thank you for their stay, the couple sent us a gift for the Beacon. It was a hand-lettered poem by the metaphysical poet, George Herbert, the first of Denni's now famous calligraphy:

Love bade me welcome. Yet my soul drew back
    Guilty of dust and sin.
But quick-eyed Love, observing me grow slack
    From my first entrance in,

Drew nearer to me, sweetly questioning,
    If I lacked any thing.
A guest, I answered, worthy to be here:
    Love said, You shall be he.
I the unkind, ungrateful? Ah my dear,
    I cannot look on thee.
Love took my hand, and smiling did reply,
    Who made the eyes but I?

Truth Lord, but I have marred them: let my shame
    Go where it doth deserve.
And know you not, says Love, who bore the blame?
    My dear, then I will serve.
You must sit down, says Love, and taste my meat:
    So I did sit and eat.

It was signed, 'With great thanks from Denni and Gerry.' It is unlikely that Gerard was aware of the euphonious similarity to a certain ice-cream company, but it is certain that our mischievous Denise was! It now hangs in the hallway to welcome other guests whose souls are freighted with burdens too heavy or complex to bear.

Case 4: DOUBLE CROSS

The man who entered Ash's consulting room that morning impressed me. A full head of silver hair, warm dark brown eyes, a firm handshake as Ash introduced us, and general air of prosperous benevolence spoke of an executive at the head of his profession. Yet I was surprised to learn that Francis Keates was but a private financial consultant, albeit to some of the more glittering names in the business world. I could somehow see him heading up an international corporation with great probity and confidence.

'I hope you can help me, Dr. Ashington. I've never been in such a hard place,' his deep voice was troubled. 'Since I saw you speak at the Harvey Institute, I felt strongly that I could ask your help.'

'Tell me,' Ash leaned back in his deep chair to listen.

'I advize clients in the city as an independent financial consultant. I am good at what I do and get on well with my clients. My reputation depends upon my results. But over the last few months, things have gone from bad to worse with me. My judgement has been completely off-beam, so much so that some of my best clients have lost a good deal of money as a result of it. Clients are beginning to leave the sinking ship as word gets out. In short, I shall be ruined within the month.'

'What has happened to shake your confidence?' Ash asked.

Keates related a series of humiliating events, the kind that a financial beginner might have encountered, but not one of his years of experience.

Ash pressed home his question, 'When you were about to perpetrate these decisions, did you have any sense of unease or precipitation?'

Keates clasped either wrist, his silver cufflinks refracting the light around the room, 'You know, it's as if I had become a young man again, with all that dare-devil sense of achievement. At that age, you think you're God's gift to the world, and that you will never be overcome. — It was rather like that. It was as if I had been infected with a sense of invulnerability and over-confidence.'

Ash was very pleased with this answer, 'So, has anything unusual occurred over the last few months?'

The indented lines between his brows grew deeper. Keates went on, 'I have wracked my brains to think of what might have caused this. ...The only alteration in my routines and habits seems unconnected to all this, and hardly likely to have brought about such a change... but I will tell you anyway, as it's of a rather serious nature.' He gathered himself to relate the story, 'My secretary has been undergoing a very difficult time, and I have been trying to help her by whatever means I can. She is invaluable to my business. — And no, before you ask, there's been nothing between us in that way. She is at least twenty-five years my junior. — I've merely been trying to help and support her.'

'In what way, may I ask?'

'A few years back, Maureen made an unfortunate marriage to an Italian from a powerful Calabrian family. He has been unspeakable to her and she left him, to live in some miserable flat with her child. He has ensured that she has no money. Her wages and some housing benefit are all that she currently has. I keep urging her to sort out a divorce, but I gather it is complicated.'

'You have advanced money to her to smooth her way?'

'I have indeed, and asked her to consider it as a bonus for all the good work she has done for me. Now it is evident that the Calabrian in-laws expect her to give up her son and send him to Italy to be brought up there. And although her husband and his family have so far done nothing tangible to hurt her, she feels under threat from them. She is living at an undisclosed address to which I send a taxi every morning to collect her. It takes her back home at night, at different times, randomly selected. Her son is living secretly with his maternal grandmother in the country until Maureen can settle down again, but it's been very stressful for her.'

'Have the police been informed of the danger of kidnapping?'

'We have informed the local station here in London and also in the country, but they cannot act unless Maureen's in-laws make some kind of move. It is very frustrating for me and terrifying for her. — I have a strong sense that I must protect her.'

'If I may ask, what kinds of things has she been experiencing to make her so frightened?' Ash asked.

'She has been having some frightful dreams that terrify her. I am familiar with simple meditation and have practised a little in that way, you know. I've shown Maureen how to visualize herself in a cloak of blue light to protect herself against any such psychic interference.'

'That is good,' said Ash, 'But such protections must be continually re-enforced and upheld by practice and prayer. Does she have the training for this?'

'Probably not. I have little knowledge of such things myself.' He spoke without embarrassment, confidently regarding Ash as someone who would understand. 'But, Dr. Ashington, I don't know how or why, but I *feel as if they know* I've been helping her....' He broke off, laughed nervously, with an involuntary turn of the head over his shoulder, as if he was being followed.

'Listen to me! — "They!" — It sounds paranoid, I know... almost as if I've caught Maureen's own fear. But since I showed her the cloak of light meditation, my own dreams have been full of headlong pursuit through narrow streets. I feel as though I have been run into the ground for several weeks now. It has been a relief to wake up, I must say. But this last week, the dreams have worsened.' He licked his lips nervously, 'My pursuers have been getting closer and closer. Last night, men with swords chased me into a dead-end ally and ran me through. I woke up clutching my chest to staunch the blood. Look!' He unbuttoned his shirt, lifting his tie aside to reveal a raised red scar just over the precordium that looked exactly as if, some years ago, a blade had been thrust in, twisted, and withdrawn.

I had seen similar psychosomatic trauma in the flesh a couple of times before, but even I had to whistle at sight of it, 'Did this appear after the dream?' I asked.

'No, it's a birthmark — but I thought I should show it you. It's on the exact same spot as I felt the blade go in. — Tell me, doctor, how can I best protect myself? I don't think my heart will stand too many more dreams like that. I have begun to think that my birthmark may actually be some kind of presage of the way I shall die. — I really fear it, I tell you. This is why I've come to you. I feel that there are things going on that I cannot understand or defend myself from.'

Ash rose, 'Mr. Keates, I would like to assure you that this is not something that lies in the future as any kind of presage of things to come. But I would like you to come into the Beacon so that we can clear this matter up. You would be quite safe there.'

He grew agitated, 'I will cancel any remaining clients willingly, but I cannot leave Maureen unprotected. I feel... well, responsible for her. I am the only friend who can support her.'

Ash considered, 'Very well, then. May I suggest an alternative that may enable us to help you? Is it possible for my assistant, Dr. Rivers to accompany you for the next few days? I would very much like you to have someone on hand at night, if you have room at your flat?'

Keates regarded me keenly, like a general assessing the mettle of an unknown soldier, 'I would very much welcome his company.' He thrust out his hand and I took it. His hand was firm, dry and warm, and I felt an immediate sense that we would get on well.

After we had made some necessary arrangements and Keates had gone off to his office, Ash murmured, 'This is a nasty business, Jack. Are you prepared to go into danger?'

'Do you really fear for him so much? — Surely he really needs police protection if this is a Mafia affair, not me? While I could slug an intruder with a quick left hook, I could barely offer Keates the security he needs.'

Ash's grey eyes glinted, 'The police couldn't help us here. Did you not see how he glanced over his shoulder every so often? The danger is spiritual, not mortal, though I fear it may prove so for poor Keates if we don't get to the bottom of it. This is an affair where money, honour, love and obedience are bound together in a singular way.' He spoke as if to himself, then he brightened and asked me, 'What do you make of our Mr. Keates? Give me your assessment!'

'Well, he seems a solid, dependable kind of fellow. His reputation for honesty and financial acumen seem well deserved. I wouldn't mind taking his advice, if I had any money to invest, I must say. But...'

Ash leaned forwards, 'Yes?'

'I don't want to speak ill of him, but there seems a great disparity between his—what you would call 'aura,' I suppose—and his station in life. Surely he should be heading up some big corporation, not common money-grubbing.'

He clapped his hands sharply, 'Precisely! Does he not have the very appearance of someone who has either accepted second-best or else sunk down in the world? No, I think our Mr. Keates has the ability to be something much greater than he is. It is almost as if he has held himself out of the limelight.... It makes me suspicious in the best possible way.'

I wrinkled my brows, laughing, 'What *do* you mean?'

'Well, that air of benevolence and acumen is not assumed in any way, is it? His manner makes people instinctively trust him and give him respect. Such a man of honour would go far in any other era but this one. He lacks the cut-throat tactics that hoist financiers to the head of their profession. In addition, he has a deep interest in meditation and healing that seems innate to his nature. No, Jack, I think we are dealing with a matter that is not of this lifetime at all.'

'But the Calabrian link—have they come after him because he's insulted their honour—you know how those people are about their wives and children? And why wouldn't they try to do him over rather than give him bad dreams? And how would they do that anyway?' I was trying to puzzle it out.

'The secretary's family is Calabrian, from the south of Italy. It's a society built on the bonds of honour and obligation. Many families grow powerful as a result of the influence that they can assert. We must consider such a society in a very different way to our own. Vengeance won't necessarily appear as physical violence but through a brooding malice that people used to call "the evil eye." The *malocchio* is still very much feared in Mediterranean countries—people carry charms against its power. We may well be dealing with a straightforward case of witchcraft.'

'What is the evil eye? It all sounds very medieval to me!'

'Ah, Jack! Be on your guard, it's not gone away. Have you never suffered as a result of a colleague's envy?'

I nodded, having been indeed made very uneasy and uncomfortable when a supposed friend and colleague was up for the same post as myself; he did all that he could to blight my career path with slander and evasion after I was the one preferred, to the extent that I almost wished he had been given it. I took a transfer to be out of his way, so unpleasant had things become.

Ash primed me, 'Stay by Keates' side, shadow him like you would a senior registrar. He will be showing you his world, after all. Take a nap in the late afternoon if you can, because the main difficulty is likely to come to him at night.'

'What do you expect me to do then?'

'This kind of dream may result in some quite noisy and disruptive movement, so you will be alerted. Sit by his side and speak to him by name, hold his hand but do not try to restrain his upper body if he is lying down still.'

'What am I to say to him?'

Ash wrote speedily on the pad in his clear italic hand, *'Have not I commanded thee? Be strong and of a good courage; be not afraid, neither be thou dismayed: for the Lord thy God is with thee whithersoever thou goest.'*

'Just say this over and over to him. It's from the *Book of Joshua*. If my sense of what is going on is borne out, then for Keates, it will be an instruction that takes him over the Jordan into the Promised Land.'

I didn't understand, and said so, but Ash wouldn't be further drawn. A verse from the Bible sounded to me like a rather flimsy response to such violent nightmares.

§§

Keates had kindly fixed up his flat near Temple to make me comfortable. The rooms were modestly furnished with good quality furniture but very little decoration or ornamentation. These could have been the rooms of a monk or soldier. Over the mantle-piece there was a singular ornament— a Renaissance Florentine apothecary jar. On it was painted a black shield with a pair of overlapping silver Xs, very like crossed swords without hilts. It was something Keates had picked up in an antique shop apparently, he said. Catching me admiring it, he said, 'That sign's become my good luck token.'

He held up his hand, slipping back his shirt cuff, and there it was again, the shield with the overlapping crosses, engraved into the bracelet of his watch. I had noticed it earlier when he came to the practice. I thought no more of it until much later, but it had also been on his cufflinks the day he came to Harley Street.

I proceeded to shadow him throughout his day, learning a little more about the mysteries of finance. He instructed me, while he was with clients, to pretend to take notes and that he would introduce me as a colleague in training. At the end of the working day, we would go by tube homeward from Canary Wharf where his office was and collect some ingredients to make supper, except on Friday when we brought in some Chinese take-out. Keates was a reasonable, plain cook and I enjoyed his company. Two nights passed without incident.

Since I thought I ought to know a little more about the Calabrian connection, I'd phoned an old friend who had served in military intelligence during the Gulf War and was now working as a private investigator. Only two days into my shadowing assignment, Ray and I met up in the Cheshire Cheese in Fleet St. He had worn well, if you didn't count the prosthetic hand that had to be fitted after he was caught in a shelling incident, and the sardonic lines etched a little deeper than before. Over a bottle of Merlot and a steak pie he filled me in.

'So you asked me to find you information on two counts. First of all, you should know that the 'Ndrangheta, like the Neapolitan Camorra, and Sicilian Cosa Nostra, is a criminal network that serves the family of those who head it up. Every new group or *locale* has to get authorization from the *capo* of the society to run his operation. Maureen Ascioti's husband, Franco, is one such regional leader.'

'Damn! I wonder if Keates knows that?'

'I would imagine he does, as her employer, but he's a brave man. My researches discovered that Franco Ascioti and his brothers are known throughout Europe for crimes ranging from cocaine smuggling to people trafficking, and are a very nasty lot, by all accounts. Several unexplained deaths have been laid at their door, and there are outstanding prosecutions for members of the family who've gone into hiding over the last year. The word on the street is that Nicolo Ascioti, Franco's cousin, is the one who's lying low.'

I had stopped eating, 'Maureen's been living under her mother's maiden name of Hardy, in an attempt to keep herself and her son out of their way. Do you think she is any immediate danger?'

Ray swirled the wine in his glass, 'I checked the records and I think not, as it looks as if the civil divorce would go through, but the boy is another business. They are likely to try kidnapping him. As he's only nine, he's probably earmarked to be inducted into the 'Ndrangheta by his father and associates as a *giovano d'onore* or "boy of honour" within the next few years.'

'Good God! Is the mother's location secure enough?'

'Neither your client, his secretary nor her mother are exactly invisible. I did a check and any determined person could find and follow them. If the 'Ndrangheta wanted to get any of them, they certainly could. I'm astonished they've not moved before now... they may have her or the boy under surveillance, and just waiting to move in.'

I now utterly doubted whether I had been entirely primed or prepared for my body-guardianship.

Ray emptied his glass, 'From those I've spoken to in the world of finance, they are considered to be the wealthiest and most organized of all the Mafia style organizations, and it's very hard to get free of them. The secretary probably needs to change her identity and clear off out of it — classic relocation candidate, I reckon. Pity she's not come forward to inform on them, as she'd certainly have helpful information for Interpol.... then she could be on a witness protection programme and have a life again....'

This dismaying news put a whole new complexion on my task, but I thought I better know the worst, 'You know the kind of work I do, Ray — getting to the bottom of — well, the unusual stuff. In your opinion, can you see any possible basis for any — well, nasty magical activity.'

Ray never even blinked, 'If you mean *La Santa*...?' He shook his head, 'Well, it's not my kind of thing, of course, but I suppose so.'

'I don't know what that is, I'm afraid? Please explain....'

'It's a secret enclave within the 'Ndrangheta — a secret society within the secret society — only members of the innermost circle belong. I don't know much about it, really. Freemasonry seems to be a way to gain entry, that and some kind of tests that the putative *santisti* have to pass first. They might be the source of such things, but I've no data on that kind of activity.'

I phoned Ash the minute I'd left the wine bar. My anxiety must have seeped into my voice, as he pitched his own lower with, 'You sound rattled, Jack. Has there been evidence of dreams or anything else?'

'Not yet. I've got my bedroom door open so I can hear what he's doing in his sleep. As to the rest, I am ready to start at shadows after all that Ray's told me today. When we took the case, Calabria sounded far enough away to allay my fears, but if this lot are all over Europe, apparently, they are as likely to be in London as elsewhere.'

'Sit tight! I think things are going to come to a head in the next few days. If that happens, get Keates and his secretary, and bring them down to the Beacon as fast as possible.'

§§

I was, of course, curious about Maureen Hardy, who seemed as much a part of this case as Keates himself. She was filing notes the first time I came to the 17th floor office. The spring light fell about her shoulders but it felt like her own, personal spotlight. They say that the film camera loves certain people, turning them into celebrities, seeing their quality and relaying it truthfully to the audience.... Well, as she turned to greet us, I had several revelations at once: that this was how Dante must have felt on beholding Beatrice; that a vulnerable woman of such beauty would assuredly call out to the honour and protection of someone like Keates; and that she would have been seen as the perfect trophy wife to her criminal husband. Maureen was in her mid-thirties now, but ten years ago, it was easy to see how she could have been anything she wanted to be, with her long blond hair wound up on top of her head, and those remarkable eyes — almost a celadon green — she could have been a model or an actress who would never have been out of work.

She shook my hand as Keates introduced us, and I felt how she looked into me and saw me, as I am — it was like being introduced to Eve. Blushing, I scuttled into Keates' inner sanctum to hide my confusion.

I was to learn that, in normal circumstances, Maureen could be modest, charming and witty; but that morning I met her, she looked stressed and worn out. Like Ash, I felt instinctively that we needed to get them both to the Beacon without delay.

'Not a good night, Maureen?' Keates enquired kindly as she came in with his appointments for the day.

'No, sir. A very poor one,' was all she would say to her employer, 'Mr. Graham of Langhams phoned to postpone his appointment to three, I hope that's alright?'

I was curious to see how Maureen and Keates were together, and I covertly watched as they conferred about the day's clients. It's my experience, if there is a woman in the business, that strong emotion and sexual attraction will motivate a wide gamut of human behaviours. But I might have known I could depend upon Keates' word: their interaction was innocent of any base intentions, it seemed to me. He called her, 'Maureen,' or 'my dear' in an avuncular way, while she called him, 'sir.' There was, of course, at least twenty years' difference in their ages. Now, of course, I itched to have the other half of the story, for it felt to me that we only had a partial understanding of what was playing out here.

I only had to wait till Maureen was packing up at the end of the following day, when she approached me, tentatively, 'I was wondering, Dr. Rivers, if I might speak privately with you? Mr. Keates has told me how helpful you've been about his dreams.....'

'Of course — please call me "Jack."'

She gave me a peculiar look, and then looked away, saying, 'Thank you, but I would prefer "Dr," if that's alright?'

It was in that moment that I understood how she had always protected herself from the unwanted advances of men, and that she had probably always had to do this, since she was a young girl.

Suitably chastened, I asked, 'Where should we talk — here?'

'My taxi will be coming in a moment — perhaps you would kindly come home with me? — It would be best.'

This put me in a quandary, as I had promised to remain with Keates for the duration, so I went back into the office and asked him, 'Maureen has asked if she could consult me, but she would prefer to do that at her flat. Are you going to be alright if I take a couple of hours now?'

Keates froze briefly, then in a considered voice replied, 'Of course! It's only right that Maureen should benefit from your services.' Keates reaction was perfectly polite and amenable, but he looked like a man who had received a low blow. Suddenly, I had the feeling that I had uncovered some deeper layer to this case that I had no means of understanding. His kindly protection of Maureen *did* come with a certain self-interest, then? I had the strange sensation of crashing through an invisible barrier where I was unwelcome. Had I somehow overreached myself? I quickly examined my actions, but I really couldn't tell how I had made a misstep. Rather more alarming was the fact that the possessiveness flooding out of Keates seemed to emanate from a much younger man.

Thoroughly confused, I got into the taxi with Maureen, only to have the weirdest sense of running away with her, even though we were just going to have a professional consultation. We spent most of the journey in silence or in light, social chat. All the time, I had the nagging sense of Ash at my shoulder. I suppose I should have phoned him, but I felt somehow immobilized or entranced. I was suddenly in a game where I knew none of the rules.

The taxi conveyed us to a leafy north London lane. The old cabbie, who was used to driving Maureen to and fro every day, turned and asked her, 'Do you want me to see you in tonight, Mrs. Hardy?'

She smiled gravely, 'No need today, Mr. Peters, I have an escort.'

I found myself holding out an arm to conduct her into the flat, like a fool on his first date; she took it and then we went in, with me feeling like the cat that got the cream.

But once over the threshold, I knew instantly that I was being watched. It was as distinct as stepping into the Beacon. There, you stepped over into calm and peace, but here I had crossed an invisible threshold into some confusing oppression. Like a fool, I just ignored and discounted the feeling. The ground floor flat had a mirror in the hall, by the door, and I caught sight of myself and Maureen: my badly-dressed, clumsy body and her exquisite figure side by side. Despite this grotesque evidence, it was as if the mirror had put us together — prince and princess, man and wife, lover and beloved. Part of me basked in this understanding, while another part was recoiling in professional horror.

She ushered me into the cold sitting room, switched on the gas fire, and went to make tea. I took in the sparse, cheap furniture and the few personal belongings. A photo of her son as a boy of about three smiled down from the mantelpiece: an arm curved about his shoulders, but the photo had been cut, so that the body wasn't present, and I assumed it must have been his father's. I shuddered at the sight of it, aware again of the sense of being watched. Like Keates, I knew I was looking over my shoulder at what wasn't there.

I stood before the fire, struggling with myself, trying to talk sense into myself. Reason told me that since stepping into the flat, I had activated the invisible watchers, and had stepped most unsafely into territory where I was not at all qualified to proceed. But what was it about this woman that caused this extraordinary reaction? In that moment, I think I fully understood the motivation of men who loved women inconveniently in past times, and just how readily the accusations of witchcraft or enchantment could leap so self-justifying to their lips. My whole being was under the assault of an attraction which had no warrant in nature, and was certainly endangering any professional relationship I might normally have with a client.

On the wall there was an image of the Virgin Mary and draped around the image was a rosary. Even at this pass, I forgot or failed to consider how I might guard myself against the twin assaults of this electric attraction and the sense of being watched. The words from the *Book of Joshua* that would have been so useful to myself, the very words I had committed to memory in case of Keates' need, had retreated so far that I might not have been a baptised Christian at all, so strong was the compulsion upon me. The tea arrived and still I struggled to be a professional. I purposely positioned myself in the most uncomfortable of armchairs at some distance from what I took to be Maureen's normal seat on the settee where there was a tell-tale muddle of knitting and a coaster for tea at one end, opposite the TV.

But still, I took my tea from her hand as if it had been the Holy Grail. In attempting to sip from it before it was cool enough, I thus spilt it down my jacket. She leapt up to fetch some kitchen towel, returning to administer it, but I tore the wad of paper roughly from her. She stepped back in alarm.

I took refuge in boorishness, 'I'm so sorry – how clumsy I am! Look, Mrs. Hardy, I am feeling a bit under the weather – please forgive me.'

Her alarm subsided and she looked into me again, 'You feel it too, then?' She sounded relieved.

'What do you mean?' I hoped fervently that we were not in for a very embarrassing conversation, squeamishly unprepared for the upheaving of my romantic youth all over again.

Fixing me with an observant eye, she asked, 'You felt it as we stepped over the threshold, didn't you? – that sense of being under observation?' She ignored my sigh of relief, and went on, 'This is precisely what my dreams are full of. Mr. Keates has shown me how to guard myself, but it doesn't seem to be working any more. It's just getting worse.... Do you think I am mad?'

I drew myself up, occupying more certain territory now. Sounding like some pompous senior registrar, I pronounced, 'I have worked in a variety of mental establishments since I was in my mid-twenties, and I have never seen anyone look less mad than yourself, Mrs. Hardy, I assure you.'

She sank onto the settee, ignoring her own tea, 'I can't help it, you know. I tried to get Mr. Keates to come here time after time, but he wouldn't. He said it would be safer for himself and me to have quite separate arrangements, if we were to throw my husband off the scent. I agreed with him, but I always wondered.... Now that you've felt it for yourself, I am so relieved.'

With the utmost care for procedure, I stepped into Ash's shoes and began to interview her properly, 'Did you have this sense of being watched in your last place?'

'Not to this degree. But since coming here, yes, I have.'

'Do other people you invite here also feel this?'

She looked down, 'I've only had a plumber over the threshold since coming here, but I could tell that he just wanted to fix the leak and get out quickly.'

'Since I'm unfamiliar with your story, perhaps you could kindly fill me in?'

She briefly related her life story: the daughter of a retired naval man and a horse-mad woman who stemmed from an old recusant Catholic family, she'd grown up wanting to paint and had ended up going to the Slade, before moving around Europe. It was while in southern Italy that she ran into Franco Ascioti, with absolutely no idea of his background. He had been handsome and charming, and his family well-mannered, if not so welcoming. With her sparse Italian and youthful inexperience, she had little notion of what she had fallen into, although her father was astute enough to mis-like Franco and his brother, the Nicolo Ascioti whom Ray said was lying low.

She didn't look at me as she related the story, but held the photo frame of her son to her breast, 'You have no idea how rare it is for men like Franco to marry out of their kind. He made me into some Jackie Kennedy or Grace Kelly in their eyes, but they never accepted me as trustworthy—I didn't come with any of the usual ties of loyalty and fear to control me. That was the job of my female in-laws: the aunties and cousins and the awful old matriarch of the clan…. And how they wove them round me….' She lay the photo face-down in her lap, as if to protect her son from this telling.

It wasn't really until she was already pregnant with Nicolo that she realized quite how the land lay. Her mother in law and her sisters began their assumptive role as guardians of the next heir to the dynasty, sequestering her movements and instructing her in her proper position as the wife of the regional head in that locality. Periodically men would come to the big family house, to pay obeisance, while other people from the household went missing or were found dead—always a long way from the house, of course. In horrified realization, Maureen had begun to pull away from her husband, starting to seek ways of withdrawing herself, but she had already become a virtual prisoner of the family she had entered.

'You have to understand that women don't exist or have any status in that society. It was made clear to me that if I strayed one inch, there would be reprisals. They made sure I knew about other wives in other 'Ndrangheta families, like Paola Mancusa, who was made to drink acid after she tried to leave her husband. *L'unica veramente importante per un Mafioso é e deve esserre la madre dei suoi figli.* "The only truly important woman for a Mafioso is the mother of his children."'

Bitterness and tears fought for control of her voice, 'No, Doctor, I had one function and until that was fulfilled, I had kissed goodbye to any freedom. I gave birth to my son under such a cloud of depression and wretchedness, you cannot imagine. The doctor put my mood down to post-natal depression, of course, but he knew. I made sure that there would be no more children, and when none came over the years, Franco began to cool towards me considerably: the unkindnesses began, the humiliations and beatings and… well, other things I'd rather not talk about. I pretended to be very upset about being barren, and made enquiries about fertility clinics. I found one that suited my purposes and offered, while Franco was doing business in Rome, to go to see a doctor there. I asked if we could have a little holiday, so that I could take Nick with me.

'He didn't suspect anything from his meek little wife, you see, and I had to be so cunning. I had kept my British passport sewn into my clothing, so he could never find it, pretending I'd lost it, over the years. But actually I'd managed to send my passport to my parents and get Nick put onto it: my mother had it sent to the clinic for me to pick up, along with enough money to get out. I slipped out of the clinic, doubled back to the hotel where a nanny was supposed to be looking after Nick, but was actually entertaining her boyfriend in our bed instead, and so we managed to sneak out, taking a taxi to the airport.'

I held my breath listening to her courage.

'At the airport, I bought a ticket to London under my maiden name and then asked to speak to a stewardess. I explained how I had to get back home and that my husband's family might be coming for me. She believed me and hid us in the back-quarters of the British Airways lounge for a few hours, eventually putting us on a later flight. My mother's neighbour came to collect us at Gatwick and drove us to a secret address — my mother was still dealing with my father's last illness then.'

'That was a truly amazing escape!'

'That's what we all thought, but it wasn't that easy. I took my maiden name, registered Nicolo as John Hardy — it's his middle name — for the local school, and lived in a mean little flat, which is all we could afford. My father's last illness took all our family money, and I knew I'd have to find work. That's when Mr. Keates took me on. I have no doubts as to the danger I am in, which is why I vary my working hours. Although I escaped from Franco's family, I haven't really. It is only a matter of time, I imagine. Every night I dream I am being examined, looked at, fought over. Calabria may be in Italy, but it's here too in London, wherever I live. The dreams persist, and everywhere I live, the feeling of being watched follows me....' She ran out of words, looking at me hopefully.

That look of trustful hope would have broken a stronger man than me: I felt so ashamed of my former feelings, that I was too flustered to answer reassuringly. I asked a few footling questions about the frequency and detail of her dreams, and then rose to depart, 'My colleague, Dr. Ashington, is far more experienced in these things than I. May I have your permission to share this with him?'

'Of course.... I'm aware that there are all kinds of complications arising from my situation. I am worried for John... Nicolo, and for my mother — she's far too frail to be dealing with this. I'm also clear that Mr. Keates has suffered some difficulties of his own over all of this, too. I am at my wit's end, that's all. I don't ever seem to get free of my foolish actions...'

'I think it is more to do with the family that you married into,' I said softly, 'but my colleague will have some better ideas, I think. I wish you would come to the Beacon where you could be free of this.'

'While Mr. Keates needs me, I will do what he thinks best.'

I asked her not to accompany me to the door, and let myself out, anxious to see if I could sense the difference outside her flat. The sense of being watched flattened out like a line on a monitor as I crossed the threshold, before activating again on the street, although at a much lower frequency than when I was inside. It was as if I had infuriatingly contracted an infection, and began to swear like a man with Tourettes Syndrome on the pavement. Several passers-by gave me a wide berth.

As I tried to hail a taxi, I made a mental note to ask Ray to come and case the joint, frisking it for devices, but even as I thought this, I knew that we were talking about some other kind of surveillance. Ray would find no hidden microphones, or bugs. This was a case for Ash and no mistake.

By now, the sense of Ash was becoming unbearable and it somehow broke through the fog of anger and irritation. No taxis being in sight, I walked to the nearest tube and I rang him from a public box there, 'Ash?'

His hand must have been on the phone, he picked up so fast, 'Goodness me, Jack! What is going on? Your signal spiked off the scale about an hour ago. I thought you were with Keates, but he hasn't seen you. We've been quite alarmed.'

I was puzzled, 'But didn't he tell you? I'd been with Maureen in north London, getting her history.'

There was a telling silence, 'No, he didn't... Has something happened between you? Keates sounded very tight lipped on the phone. I got the impression he felt you had run out on him, or even betrayed him ... Are you alright?'

Using the phone box like a confessional, I related the events of the last hour and half, ending with, 'I've just had one of the weirdest experiences of my life. If Keates and Maureen are feeling anything like me, then I am truly sorry for them.'

He asked a few more questions and then came back to it, 'So what happened between you and Keates?'

'I told him I was going round to Maureen's place, that's all. —Really, that was all.' I withheld my shameful sense of attraction for Maureen in my account to Ash, for a man has to have some sense of self-respect.

'How did he respond?'

'Like I had stolen his girl.'

'And had you?'

My scorn at his question was not very convincing, largely because of the long pause before I answered him: 'Of course not!' Bless him, Ash made no comment but asked, 'So how would you assess the situation now?'

'Out of control and dangerous, but I couldn't tell you how or why. It feels as if something imploded and the world is in some kind of free-fall. And I would include myself in the 'out of the control and dangerous' department....'

'Right! Then I suggest you go straight back to Maureen and pick her up. I will get Keates myself and meet you at Harley St. They should both come to the Beacon immediately and we can do some triage. Tell her to pack a bag.'

I ran round the corner to halt a taxi and back we went. I knocked and was admitted. Maureen simply nodded, returning almost immediately with a suitcase. 'I keep it packed ready,' she explained when I exclaimed at her speed. That small carry-on bag said it all. We locked the flat and left.

§§

The rendezvous at Harley St. was awkward on many fronts, not least my meeting with Keates. A churlish simmer of resentment sat on his pleasant face, while Maureen seemed agitated and afraid. I knew that Ash would scan me on arrival, in his usual fashion; that my hang-dog features would doubtless speak for themselves, and that I would be found out.

But his only remark to me, as we loaded the car with luggage was, 'I see that we have three clients not two!'

'Is it that obvious?' I snapped, feeling rubbed up the wrong way entirely.

He put his hand on my shoulder, 'Jack, don't take this on yourself. I blame myself for sending you into such an explosive situation.'

We drove down the motorway in awkward silence with Francis and Maureen sitting as far as possible apart from each other in the back. An inchoate miasma of such desperation and fear filled the car that it was hard not to be affected by it.

It was too late to do anything meaningful on arrival at the Beacon, we were all too tired, and after Wendy had shown them their rooms, our guests went straight to bed. I chuntered off to the kitchen to get a Horlicks, as I doubted I would sleep at all, I was so churned up.

Gillespie was winding the clock and yawning as I came into the kitchen, 'Man, you look as if you went nine rounds with Mike Tyson! Come away in. Och, leave the wee saucepan where it is, you need something stronger than milk!'

Which is how I ended up in Gillespie's snug, helping him finish off a bottle of *Highland Park*. Wendy came in after dawn and drew the curtains on us both, still slumped in our armchairs, the bottle between us on the floor. She discreetly said nothing, but returned with a pot of very strong coffee and some aspirin.

Thus fortified, I went straight to Ash's study to give a better account of myself than yesterday's effort.

He listened thoughtfully to my confession, which it really was this time, for I left nothing out. 'I am glad it wasn't worse,' was all he would say afterwards.

I ended up mumbling, 'It's bad enough that I broke trust with you and with all we believe in, not just with our clients. Had I been a younger man, I don't know how it would have ended.'

Ash's long gaze held no judgement, 'Don't beat your breast so much, Jack! You were under a very strong compulsion and your experience has fortunately saved us a lot of havering, as Gillespie would say. Having you as my assistant is proving more than worthwhile. You are like psychic litmus paper. Now we know who we must treat first.'

'Who, Keates?'

'Not at all—Maureen! Her presence was the ignition for this situation, by your own account. Did you not sense it when you first met—I have never heard such a line of superlatives from your mouth—Beatrice, Eve, Juliet—No, I will see your paragon this morning and Keates in the afternoon. As for him, I think you need to go and make it up, as a friend, before you accompany him as a professional.'

'But I don't know what to say to him!' I protested.

'Yes, you do! You simply apologize for abandoning him, and turning instead to Maureen's trouble. He understands the necessity for triage—that some cases are more urgent than others. If he doesn't get it, then you have my permission to blame me for setting you on....'

I bumped into Wendy on the stairs and told her that Ash would see Maureen after breakfast.

'Well, I don't know when that will be, as I just looked in on her and she's very still deeply asleep,' she frowned.

Keates was already awake and taking the air in the garden, so I bearded him there, under the cloud-swathed shadow of Hartsworth Beacon. He was immediately prickly and disinclined to greet me, but I said my piece and apologized for leaving him alone. In all justice, he listened to me. When I spoke about the danger that Maureen was in, tears came to his eyes, and he nodded, 'I see that you acted strategically now. It is just that I've been so worried for her for so long ... I am not a young man any more, you see...' He didn't need to finish, as we both peered down the corridor of that thought, and the 'what might have beens' that huddled there.

I could only think of one thing to say to him, 'Mr. Keates, I regard this place at the Beacon as holy ground, as dear to me as my life. I swear to you here and now, on the very soil' —I picked up a handful of it—'that Maureen is nothing more to me than a client. She is a lovely woman, but she is not mine and never will be mine.' That last part got away from me rather, surprising me, but I knew it to be true as I stood in that protected place. I think it is what redeemed me in his eyes, for I'd never sailed so near the wind with any of my charges as I'd done the previous day. My Saxon ancestors stood with me and witnessed my words, and they would hold me to them.

Keates was moved, 'I thank you for that. I know you are an honourable man.' I realized then that, for him, Maureen was as holy ground too, but too precious to be touched. Or maybe, he had been much stronger and wiser than myself? Whichever it was, knowing his true feelings, my respect for him rose and our friendship was mended. We gripped each other's hand and went into breakfast together as the clouds lifted from over the Beacon.

Ash saw Maureen alone, which I thought was for the best, considering yesterday's performance. Afterwards, he came looking for me after alerting the MacLeans, 'Are you free to take some dictation, Jack?—You will need to put the token on the door, as we need to look at something.'

When we were in his study, I asked, 'How did it go?'

'What we are about to do may trigger a response, so I want you to phone your friend, Ray, if you would? I think Maureen's mother and Nick need to be moved immediately.'

'Have there been developments, then?' I asked, alarmed.

'Not yet, but there most certainly will be, I think. I learned from Maureen this morning that she instigated divorce proceedings last week.'

I must have looked blank.

Ash patiently explained, 'Divorce between an Englishwoman and a foreign national whom she has married in the husband's country cannot proceed until she has returned home more than six months. Last week, she began proceedings under British law … so things will be coming to a head in any case.'

I remarked, stupidly, 'Of course, she has no assets—they are all on her husband's side, but she does have her son….'

Ash leaned forward, 'Someone in a position of authority like Franco Ascioti, from a traditional family, is unlikely to countenance the shame of a divorce—'Ndrangheta capos are model husbands with perfect wives, you understand—if a divorce did happen, he is unlikely to allow an ex-wife to live, it would be against his honour and that of the family. I suspect that his next move would be for him to eliminate Maureen and take the boy.'

The reality of the danger finally established itself, 'Good God!'

'I just want to ensure that Maureen's mother and the boy are moved to safety.'

'But where to?'

'There is a place in Lanarkshire that I know where they can be safe. I've made the arrangements and alerted the police just now. Now we need to ensure that Mrs. Hardy and her grandson can be moved there without alerting anyone else.'

Ray was immensely practical, taking the Lanarkshire address and arranging for a message to be sent immediately to Mrs. Hardy by a courier; it included a family reference from Maureen that only her mother would recognize. She was to pick up Nick from school and proceed to a garage where Ray would meet them in the MOT centre, after which he would drive them north, but they were to take no obvious luggage.

It was very hard to concentrate after all these arrangements were set in place, as the tension and danger felt palpable, yet Ash was still capable of lying down and going into a deep state. I sat beside him with pen and pad waiting to take dictation, in a state of agitation and fear.

After emitting a series of deep overtones, Ash slipped into a deeper state, his breath barely registering a rise of his chest. Knowing the routine now, I watched for the movement in his feet that told me he had reached his destination and, sure enough, he began to report in a distant voice, 'I am in a long corridor now, dark with heavy curtains. On the walls of the corridor.... many photographs of different eras.... from the seventies and eighties but older ones too.... Daguerrotypes.... Profoundly disturbing, these.... severe women swathed in black, corrupt old men, youths and girls who have never been young.... yet all the images have the same characteristic... the eyes are fixed so that, wherever you are, however you look, they see you.... are still seeing you....' His body twisted violently and he emitted a cry of distress. Immediately, he seemed to baton himself down, and a series of piercing overtones ensued... Alarmingly, his body shook with sudden spasms, very like febrile convulsions, then his breath resumed, long and deep, as a returning wave to the shore. He remained thus for another few minutes before his eyelids fluttered and he was back in the room. I insisted in taking his pulse when he sat up, 'That was most alarming.'

He smiled, 'It was a little more active than some of my trips, surely!'

'It looked as if it was a bit of a struggle?'

'The images down the corridor were all staring at Maureen.' With a naughty face he said, 'But I turned them all round, so they were facing the wall.'

'Well, this is certainly the time we need them not to see... What were they? The Ascioti family?'

'The living and the dead, both!' He gave a delicate shudder, 'These are the ones whom Maureen, Keates, and yourself have been aware of. Anyone who steps into the arena of the Ascioti family is like someone who's been bugged. I have just done the equivalent of going into the central junction box and turned off the power. Hopefully it will have debugged everyone in this case.'

'Myself as well?'

'Yes, but my action will have set off the alarm... while Maureen, and Keates as her protector, were under surveillance, the family had a hold on things, but now, things are going to get nasty. The ants' nest is going to spill out, as they try to pick up the signal.'

'What about Maureen? — You said she was the trigger for all this?'

'I think we will find out more this afternoon,' was all he would say.

After a subdued lunch during which Maureen could only manage a cup of tea, and no-one said a great deal, we got to work. Since we had agreed that Ray himself would only phone us when grandmother and grandson were safely over the border, which could not be until much later in the evening, things were tense. I trusted Ray implicitly, but it was less easy for Maureen, who had not met him. While she herself had had a good night, with no dreams, she was very much on edge. Ash, on the other hand, had eaten like a horse, cutting off slabs of cheese and even gone back for several more slices of the rustic bread. For myself, the sense of being watched, which had been a mere low level irritation since I returned home, had entirely faded since that morning. Everyone left to go about their own devices, leaving the better part of Wendy's good salad wilting on the table.

Over lunch, Keates had looked questioningly at Ash, received a nod, and had immediately stopped eating. Like a man being told he was about to go over the top in a few minutes, he gathered himself, and rose when we left, Ash leading upstairs. Wendy darted out of the scullery as we left, saying, 'I'll keep on eye on Maureen. Gillespie is nearby if we need any backup.'

We filed into Ash's study, where we did a brief overview of the time that had elapsed since the last meeting.

'How has your judgement been since our last meeting?' Ash asked Keates.

'Much better — steadier.'

'And the dreams?'

'Since Jack came to stay with me, it was as though I had some relief...' He said, with some reluctance, 'I'm sorry that nothing very conclusive happened while he shadowed me.'

Ash treated him to one of his long stares, and to a length of silence, 'Has it not?'

In the trailing silence, Keates turned colour twice, flushing red with embarrassment and then white with anger, struggling with himself, 'Of course, many things have happened....' His eyes sought me out, as I sat making notes, and I felt awful again.

Setting his head on one side, Ash invited him to continue. I jumped into the silence, half rising, 'If it would be easier for you, I can leave....'

Again, Ash allowed Keates to make that decision. He lowered his head, like a man defeated, 'No... I would like you to stay... I think you have experienced some of what I have been carrying... It is only right you should be a witness...'

'Tell me, from your side of things, what did you realize?' Ash ignored me and focused on Keates.

'I knew I needed help, and I was initially pleased to have Jack with me; I valued his presence at a time when I felt both weak and confused.... but...' He rose, walking up and down in agitation, then, fixing me accusingly, 'That day when you asked to leave me to go to help Maureen, I had the most irrational reaction... it was as if you had betrayed me... that you were leaving to take her away....' He shook his head. 'It made no sense... It was as if the thing that was most medicinal to me had been snatched away and, worse, that I had deserved it.... It was like being a teenager again, unable to work out what is happening, ridden by strange passions... and then I knew that I loved Maureen with a terrible, possessive jealousy... but that wasn't right either...'

I asked permission of them both, 'May I continue?' It was Keates who nodded to me, 'I can only say that on that day, I also felt as if I had stepped over some unseen threshold... that I was indeed taking her from you... in the taxi on the way there, I was confused and overwhelmed by feelings that didn't seem to be mine at all. I felt those watchers that are set over her when I entered her flat, and I also experienced the protective urge that you felt, only it came with the mad supposition that she was indeed mine.... It was all nonsense, of course.... I still don't know what came over me....' I stopped abruptly. Keates had spoken about Maureen as something medicinal... and I suddenly remembered the emblem on the apothecary jar in his flat: the very same emblem that was engraved on his watch and cuff links.

'Francis, could you please show Ash your watch?' Keates peeled back his sleeve. Ash's reaction was an unsurprised nod, 'The double saltire of St. Andrew – the double cross.'

Keates did a double take, 'A double cross? – Oh, my God! I've never made that connection all these years!' He looked perturbed and downcast.

Ash leaned keenly forward, 'What is the double cross in this case, Mr. Keates?'

Evasively, he failed to meet Ash's gaze, 'It is in my dreams... and imaginings....' he muttered.

Ash's attentive silence encouraged him to continue, 'Very well, then. It is part of a story that I used to tell myself as a child – I probably picked it up from some children's novel or other – I always enjoyed historical fiction.' Keates absently spread his hands, 'In the story, I was an impetuous youth who had his family's trust, but I got into bad company and ended up implicating my family in some kind of dishonourable enterprise. The details were all a bit vague.'

'What historical period was the story set in?'

Keates looked over our heads, as if envisaging the scene, 'I remember that it seemed to be dressed in some kind of Romeo and Juliet-ish style – again, it could have been some early television programme memory or other. There were lots of Montague and Capulet-ish run-ins, with trading insults or sword play. As a boy I rejoiced in this verbal passage of arms, making it more and more outrageous and insulting.'

'So, Northern Italy?'

'Yes. But I remember trying to tell the story differently or to stop the youth from betraying his family, but it always ended up the same way... with a sword fight in a dead-end street, with my back to the wall and my enemies at my throat.'

The hair rose on my neck. Now, I know that children fantasize about all kinds of things, but they do generally tell themselves better stories than this, ones in which they feature as the triumphant hero, not as the dead betrayer. I turned to see what Ash made of this response. He had his hands on the paperknife on the desk, his fingers curled about the blade, 'Did the end come like this?'

Quicker that I could see, Ash rose, extending the paperknife like a poignard with a backhanded, downwards movement to the exact point above Keates' chest, stopping short only at the last minute.

'*Porca Madonna!*' Keates slammed backwards into the mantel-piece, his palms guarding his body from the blow, '*Bruto filio di puttana...*' he spat.

Utterly appalled at his actions and Keates' response, I stared as Ash put the paper knife quietly back on the desk.

'Goodness me! What just happened?' Keates appealed to Ash, who helped him sit down and poured him some water.

'Mr. Keates, I judge from this demonstration that your childhood story is no story, but rather the memory of an actual event that you have experienced in another life.'

Our client's eyes searched wildly from side to side, trying to understand what Ash was saying, 'You mean that my birthmark is a remembrance of something that actually happened, just like in my dream?'

'Yes. And the recent business of protecting Maureen reactivated this memory and has given you the means to close the circle finally — to make good.'

'But how?' His voice bewildered and hopeful at once.

'Jack will tell you that, before lunch, I did some investigations on behalf of Maureen, which he kindly witnessed for me. While I was "out researching," I was given two names that I think relate to your dreams and to a situation that has been playing out here. — Ignacio Andrea, the nephew of the Florentine banker, Antonio Andrea, and the beautiful Genevra Batisti of Pisa.'

As these names were uttered, a tumble of expressions passed over Keates' face: at times resembling someone much harder, younger and impatient, at others registering the sorrow and regret of an older, more chastened man. Finally, his features settled into his own, mature self, 'Then it is true?' he cried out, in tones of wonder.

'What was the nature of the double cross? How does the story go? You know it, Francis... tell us... how did it play out?' Ash was like a trainer urging a young athlete on.

In a dreamlike voice, Keates hesitatingly outlined the story. How young Ignacio had fallen into bad company, running up debts both of money and of honour. While deeply sunk in this misfortune, he had fallen for Genevra, the daughter of a minor nobleman, and god-daughter to the then pope. However, Genevra was to have been married to another. Ignacio was entrusted with conveying the young woman's dowry to the home of her intended, for the Batisti family, having been in debt themselves, had raised a loan from the Andrea bank for this purpose, to uphold their family honour. Not content with stealing the dowry, Ignacio also made off with the bride. But they did not even enjoy one night together, for Ignacio's betrayal was swiftly brought to light, and Genevra's betrothed, aided by the Papal guards, pursued him through the backstreets of Pisa until they found him and ran him through.

Keates ceased his recital and looked at us both, 'I know now that I was young Ignacio, that my life was a morass of betrayal of family, but I feel that I have been purged of his rapacious greed. — You know, the love of Genevra was a pure thing: she offered him hope and love, and he deceived her family and the church, the foolish wretch! — Well, it is all done with now.' He removed his watch and his cuff-links, as a man might remove manacles. With the sleeves of his shirt hanging loose, he gazed restfully out over the Downs, as if he had been offered a wonderful privilege.

We gave him a few moments to register his ritual gesture of renunciation. He turned, rolled up the cuffs to his forearm and said, 'Thank you, dear friend.' Keates shook my hand, 'I know now that I saw you as Genevra's betrothed. I am grieved to have offended you with those old suspicions... you were innocent of all blame.'

Turning to Ash, he said, 'You are a true soul doctor. The story you've coaxed out of me is not a happy one, but I feel it can leave me now. — You are right, the double cross of my earlier life has a chance of redemption in this one. As for Maureen...' a shadow passed fleetingly over his face, and left it, as he finally mastered the ancient passion and greed of young Ignacio Andrea, 'As for Maureen, I will dedicate my life to serving her in whatever way she requires, to her protection if she wants it, or in any other way. The danger surrounding her and her family is more pressing than mine now... does she need to know any of this?' he appealed to Ash.

Ash shook his head, 'None of this needs to be shared with her. For her, nothing has changed, except the consequences of her current marriage and their implications. What do you want to do, now?'

'I want to offer her a safe place for herself and her family. If she can be protected, then that is my first concern. I will take early retirement, sell up my office and dedicate my assets to her care. — I had already remembered her in my will. — Would that suffice to make up for what Ignacio Andrea did, do you think?'

Ash breathed, 'Perhaps.' Something in his demeanour gave me pause, but Keates didn't notice, he was so full of his plans. As he left the room, running down the stairs to Maureen, I made to follow, but Ash pulled me back, 'Leave him! Justice will work itself out accordingly....'

I frowned, 'Justice?'

He said to me, 'Do you understand what part you've inadvertently played here?'

'Well, you said I was like psychic litmus paper — but is there any way of limiting that effect? I don't think I could possibly go through that sort of thing again — it was the weirdest experience....'

'I did warn you that you were going into danger...'

'Yes, but you never told me that I would be stepping into the shoes of some long-dead Italian whose bride had been stolen... and going head to head with my rival...'

Ash took me by the shoulders and looked into me, just as Maureen had done when she first met me, then he scanned over my head, 'You are completely clear, Jack... I imagine....'

But I never heard what those imaginings might be as there was a commotion coming from downstairs. Wendy's voice raised in horror and Keates barking orders up the stairs to me, 'Give me the keys of your car, Jack!'

'What's happening?'

Wendy peered up the stairs, clutching the newel, white as a sheet, 'It's Maureen… while I was out the back, she called a taxi to take her to the station. She took the details of the Scottish house from the desk.…'

Keates broke in with, 'She's gone to be with her family… let me follow her, please.…' He held out his hand and I, fool that I was, threw my keys down to him. Ash's attempted intervention was quickly withdrawn, his expression unreadable.

We stood at the door helplessly watching Keates drive off down the lane. Wendy ran into the drive after him, one hand clamped to her mouth in despair, as Gillespie came round from the garden with a bundle of sticks. At the sight of our faces, he dropped them to the ground with a clatter, 'Do ye want me to follow him?'

Ash shook his head, gravely, 'It's too late for anything but calling the police now.'

Although Ash assured Wendy over and over that it was not her fault, she could nevertheless be heard weeping quietly in the art room, where she had taken herself off. Nothing we could say helped: she blamed herself for leaving the address in plain sight. She sat trying to hug Cinnamon who merely wriggled off her lap into the garden in protest. The police had been informed of all the pertinent details and now dark had fallen. The house was waiting. Ash, myself and Gillespie took turns to sit by the phone in the kitchen. Any local calls were swiftly answered and as quickly ended, as we waited for news from anyone.

Gillespie had checked the timetables for the train times north: it was likely they had got on the 16.17. but from Christminster to Waterloo, Waterloo to Euston, with a change at Motherwell, the train couldn't possibly reach Lanark Station until 06.12 the next morning, so were in for a long wait before we knew anything, we reckoned. As for Ray, his journey would take him about 6-7 hours by road, so we wouldn't hear from him till about midnight.

Ash listened to us rationalizing the possibilities, with a worried frown, 'The work of today will have precipitated things, I'm sure, but we can't know how.'

I asked quietly, not to unduly worry anyone, 'You think the Ascioti's will make a move?' He nodded.

'But how? — We've been so careful about Ray. If Keates caught the train

Maureen will be on, then they will arrive tomorrow....

Gillespie pointed out, 'But he has your car, Jack, so your man could be in Lanarkshire tonight!'

The permutations were too various, and we were just working ourselves into a state.

Ash went to speak to Wendy and get the sequence of events clearly. He returned, having given her a sedative to help her sleep. 'Wendy says that she thinks Maureen could have made another call after phoning for a taxi from the guest ....'

'The number might still be in "last number called" in the booth,' Gillespie hurried to it and dialed the call back, writing the number down. 'London — shall I dial it?'

'But what if it's someone who will be able to work out where we are? Should we even be doing this?'

Ash pointed out, 'If they were that clever, then they already know where we are, Jack.' He nodded to Gillespie, who dialed the last call back.

Over the speaker we heard a male voice answering in Italian, 'Pronto? Chi parlo?'

Gillespie assumed his thickest accent, 'Is that the dry cleaners? I left my winter coat with you....'

The respondent put down the phone without another word.

We stared at Ash, 'Who could it have been? — Surely she's wasn't so stupid as to make calls to her husband's family?' I asked in bewilderment.

'We spoke about the divorce — she said she would have to open up channels to broach it... even though that would be her solicitor's job. We have no idea what has been precipitated here.'

Now that we had this intelligence, the atmosphere became much gloomier even in the cosy warmth of the kitchen. The ticking of the clock seemed so oppressively loud, that I stood to silence it when the phone went.

Ash got there first, Gillespie at his shoulder, 'Thank you, Ray! That's good to hear! Listen, we may have a complication...' He filled in Ray about developments. Both Keates and Maureen are on their way up to you — we're not sure by what means — train or car. But there is a chance that you will receive earlier guests than those, so I would phone the police now and get some protection.'

I could hear Ray's steady drawl from the receiver. He was good at defending himself, but he had just driven nearly seven hours through the night and sounded tired. I imagined the remote place that Ash had selected, a shepherd's bothy done up as a holiday rental, situated on a private estate, and how Ray must be fixed, in so isolated a spot, with two vulnerable charges to protect, with none of us there to watch his back. I felt his exhaustion in my own body, drained of its last resource.

Gillespie took the first midnight watch, with Ash following him, and myself on the dawn shift. I remained wakeful, and so when I heard Ash come down at 4 am, I finally ambled down to join him. He was sitting at the kitchen table with Cinnamon draped over his chest and round his neck like a scarf. He shook his head, 'Nothing more yet.'

I must have slept, for when I next raised my head from the table it was light. Ash was stirring his coffee, yawning. The first light of dawn penetrated the kitchen, lighting the golden stubble that was testament to his vigil. It was 6.15am by the clock. He heard me stir and made another cup, 'I have a very bad feeling, Jack. We are going to have to be strong, I think.' His face was drawn, his eyes lacklustre from watching.

We sat sipping the bitter brew, too tired for conversation. The phone call, when it came, sprang into the quiet room without warning.

Ash grasped the receiver. As he listened to the caller, without speaking, I saw his eyes close with resignation. He asked, 'And Maureen and her family?' At the response, his eyes opened again with relief. 'Thank you, officer.'

I knew before he turned to me, with the utmost pity in his voice, 'Maureen and her family are alright, Ray is injured — not seriously — and in hospital, but Keates is dead.'

I am used to losing patients to over-doses and to suicide, but Keates was another matter. Ash gave me the barest details that the police had relayed to him, but it wasn't until afterwards that we were able to piece the whole story together. It was clear that when Keates took off in my car, he had missed by minutes the train that Maureen had been on, determining instead to drive the whole way. This meant that he arrived in Lanarkshire after Ray, but many hours before Maureen, whom he had gone to meet at the station, while we were still drinking coffee at the Beacon. Maureen had been followed, not by the Ascioti family but by a series of Albanians in league with the 'Ndrangheta. Apparently, they ran the drug-and-people-trafficking racket in Britain. They'd had orders not to harm Maureen until she led them to her boy.

Ray later told us the story, 'It was not until Keates drove up to the bothy, that they made their move. I heard his car arrive and came down to see who it was. Unfortunately, the boy was already awake and banged on the upstairs bedroom window when he saw his mother, which is how the two Albanians knew he was within. As soon as they made a move on Maureen, Keates threw himself in front of her, which is how he came to take the bullet intended for her.

I was grappling with Nicolo Ascioti, who had come for his nephew. He knifed me in the side, but I managed to headlock him and twist. He fell and hit his head, so by the time the police arrived, he was taken up unconscious.'

Maureen, her mother, and son, were taken first to the local hospital, and then into protective custody. Thus it was that she and her family entered into witness protection, as a unique witness to the inside workings of the 'Ndrangheta. Within a very short time, Nicolo Ascioti was extradited and, with other members of his family, was arrested and sent to Rome where, in one of the biggest show trials of the 'Ndrangheta network that Italy had ever seen, he and several members of the Ascioti family — including Franco, Maureen's husband, were imprisoned along with many of their henchmen.

As for myself, I could not help feeling a certain culpability in Keates' death, finding myself increasingly irritated with Ash's calm neutrality.

I remember attacking him with, 'You said that justice would work itself out — is this what you meant? Did you foresee this?' I did not spare the blame, but he answered mildly enough, 'No, Jack. I had no idea how it would fall out. Thank goodness, I am not the balancer of the cosmic books, I leave that to a higher power. Do you not remember Keates' assertion, that he would dedicate himself to Maureen's welfare? The moment he uttered those words, that was when I did realize that something had shifted, but no, I had no notion of how that would play out. In the scale of time and honour, one death has paid for all.' Of course, Ash took the longer view of time, seeing the effect of many lifetimes, but he was mourning as much as the rest of us. Gillespie had a hard time with Wendy, who continued to blame herself for not locking the office door.

With many of our cases, the final outcome remains unknown. We see people in their most extreme conditions and hopefully put them on the road to a new life, free of their burdens. In this case, there was more than the usual sense of hiatus. We did not expect to see Maureen again — she would have a new identity, a new location, and there was much that we could never know. We never discovered how the Asciotis learned of Maureen's movements: the police concluded that she must have been under observation from the time she made that phone call from the Beacon.

The funeral of Francis Keates was a quiet affair, held at Temple Church in London. It was well attended by his fellow financiers. Respectful tributes to him from the City were paid and his body was given the honour of being carried by liveried officers of the Guildhall. As Ash and I turned to leave the church, I saw a woman standing at the back of the church gravely regarding the stark stone effigies of the Templars who lay with folded hands contemplating eternity. She wore an enveloping black veil and gloves over her grey clothes, but it was undoubtedly Maureen.

I made to approach her, but Ash drew me aside, warning me, 'Don't draw attention to her!'

'Should she be here?' I whispered back.

'No, indeed. But is it not Genevra Batisti, to the life, paying the tribute she was unable to give her abductor in life?'

It was then she saw us. I knew only by the trembling of the veil. With one graceful nod to us, she turned and left, which is when I realized that she had not been alone. Her bodyguard, with the build of an ex-policeman, gave us one sharp look and followed her out. It was a relief to know that she was protected. She had left one single flower upon the nearest effigy before she departed.

After the wake, held at the Guildhall, Keates' solicitor read the will in a little back room, bare of everything save chairs and a table. The will read like that of a medieval man, commending his soul to God, and the disposal of his goods for the needy of the parish. Keates had left the majority of his assets to Maureen, but there were a series of small bequests that would ensure he was remembered warmly in the city for generations to come. He had also not forgotten the Beacon, which received a trust fund, to be specifically used for the care and support of any person, without means, to receive our treatment and full accommodation. It was generous enough to fund several guests a year. Maureen was not present.

Back out in the early summer sunshine, Ash demanded that we walk to the river to blow away the cobwebs. We strolled down through Temple Gardens to the Thames. As the little river launches plied their way up and down the flooding tide, with their complement of tourists and commuters, Ash felt in his pockets, taking out the cuff-links with the double cross upon them. Reaching over the embankment wall, he cast them far out into the flowing tide, 'Farewell, Ignatio Andrea! Your treacherous days are done. O eternal powers, welcome the faith and trust of Francis Keates, who has brought justice!'

The waters received them easily and kindly, as I hope he is also welcomed where he has gone.

Case 5: ODIN AND THE RUNE WRECKERS

He had only one eye and claimed to have hung nine nights on a windy tree... Looking at the state of him after the gig on Saturday night, you might well believe it. How did Erik Ragnarok — aka plain Rick Stevenage — of the *Rune Wreckers* swing into our orbit? It wasn't what you'd call an obvious connection. How come this worn-out, heavy metal guy from an eighties band had even heard of a classical music-minded healer like Ash? The *Rune Wreckers* were a by-word for over-the-top antics onstage and off. If it wasn't the violence, it was the drink. I was astounded that any insurer would still replace their guitars after so many destructive wastings.

Seeing the two men together, Ash so straight, slim and tall, and Erik so very ravaged with touring and brawling that his body resembled a wind-blown tree on a blasted moor, you wouldn't have made the connection. Watching them together, as Ash pushed Rick in a wheelchair up to the dell (which is really a part of Hartsworth Beacon but still within the grounds of the Beacon), I remembered the morning, was it only last week, when the connection between them was re-forged in bizarre circumstances?

I hadn't given a thought to Erik's band for many years until Ash breezed into breakfast that late spring morning with a fat envelope in his hand. Over the grapefruit, he emptied it out to find a letter together with two tickets and back-stage passes for the *Rune Wrecker's* latest gig at the Round House in London. While sipping coffee, he passed them to me, 'Any use to you?'

The passes were printed on black card with white lightning-style script and a huge red eye that seeped blood. I groaned. 'Ash, I think my days of heavy metal are well passed, thanks. — Why not offer them to Wendy and Gillespie?'

Moving the orange juice skillfully beyond my reach, Wendy responded, '*We* are more likely to be seen at the Arlington Folk Festival, thank you very much. Gillespie is very fond of the Highland Fiddlers.' She wrinkled her nose at the lurid passes, 'Who goes to that kind of thing these days, anyway?'

'Ageing head-bangers? It certainly didn't appeal to me,' I remarked.

Looking up from the letter, Ash declared, 'Well, I think you and I will be paying a visit to the Round House, after all, as it seems to be the only convenient break in Rick's schedule. He's going on to Rotterdam, Hamburg and Stravanger after London, but I rather think we will need to see him before then. — Before things get any worse.'

Later, in the library, I read the letter. Such a careful hand for such an unregenerate character, I thought.

Dear Rickie,

It's been a few years since we sloped off behind the bike sheds for a fag, old lad, how are you doing? My mate Foley says you've gone and got yourself a whole new world of medical miracles going on down south. I sure could use some help right now.

Being on the road and all most of the time, I don't get a lot of chance to see folks, so I wondered whether we could meet up in London town?

I got this act with the Rune Wreckers—it seemed a good idea when we started—but something keeps phasing out in me. I do an Odin on the tree act, but somehow I don't get past Jotunheim. We rehearse the songs I'm supposed to sing from the tree, but, honestly, something like a bad trip is coming through instead. The boys are freaking out about it, so I promised I'd write, like. It's taking too much of me, as you probably know from the news.

I don't know if it's something you handle, but I need something soon. No point me coming to your rooms in London—I looked you up after Foley told me what you do—fancy you making it to Harley Street! —You need to see it all in action, cause I can't make it happen unless I'm up there on the tree. Then you can do your stuff, maybe?

Grinder, Jobscald, Loki and the rest of the boys would love it if you'd pay us a visit. Enclosing a couple of passes for you and a friend. Foley never told me if you got a girl? Lindie and me never did get married, but she can't stand my guts anymore now and went all Christian Metal on me since I took to the tree. Well, some you lose, like they say. Pity, cause she was the best!

I got the weird on me now, old friend. Any help you can be, best make it quick, like. I don't think I got many more performances left in me.

Yours,

Rick

Ash took the letter back from me, 'You see, he asks for help three times?' He sounded sad. 'Do you get the reference to Jötunheim? It's not really my field.'

As I said before, I've always had a warm interest in Norse Myth, so it was a rare pleasure to expound something that Ash didn't know. 'Indeed! Odin has to go through Jötunheim, the Land of the Giants, to get to Mimir's well where all wisdom lies. — But what's all this about the news?'

Ash opened the folded up paper from the letter: it was a headline page from the *Daily Mirror*, 'Oh Dear, Odin! — Rune Wrecker Wrecked' showing a picture of Rick looking dire, after coming out of hospital only last year. A woman — presumably his partner, Linda — glared at the photographer as if she would take his liver out. During Rick's act, a spotlight on the lighting rig had exploded; because of his proximity to it, the accident had caused him to lose an eye. Looking down the article, it was clear to see that the onstage stunts had become very dangerous and that many theatrical managements were unwilling to take the *Rune Wreckers* onto their programmes any more.

'Strewth! One eye missing? That is a shade too mythic, even for the legendary *Rune Wreckers*. — I agree — we should go and see for ourselves, but can't we get to see him before the gig? What he proposes sounds like triage rather than a consultation. It would be good to get a base line before we proceed to picking up the pieces, surely?'

'I think this is one of those cases where it has to be on his terms, rather than ours,' Ash said quietly, 'Whatever he says in the letter, we won't get near him very easily in the normal way. The fact that he wants us to see for ourselves tells me that he knows the extremity he's in.' This cut clean across Ash's normal procedures of preliminary assessment, so I was surprised.

'You have enough of Rick's base-line to proceed, then?'

'Yes! We were at school together.' I was intrigued, as Ash's past history was largely mythical in itself.

'But you hate loud music!'

'Indeed I do. But this is going to be a necessary witnessing.'

§§

Even for myself, having been to many a rock concert in my youth, it was pretty difficult to manage, but I was amazed that Ash was able to tolerate the bestial wave of sound that issued from that stage. Could this be the same guy who would listen to Rachmaninov stretched out on the sofa with Cinnamon curled upon his chest? (He afterwards admitted to having worn ear-plugs, 'While they didn't much reduce the impact of the beat, they did prevent damage to my eardrums.')

We were up in the gallery overlooking the huge round auditorium, with a good view of the main stage area. Below us a sea of black and metallic moshers milled and danced — if you can call it that. It was clear from the set that Erik and the *Rune Wreckers* had long departed from straight heavy metal and moved into the deeper regions of what was now called 'Viking Metal,' I discovered. The stage was arrayed with a great steel Thor's hammer which later also served as the tree of Yggdrasil. When I saw this, my heart sank. I hoped fervently that we not in for an evening of right-wing, nationalist, or neo-Nazi style music, but I needn't have feared. The evening began to be more than mythic as it wore on.

On stage came the 'boys' — ageing instrumentalists to a man — twisted Grinder and obese Jobscald, with vocalist, Loki — his mighty voice belying his slight frame. They and the rest of the act were attired in ubiquitous black with greased up hair in spikes, their faces painted with the rune of their stage name. I know my runes:

ᚷ *gebo* or gift,   ᛃ *jera* or year   ᛚ *laguz* or lake.

After a clashing build-up, Erik erupted onto the stage to massive applause and shouting. He had inscribed himself with ᛟ *othila* or heritage on the opposite cheek to the dead eye. He wore a war-coat with flashing bands of metal on its long skirts that rayed out when he spun around, giving us multiple twirls of jagged lights as he sang a long evocation. His now blind right eye-socket was painted bright red, just as on the passes. It was cacophonous, and it wasn't my ears that ached but my whole body from the onslaught of decibels.

The *Rune Wreckers* played a couple of sets, with Loki as secondary vocalist doing his share in the second set. The audience began to be quite keyed up and restless during the latter part of this set, as if they were waiting for something. and that any more music was somehow extraneous to the plot. It was clear that this second set gave Erik time to retire and get ready for his grander entrance.

Midway through the performance, the Thor's hammer at the back of the set began to open up, extending to become a tree with branches. Sparks scattered over the stage as Erik returned to the stage with a huge black cloak, swathing him from head to foot, and with a brimmed hat pulled over his eyes — the very spit of Odin. His appearance, so plain after such a colourful (in the metallic sense) opening took effect and the audience seemed to lean forward in anticipation.

What had been, so far, a good floor-show with some tolerable performances then departed from entertainment, turning into something quite different. While the *Rune Wreckers* started chanting a ballad about Odin, Erik mounted the tree by means of the incised ladder which formed part of the Thor's hammer — now the trunk of Yggdrasil. He fitted his arms into straps so that he could sing suspended from the tree. Great shimmers of pure metal sound erupted like fireworks, shivering the air. Then, as Odin, he began to — well, there is no other word for it — rave in prophecy. You couldn't understand any of what he said, but it sounded pretty authentic to me.

To a professional eye, he could have been having a fit or a psychotic episode—it resembled this, but something else was happening too. His voice began to take on the distinct timbre of someone much heavier and older. An archetypal and ancient happening was unfolding before us and the audience was already attuned, waiting for it to happen.

The largely male head-bangers in the hall stopped their moshing at the sight of this, several being much moved by the seemingly simulated sufferings of Odin. It was almost like watching the Crucifixion, although the words projected up behind him were wholly Norse:

Veit ek at ek hekk vindga meiði a
netr allar nío,
geiri vndaþr ok gefinn Oðni,
sialfr sialfom mer,
a þeim meiþi, er mangi veit, hvers hann af rótom renn

I didn't need to know any Norse to get this, because the rhythm of the words being insistently sung by the *Rune Wreckers* in chanted chorus, was resonant with my understanding:

'I know that I hung on a windy tree
nine long nights,
wounded with a spear, dedicated to Odin,
myself to myself,
on that tree of which no man knows from where its roots run...'

I felt, rather than heard, the tension in Ash's body beside me as the prophesying began. Glancing sideways, I saw that, like the audience, his whole body was leant forward, transfixed by this spectacle of his old school mate suffering on Yggdrasil. Then, looking more closely again at the tree, I saw what Ash had seen, realizing that Erik was really in pain, not faking it. His body was convulsing like a combatant stricken by a mine or a woman in the throes of labour: there is a point of pain where the human body and soul struggle to part company and Erik had been in the grip of appalling pain for about five or six minutes now, I realized.

Metallic awe was the centre piece of the evening. At that moment, a couple of hardened metallic harpies with wing-like cloaks were lowered from the rigging; with wild black hair and eye-liner an inch thick rimming their staring eyes, they were streaking it down their cheeks as they hovered beside him, wailing over Erik's sufferings, like a pair of raven-angels.

Suddenly, the reality of it overtook me and, before I knew it, tears and sobs were bursting from me, despite, or fuelled by, the outrageously overpowering volume of sound. I was *really* present at Odin's struggle in a way no book could create, my imagination raw with the reality of it. In my own head, the words I'd read so often were rising like ribbons of runes and wrapping me round:

> *No bread did they give me nor a drink from a horn*
> *downwards I peered;*
> *I took up the runes, screaming I took them,*
> *then I fell back from there…*

Almost the same moment those lines came to my mind, so Erik drew from his cloak an electrical confetti of runes that spilled from his hands and fell to the stage, as wisdom fountained and spewed out into that place. At that point, it was just as well that there was a high barrier between the audience and the stage, as the moshers all pressed forward as if they might catch one of the runes. My mind snapped back into reality as I saw the very real danger of the front rows pressing towards the stage becoming crushed in the stampede. Stage crew and front of house folk were equally alarmed, and I saw the front of house manager raise a walkie-talkie to his mouth — though how he could have heard or been heard wasn't really feasible in this cacophony of sound.

The music wailed on to its catastrophic climax. I wondered how it would be possible to step down the atmosphere before more damage was done. The metallic discordance had entered into a rhythm so persuasive that there seemed no means of bringing the audience back to its senses.

Loki's face was turned up to where Erik writhed on the tree. His hand was lifted from his guitar and he was making urgent gestures to the other instrumentalists to stop. It was the ensuing silence that turned the tide of danger — a silence as potent as the cacophony had been. The audience pressing forward suddenly halted their dangerous career as if an invisible barrier had been raised.

Then in the silence, with perfect timing, Loki hit one gentle electric chord and, using the sustain of it like a drone, began to sing to Erik, not Odin. He was improvising, not performing some rehearsed song, I'm sure of it:

> *Come down, my friend,*
> *From your wanderings far.*
> *We see your pain, we reach for your star.*

Come down to us and live again.
Leave your suffering, leave your pain....

Behind the quiet singing we could all now hear the stark agony of the man tied to the tree. His awful groans were too real. The rigging crew above him were working furiously above Erik to lower the whole tree, as he clearly had no ability to climb back down himself.

Ash's knuckles were white with gripping the rails of the gallery. He turned, indicating with his head that we should go below. As we raced down the stairs to the pass-door, stage crew were filing on below to receive the tree with its terrible burden. We were past the point whereby the audience's suspension of disbelief could be sustained and now, as we pushed through the audience, there was beginning to be anger and incredulity that the performance had stopped. They had swung so high, it was impossible for them to come back down so quickly.

Almost at that same moment, Jobscald began a series of deep bass chords and rumbled a slow, emphatic chant, that fitted the deposition of Erik to the stage. The two harpy-raven women, now lowered to the stage themselves, unhooked themselves to come and stand in front of the awkward spillage of the tree's fruit going on behind them, raising their wings and taking up the chant,

Odin, Odin, Odin
The wise one has spoken,
All that is needful to know.
Huginn and Muninn
Will keep you in wisdom.
Fierce is the joy of the man
Who holds to the runes and
Understands them.

This time, the music was loud enough to cover the groans, and Erik's departure from the stage. The rigging crew swung a curtain across the scene of deposition. While Grinder, Loki and Jobscald continued with one of their standard numbers, Ash and I arrived in the back stage area and met the team carrying him out. Erik was still tied to the tree which was being carried with great difficulty into the tight space. The team resembled pall bearers with an unwieldy load.

Ash was in charge within seconds, taking Erik's pulse and examining whatever parts of his body were accessible. While the stage manager called an ambulance, myself and three of the crew tried to remove his limbs from the straps which had become impossibly twisted; in the case of his right leg, the strap had begun to stop the flow of blood. Already the leg was swollen up and we had to resort to a knife, desperately sawing through the strap upward in a vain attempt to free him, but the webbing had obviously been made of some impervious material. What had started out as a good nod towards health and safety was now becoming a hazardous constraint to circulation. One of the crew working on the straps with me was swearing and praying in alternate desperation and hope. Finally, we freed the endangered leg. One of the harpy-ravens immediately cast herself down beside Erik, attended to the leg, massaging the tissue and encouraging the flow of blood again with skilful fingers.

She met my anxious glance with unwavering eyes, 'Heather — Professional masseuse!' she said. The eyeliner had run down her face so badly, it actually looked like feathers.

'Jack — mental health professional. You did well, there!' I said to her, admiringly.

'Not your scene, this, is it?' she smiled slowly, speculatively glancing at my clothes, which were not heavy-metal standard.

'Not normally. But I live and learn. — It was quite a show.'

Erik had finally stopped convulsing and his groans were subsiding. Ash, kneeling beside his head, was speaking to the Stage Manager, 'No, he's not fit to continue. Let the rest of the show go on, if they can without him.'

The *Rune Wreckers* seemed to be keeping up a manful amount of music front of house and would have to just struggle on alone.

Erik opened his eyes, seeming to register finally where he was.

Ash grasped his arm, 'Rick, how are you now?'

He licked his lips and muttered. '*Heroes they seemed when clothes they had,*
But the naked man is nought....'

Ash frowned up at me for confirmation.

'It's from the *Havamal*, the *Elder Edda*. — Old Norse poem,' I said.

'Time to go now,' Ash said to him. 'We'll be there with you.'

The ambulance had arrived, and we went with the paramedics to the University College Hospital.

§§

Hanging around in A&E on a Saturday late is a special purgatory. Only junior doctors are on duty, any test results are slowed down by the lack of staff, while the volume of patients increase minutely as the evening wears on. Erik was seen remarkably quickly after the triage nurse assessed him, but he was still behind a stabbing, two strokes and a heart-attack, and only a little ahead of the minor accidents caused by drunkenness. The massed inebriates of Camden Town seemed to have assembled that night, with two of them covered with blood and continuing an argument that could only be called 'a mutual assault.' The family room was already host to the bereaved parents of an earlier fatal ATC so, exiled to the waiting area, Ash and I wedged ourselves in between the coffee-machine and a maudlin Glaswegian with a broken nose who swung from belligerent to charming ever so often.

We had played the 'medical advizer' card but even Ash had difficulties being recognized when there were, manifestly, no notes or prior consultation to back up this assertion. We just had to wait. Erik's letter asking for help wasn't much use here. We both knew that we were unlikely to be consulted or given any results or prognosis.

A male nurse with ginger hair sought us out, 'Does Erik — er, Mr. Stevenage, have a nearby next of kin we can call?' The staff had been told to keep discretion about Rick's identity.

Ash said, 'His ex-partner, Linda, is unlikely to come, but you can try — maybe he has a contact for her. I know that both his parents are dead.' At that point, Heather showed up, her face hastily scrubbed down and without her Valkyrie wings, looking pale and tired, as she made her way towards us.

The nurse turned to her, 'Does Mr. Stevenage have someone we can call? — I believe he has an ex partner?'

Heather incredulously enunciated the name, like the world might come to an end first: 'Linda? I very much doubt it.' To demonstrate, Heather searched her phone and pressed 'call.' Explaining the situation briefly, telling Linda where Rick was. We all heard the outraged shout and the sound of the receiver being slammed down. Heather held out the phone with a 'see what I mean' face.

'Is there anyone else we can call?' The ginger nurse frowned.

'Steve from the band is on his way….' Heather's eyes ranged around the waiting room, and saw a couple of newsmen arriving like predatory crows. Turning her back on them, Heather said quietly through the side of mouth, 'But you might want to clear the area first.'

The ginger nurse tutted with distress at the sight of the assembled newsmen and strode off to get security to keep the paparazzi at bay outside. But, at that very moment, Steve, aka Loki, was descending from a taxi, still in his *Rune Wreckers* gear, complete with rune-pasted cheek and semi-naked chest. Soon the whole of London would know where Erik was, and A & E would become ever more besieged. Loki was immediately surrounded by newshounds intent on the pickings, but by machetéeing his arms aggressively, he was ably swarming through their ranks.

He came towards Heather, acknowledging myself and Ash with an aggressive, 'How's he doing?'

'Not so good,' said Ash.

'Are you the guy Rick said he'd be writing to?' He twisted his neck up to Ash. Close too, Loki was all sinew and sweat, and about five foot two.

'Yes, he asked us to come and see the performance.'

'Thank goodness! What do the docs say?'

'We don't know,' I said, 'They won't discuss the case with a non-relative.'

Loki clenched his fists, 'I'll make them listen.' And strode off to the desk to get attention. 'That's my mate in there, and those are his shrinks!' He had a very loud, carrying voice. Since his entry into A & E, the other disruptives had fallen strangely silent, as he clearly upstaged them all in his ragged black gear, spiky white hair and rune-paint. Now everyone stared over at us with blatant curiosity and suspicion. Loki's demands certainly made the staff run around at an increased pace in the next few minutes. A burly porter stood ready, in case any violence was offered.

Increasingly, it looked as Ash and I were being recognized as the best bet for a 'who you gonner call?' A white-coated junior doctor from Nigeria finally appeared, 'I gather you are Mr. Stevenage's therapist?'

'And friend,' Ash asserted, handing the doctor his card, Harley St. side up. 'Rick's fellow band-members are concerned for him. If you will take us through to him, I promise we will ensure that they are informed and — pacified?'

Dr. Omowale was clearly a sensible man, 'Come this way.... Dr. Ashington. Mr. Stevenage is doing a little better now. Please don't keep him talking long. He needs badly to rest. We will be sending him upstairs as soon as a bed comes free.... Unless he has private health care?'

Rick — definitely no longer Erik — lay rigged up to the monitors. I've seen dead dogs look better than he did that night. His face was grey, the veins standing out in relief. His whole body seemed shrunken, diminished after his over-the-top performance. His leg was elevated and looked a better size, but the monitor on his vitals was fluctuating all over the place.

Loki seemed to have become stuck at the door of re-sus, seemingly unable to credit what he saw. 'It's Reykjavik all over again!' he said, in an entrancement of Nordic gloom. '*That* was bloody awful because we had to do it in Icelandic. At least *this time* we can do in English,' he comforted himself ironically, striding forward to stand over Rick, shaking his head furiously, his mouth gurning with suppressed emotion. Mistaking his anger, I thought he was going to hit something; so did the ginger nurse who swarmed forward. But Loki just looked down on the bed with utter contempt, spitting, 'You poor, bloody fool! I told you I wouldn't play this game again!'

In the middle of re-sus, Loki began pulling off the remains of his tattered black top, furiously trying to scratch off the impacted rune-paint, distancing himself from his friend and his antics by the classic gesture of a renunciant. Standing half-naked over the bed, his thin chest quivering, Loki said in a quavery voice, 'I sung my last for you, Erik!' Then, bursting into noisy tears, which started to dislodge the rune-paint properly, 'I'd have sung you back from hell, you know that.... I just... can't go there any more... It's killing me, I tell you!'

Dr. Omowale stood very close to Loki, blocking his view of Rick, 'Sir, you are not helping this patient with all this noise, please wait outside.'

Loki strode off, turned suddenly at the door, saying, 'Patient? He doesn't know the meaning of the bloody word!' With which, he disappeared back into the maelstrom of newsmen. His likeness afterwards appeared in the morning papers like an avenging fury, complete with the headline, 'Im-patient Wrecks the Runes,' and a nasty sidebar about Loki's past exploits.

We remained until we were assured Rick would be staying in for the night. He and Ash had had a brief consultation behind the screens, while I kept the curious at bay on the other side of them. Ash emerged thoughtful and rather subdued.

As we left A & E, we saw a tight group of Heathens, identifiable from the Thor's Hammers and other spiritual insignia round their necks. I recognized some of them from the Round House. They stood aloof from the media circus developing at the door. A quiet woman of about forty-five years approached us. Taking Ash's hand she said, 'We saw what you did! Thank you for looking after him. — How is Erik?' She had a Bradford accent.

'Poorly, but stable,' said Ash. 'He won't be able to see any of you, unless you are family.'

A tall youth with a complex, interwoven tattoo on his neck piped up emphatically, 'We *are* his family.' Ash put a hand on his shoulder and nodded.

The others crowded us with affirmation, 'Yes, he's kindred.'

It was unclear whether they meant they considered Erik as spiritual family, as an inspiration, or whether Erik was indeed a member of their group. They certainly didn't sound like the kind of proprietary fans who would have torn off Erik's shirt for a souvenir. Their genuine concern contrasted favourably with the venal newshounds waiting for the next gobbet of filth to fly in their direction.

Ash assessed the group swiftly, with that characteristic 'looking over their heads' look, then gave the quiet woman his card, 'Then—you might be able to help him when the time comes.'

Many in the group were shocked. One swore, but the woman's level gaze didn't flinch, 'Thanks. —We'd all drop anything to be with him.' She scribbled down her name and phone number on the back of an HIV leaflet filched from the stand. 'We're all he's got, apart from the band. He came to me last time this happened.'

Ash read the backside of the leaflet and gravely shook her hand, 'Thanks, Kirstin. I promise we'll call you.'

As we walked through the rain to the nearest tube back to Harley St, where we'd have to spend the night, I asked, 'Is he really that bad?—The medics sounded hopeful back there.'

'I honestly don't think he's got long. He is being sucked dry.'

'By what?'

'By the power he's inadvertently taken on,' said Ash. 'That was no performance, it was a complete embodiment of Odin! But Rick doesn't have the stamina to maintain that kind of thing. Every time he embodies Odin, his whole vehicle weakens—it should be the other way round when spirits embody... '

'You mean, people do that sort of thing for a living, then?' I was curious, listening closely as we chugged home on the tube.

'There are lots of shamanic traditions where it happens. It's something that occurs when there's a good connection between the shaman and the spirit in question: not an involuntary possession, like most people think, but a consensual manifestation, using the body of the shaman as a vehicle. —The Mongolians call the shaman the 'spirit-horse,' or one who is ridden by the spirit. —Embodying shamans report that when the spirit leaves, it leaves its sparkle behind—so, if things were well between him and the spirit, it really shouldn't drain him like this. Another bout like that and a stroke could take him off.'

At the stop before ours, I noticed that several passengers had leaned closer to listen to our conversation in utter disbelief; they were obviously deeply disappointed when we alighted at Tottenham Court Rd.

§§

After a shower and a good night's sleep at Harley St, we were ready to attend to things. I had offered to go back to the Beacon that morning to take care of things there, but Ash vetoed this, 'No, I'll need your expertise, I think.' So Maggie was relaying Ash's messages relating to our residents' care to Wendy and Gillespie. After breakfast, Ash asked me many questions about Odin and the runes. It felt magnificent to be the one with all the knowledge, for a change. Ash listened closely to all that I said, then asked, 'So what do you think was happening last night?'

'Well, I had the uncanniest feeling last night. When Rick was hanging from the tree, it was as if Christ and Odin fused in my consciousness. I felt... well... brought to my knees by the pity of it, and simultaneously exalted by the sacrifice being made.' I had to swallow hard again, as words summoned up those feelings again. 'It was like... well, Good Friday and Easter all rolled into one, I suppose—only in a pagan way.'

'So, for you it was a true embodiment?'

I nodded, trying to excise the awful remembrance of Rick dangling from the tree.... I opened the book I'd brought from my bedside, the *Havamal*, an Old Norse poem that gives the wisdom of Odin, and showed it to Ash. He scanned it quickly, asking me questions about it. I explained that, while most of it was just good advice for anyone, some portions were about the runes themselves and the power they had to evoke things.

He asked, 'So the inscribing or utterance of the runes can be a form of invocation?'

'Certainly, though they were often used as ordinary identification signs— like the ownership on a comb or a spindle whorl... but most people used them for protection or like a kind of prayer...'

'And if they were used with intention and knowledge...?'

'Then they would bring things about... but it was considered to be a skill that some folks did better than others. One part of the *Havamal* says about the runes:

Know you how to cut them and read them?
Know you how to stain them and try them?
Know you how to invoke them and make sacrifice?
Know you how to send them and to slaughter?
Better it be not to invoke than to sacrifice too much.'

Ash quickly grasped my explanation and ran his eye down the succeeding verses that dealt with the runes, 'And what was the rune Rick had on his cheek again?'

'Othila—the rune of heritage. It stands for your homeland and inheritance, so it's to do with the ancestors and the protection they give you.

He suddenly stabbed his finger at the page, 'Well, I think this was what Rick was doing, whether he intended it or not:

I know a twelfth one if I see,
up in a tree,
a dangling corpse in a noose,
I can so carve and colour the runes,
that the man walks
And talks with me.

I read over the verse. 'Umm! People think that this one is about invoking the dead and bringing them present so that you can talk with them.'

Ash put his head on one side and looked long at me, then with rare irony asked, 'Have I been practising with the help of a necromancer all this time?'

'Not at all—just an Anglican, me, with a few Norse leanings... but what did you mean about his trying to do something by necromancy?'

Ash refreshed the sanctum light on his shrine, 'Well, I know Rick's back history very well. He landed in my class at school because his father lost the family business and the land that went with it. He grew up in a mean, two up-two down with his mother and little sister, down by the seedy side of the canal. His father drank himself to death and left them with nothing.'

I tried putting this together in my head, 'So you think he's been reacting from the trauma by trying to offer himself like Odin and get the power of the runes to restore the family heritage?'

'Or to appease or compensate for his father's shame, perhaps?'

'He's got a weird way of going about it then, is all I can say!'

'If you live by mythology, you can also die by it,' Ash remarked gravely. 'Let's go and see if we're on the right track.'

§§

Back at the hospital, things had both improved and got worse. Rick was properly conscious and raring to be discharged as soon as possible, but most of London's paparazzi had meanwhile taken up residence outside the hospital and it was going to be difficult to get him out.

'I'll come down to the Beacon with you guys, no problem, but getting me out so that they don't follow us is going to take some planning,' Rick grinned and speed-dialed. He spoke one word into the phone, 'Ragnarok!' Putting the

128

phone back into his locker with a secret smile, he said to Ash, 'Rickie, there'll be a flash mob at the front door about 11.15, I'd say.'

It was weird hearing Ash addressed as 'Rickie,' but apparently this is what they'd always called each other — Rick and Rickie. With the help of the ginger nurse, and with screens surrounding the bed, Ash was attired in a set of green scrubs, complete with glasses and surgeon's cap. As soon as the flash mob of heavy metallists hit the front door in a very substantial body, Ash was already wheeling Rick on a trolley to the waste disposal bay where I was hovering with the car. By the time we'd got onto the M25, I was fairly confident that we'd shaken off any possible pursuit. So much for my confidence!

Ash let Rick talk, following our usual procedure, but after a few miles, he grew increasingly quiet and was having some trouble breathing. He lay down in the back of the car with a cylinder of oxygen, with Ash monitoring him. Wendy and Gillespie were ready for us, giving Rick a warm welcome. Away from the perilous world of performance and settled into his room overlooking the dell and the magnificence of Hartsworth Beacon, it would have been hard to connect him with the demented being hanging from a metal tree of a couple of days back.

I'd already established from the drive down that Rick's fabled bad behaviour was in fact largely publicity fabricated by his agent, Andrew Collings, who'd taken over the stage management of the *Rune Wreckers* and their failing career at the turn of the millennium, making them into the attention-grabbing headlines so beloved of the tabloids, as Rick told us in the car: 'Andy'd just arranged to have some big dude come and tackle me after the show, or else get me pretending to be drunk, and stage some fight between us in a public place. Nice lad, that stunt guy — ugly as shit but very nice-natured; keeps ferrets, I gather.'

The next day, in the garden room, Rick lay propped up on the vast settee in the afternoon sunshine, listening to a thrush singing on the cherry tree beyond the French windows. He looked at rest, but his whole body bore that deflated appearance that often signals a poor diagnosis. Without turning his head away from the prospect, he said, 'Well, me old lad, I never thought you'd literally come to the rescue when I wrote you that letter!'

'What made you know you'd need it?' Ash had begun the interview without any formality, I realized.

'When Lindie left me — she told me straight. Either I stopped with the runes and the act on the tree, or she saw me going to hell.'

'It's never easy when someone gets religion,' I agreed.

Rick turned to me, tears brimming in his one good eye, 'Yeah, but the point is, we both got it — that was the trouble! She got Jesus and I got — well, Odin!

—It started as a stunt. Andy said to go over the top a bit, so I just thought of the first thing that would do it without much trouble—well, that's what I thought. Me and the boys had been going more and more Norse over the years: it fired up the fans, right enough. I'd been reading stuff, but it was when the reading turned to doing.... We kind of fell into it... and, you know, Rickie, it was real—*really* real!'

Ash nodded in agreement, 'Oh, yes! Odin is just as real as Jesus. What happened?' It was a good job the Rev. Hallam, our local vicar wasn't in the room!

'We'd sing the songs and do the business, but anytime I got near those runes or the Ash Tree, then I'd kind of blank out and Odin would be there instead. —Are you going to do some kind of exorcism on me, then, old lad?' There was a childlike trustfulness in his eyes as he stretched out his rugged hand. Ash took it between his. He never normally touched clients without good reason and judgement, spurning the 'hands-off' necessity that arose among therapists in the wake of abuse cases. Looking at the bond between them, I felt it was myself who was infringing on intimacy. Their two hands reminded me of the old symbol of friendship and brotherhood, the clasped hands. I tiptoed out, leaving Ash to solace his childhood friend.

No exorcism on Rick was necessary but we did need to do a forced ejection the next day when Andrew Collings, his agent, showed up unannounced. The first we knew of his coming was a screeching of brakes as his car came to the end of our lane rather faster than the bends leading to us allow. There was a beating on the door which Wendy went to answer. Collings stood in the porch, 'I've come to see Erik!' he announced, pushing past her. 'Which room is he in?'

From upstairs, I could hear Wendy's raised voice, 'I'm afraid Mr. Stevenage isn't accepting visitors yet. He's not well enough. Would you please leave? You can make an appointment and we'll let you know when he's fit to see visitors. —No! You cannot go up there!'

I had already reached the top of the stairs as he came barging up, taking the stairs two at a time. Dripping cholericly in a checked Gieves and Hawkes shirt that was a size too small for him, he confronted me, as I barred his progress. Contemptuously, he tried to get past me, 'Get out of my way!' He had that well-tanned superciliousness of someone who knew his own mind to be better and his own needs of a higher priority than anyone else's.

Now one of the reasons I've always been welcome in mental health has been not entirely for my aptitude with the ill, but also for my build, which has been useful for restraining the more unruly cases. Our intruder might have been about my height, but he was clearly not in such good condition. Foolishly, he attempted to push past me with violent hands. By the time Ash came on the scene from the East Wing, I had got Collings in a headlock.

'You can put our guest down now, Jack! At least let him tell us who he is.'

Taking my employer literally, I swung Collings round and deposited him safely on the landing, rather than down the stairs, where I would have preferred to put him. Our intruder's own struggles brought him to rest unceremoniously on the carpet on his backside. Ash proferred a hand and hauled Collings up, 'I am Dr. Richard Ashington, head of the Beacon, and you are?' Ash retained his hand, thus forcing the intruder to look into his steely grey eyes.

'I am Andrew Collings, Erik's agent, and you will let go of my hand immediately!' he retaliated.

'How did you know where to come?' Ash asked the question that had been puzzling me.

'Jobscald told me, of course. The bloody tour's had to be renegotiated, thanks to your interference.'

Ash let go of his hand, 'I won't stop you seeing Rick, as you are his agent, but I must insist on remaining present: he is not well.'

'What's wrong with him? Surely you can give him something and let him get on with it — the fans in Stravanger are going to slaughter the *Rune Wreckers* if they show up without Erik.'

'I can't discuss your client's illness without his permission. Rick needs to be kept very quiet indeed, so I would ask you to keep your voice down, or you will be shown the door.'

With sweat pouring down his bulging cheeks, Collings wrenched open his shirt by another button, revealing a chest that was the same brazen hue as his hands and face. 'I demand to see him!'

Ash asked, 'Jack, can you please go and see if Rick wants to see his agent or not?'

Rick was coming out of a doze, 'I thought I heard Andy's voice. Is he playing up?' He looked sheepish.

'You don't have to see him if you don't want to. Ash and I will keep him away.'

'Nah, don't bother. Tell him, five minutes is all he gets. — And I'm sorry I had to tell the boys how I was, but they have to decide what to do about the tour, so I was kind of expecting him.'

Collings sprang through the door unbidden, with Ash in hot pursuit. The agent began to bully his client with, 'Well, Erik, time for you to stop this malingering and get back to the coal face!'

Rick was immoveable, 'No can do, old mate, sorry and all. Limbs won't obey me like they used to.'

Collings expressed his disbelief and began trying to get Rick to stand up. Rick promptly wavered and fell to the floor like a rubber man. While I got between him and Collings, hauling Rick back into bed, Ash called the police, 'We have a disturbance at the Beacon, Sergeant Hobbs, could you send a couple of your men round please? — Yes, an intruder who is harassing one of our patients!'

As I dragged Collings backwards out of the room, he was yelling, 'You can do the act from a motorized wheelchair, you know…'

'Not this year, Andy, sorry!' Rick grinned as we supplied our own floor show for his amusement.

Gillespie and I manhandled Collings down to the front door where he lashed out, knocking over the copper lustre jug of gladioli that stood in front of Melanie Rydale's photo, and breaking the glass of the frame: He then managed to fall on the broken glass as well so that when Constable Davey and his companion showed up it looked as if we'd been slaughtering sheep in the porch.

Ash gave a terse account of Collings antics while he, refusing any medical treatment at our hands, was conveyed ignominiously by police car to be sewn up at Christminster hospital.

Wendy tutted at the wreck of Melanie's shrine and fetched the dustpan, while Ash shook off the remaining glass from her photo and stolidly reset the shrine to his requirements. Gillespie spat on the drive, 'Good riddance to bad rubbish!' But I feared we had not seen the back of trouble.

§§

The following morning, I came downstairs to find Gillespie poised unmoving, with wary watchfulness, with his rake by the kitchen door, staring at the road. 'That's twice today I thought I spied a body by the gate. But every time I go out, there's nothing.'

The one good thing about the Beacon is that it lies at the bag-end of the lane, and only the occasional walker who'd missed the public path to Hartsworth Beacon comes this way, apart from tradesmen or clients. You can both hear and see anyone coming, as the walls of the property create a kind of sound-trap. I peered through the window, but couldn't see anything either. Not a car nor a push bike in sight.

Ash had applied for an injunction against Collings making a return visit, but I had a very uneasy feeling.

'Someone's watching us, I reckon,' he said. 'If it's one of they daddy-rats (Gillespie's mishearing of 'papa-ratsies,' sic.), I'll skelp the bejaysus out of them with this rake.' Both Gillespie and Wendy were primed for any further intruders, knowing who we had as a guest, so we were being careful about unexpected visitors. 'Keep watchful!' I said, and took a turn about the grounds to satisfy myself that we had no intruder or peeping tom cameraman.

Rick wasn't so good that day. Wendy and Ash took turns to sit with him. The next day, the press arrived in force, proving once and for all that Collings meant us to suffer for his discomforture. Page five of the *Daily Nuisance* (as we usually called it) sported an inset picture of Ash borrowed from some conference, and a larger picture of myself in the garden glaring belligerently right into the camera, taken the previous day. They'd made me look like some Victorian strong-arm warder from the asylum. Not the kind of advert for the Beacon that we wanted, really! Additionally, there was the usual ill-informed paragraph about our work that made out Ash to be some kind of charlatan.

Wendy's comment on surveying my incipient paunch in the paper was, 'More exercise, less beer, my friend!' My own comments cannot be recorded here, but suffice it to say, Gillespie had my full permission to use his rake on any further daddy-rat presenting itself at our door. Needless to say, the next few days we had a party of assorted, bored journalists and camera-folk camped out beyond the flint-faced wall of our perimeter. The police had to be called once more and there was much unpleasantness. But there was also lots of local support to balance it, with Farmer Jelley kindly leaving his tractor partially across the entrance to our lane, thus giving the paparazzi a good long winding walk with heavy equipment to diminish their ardour for gossip. While Janet Bagley's postbag was much heavier than usual, complete with fan-mail for Rick, she manfully equipped herself with a push bike in the back of her van and somehow managed to convey it to us.

Inside our besieged premises, we kept the road-side windows curtained, to avoid any further nuisance, with much cursing. Wendy had to deal with most of it, appointing herself door-warden with, 'Well, they don't know me, I'm no-one, and at least I won't be arrested for assault with a long-range haggis' — this in the face of an irate Gillespie who entertained notions of retaliatory siege-warfare. Since 'a soft answer turneth away wrath,' was her philosophy, she dealt with the motley crew at our gate with equal portions of icy politeness and non-cooperation, with the continual reminder to our unwanted door-steppers that we were a place of sanctuary and recuperation for the sick, and would they please keep the noise down. They continued to litter our walls with fag-ends and telephoto lenses for a few days more.

When Rick was able, we met up in Ash's room at the back of the house, with its stunning view of Hartsworth Beacon, lush and green in late May.

'Let's get to the bottom of it, Rickie! I'm just causing you and your lot grief by staying here,' Rick was impatient to get on off, just like he had been at the hospital. 'So, what do you prescribe?' His breezy manner belied his pallor and weakness.

Ash didn't engage with the banter. 'Where would you go to, Rick? Would Linda have you back?'

In response, Rick chewed his lip, his empty eye socket drooping bitterly. 'I could hole up at Jobscald's brother's place, I suppose, up in Whitby. He's got a caravan on the headland.' It sounded pretty bleak to me, I must say.

Ash just looked at him, 'And when you have trouble breathing will Jobscald's brother come over with oxygen, and sit with you?' We all knew, he wasn't fit to look after himself, and that this wasn't something a course of tablets was going to cure. Rick dropped the act, 'There's one place, if they'd have me back... I went there after the eye and all.'

'Kirsten's, down in Malmesbury?' Ash suggested.

Rick smiled brightly, 'You know her? — She's the Steerswoman of the Hearth of Troth. She and her folk were good to me when I was bad after I lost my eye.'

Ash said, 'I won't throw you out of here, my friend, you know that, but if you would prefer to stay there, I am very happy for you to go — she seems a very good woman. But, you have something more to do yet, I think?'

Rick was puzzled, 'What do you mean?'

Ash quoted,

'Much have I travelled, much have I known,
Much have I tested the gods.
What will Odin have at life's end
When the powers perish?'

I looked about as gobsmacked as Rick, for Ash was quoting the *Lay of Vafthrúdnir*, when Odin goes in disguise to dialogue with the giant. Clearly he had been making free with my Norse library to good effect.

Ash said quietly, 'You've given Odin an offering that was most costly to you, but the return for Odin's loss of an eye was wisdom, and I don't think you've accepted that yet.'

Startled, Rick sat up straighter, looking quizzical, 'What do you, mean, old lad?'

'You have a choice, when the powers perish: you either go with them and end gloriously, or you chose the wiser road. The longer you hold onto Odin's sacrifice, the more you diminish yourself. If you'd had years of training and preparation, it would be different, perhaps, but you've not exactly lived a temperate life. What do you want for yourself now?'

Rick stood up and stumbled to the window where the fringe of trees around Hartsworth Beacon was crowding with richness of new green as the oaks and ash trees caught up with the beeches. After a moment, he turned, holding onto the back of the chair, 'Blimey, Rickie! You *have* come a long way since the old days. You sound like you're offering me a choice between life and death. You become some kind of god yourself, then, me old mate?'

Ash shook his head, 'No, just trying to get you to answer my riddle!' Then he looked at me, 'Jack, what does the giant say to Odin when he asks that question,

"What will Odin have at life's end
When the powers perish?"'

I ferkled about in my memory for the right verse, which spoke of Fenrir the Wolf that devours everything and brings Ragnarok with the end of everything:

'The wolf will devour the Father of Men
Whom Vidar will avenge:
He'll cleave the wolf's cold jaws
In his battle with the beast.'

Ash looked straight at Rick, 'And who is Vidar?'

'Vidar's Odin's son, of course,' he replied looking at me in puzzlement; neither he nor I knew what Ash was getting at, but there was a palpable gathering of power in the room.

'So I ask you another time,' Ash quoted again:

'"Much have I travelled, much have I known,
Much have I tested the gods.
What word did Odin speak into his son's ear
Before he was laid on the pyre?"'

'I don't remember the rest,' Rick said, and appealing to me, 'Do you know,
Jack?'

'As far as I remember, the giant replies,

"No one knows what you said in the days of yore
Into your son's ear.
With a dying mouth, I told my ancient lore,
Speaking of Ragnarok.
To you, the wisest of men,
Have I contended in wisdom."'

Rick threw up his hands, 'This ain't getting us anywhere, mate! What are
you driving at?'

Ash was standing now too, 'My friend, Odin dies and Ragnarok is on its
way, but what does Vidar do?'

Exasperatedly, Rick said, 'He puts either foot in the wolf Fenrir's mouth
and becomes the leader of the world after that. So what?'

'You are facing the perishing of the powers, but you're not on your pyre
yet. Don't you want Vidar to stand by you now?'

'I don't have no bloody Vidar!' Rick shouted back at Ash, and with contempt
spat, 'Honestly, Rickie, you are a piece of work!' I thought Rick would strike
him, but Ash stood his ground, reaching into his pocket and proferring him
a photo, with great gentleness, 'But you *have* got a Vidar, and you will have a
wiser word to share with him yet, if you chose to.'

Rick was transfixed, his dead eye working with emotion, 'How? Where?'

'All the time you were working for your lost hearth and home, for your
kindred, you had a son all along!'

Rick took the photo Ash proffered with trembling hand. Peering over his
shoulder, I recognized it as the tall young man with the tattoo about his neck.
He was, I now realized, the living spit of Rick Stevenage.

Rick held the photo to his heart and in bewilderment asked, 'Why didn't
Kirsten say anything to me? Why did she keep him secret so long? She and I
had a night of it yonks ago.'

Ash didn't spare him, 'Because you had Linda, and Kirsten didn't want to get in the way, or make any claim on you. Because of the life-style you led. She didn't want your boy growing up to ruin his life....'

'.... like I did?' he muttered bitterly, then realization struck again, 'Bloody Hell! I'm a dad!' He embraced Ash fulsomely but, sensing some reserve, drew back. 'What? ...There's something else! ... Tell me!'

Ash laid down the rules, 'Kirsten will have you in her home for keeps, she says, but not if you continue to tour and carry on as you've done before. — And as your friend and medical adviser, I have to tell you that your life will not be a long one, but that it will be considerably shortened if you persist. —She won't tolerate drugs or violence, and she expects you to be a proper father to Carl.'

Rick promptly sat down, properly gobsmacked, 'Can I speak to her?'

Ash smiled, 'She's been waiting for that call,' and handed him the phone.

Down in the kitchen, over a much-needed cuppa, I asked him, 'How did you know about Carl?'

'Didn't you see the likeness?'

I shook my head.

'The minute I clapped eyes on that young man, I knew instantly — he looked just like Rick when he was young with me. No mystery, really. I just needed a way to broach it, and you gave me the way with *The Elder Edda* you lent me.'

'Do you think he will make a go of it? —I mean, it's a lot to give up.'

'It's not going to be plain sailing, perhaps, but love and stability will give him more years than he perhaps either deserves or expects. Kirsten is right named a steerswoman — and I expect she will find him a handful, but she loves him as badly now as she did when she was just a big fan of his.'

'But will Odin let him alone?' I wondered aloud.

'I think his tree-mounting days are over, let's say.'

§§

The press release was given outside our front door, a week later, that Rick Stevenage was leaving the *Rune Wreckers* for the sake of his health, but that the band would continue. This statement made a nine days wonder in the world of Viking Metal and beyond, but life at the Beacon was able to go back to normal again. Gillespie swept away the fag-ends and other detritus from our front premises with a savagery that bespoke a Herculean cleaning of the Augean Stables, at the very least. Wendy made a big batch of cheese scones and a huge Pavlova for tea, while I shelved my copy of the *Elder Edda* with a sigh. We had endured the coming the *Rune Wreckers* to the Beacon, with Jobscald and Grinder having a harder job of it than Loki, who had already got the lie of the land. They would go on, in the hope of an unfading and disreputable career.

We had tolerated the descent of Andrew Collings who, furious at the loss of his prime asset, threatened us with an investigation into the work of the Beacon and the life of Ash in particular, quite apart from setting the press upon us. Finally, we had welcomed a small delegation of the Hearth of Troth who came with their own ambulance driver to bear Rick away to reunion with Kirsten and Carl. The paparazzi had done their best, but a number of them strangely never made it to Malmesbury due to an overwhelming bout of diarrhoea caused—though it has never been conclusively proved—by a couple of bottles of whiskey that seem to have been doctored by a strong laxative by a certain member of our household who had left the bottles in open camera bags.

The press still turn up in Malmesbury, from time to time, to find a recuperating Rick who is now so ordinary in the service of Odin that the newspapers have finally given up trying to work out an interesting angle. As for the Beacon—it has been just too remote and uncooperative for further assaults on our premises, so the Daily Nuisance merely resorts to what it does so well already—just making stuff up about us.

Case 6: EXCHANGE AND MART

Frisdon on Sea offers the kind of sleazy feel-goodness that derives from the proximity of others enjoying themselves. It certainly can't be based on the sharp pebble beaches down which holiday-makers gingerly teeter with bare toes, nor upon the paucity of parking places near the sea-front which have to be aggressively fought over or else the whole family has to walk miles from the multi-story. There is, it has to be said, a certain masochistic British amusement to be had in sheltering in one of the many roofed benches, being battered to pieces by a bracing wind, while regarding the grey and unrelenting English Channel over one's greasy chips. Personally, I've never been able to understand the attraction.

Even lower on my list of sea-side requirements is the amusement arcade and the fun fair, which is neither fun nor fair in my opinion. Call me snobbish if you will, but I've never enjoyed the pullulating company of the weekend masses who could easily be categorized as a special suit in Happy Families. The pack would have to include Mr. Severely Put-Upon, the Provider, with his shirt unbuttoned and his crack-revealing trousers, wearing a kiss-me-kwik bowler hat. He is paired by Mrs. Bleached-Ends, the Check Out Cashier, with her skimpy top and D cup bra showing. They are accompanied by Miss Scowl, the Rebellious Teenager, loitering in her parents' wake with a pierced navel and a roving eye for the boys, and by Master Howl, the Fractitious Toddler, hoisted upon his father's shoulders with a dripping ice-cream in his fist.

So when Ash told me we were going to the sea-side, you can imagine my joyful anticipation.

'Cheer up, Jack. It can't be as bad as all that!'

'Oh yes it can,' I sulked. 'I was brought up in Dorlingmouth, arm-pit of the universe. Did you know it had one of the highest suicide rates in the country? And I know why.'

Ash merely smiled at this revelation of my unreconstructed psyche. 'Very well then, so we won't go on the Waltzer!'

I ground my teeth.

But even Ash was forced to admit that Frisdon's amenities were less than adequate when we finally gave in and parked on the top floor in the multi-story car-park. 'Nice view!' he remarked irrepressibly as we headed for our destination.

We were following up a request for help from Myrtle, our cleaning lady, whose cousin, Karen Shillington, had recently been taken in for observation at the local hospital. 'I been to see her, Dr. Ash, but honestly, it's no use. She just lies there. She used to be so lively. Now she's like — an empty house. You know, no one at home. Can't you go and see her, Doctor?' she appealed to Ash. 'Hospital can't do much for her, my aunt says. She's back home now.'

The tower block we needed was facing the down-at-heel pier. It was redolent with the saturations of cheap cooking fat, mingled with cigarettes and candy-floss, emanating from the fun-fair below. There had been talk of up-grading the sea-front by repossessing such high-rise monstrosities and turning them into bijou apartments for the jet-set, but I somehow doubt it. For one thing, there is no form of double-glazing made to keep out the rancorous shouts of inebriated excitement rising from youths on the Waltzer or being hurled about on the Higgledy-Pig which oscillates you in three directions at once — allowing for a speedy evacuation of their riders' stomach contents, I should imagine! The continual whine of the electronic motors and the multi-flashing lights at night would be bearable only from afar.

Our client was marooned up on the thirteenth floor since the lifts weren't working. The over-weight mother let us into a room so pink that it hurt the eyes. It had clearly been decorated when the teenage girl lying propped in front of day-time television had been much younger, for the running frieze around the walls had Barbie posed in various unlikely attitudes — playing tennis, camping, marrying Ken, posing on the cat-walk and out riding. There was something rather reminiscent of a Miss Havisham time-warp in the room. Looking at the mother, Rosalie Shillington, I realized that the room's taste reflected what would have been desirable in her own, rather than her daughter's youth. There was a pride and sorrow in her face now as she tidied the bed around her daughter whose eyes were dead to the flickering images on the screen.

Karen was slim, with golden brown hair, some of which was arranged in pink and purple wraps. She was sixteen, but a young sixteen I'd have guessed. Her vacant gaze was a stark contrast to the photo on the wall, taken quite recently, where a mischievous Karen peered out from behind a garden fence. As Myrtle said, an empty house. Her thin limbs lay idly, in a travesty of teenage indolence. In contrast to her daughter, Rosalie Shillington had the same pretty eyes and delicate wrists, but these features were sunk in rolls of fat. The mother couldn't be much more than a child herself.

With Mrs. Shillington's permission, Ash gave Karen a cursory examination, shining a light into her eyes, testing her pulse.

We withdrew from the bedroom and sat in the lounge over a pot of Typhoo tea on the three-piece suite with its garish throw of the Last Supper, while Ash asked a few questions of the mother. Just under a month ago, her daughter had been quite normal. The next morning, on 26th March, she had lapsed into her present vacant condition. The hospital had ruled out drugs or any known medical condition. They had sent Karen home and put her on the waiting list for further tests. 'But I don't want them to give her electric shocks — they do that, don't they?' She appealed to us as to sources of higher authority. 'I asked Myrtle and she said you'd come. I'm ever so grateful, doctor!' Mrs. Shillington was effusively eager to assist us. She pushed a plate piled high with assorted biscuits and sugary foil-wrapped chocolate snacks towards us, absently thrusting two bourbon creams one after the other into her own mouth.

'Tell me, did Karen go out that night on the 25th March? Or have anyone over?' Ash asked.

'No. She said she had homework and went to her room. I didn't see her again that night — only looked in to kiss her goodnight, but she'd already dropped off to sleep. When I went to wake her, I could see she wasn't right. It was like she'd got lost in the night and couldn't find her way home.' She began to sniff.

'Can she do anything for herself?'

'She'll eat and drink if I hold it to her mouth, she'll come to the loo alright, if I lead her, but I have to wash her myself. The hospital said she wasn't ill enough to take up a bed.' She sounded bewildered at being so abandoned.

'That must be a lot of work for you?' I said.

'Well, fortunately I got a big family to support me,' she said, smilingly bravely. 'They come round between my shifts at the Co-op.'

The Armitage clan were obviously determined to do the daily maintenance and one of them came round most evenings to give her a break. On the mantelpiece there was a large photo of them all, grouped around a priest at some church function. In it, you could see what a pretty and lively girl Karen had once been.

Ash indicated the photo of a ruddy, ebullient man with bright blue eyes in naval uniform, 'Is her father away at the moment?'

Distantly, the empty-headed happy tune of the Wurlitzer swelled up to fill the silence. Rosalie's lower lip began to tremble, 'Ran off, Ron did, with some piece of skirt. But the navy got the maintenance people onto him, I'll say that for them.' Despite her bitterness, she clearly couldn't bear to put the photo of Ron Shillington away or believe that she was totally abandoned. It can't have been much of a life before, stuck in this concrete monstrosity. Now, it must be purgatory.

'What do *you* think brought this about?' Ash asked her.

Rosalie Shillington pursed her lips, 'Dabbling in the occult. That's what I reckon, doctor.'

Ash enquired for evidence of this assertion. Rosalie went into the bedroom, hunkered down with difficulty on her knees and drew out a shoe-box from under Karen's bed. In it was a book entitled, *How To Be the Best Teenage Witch Ever* which seemed to consist largely of love-charms; in addition there was a Fairy tarot pack with images of air-brushed Californian-looking pixies, and a series of supposedly semi-precious bead bracelets, most of which were made of mass-produced plastic. There seemed little here to tell of any potent occult force that could have caused such an effect upon the catatonic girl on the bed.

'Is there anything else of hers that might be relevant? Something that could help us?'

Reluctantly, she drew open Karen's bedside drawer, 'Well....'

Ash asked, 'May I?' She nodded. Inside was a locked five-year diary with no key and a box of some cheap jewellery.

'Have you looked?' he asked.

Rosalie shook her head, 'I don't like to.'

Ash laid the diary back in the drawer. 'Would it be possible for you to draw up a list of Karen's best friends, please? I'd like to ask them a few questions.'

Rosalie backed out, leaving us in the bedroom.

'What do you make of her?' I asked him.

Ash turned up *Ready, Steady, Cook* which was just starting on the television. 'I'll tell you later. Tell me, what do you notice about this room? What's uncharacteristic?'

I looked again, taking in the row of Beanie Babies arranged around the dressing table and the juxtaposition of pop-idols and Buffy the Vampire Slayer postcards over the mirror. It looked like a typical teenager's room. A pink radio and pink portable CD player completed the colour coding of the room.

'No religious artifacts,' I said, for the lounge had its Catholic emblems and icons on every wall.

Ash raised his eyebrows in exasperation, 'She *was* aiming to be the best teenage witch ever! Try again!' He was skimming through her wardrobe, finding nothing of significance.

Then my eye fell upon the pile of teenage magazines on the floor. Stacked between the glossy pile was some dull newsprint that I immediately recognized as the advertising weekly, *Exchange and Mart*. This was the weekly journal where, long before the advent of EBay and the internet, people advertised their items for sale.

'What about this?' I asked, pulling it out. 'What's a girl this age doing with a magazine like this?'

Ash's eyes gleamed, 'Well done, Jack! But what if she used it to sell off some childhood toys—a full set of My Little Pony perhaps or fully-posable Barbies?'

I shuddered. Under cover of the inane cooks battling it out on the screen, I asked him, 'How could a few tarot cards bring this on?'

'I don't think it did, but...' he pressed one finger to his mouth and looked significantly at the door.

Flipping through *Exchange and Mart*, I came across one page where an advert was ringed with a pink magic marker, 'Ash! Look!'

He read aloud under his breath, 'Beautiful crystal, genuine smoky quartz for health, love and happiness. Limited offer to the right witch. £20 including p. & p. Box 943.'

'That's pretty steep for a crystal!'

'The question is where is it? asked Ash.

'Maybe, she didn't send for it,' I suggested.

'Look at the date of the magazine, Jack—a fortnight before this happened.' He went through to the lounge, 'Mrs. Shillington, did Karen receive any packages over the last month?'

'Nothing, only the free Olympic Beanie Baby—she'd been saving up the twelve tokens for it and I gave her the money for postage.'

'Did she have any money or savings from a job?'

'Well, she did have a paper round, but she spent most of that on little things—you know, cosmetics and hair things. There's only the £25 her gran sent towards her holiday and we put that in her bank book.'

'Is it still there?' Ash asked.

Rosalie searched the bureau, opening the pass-book with dismay, 'Oh my Lord! She drew £20 out on the 11th.' She sat down suddenly in the chair, 'What does it mean, doctor?'

'Do you have that list of friends for me, Mrs. Shillington?'

'You think Karen bought the crystal?' I asked him, as we pounded down thirteen flights.

'She certainly withdrew the money. Possibly she arranged for it to be sent to a friend's house. We need to speak to her friends.'

'What's all this teenage witch nonsense?' I demanded.

'Young women fighting off malign powers and casting spells that really work appear on television every night, Jack.' God knows how he knew so much about the media with no TV in the house! 'It's glamorous and entrancing. Absolutely nothing to do with the modern Wiccan religion, and as far removed from malign witchcraft as you can imagine.'

'What about the diary? That might give us some clue as to the state of her mind before this happened. What do you think it is?'

'That girl is in a state of trance. Whatever induced it is still exerting its influence.'

I asked, dubiously, 'You really think it's the crystal that's caused this?'

'Precisely! We will look at the diary as our last resort, after all, teenagers don't have much privacy. If she thinks her mother sneaked a look at her diary, she'll not trust her again. For all her faults, Rosalie Shillington is a good mother.'

'I agree with you. But, if it's the crystal that caused this, who would send such a thing through the post to a teenage girl? And why advertise it? What could anyone possibly gain from such a thing? It doesn't make sense!'

'That's what I mean to find out,' said Ash grimly.

§§

We called first on her best friend, Midge, introducing ourselves as friends of the family who were trying to piece together the mystery. The contrast between the cleanliness of the Shillington's flat and this place couldn't have been greater. A general air of neglected housework and stale cigarettes permeated every corner of this squalid flat. In the middle of the pokey room was a disproportionately large new wide-screen TV, now showing a quiz show. As a concession to our arrival, the volume was pitched down to an irritating buzz. Midge's mother, a thin hard-faced woman, sat suspiciously on the arm of the settee with her legs tightly crossed while we asked her grubby daughter questions. I think it was only the fact that we were doctors that we were let in at all. The room was stiff with the mother's disapproval and the girl's repressed emotion. Midge maintained her spiky evasion, answering all questions with 'yep' or 'nope,' when she wasn't mutinously silent. Ash perceived the problem and asked Midge's mother for some tea. While she reluctantly prepared it, he asked the girl, 'Is there something you want to ask me?'

Midge flicked a look at the kitchen door, asking in cool, unconcerned tones, 'Will Karen die?'

Ash looked through and into her, in that way of his, 'We all will eventually. But no, I don't think her *life's* in danger. However, would *you* like to live like that for another sixty or seventy years?'

Midge thrust out, then sucked her lip, 'Orright. I'll tell you, though I was sworn to cross my heart and die. But not here, orright?' she flicked a look to the kitchen and leant forward, whispering hoarsely, 'Outside the arcade. Alf an hour.'

Ash nodded. We consumed our tea in record time and left to make our assignation. On the way I begged him to think of our professional reputations, 'I mean, we can't go off and meet with a teenager outside some arcade — we'll be picked up as drug-peddlers or something!'

'It's either that, or Karen stays as she is. Midge knows something vital, I'll be bound.'

We looked very conspicuous outside the arcade, being neither old enough to be coach-bound pensioners or young enough to be the kind of youths loitering around there. In such a context, Ash looked exactly like some high-class dealer in his cashmere sweater and leather jacket, while I looked even worse. One glance at my dishevelled reflection in the arcade window suggested a lorry driver looking for a quick pick-up.

'Buy some cigarettes,' Ash suggested.

'But I don't.... oh, ok!' I bought some Marlborough Lights and box of matches. Ash took one and pushed the box back to me, 'It's alright, you don't have to inhale!'

Ash exhaled twin streams of smoke from his thin nostrils, though I would have sworn he was a life-long non-smoker.

Midge approached, ignored us dramatically, then walked past us looking over her shoulder in a vampish way that made me feel no better. 'Follow her,' Ash breathed. We began strolling up the sea-front in what felt to be a foolhardy enterprise. She stopped in the lee of the war memorial, waiting for us to catch up.

To my surprise, Ash offered her a cigarette which she coolly accepted. He got straight to the point, 'Tell me about the crystal?'

Midge looked relieved, 'She was desperate for a smoky quartz crystal. It said in her book that you could only get to be a genuine witch if you had one. She bought one off a stall in the market, but it wasn't a real one. They'd injected ink into it, you could tell when you held it to the light. It was no good 'cause you couldn't see through it. Then I saw one in my dad's *Exchange and Mart* and showed her. She gave me the postal order and I sent for it — her mum would've given her stick for spending her holiday money on stuff like that. Dead religious, her mum.'

'What happened when it arrived?'

Midge grew evasive again. 'We — she did a ritual — just like on *Buffy*. It even thundered during it — it was scary. She had powers.... The ritual really worked. She said I could wish for stuff.'

'Did you get what you wished for?' Ash enquired.

'Yeah! This boy I liked asked me out. Brilliant!' But if it was really that good, then why did she look so guiltily miserable?

'Then what happened?' Ash continued.

Midge thrust both hands into the pockets of her dirty fleece jacket, 'She started to go strange — didn't want to come out. I went round and said, "Let's use the crystal," but she went funny. She just wanted to get rid of it. She kept it in a red box.... I think she buried it.'

'Where?' he asked, but from Midge's expression and continued silence Ash discerned the truth, 'When did you dig it up, Midge?'

'I never!....' then she turned towards the sea, saying sheepishly, 'Well, it's gone now...'

Ash followed her gaze, 'Is it truly gone, Midge?'

She turned on him, 'What's it to you? What're you bothering with it for?'

He kept his voice level and undramatic, 'Because I'm concerned that no-one else should end up like Karen. If it did that to her, then it's capable of doing the same to anyone else who uses it.....' Leaving this thought hanging in the air, he briskly consulted his watch, saying, 'Jack, we mustn't waste any more time here. Let's get back.'

Midge's expression was a mixture of fearful self-concern and teenage cool. But as Ash pulled his jacket tighter against the wind, the teenage cool won. He pulled a card from his pocket and gave it to her, 'This has my mobile number if you need to speak to anyone about this, and an address if you need to get rid of anything — troublesome. It can always be sent on to me and I will see it safely disposed of. Thanks for being so helpful.'

We walked back up the promenade, leaving Midge staring out to sea, bristling with insecurity. I asked him, 'Where would a girl in a high-rise block of flats possibly go to bury a crystal? They don't even have a window box up there! I've never heard such a farrago of nonsense!'

Ash grinned his Cheshire Cat smile, his features broadening with glee, 'Oh, Jack! What would I do without you? Practical to the last detail. Yes, where indeed?'

'You think Midge's still got it, then?'

'Quite possibly. Her side of the story sounded like a massive piece of self-justification. I think she was trying hard to let herself off the hook.'

'God preserve us from teenage witches!' I breathed.

'Amen!' he responded.

On the way back to the car, Ash suddenly clutched my arm, 'Jack! We need this week's *Exchange and Mart*.'

We turned into the corner newsagents, pushing through display racks of plastic flip-flops, beach-balls, buckets and spades to find any newsprint. Ash started scanning the latest issue of the magazine then and there, only to be rebuked by the sharp-tongued owner, 'This ain't a library, you know! Sixty pence, if you please!'

While I handed over the money with as good a grace as I could muster, Ash was fizzing, 'Look! It's in again!'

Sure enough the same identical advert had been placed under 'Collectors' in the Home and Leisure section. I was puzzled, 'But why is it in again? Oh, I know, the advertiser probably paid for a month rather than by the week. —They'll be a few more teenage witches this week, then!' I quipped.

But Ash wasn't smiling. He looked grim as he thrust the key into the door of the car, 'But what if the advertiser has more of these crystals? Jack, I think that we're up against something very dark indeed. Who would want to ensnare the souls of young women by such a dirty enterprise?' He shook his head, as if to shake the newly-formed thought from his mind, 'No, Jack. I think we are dealing with a soul-thief.'

I stopped walking, 'Hang on! I've gone along with a lot of your weird ideas, but this takes the biscuit. We aren't living in some voodoo compound but on the South Coast of England, for God's sake!'

Seriously he said, 'When it comes to evil intentions, no place on earth has a monopoly on malignity! Soul-stealing is an ancient art, enhancing the prestige and power of the petty-minded, making them feel big. Usually the soul-stealer is someone who's been abused or diminished himself. It's a form of vampirism that's all too common, when the weak come under the aegis of the strong. The employer who holds his employees in fear, the lover who makes a slave of the beloved, that's the stuff of everyday life… But this is far more serious. There's a method and a foul intention behind this advert. God knows how many young girls have answered it.'

§§

Back at the Beacon, Ash asked Myrtle, 'Your cousin is going to need your help. Are you willing to write a letter?'

Myrtle threw down the duster, stripped off her rubber gloves, declaring, 'Anything, Dr. Ash! What do I write?'

We concocted a letter between us.

Dear Box 943,

I am a teenage witch who lives to do spells. Please send me the smoky quartz crystal you advertised as quickly as possible. I want to cast a spell under the next full moon.

Here's a postal order for £20. Please send the crystal to Deborah Davidson, 6 The Port Holes, Asterton Rd, Frisden FR2 5TY.

Myrtle had wanted to write her own name, but Ash was adamantly opposed. Written on a cut-down block of scrap paper with a mis-matched blue envelope and first class stamp, with Myrtle's laboured scrawl, it could indeed pass for the letter of a teenage girl. Ash provided the postal-order with a stern warning, 'Now Myrtle, warn everyone at home, not to open any parcel whose origins you're not sure of, alright? And don't let anyone in your family send back a parcel for Deborah Davidson. Just bring it here. It's essential that it's unopened, is that clear?'

Myrtle nodded her curly head vigorously. 'You're going to try and catch the person that did this to her, aren't you?'

'I am indeed!'

Over the next week, Ash grew notably more tense. He attended his London practice on only one day, having got Maggie to move all his appointments over, and motored back the same night, impatient to see what telephone messages or post had come. In my ignorance, I attached much less importance to this case than he did and was inclined to be sharp with him, I'm ashamed to say. 'If it goes on at this rate, I shall end up treating you for depression,' I remarked, taking one look at his long face.

But his level grey eyes didn't lighten with a smile. In a voice like stone, he said, 'I got Maggie to fax a few hospitals around the country to ask if they'd seen any cases like Karen's.'

I threw down my newspaper, 'And......?'

'I've had six replies — one from Durham, two from South Wales, three from London and one from Dorset. They each report a young woman in the same condition. And I only contacted hospitals where I had some colleagues. Think of how many other girls may have answered that advert.'

This seemed to me to be a great step forward, 'So now it can become a police matter then, as soon as they investigate the advertiser.'

Ash threw back his head in exasperation. 'Don't you see, Jack, that as soon as the police become involved, we lose all chance we have to put an end to this.

If they make an arrest, what charge are they going to bring? There's no law against selling harmless goods through a reputable trade journal. What jury's going to convict a man for sending crystals to young girls? Who will be able to prove that the crystals have been charged to create this result? Any lawyer would make hay with that argument in a few minutes and the case would be thrown out of court!'

'Alright, alright! I take your point, but what good can we do now? You said to Myrtle that you would catch the perpetrator, but how?'

'I'm powerless to act until I get one of the crystals he's been sending out.'

'*He*? How do you know it isn't a woman?'

'Oh, this is a man, I'm sure... it has the right pathology, don't you agree? I mean, teenage girls......?'

'Look, Ash, I know I'm pretty dense about all this, but, well, I mean, it's not as though he has their bodies, is it? What possible pleasure could a paedophiliac occultist take with their souls? Isn't this just some New Age crystal freak?'

With infinite patience, Ash asked, 'What powers your watch?'

'It's got a quartz mechanism, I think.... oh, I see, crystal!'

'Precisely! Crystal is also used in radio transmitters and receivers. When crystal is shaped in certain ways, as in your watch, it generates a charge or voltage on its surface. In your watch, it's shaped like a tuning fork, chemically etched to enable continual oscillation around its axis — that's what keeps time. In a radio transmitter, the same principles apply. I believe that these crystals — and we know that many have been sent out — have been charged with certain instructions. These instructions are probably dormant until someone activates them — probably by some ritual action. Whoever is doing this, has created perfect soul-traps. Once the crystal has received, it transmits back to the sender.'

'So he's collecting souls and posting them home by means of a crystal?' It sounded the most preposterous thing I'd ever heard. 'Why?'

'Jack, I've been trying not to consider that. We're not dealing with anything as straightforward as a paedophile. Whoever has set up this elaborate scheme is someone who knows what he's doing, someone with magical knowledge. My guess is that there's a master crystal that these other crystals have all been tuned to in some way. With the energy of those young souls trapped in it, the sender could enhance any intention man can envisage in his most depraved dreams. Whatever his true purpose, he has effectively created a power-base of souls: power that he can use for who knows what end. And he has all their addresses.....'

I began to see why he was so worried. 'But, he has Myrtle's address!'

'Yes, but not her name. And he's not going to have her soul!'

'But shouldn't a watch be kept on all these young women?'

'If they are in the same state as Karen, I expect they are under family protection or hospital care. But we don't know how long that advertizement's been carried in *Exchange and Mart*. It would very much depend on whether the crystals were still in or around each of the teenagers affected. It's possible some were never activated, due to boredom or fear. I wish to God I could get my hands on the one Karen had, but I imagine that Midge isn't going to oblige us by producing it!'

I privately thought that Midge was greedy enough to dig it out again from wherever she had hidden it and work some new life-enhancing spell, but perhaps fear had won out. Part of me was reeling at the thought of teenage girls whose soul-parts were in thrall to some predatory magician. Having seen Karen, I could see how the legend concerning zombies might have first come about. 'I was thinking, aren't zombies the un-dead? I mean, Karen and the others are still alive.'

'If that's what you call living! No, not always. Some zombies are people whose souls have been stolen, leaving their bodies free to undertake certain tasks.'

'But these girls are just lying there. Who would want to do such a thing?' My brain just wouldn't accept something so outrageously preposterous and yet so palpably real.

'Someone who loves power more than his own moral health,' Ash answered me. 'The advertiser could well be planning a part two to this, posing as a healer to help what must be dozens of anxious families who, like Mrs. Shillington, have had little help from the hospitals. — No, this desire to be a teenage witch is what's fuelled it, I'll be bound. We must pick up that book that Karen had. I want to understand the mindset of such an irresponsible person who would write such a book. Then maybe we'll see what triggers young girls to behave so recklessly.'

Two days later, Myrtle came in, triumphantly bearing a brown-paper wrapped parcel, 'It's come!'

Ash carried it carefully to the light, examining the wrapping and the post-mark, 'It's got an SW10 postmark.'

'Fulham then?'

'Well, it was posted there,' he said, putting the box under one arm.

'Aren't you going to open it then?' Myrtle was disappointed.

'Yes, but not while you're in the room, Myrtle. This is a very dangerous item — think of it as a kind of contagious virus. Much better opened in clinical conditions.'

As we went upstairs to his study, he asked me to draw the curtains and put into my hands a Byzantine convex mirror that I'd always admired from the wall. Childishly, it gave me a warm, safe feeling, reminding me of the mirror in the medieval Flemish portrait of the Arnolfini Marriage, where a convex mirror captures the whole room in one splendid optical illusion. Ash's study was full of small marvels of this kind and this mirror captured them all in its compass. 'What's this for?'

'Rear-view mirror!' Ash said cryptically. 'Hold it outwards, like this and keep quiet.' He rearranged it so that I held it pressed to my solar plexus, facing out towards the parcel. It felt like having a plate of armour defending me against the offending package.

Having thus positioned me, Ash then circled the room, turning to each direction in turn, uttering a series of high-pitched tones that seemed to emanate from the top of his head. Under each of the tones was a simultaneous deep, powerful note that sounded as if it came from beneath the earth. It made my hair stand up on end to hear it, for I had no idea my employer was capable of producing such unearthly sounds. As he turned to each direction, he made a series of decisive gestures in the air before him. In the darkened room, it seemed to me that these hand-movements left a faint but unmistakable trail in the air. I realized that these ritual gestures and the extraordinary double-noted tones had created a kind of bell-jar in the room, for the sounds outside in the grounds and from downstairs seemed to become hollow and far away.

He undid the parcel carefully, laying aside the paper. Inside was a box. With cautious fingers, he opened it, disgorging a swathe of bubble-wrap in which the crystal was encased. Between one sheet of bubble-wrap and the next was a folded sheet of paper. He swiftly read it, pulling back the corners of his mouth with grim disapproval.

He removed the last covering sheet from the crystal and tipped it in a bowl of salt that stood waiting to receive it. It looked like nothing special to me. The kind of thing you'd see on a New Age stall in the market any day of the week. It was a pale flint-like colour. From its base, two crystalline arms thrust in either direction. It looked utterly harmless.

I opened my mouth to speak, but he put up a warning hand. Turning the salt bowl, he examined the quartz from every direction. He placed his hand over each of the crystalline arms in turn, as if feeling for life-signs, then nodded, satisfied. Reaching under the desk, he brought up a metal bowl and inverted it over the quartz in its salt dish.

In a whisper, he said, 'We can talk now. I didn't want to disturb the vibration. Look!' He thrust the folded note at me. It read,

Dear Teenage Witch,

Congratulations on receiving one of the most powerful crystals in creation! It will grant you three wishes, but choose carefully before you make your spell!! The full moon is the best time to call upon your good fortune, so when you're ready to ritual, just chant this word three times and your wish will be granted.

ZEDELIAC.

I gave a low whistle. There was no other information, address, phone number or email. 'He's seems to have covered his back pretty well,' I observed, flatly. 'We'll never get at him through this.'

'On the contrary, Jack. He's given us his call-sign. It's like the key-word to his code, if you will. As long as we don't use the word, we're alright. With it, I'll be able to track the vibration of the crystal back. He's given us a back-door, the dangerous fool!' For the first time in days, Ash looked jubilant.

I read the note again, 'This is a very nasty trick. Think of some naïve teenager reading this! It's a psychological mine-field of auto-suggestion. You open the box and you're inside a fairy tale with his three wishes. As for that word, your tongue just longs to say it, doesn't it? What does it mean?'

'It may be one of the barbarous names of demons used by medieval magicians. They're two a penny in any grimoire. It may mean nothing at all, of course. It's the intention that's behind it that's important. You could chant "Marmite" or "Creosote" to precisely the same effect as this. Tell me, as a matter of interest, what does it do for you?'

I framed my mouth to say the name, then snapped it shut, 'Ash, are you trying to make me the slave of the crystal or something?' He grinned. I closed my eyes and tried to say the word mentally without making a sound. As the images and feelings rose I said, 'I feel confident, even powerful. I get a smell of roots dug up out of the earth, some prickly plant like a thistle. The thistle flower turns and gets bigger, its seed-head grows, it blocks out the sun. I feel tired and sleepy...'

'Stop!' Ash commanded. 'You are too psychically sensitive to go down that route, but I'm not sorry I asked.' He appraised me with one his deep looks, 'You are proving to be an invaluable colleague, Jack.'

'Is that why you chose me to work here? For my truffle-hunting nose, enhanced instincts, and my tendency to lapse into trance at your suggestion?' I had rather wondered about this, the longer we worked together.

But my supreme irony was rather spoiled by his answer, 'Partially! As well as for your professional skills and personal qualities,' he assured me, seeing my dubious expression. He went about the room anticlockwise making another set of decisive hand gestures which seemed to unlock the bell-jar atmosphere that had come over the room. He threw back the curtains. I was once more aware of Wendy in the garden talking to one of our guests and the sound of Gillespie raking the gravel in the drive.

Turning my mind back to the problem in hand, I asked, 'I understand the crystal, I think, but how is the sender making wishes come true? Is there any real power in it?'

'As you said, Jack, it's a two-way psychological trap. What do most teenagers want, in your experience?'

I ticked them off on my fingers, 'Boys, an unlimited clothing allowance, to be thin and beautiful like a model, to be on Top of the Pops—I don't know.'

'Quite! You've already said how the word, combined with the promise of three granted wishes, gives you a false sense of confidence and power. Just think of that boosted by teenage enthusiasm and inadequacy!'

'So what now?'

'Well, we now know when he wants us to pronounce the barbarous name—on the full moon. It was a full moon on 24th March, the day before Karen probably worked her ritual. Let's not disappoint him, shall we?'

§§

It was a full moon in three days' time. We returned to visit Karen and picked up *How To Be the Best Teenage Witch Ever* from under her bed. This time, Ash made a thorough search of the room with Mrs. Shillington's permission. Karen still lay on the bed, her vacant eyes staring into the middle distance. Ash called her by name, but there was no response behind the eyes.

'Has she stirred or attempted to leave the flat at all?' Ash enquired.

'Well, she got restless during that storm we had last week. But no, doctor. She just lies there... It's doing me in, seeing her like this.' I felt the greatest sympathy with Mrs. Shillington.

Ash took her hands in his. I noticed that he rarely touched a patient, but that when he did, they calmed down immediately. It worked now. He asked her, 'Will you do something for Karen? I believe that there will be an improvement in the next few days, but we need some extra help. Do all your family go to church?'

Rosalie Shillington nodded vigorously, 'All of us go to St. Aloysius in Danby St.'

'Can you organize a prayer circle for Karen? Something like a novena to the Virgin... a kind of.... chain of prayer. Dr. Rivers and I are... near to the source of this problem, so the prayers of yourself and your family would be very useful right now.'

'Everyone's praying for her at church already. Karen's been in the bidding prayers every week since it happened.' Rosalie sounded pathetically proud of this sad distinction. 'Father Phillip said he'd asked the nuns at the Marist Convent to pray for her too.' Then she caught sight of her daughter's book in his pocket, 'Is it witchcraft that did it, doctor?'

To my amazement, he responded seriously, 'I believe that it is. But it was not caused by anything that your daughter did. We are fighting "against principalities and powers" and any reinforcements on our side are very important now.'

'Then I'll pray till I'm blue!' she said resolutely, squeezing his hands.

On the stairs, I asked him, 'All this prayer... is it doing any good?'

'Oh, great unbeliever! Of course it is! Karen is luckier than poor Midge. At least Karen's family care enough about her to pray for her. I don't think Midge's mother would automatically turn to prayer if anything befell her daughter. No, I asked Rosalie Shillington to pray because she needs to know that she is doing something positive. Her prayers help keep open a loving pathway that opens the channels to support for Karen and they are certainly needed by us, if we are to help her. The prayer circle will be our safety net.'

'So are we in danger then?' I asked in some consternation.

'Jack, why do you think I made you hold the mirror against your solar plexus?'

'I've no idea. Tell me! You called it a rear-view mirror...'

'Smokey quartz is one of the commonest crystals on earth. Used with respect and intention, it might boost your self-esteem or help keep your consciousness grounded while you meditated, or it might help you gain higher states of consciousness. It can be legitimately used for all those things, but it is a crystal, when all's said and done.... a receiver and a transmitter.... a very powerful way of enhancing an effect. It might have transmitted directly to your solar plexus and then I'd have had another casualty on my hands.'

'But I didn't notice you protecting yourself.'

He smiled, 'Oh, yes you did! The over-tones etched a protective shield over my auric field. That, together with the other protections that I called upon, made a lorica — call it a breastplate — around me. The Byzantine mirror is in my study to refract anything untoward that comes into that room. We have to be on our guard.'

'Is that why the crystal is in a bowl of salt?'

'If the sender is using the crystal as a surveillance device, then all he will see is a crystal in a sea of salt-crystals — a neutralizing environment for it.'

I boggled at the idea of long-distance crystal surveillance, 'But what are we — you going to do with it?'

'We're going to set the crystal on send, rather than receive, but only after I've set up a few more co-ordinates. Now we're going to meet Midge. She phoned this morning.'

It was a very pale and agitated Midge who paced outside the amusement arcade that lunchtime, peering anxiously through the Easter holidaymakers thronging the promenade. At sight of us, without preliminary, she thrust a carrier bag at Ash, 'Here it is. Take it away! I don't care if I never see it again.'

Ash received it carefully. Inside was a bundle wrapped in newspaper. 'What's happened, Midge? Did you try to work another spell?'

'It's all used up now. It don't work anymore,' was all she would say. She was already backing away.

'Midge, before you go… has anyone else touched this crystal except you and Karen?'

'I don't want any more trouble!' she half-shouted at him. Curious eyes turned towards us. Soon we would be arrested for molestation, if we weren't careful.

'There won't be any trouble from me. I only want to make sure anyone who touched this is safe,' Ash spoke softly. 'Tell me.'

But Midge had jumped down onto the shingle, away from the crowds. Ash heaved the carrier bag at me, ran after her and caught her arm. She spat and shouted at him, then collapsed in tears. When I caught up with them, she was clinging to him with the desperation of someone drowning, the story spilling out of her.

'Karen didn't want to do the ritual! I made her! We were on the beach and the moon came out. She said she was frightened. I made her say the magic words three times, like it said in the letter and in the book. Her face went all strange. Then she threw the crystal under the pier and ran off. The next day, she went funny.'

So Midge had been the instigator of this tragedy!

'You found the crystal?' Ash prompted her.

'I thought the tide would carry it off, but when I went to look it was still there. The sea must've carried it higher.'

'And what happened when you used it next?'

Her face contorted and I thought that she was about to faint, 'Mr. Dawkins, my science teacher, had a heart attack....'

'Was that what you wished?'

She shook her head, then nodded, thrusting Ash away to be sick on the pebbles. 'It just brings bad luck,' she heaved. 'Take it away!'

While she sipped from my water-bottle and cleaned herself up, I whispered to Ash, 'How come she's alright and not in a state like Karen?'

'The crystal transmission may not work on everyone. Midge is much tougher, more streetwise than our Karen. I think she's had enough of a shock to put her off witchcraft and spells for a long while.'

Ash knelt beside her on the shingle, 'It was very brave of you to phone me, Midge. Now listen, I'm going to make the crystal safe so that it won't harm anyone else. I'd like you to make up for what happened by helping Mrs. Shillington — you don't have to sit with Karen, but maybe run some errands for her mother.'

She nodded, still looking very sick, 'But Mr. Dawkins....!' she wailed. 'What if I killed him?'

'I will send Dr. Rivers round to check on him... and then maybe you could go with some classmates and visit him?'

She shrank at the suggestion, but Ash was adamant, 'You've learned what happens when you focus your intentions, Midge. Now you must face up to the consequences of badly-thought out wishes. Try putting half as much intention into your science lessons and Mr. Dawkins will be more than pleased with you. Now, are you fit to go home?'

We saw her to the entrance hall of her flat, a very chastened teenager indeed.

When she'd gone in, I turned on him, 'You were very hard on her, Ash! You let her seriously think that she had caused her teacher's heart attack by her spell!'

'She may well have done, or it might have been a complete coincidence. But I don't think there's any harm in a lesson about living responsibly, do you? Murderous intentions kill, you know, Jack. I don't imagine she gets any moral guidance at home, poor Midge!'

§§

The night of the full moon was upon us. It shone high over Hartsworth Beacon, etching the ring of beeches at its summit with a sharp filigree of silver. Ash's study had been stripped for action, the furniture pushed back or removed. This time it was clear that we were in for a more serious magical working than last time. I had been aware over the last two days of Ash's unearthly overtoning resonating through the house, so much so that two of our guests had enquired of Wendy if we were using some strange kind of garden equipment. I had been instructed to bath in salt and don clean clothing as part of the preparation.

The crystal that we had sent for was set up in its dish of salt, under a metal bowl, while the crystal that had brought Karen to her current sorry state was lying on the desk wrapped in a piece of silk. I had been given my instructions and waited with trepidation as Ash sealed the study as he had done before. He himself had put on a long loose robe of white silk that accentuated his height and authority. I could well believe he was a magician, in such attire, as he swished about the darkened room. There were two candles on the mantelpiece and two more on the desk which had been positioned in the centre of the room like some great altar. Privately, I thought that things could have been managed without all this esoteric nonsense, but I held my peace.

'I've prepared this for you, Jack.' About my neck, Ash placed a talisman made of inscribed vellum strung on a length of waxed silk. 'May this talisman protect and defend your soul!' Then he gave into my hands the crystal that had been sent to Karen, still wrapped in its silk. 'Bring this to me quickly when I ask.'

Then, uncovering our two-armed smoky quartz in its bowl of salt, he began intoning in a particularly piercing way, until the whole air seemed to shimmer with the vibration. He repeated the syllables CAIL – ED – EZ over and over. To my astonishment, the crystal in its bowl of salt seemed to oscillate. Surely I had been staring at it for too long? But no, there was a distinct movement, almost as if his chanting was causing the crystal to physically shudder. Then he began to chant Karen's name, with overtones so vibrant that it was like being under a high-powered water hose. I wanted desperately to put my fingers in my ears, but then he called, 'Bring it quickly!'

Our crystal now seemed to be full of milk that was pulsing and growing to a point like a geyser about to blow. Ash seized Karen's crystal and held it over the pulsating stone as if it were a hyperdermic. Only instead of injecting liquid, the milkiness of the new crystal seemed to transfer itself into Karen's crystal. Swiftly, he wrapped it in its silk and placed it in a Chinese draw-string bag.

'Is that it?' I whispered hoarsely.

'Not quite!' To my alarm he poured some lighter fluid into the metal bowl and threw in a match. Blue flames leapt up kindling the darkness to deeper intensity. Then he began to tear pages out of *How To Be the Best Teenage Witch Ever*. It made a merry blaze in his study—surely not the best place to burn books, I thought? As he ripped and burned, he intoned, 'Unclean!' I wondered if he'd gone stark mad, for this seemed more in the line of a medieval conjuror than the Ash that I knew.

Bending once more over our crystal, he ordered, 'Put your fingers in your ears!'

I hastily complied as he prepared to chant again. This time, I *felt*, rather than heard the vibration of his chant. It was on such a deep tone as to be virtually subsonic. He directed it at the crystal which seemed to pitch and heave in its dish of salt like a boat in a heavy sea. It finally seemed to lift itself up as if to escape, at the same time growing in density and size. Something was flowing out of the crystal and forming over it, in the shape of a man. Smooth-skinned, but with an unpleasant, almost mercurial oiliness to his flesh, he was holding up both his hands to ward off the terrible subsonic chanting that I felt would pull the room apart if Ash kept it up. Finally, Ash took a swift breath and increased the intensity of the destructive tone. The room itself was beginning to pitch around me and I had broken out in great sweat. It was as though all the molecules that made up that room were breaking out of their normal cohesion and were threatening to dance into orbit. Panic was not far from me, as I regarded that malign shape standing against Ash. I think I was praying aloud by the time that the chant abruptly stopped. The shape vanished and the room settled back into its accustomed place.

There on the desk lay our crystal, split completely into two pieces. Ash tipped it into a bucket under the desk and poured salt over it until it was completely buried. At that point, my legs gave out under me and I slumped to the carpet. Never did *terra firma* feel so welcome!

Ash regarded me with concern, 'Sorry about that, Jack. It took rather more volume than I was expecting. How are you feeling?'

'Nauseous, if you must know. What the hell did you do?'

'Turned round the polarities of the crystal, that's all. I used the call-name in reverse and that summoned the soul of the sender to this room. That's what we saw. There's no doubt that he is the author of this wretched book.' He gestured to the desecrated remains of Karen's book. For the first time, I read the name on the cover and understood. *How To Be the Best Teenage Witch Ever* was written by the unlikely sounding Alice Zed. Finally I saw the connection.

ALICE ZED was an anagram of ZEDELIAC.

For the first time that evening, I laughed, 'He must have been well-pleased to see his book being burned!'

'Quite! — I'd nearly missed the connection between the book and the name in the letter myself. It was very foolish of the sender to give us an anagram of his pseudonym.'

'Have you killed him?' I wondered aloud.

'No! But the mother crystal in which he had been holding the souls of those would-be teenage witches is certainly shattered like this one here.'

'What about Karen's soul?'

'Safe in this crystal which I'd retuned before we began tonight. As for the souls of the other victims, I hope they will be able to find their way back home again.'

'Don't you know?' I had naively supposed him to be omniscient.

'I think the sender will have enough on his plate right now, Jack. His little larder of souls is empty now. They will certainly be free from his foul manipulation. Now, let's finish off here and see how Karen is doing.'

Rosalie Shillington had just come off shift from the Co-op when we arrived. She looked weary, but she brightened as she opened the door to us. For once, the TV was switched off for, as chance would have it, Myrtle had been with Karen all evening, reading her *Wind in the Willows*. She gave us a little wave as she read on to the vacant girl, relating how Mole had sniffed the smell of the home he'd abandoned so suddenly one spring day to go and join Ratty on the riverbank. Ash let Myrtle read on until she came to the part where the young carol singers come to the door before interrupting, 'Thank you, Myrtle. I think it's time that Karen came home too.'

Rosalie Shillington pressed a hand to her mouth in fearful hope, 'Oh doctor, do you think so?' Tears sprang to her eyes and brimmed over.

'Let's see if your prayers have been answered,' he smiled.

He drew out Karen's crystal from the silk wrapping. It still had a milky opacity to it. Placing the tip of the smoky quartz to Karen's chest he began to emit a single pure tone. What happened next was so extraordinary and yet at the same time so natural, that none of us could believe it. It was as though Ash had poured her soul into her down the length of the crystal as easily as you squeeze toothpaste from the tube. Even as I watched, I marvelled that the smoky quartz crystal that had caused such anguish could be turned into such an instrument of healing.

As intelligence began to flicker behind Karen's eyes, Ash called her by her name. Clearly, whatever had been trapped in the crystal had been transferred back to the teenager. She stirred moodily and snapped back into herself. 'What's for supper, mum? I'm starving!' Then, catching sight of us, she demanded, 'Who are you?'

Since that time, Ash has become somewhat of a reluctant saint in Mrs. Shillington's canon. She insists that it was just like the raising of Jairus's daughter in the Gospels, and has no words of praise too high for his healing capabilities. Karen made a full and immediate recovery, to the bafflement of the hospital, who have doubtless written her case off as 'the spontaneous remission of a hysterical illness.' As for the other young women around the country who had been in a similar condition, all have made a similar miraculous recovery. Midge's apparent death-wish against her science teacher was unfounded, for he turned out to have had a history of heart-disease in the family and is now making a good recovery. Mr. Dawkins is unlikely to suffer from any ill-wishing in the future. Somehow, I think that none of the young women involved in this curious case will be pursuing careers in teenage witchcraft.

Case 7: THE HOLIDAY LET

There are many unusual cases that we have treated here at the Beacon, but few are as strange as the one I record here. It might be thought of as one of our near failures. Although others might regard it as nearer to black magic. Certainly, the law would have had difficulty in sorting out the legalities, but fortunately, they were never called in to comment. I cannot, in all fairness, exempt myself from blame. It was entirely due to my ignorance that it came about at all, I see now.

Driving back from London late one autumn, I noticed that the derelict cluster of farm buildings at the top of our lane were now bristling with scaffolding.

'What's going on down the lane?' I asked Wendy who was making tea for two of our guests.

She made a face, 'Farmer Jelley's got financial problems. It's either sell off some land – and you know how farmers hate to do that – or else find some other way. There's grants available for the renovation and refurbishment of existing dwellings, apparently, and so he's opted to turn the old sheds into holiday cottages. Ash is hopping mad about it.'

I whistled, 'Will Ted Jelley get planning permission?'

'Already has it, apparently,' Wendy said flatly, slamming down the plates on the trolley.

I was curious to see Ash in a temper, since I had never yet seen anything bother him so badly that he ever lost it, so I wandered up to the solar to see if he was about. He stood in the light of the westering sun, staring down at the line of the downs in the distance, lost in thought.

He turned, 'You've heard about the proposed cottages? It's a confounded nuisance when neighbours take such decisions. When Melanie first moved here, things were different. I don't want the peace of the Beacon jeopardised by a lot of irresponsible holiday makers.'

I hid a smile, 'But what about the hikers who climb the Hartsworth Beacon every weekend? They often take their radios and children...' I pointed out.

'That's different. It's not an everyday occurrence, for one. No, holiday makers have a way of disrupting the peace of this place. That's all.'

He sounded petulant and unlike himself, so I pronounced, 'In my professional opinion, you sound tired!'

'I am, to tell you the truth!' Throwing himself into the depths of the great sofa, he laughed at himself, 'Perhaps I do need a holiday?'

'Why don't you take one soon? I can manage here. Didn't you say that you had had an invitation to your friend's place somewhere in the Peloponnese?'

'Maybe early next year,' was all he would say.

Following a few words that passed between Wendy and Elaine Jelley in the local shop, Ted Jelley came round to the Beacon himself to explain the situation. He sat on the couch, flat cap twisted in hand, 'Market forces, that's what is, Dr. Ashington, market forces! Painting me into a corner they are, this bloody government. I just called to say that it's only holiday lets, you see, so it won't be all year round. The builders have their instructions to keep down the noise so as not to disturb you. My girl, Elaine, she'll be looking after the cottages, so any problems, you ask her. They'll be ready come Easter. Got bookings already.'

Ash was perfectly polite to Ted, but you could tell he wasn't to be placated easily. A rather uneasy truce is all that was negotiated between them in the end.

Just before that next Easter, the transformation had been complete. Derelict farm sheds had indeed become a very pleasant block with two two-bedroom cottages and a single studio with a shared courtyard, and a lawn at the back with swings and a slide for the children. Ash looked over the conversion, deemed it acceptable, and then, rather surprisingly, went off on his own long-promised holiday after all.

At that time, we had just one young woman staying at the Beacon. She had been checked in by her brother who had made it clear that Ash's kind of hokey treatment was a last resort for his sister. This attitude strangely never made Ash despondent or annoyed. When I asked him why not, he merely said, 'I hold no investment in the client's recovery. If healing is possible, we will investigate all possibilities. If it is not, we will do no further harm.' It was the kind of statement that made me glad I had no medical colleagues staying! This kind of ruthless neutrality is what puts backs up no end although, in his defence, it must be said that his compassion was equally bestowed on all our guests.

I hadn't been present at the young woman's admission, but her history didn't seem a very promising one to me. Lank and listless, with that uninhabited look that certain mental patients have, she was disturbing to the eye. Her skin had a sallow tinge and she held her hands at waist height in what appeared to be a rather predatory way, with the nails curved towards her palms.

Before he went, I asked Ash, 'What's her history?'

'A very sad case,' he said, looking down in the garden where Wendy was pushing her about in a wheelchair to show her the newly opened daffodils. The young woman, bundled up in a thick coat and scarf, with a blanket over her knees, stared at the bright yellow flowers dancing in the March wind with no show of feeling or recognition.

'That's Alison Brady,' Ash said.

'What? The girl who was kidnapped in Indonesia with her mother?' I looked again, with new eyes. The daughter of Peter Brady, the wealthy art dealer, had been snatched from outside their hotel in broad daylight in Western Java where they had been holidaying, and held to ransom by a group of fanatics anxious to raise their political profile and make some cash. Since Brady was a rich US national, the terrorists obviously thought it worthwhile. Held captive for months, Alison had finally been tracked down by the Indonesian government who had gone in with a crack squadron. Unfortunately, they only succeeded in bringing out Alison, then only 12, but there had been no sign of the mother. A subsequent investigation in the region revealed where Mrs. Brady had been buried. She had been a diabetic, and without medication had probably slipped into a diabetic coma and died.

Since that time, Alison had been in and out of private institutions, and no one had been able to help her. Peter Brady had more or less become a recluse after his wife's death. He had been unable to cope with Alison's unstable condition and vacant appearance, and the business was now in the hands of her older brother, Will.

Ash said, 'The brother brought her here as a last resort, before she gets finally committed. The family have done their best for her with private nursing homes and private nursing care. Certainly, if money could bring back her soul, the Brady millions would have seen her right.'

'What can we do for her?'

'Keep her stable, monitor her condition, make your observations. I don't think there'll be any big change yet. I've drawn up her chart and the likelihood is that we won't see any improvement until after the next full moon.' I knew that it was Ash's custom to set up an astrological chart, especially for any guests unable to tell us much about themselves. It gave him a wider part of the picture, he said, though I was frankly doubtful about the whole proceeding. My doubt must have shown, as he added: 'It's not like reading your stars in the newspaper, Jack. That only gives a superficial scan of people's sun-sign.'

'Sun-sign?'

'Your birth sign—you're Taurus, I believe?'

'It's all nonsense, in my opinion,' I said, flatly.

'You know how much I rely on your Taurian pragmatism, Jack. But you did promise to keep an open mind when you came to join us here.'

'So I did! Well, if looking at her astrology will shed any light on the poor girl's predicament, I for one will be glad of it. It's depressing to everyone to see her in such a bad way.'

Alison seemed stable enough and so Ash accordingly took his holiday, leaving me in charge.

§§

On the morning that Ash's first postcard arrived, I was sitting with Alison for a couple of hours to relieve Wendy. The twenty-year old had the vacancy of an empty house. Wendy had attempted to cheer up her appearance by braiding her hair in a fancy way and dressing her in one of the many pretty dresses that her brother had bought her. But it was like dressing a doll. After attempting an interchange with Alison, I finally resorted to taking her for a walk in her wheelchair. At least one of us would get some exercise! I would wheel her out and talk loudly about whatever came into my head, or even sing, when no-one else was about, so that she had a bit of stimulus to her dull life.

The day was blustery as we wheeled down the lane towards Jelley's farm, but Alison was snug enough under her blanket. I thought that she might like to view the newborn lambs in Jelley's barn. Since the holiday lets had opened, we had monitored the noise and nuisance level, but it seemed pretty low to me. The Jelleys had been good neighbours to us in the past, and I felt that I should do my part in reciprocation.

Elaine was bottle-feeding an orphan lamb when we arrived, its urgent mouth sucking upon the teat. Several other lambs were pushing against the enclosure that Ted had erected, their spongy noses and pleading baas making loud appeal. Elaine is a good sort who would do anything for you. After her husband left her, she dedicated herself to her father's farm and to local community work. A comfortably-made woman with no children of her own, she was evidently glad to have the holiday cottages to fuss over. Her face froze at the sight of me initially, but I showed that our brief disagreement was water under the bridge. Apart from anything else, Elaine was unable to keep up any animosity for long, and her natural sympathies flowed towards Alison.

'Is this the poor girl Dr. Ash was talking about? Father thought he recognized her from the papers. Does she not talk at all?' asked Elaine, quietly.

'Not yet, I fear. She seems to like these ones though.' I nodded towards the pushing lambs. There actually seemed to be a trace of interest in Alison's features, so I left her in the shelter of the barn while Elaine showed me the wondrous new cottages.

'We're so pleased — you know Primrose Cottage is booked right through to the summer. A lady author from up north who wanted a quiet place to write her book and she took the studio for the whole month, though we don't see much of her,' said Elaine. It was pretty clear that one of the cottages was occupied by a young family, whose children were getting the full use of the swing and slide, as well as giving full vent to their lungs in the process.

'Your lady novelist won't be making much headway against that lot,' I mused.

Elaine glanced towards the studio, 'She says it doesn't bother her, but I did leave some ear-plugs on her kitchen table in case!'

I wheeled Alison back up to the Beacon and thought no more of it until later that week when I walked further down the lane to post some letters.

An attractive but very thin woman with short peroxide-blonde hair stood staring up at Hartsworth Beacon. She was exceedingly pale, like someone with acute anaemia. Something about her dramatic attitude caused me to slow down, so as not to intrude upon her. She wore a bright red jacket that drained her skin of colour, making her seem even whiter. The same shade of lipstick made a slash of her mouth, and her eyes were rimmed with intensely black eyeliner. From the set of her shoulders, you could tell that she was determined and impatient by nature, yet she also had a stillness and watchfulness that reminded me very strongly of Ash. For a moment, as I stepped nearer to the post box, I almost thought she could have been a relative of his. But when she turned full on, it was evident that I'd been mistaken. Her colouring and bone-structure were utterly different. It was only in the intent, long gaze of her eyes that she resembled my employer.

'Good afternoon,' I said, politely.

Without any introduction, she said to me, 'It would be better if the collecting times were more frequent.' The tight resentfulness from that mouth was at odds with the quality of her voice, which made me want to run back and fetch the car so that I could personally bear her letters to the Royal Mail with greater speed. This confusing reaction sat uneasily with the physical aversion I felt at being in her presence. But, riding over all, was my professional observation that this woman was exceedingly ill. Her pallor had been extreme at distance, but close-up, it was clear that her thinness was not due to fashion but to some wasting illness; her weight was scarcely sufficient to bear her to the post-box. I'd seen healthier-looking anorexics.

I restrained myself to impersonal remarks, saying, 'Twice a day is pretty good for round here. If you want letters to go more quickly, you have to drive into the village.'

'I don't drive.' Again, the timbre of the voice made my whole being vibrate with the desire to serve her. She had the ghost of a Sheffield accent beneath the vibrant timbre of her voice, but that was all that gave her the reality and substance that her physical frame lacked. She turned to look at me properly. Her appreciative stare made it clear that she found me interesting, but I had no illusions about my possible attractiveness to women. I had been around the block with Amy, but my instinct was 'once burned, twice shy.'

Bidding her an abrupt good-day before I said or did something foolish, I strode back to the Beacon, wondering about my reactions to her. It was only afterwards that I considered, what could be so urgent that a woman so sick should venture to the post in person?

By means of the milkman, Elaine had sent myself and Alison an invitation to view the lambs and their mothers when they were to be let out of the barn into the field later that week, what with the warmer weather, so we wheeled down again. It did my heart glad to see the innocent creatures following their mothers curiously into their new environment. Once they'd cautiously explored the space, they soon began to gambol and play, leaping on rubbery black legs and chasing each other. This time Alison's whole body quivered in a spasm that seemed to be a natural reaction to the spring-time spectacle before us. Much heartened by this sign of progress, I accepted Elaine's offer of tea and fresh-baked scones. As we sat together in the kitchen beside the range, Elaine ventured a question with some reluctance, 'Dr. Rivers, I do hope you don't think I'm taking advantage of your position, but I'm a bit worried about Avril—that is, Miss Long—the lady writer in the cottage. She worries so about getting to the post every day—I think she must be posting bits of book out as she writes them, but she couldn't go today.'

'What's the trouble?'

'I don't think she's in the best of health. I'd not seen her for a couple of days, and when I knocked this morning and went in, she was still in bed. She doesn't look at all well.'

'If she's unwell, then she should see Doctor Carr from the local clinic. I'm afraid she's really outside my jurisdiction,' I said, thrusting another scone into my mouth.

'That's the thing. She's says she doesn't want to see anyone except you,' Elaine sounded most embarrassed.

'But I don't know your lodger. And how the hell... how on earth does she know about me?'

Elaine had gone crimson, 'It's all my fault. I told her about your work at the Beacon after she said she'd met you at the post-box... I'm really sorry now, but I'm so worried about her. I'm sure something's not right and I'd be so glad if you'd just come and look in on her.'

This put me on the spot, for I had no licence to minister to patients outside my brief at the Beacon, but then again, I could see that Elaine felt responsible for the care of her lodger. 'Very well, then. But it will be strictly a social call and no more. If I feel her condition warrants medical attention, then I will do all in my power to persuade her to see a doctor as soon as possible. Will that put your mind at rest?'

Elaine breathed out, 'Oh, thank you so much, Dr. Rivers! I'll sit here with Alison, if you like. I can show her the musical box that my uncle sent me from Singapore. It does make a lovely sound.'

I rapped upon the door to Primrose Cottage with the certainty that I was being set up for something. I have always had an intense detestation of being manipulated: it was the main reason that Amy and I never made a go of it, for she would insist on her own will by getting round me in a million little ways that made my life hell, so that I was either guilty or blameworthy in some way or another. Now, on the stairs leading up to the studio entrance, I felt unaccountably like Red Riding Hood knocking at granny's door, about to be faced with the wolf.

But as soon as that lovely voice asked me in, I forgot all about my qualms. Indeed, I think I must have forgotten most of what happened next. I remember Avril Long inviting me in, and I suppose I talked to her, but I don't know what about. I just remember her red mouth speaking and my agreeing with her that she was not well.

I only came back to myself while engaged in the strenuous effort of pushing Alison's wheelchair uphill. The gradient seemed to have become much steeper and I had an almighty struggle to keep going. On my return to the Beacon, Gillespie took one look at me and got Wendy to order me to bed. I didn't argue with either of them, for I was bushed and no mistake. They both said afterwards that I had looked like I'd run a marathon. 'There wasn't an ounce of energy left in you, man,' said Gillespie over breakfast. After my long sleep, I certainly felt restored. I merely supposed that the strain of having sole responsibility for the Beacon's guests had over-taxed me. It is from such neglected realizations that much worser things spawn, I now know.

Later that morning, Elaine came up with a tray of eggs from the farm, 'As a little present,' she explained to Wendy, who let her through the kitchen door with much more of her accustomed kindness than had been recently warranted. As she and Elaine gossiped over the kitchen table, some small peace was accomplished, I felt, when I finally looked in for my own cup of tea.

Elaine's face broke open in a smile at sight of me, 'My lodger's feeling so much better after seeing Dr. Rivers.' I saw Wendy's eyes widen in surprise, but she said nothing in front of our guest.

'I didn't prescribe anything for her lodger except rest—to my best knowledge,' I afterwards defended myself to Wendy, when Elaine had gone.

Wendy halted on her way to the fridge, hearing the hesitation and uncertainty in my voice, 'Do you mean to say you don't remember?'

She could see the lie in my hesitant denial. With a worried frown, she said, 'I think you should phone Ash.'

'There's nothing worth bothering him with,' I said with some irritation. Turning out of the kitchen, I took the stairs two at a time. Honestly, women! Manage, manage, manage! I found myself outside Ash's study rather than my own room, and went boldly in, to garner what support I might from the residue of his presence. Something was not right, but I couldn't put my finger on it. After all, all I'd done was pay a social call on a neighbour's guest, I told myself.

I closed the door on Ash's study. The room was resonant of my employer but void of his wisdom. However, I thought that being there would help me focus more clearly upon present reality. It was at this point that something utterly bizarre happened. I certainly remember going into the room, but it wasn't until I was charging downstairs where Gillespie blocked my way, that I realised I had no memory of what I had done in the study.

'What's that ye have in your hands, laddie?' he asked with the carefulness of a man about to restrain a wild beast.

I felt massive irritation and impatience, trying hard to get past him to the door. But he merely stationed his lanky frame before me, in a rugby check.

'I think we'll put those back where they belong,' he was saying, tugging at the folder in my grasp. He pulled the folder hard, wrenching it from my possessive grip. The papers flew up and out of it, as Gillespie took a very professional restraining hold upon me.

Wendy dashed forward, to pick up the papers that were falling about us, 'How could you?' she cried, kneeling on the floor and gathering them into her lap. It was her appalled voice that brought me out of it. Confusedly I looked at the papers in her hands and scattered around the hallway. They were rituals, inscribed with magical sigils. Private things that Ash always kept locked in his cabinet. Raising my hands to my head, I wailed, 'Good God, what I am doing?'

Gillespie ferkled in my pockets for the bunch of keys, 'I'll take those, I think.' Then I realized where I had been trying to take these very private papers—to Avril Long.

The McLains sat me in the library and gave me the third degree.

'What came over you?' Wendy asked.

'I think I was doing that wretched woman's bidding,' I reluctantly admitted. To Gillespie, I said, 'Thank God you were there to stop me.' He was impassively silent, his eyes narrowing.

'I would never have thought you capable...' Wendy said. 'Until Ash comes back, you must not go down there again, and you are not going to have the keys to the study or your car, until we're satisfied you're alright.'

Gillespie intoned, 'Post-hypnotic suggestion, I ken?'

Wendy nodded in agreement, 'Our Jack would never do such a thing without being under the influence.'

The affection of 'our Jack' gave me hope of forgiveness, but I knew I had been a fool of the worst kind. Pride had gone before me and I had fallen.

I had once before experienced the bamboozling influence of post-hypnotic suggestion as a medical student, where I had humiliatingly been subjected to what was considered a good jape, but which found me half way up the roof of the local nurse's home, a position from which I had been rescued by the fire service. This was now far worse, for I had been made to abuse my employer's trust in the worst possible way.

For the rest of the day the McLains treated me like a guest myself, with a kind wariness. I was aware of some rearrangements and phone calls, but most of all I knew we needed Ash home.

I picked up a smooth sea-washed piece of serpentine that Ash used to put into the hands of guests who became panicky. It had been left on the library mantelpiece. Like a character out of fairytale, I clutched his familiar stone between my hands with the fervent wish, 'Ash, I wish you were back. Something's not right here.' This irrational request helped me no end.

The McLains had obviously attempted to phone Ash to recall him, but he had been utterly out of reach. In their wisdom, it was decided that I would report in with them and not take any major decisions without their say so.

I was able to return to my tasks with better heart, glad that I could at least write up Alison's daily progress. Some little improvements continued. Alison's skin had begun to look less sallow. She also seemed to be responsive to my playing the guitar. Live music was much more powerful than recorded sound, it seemed, so I played a little to her everyday. Her body was responsive to rhythm and vibration. Every afternoon, she went for rides in the wheelchair: this time with Wendy or Gillespie, but not to the Jelley's farm. Despite all of this, Alison still didn't walk or talk, but these were still impressive achievements for someone who had been virtually absent for the best part of eight years.

I thought it was time for Alison to see her brother and, with the agreement of the McLains, I phoned him with the news that we were making some progress. He responded immediately and made arrangements to come that following Wednesday. Even as I marked it on the diary, I noted that the night before that date would be a full moon. I say this because it is certainly true that people who are psychologically disturbed are strongly affected by the moon when it is full. At the last mental hospital where I worked, all staff leave was usually rescinded at the full moon because of the extra work it made for us all. Charming and modest old ladies controlled by light medication would suddenly strip off their frocks on the lawn, young men would work themselves into manic or violent states where they were a danger to themselves and others, while obsessives would attempt to embody their obsession with all the fervour of West End actors.

Those days leading up the full moon at the Beacon were particularly hectic. I received two calls in the same evening from Elaine to come up and see Avril Long once again, which I steadfastly refused to do, despite Elaine's assertion that her lodger felt better after seeing me. 'If she's that bad, call in Dr. Carr,' was all I would say, and stuck to my guns, much to Elaine's irritation and disappointment.

The next night, Wendy had gone in to adjust the central heating in Alison's room, as the temperature had plunged back to winter, 'Jack, come quickly. Something's happening in here.'

I threw down my book and rushed up to her room. Alison was breathing stertorously, sounding as if she might arrest at any moment but then, just as suddenly, her breathing entered into a new phase. Even as I took her pulse, a change came over her. Her broad brow and short, upturned nose, seemed almost to melt and reform, like a character in a film, shapeshifting into a different form. But her erratic pulse settled into a new, more orderly rhythm.

'She's going into REM sleep,' cried Wendy in wonder. Throughout the whole time of her stay, Alison had not once entered into rapid eye movement, signalling the phase of sleep where the subject is deeply dreaming. It was yet another sign of impending recovery to my eyes.

I sat with her uneventfully till dawn when Wendy took over again. On my way to bed, the phone rang. Elaine Jelley now sounded hysterical at the other end, 'Dr. Rivers, you *must* come down and see Avril. She woke me up an hour ago and started telling me a story — such a story. I thought it must be the plot of one of her books, but she insists it's her own story. She doesn't even sound like herself and she won't be satisfied.'

Again, I kept my boundaries high, 'Elaine, if she's getting hysterical, give her a slap. But you really must call Doctor Carr! I can't come down, I've been up all night here with Alison. Even were I free, Miss Long is not my patient, and I have no licence to attend on her.'

Elaine burst into tears of frustration at my cowardly desertion, but I couldn't be of any use to her. I truly didn't want any more involvement with that woman after the last time.

§§

Events moved rapidly that morning. On waking, Alison had sat up with every sign of being in normal consciousness. Intelligence flickered in her eyes and she asked for breakfast, according to Wendy, 'She's hungry and has an animation we've not seen before,' she said, but somehow, the gladness with which Wendy usually greeted recovery was absent from her voice, so I asked, 'Is there something wrong?'

Wendy frowned, 'I don't know, but I think you should come and talk to her, and see for yourself.'

Alison lay back languidly on the pillows, with heavy eyelids shading her eyes, 'Thank you,' she whispered, squeezing my hand as I sat beside her. I made a brief examination — she seemed normal in every way.

'Welcome back to us at last: your brother is going to be so pleased!' I said to her, with some self-congratulations of my own.

But that was not to be. When he arrived later that morning, Will Brady was led straight to Alison's room, where they were left alone. I was snoozing a little in my chair when Gillespie came to find me, 'You better gae to the office, Jack. Mr. Brady's hopping mad about something.'

'Oh God! I hope he's not going to play the litigation card. Bloody Americans!' I muttered.

'I'll be outside the window, if you need me,' Gillespie promised me.

Will Brady strode restlessly up and down the office, awaiting my arrival. His blue eyes were boiling with rage and fear, as he turned on me, accusingly, 'What have you been doing?'

'Looking after your sister and aiding her recovery,' I informed him, God help me!

Brady snarled, 'Well, that's not my sister you have there!'

'I'm sorry?' I was taken aback by the violence of his accusation.

'The woman in my sister's body is not my sister!' He insisted.

Totally bemused, but with respect for his distress, I countered, 'But, Mr. Brady, how can you tell what your sister is like now as a twenty-year old adult? You last met the Alison you knew when she was only eleven.'

'Someone else is looking out of her eyes,' he said bluntly, 'That's all I know.' He looked fearfully at me, and that was when I knew I had made an awful blunder.

In the silence, he tapped vigorously upon the cigarette lighter he most evidently wished to use. I invited him to step into the garden where he immediately lit up and went on the offensive once again.

'When I left my sister here under the care of Dr. Ashington, I admit that I had little hope of much improvement. He was my last resort, to tell the truth. But I did not leave her here merely to pick up... a substitute.' He exhaled a cloud of smoke, then turned upon me with glittering eyes, 'I'd heard all kinds of things about your employer but I discounted them, out of desperation. If I find out that he's been meddling with Alison, messing her up with his magic or spiritualism or whatever he does, then things are going to get very nasty!'

Inside, I howled, 'Oh, Ash! Why are you not here? What is going on?' I was truly out of my depth and no amount of appeasement could satisfy Brady.

As firmly and professionally as I could, I said, 'I'm sure that Alison's return to us is accompanied by certain phenomena and behaviour that is confusing to herself as well as to you. Dr. Ashington has not had her on any medication or any other kind of treatment. We've been merely observing and accompanying her.'

'Then come and see for yourself,' Brady insisted.

Together, we went to observe Alison. Wendy was right. She was out of her wheelchair and staring through the hedgerow that separated the guests from the staff premises. She had the unaccountable air of a spy.

'Hello, Alison!' I called, in as cheerful a voice as I could muster in the circumstances.

She turned gracefully. Gone was the shambling heap of a girl who had sat vacantly in her chair. The vibrancy of life was in her body and there was vitality in her eyes. As I walked joyfully towards her, pleased and somewhat self-congratulatory at this great improvement, I suddenly saw what had so badly disturbed Brady. The look in Alison's eyes was not that of an innocent, un-awakened girl, nor even that of a young woman come unknowingly to adulthood. The soul that looked out of her blue eyes was that of a knowing woman whose experience of life was far in advance of the body she inhabited. It was like looking into the ageless eyes of Ash, only stripped of any of their compassion. It was as startling as being bitten by a charming kitten. Her demeanour, gait and set of her head reminded me of someone.

Brady caught my dismay, 'You see what I mean?'

'I'm very glad to be back,' said Alison, or the one who sat in Alison's body. I had no notion of what the normal timbre of her voice had been, since we had only ever heard Alison snore or groan in her sleep, but this voice bore the distinct trace of a Sheffield accent. Now, the Brady family had a Bostonian Irish accent. Which was how I knew....

Sheer professionalism helped me stand my ground with the brother, but when I heard that unlikely accent issuing from Alison's mouth, I feared for my very sanity.

Gillespie saw my predicament and came forward, saying to Alison, 'I think that's enough exercise for the day. Let's go back to the conservatory, shall we, my dear?' He attempted to put his arm under her elbow, but the woman in Alison's body flung him off, insultingly disdainful of him, 'Take your hands off me! I shall walk where I please.'

Brady threw away his cigarette end, his face working with incomprehension and distress. With eyes full of blame, he spat at me, 'I'm not taking whoever that is home with me. I want an explanation and soon. I shall be speaking to my lawyers.' It was down to Wendy, who persuaded him to go back to the hotel he'd booked until Ash came home, when Brady could have a second opinion.

§§

Miraculously, Ash rolled up about seven that night and not a moment too soon. Gillespie and Wendy had been led a merry dance by 'Alison' all day. She'd attempted to get into the private part of the house in order to get upstairs and she clearly also wanted the keys to one of our cars. Though it does not present me in a good light, I must admit that I slipped her a sedating hyperdermic while she grappled with Gillespie. Together, we carried her up to her room and locked the door. It was like a scene from my former life at the mental hospital. God knows what kind of headlines my actions would generate, let alone what the Brady lawyers would have to say.

I was at the door the moment Ash pulled his small suitcase from the boot of the taxi, 'We've got trouble, Ash!'

He put his head on one side, 'What, no "welcome home" for the wanderer?' He had that god-given ability to tan evenly and without burning, I noted, as he shook my hand.

'Of course, I'm glad to see you. But you've been desperately needed here. How did you know?'

He laughed in my bemused face, 'Why, Jack! I picked up your distress call three days back. That's why I started back so early. Now what's brought this on?'

'I think you know very well!' I poured out the sequence of events nevertheless, along with the McLains' testimony of my own frightful behaviour.

But his first concern was, 'You've got her securely under sedation, you say?'

I nodded with shame, but his reaction reassured me, 'Thank goodness! We still stand a chance of bringing things right.' He flung his case into the hall, calling, 'Get a wheelchair and put it into the van. We're going to Jelley's farm.'

'Aren't we going to look upstairs first?' I asked.

'No! Our need is elsewhere.'

As we drove the short distance down the lane, Ash explained, 'Alison's soul has been largely out of her body while she's been awake. But when she was sleeping, someone else had the occasion and sufficient experience to completely enter her vacant body. Having no other place to go, Alison's soul has woken up in Avril body... Brady is quite right—it isn't Alison you have upstairs but Avril.'

Seeing my astounded look, he said, 'Think of it as a holiday let.'

Ash's simple, startling explanation was so horrific to me that I felt physically sick. All those walks to the post-box and visits to the farm made a different kind of sense now. 'But what about the time *I* visited Avril Long? Was she trying to enter *my* body?'

'Oh no! You say Avril was a sick woman with little energy? Well, she merely drew off some of your own when you were so obliging as to visit her. Simple vampirism, Jack. However...' he turned into the farmyard at speed, causing Elaine and Ted Jelley to spring into their back porch, 'I think we are dealing with a woman who is adept in the magical arts, and her intentions have been little less than murderous. Avril has taken her chance of life by forcing Alison out. If your diagnosis is correct, Avril's body hasn't got long to live. We have to get to Alison now and quickly!'

Elaine virtually fell on Ash's neck with gratitude, 'Oh, Dr. Ash! Thank you so much for coming.'

Farmer Jelley remained where he was, his face like a stone, 'I want someone to tell me what's been happening here.'

"Perhaps, Elaine can tell us,' Ash suggested.

Hurrying us over to the studio. Elaine clung to Ash's arm, 'Avril woke me up at 5 this morning in a terrible state. She was so confused and terrified, it took the two of us to get her back to bed. She kept going on about being a prisoner and then when she looked in the mirror, she couldn't stop screaming. We've got her settled now, but she's been hanging on, trying not to sleep. She's so weak.... Oh, Dr. Ash, if you could see how pathetic she is... she's like a child.'

Ted Jelley was regarding me all this while with reproachful eyes, 'And I thought we was neighbours.'

'I'm very sorry we couldn't come earlier, but we had troubles of our own today. Did you call out Dr. Carr?' I said, with heavy embarrassment.

'Couldn't come till later, he said,' Jelley sounded disgusted with the medical profession at large. 'My Elaine's been near out of her wits with worry.'

Ash ignored this and took the steps in a single leap. On the bed lay the emaciated body of Avril Long. However, struggling for life within it, the soul of Alison Brady looked out of her eyes.

'Oh, will you please help me?' she attempted to rise, at the sight of us. 'I've been a prisoner in the jungle. My mother's dead. I don't know where I am. The people here are kind but... but this isn't my ... place. Everything is wrong...'

Ash took her hands, 'Alison Brady, we both know who you are. My name is Richard Ashington. I'm a doctor. This is my colleague, Jack Rivers. Be assured that you will be in your own place very soon. We've come to rescue you.'

It was then that Alison recognized me! The soul and intelligence of Alison tried to raise the almost lifeless arm of Avril Long in an attempt to greet me, only the body in which she was trapped had no power to move.

Ash directed that I lift her into the wheelchair. The body of Avril Long weighed no more than an Alastian dog in my arms, and I bitterly cursed myself for not coming sooner to answer Elaine's call.

Ash left his instructions with the Jelleys, 'When Dr. Carr calls, please direct him up to the Beacon. We're taking Miss Long where she can have access to medical equipment in case it's needed.' But once we were in the van, he whispered to me, 'But it's essential that Carr's kept away for as long as possible. We have to save Alison before he comes.'

I was still in massive shock from this extraordinary transfer of the souls of the two women into each other's bodies, and merely nodded. Helping Ash out with the wheelchair at the Beacon, I summoned up sufficient energy to ask, 'But how are we... how are you going to make the exchange?'

'That depends on several things,' he said grimly. 'Get some more sedative — not too much. And, Jack... do exactly what I tell you. The timing is going to be tricky!'

I never felt more like a body-snatcher in all my born days. The legality of what Ash was about to attempt was questionable in the extreme, but then, I doubt that any judge in the land would have the faintest legal statute to cover this particular territory.

Ash positioned the two women next to each other, the dying body of Avril Long in the wheelchair and the living body of Alison Brady on the bed. He nodded at me to top-up the sedative on Alison's body. As the sedative took effect, the body of Alison relaxed completely. In a sonorous and commanding voice Ash addressed the soul of Avril in Alison's body: 'Avril Long, what you have been seeking for, is now here.' He uttered some of his piercing overtone callings, 'In the name of Three, the Magister of the Temple calls you forth and bids you stand before him. The secrets that you have been seeking are manifest in this place.' He made some forthright gestures in the air, like a draughtsman making a complex design. It seemed to me that he drew a shape like a fence, and in it a gate that stood open.

In the dim light of Alison's bedroom, I thought I saw a stirring of a vapour, like a cloud of breath on a winter's morning. It rose and gathered, sliding up and out of Alison's body. I held my own breath. The vapour moved towards the invisible sign that Ash had drawn in the air. When the vaporous body was fully enclosed by the sign, Ash shut the gate, just like a farmer gating a sheep within the fold. There was an agitation within that invisible fence that he'd drawn, a desperate struggle to escape.

He whispered to me, 'Quickly, sit behind Alison's body and make your body like a chair.' I hopped up onto the pillows behind her so that Alison's body leant back drawn up upon my chest.

'Now!' he said grimly. He turned to the almost lifeless body of Avril, 'Alison Brady. Listen to my voice! I am Dr. Ashington. You've been imprisoned in the wrong place, but now it's time to go home to your own body. You will not remember what has taken place over the last 24 hours, but will awake as from a deep sleep. Dr. Rivers is beside you, calling you back to your life again. Listen to his voice now and return.'

He nodded to me encouragingly. Now, as a doctor, I've been called upon to do many strange things in my time, but that was definitely the strangest. In as normal a voice as I could muster, I called, 'Alison! Come over here now. I need you to come back to your body. When you wake up, I'll bring you some orange juice and porridge, and then we'll go and look at the lambs again. Would you like to do that? ... Come back here, Alison!'

This time a vapour surged out of Avril's body and made its way towards the body that lay in my arms. I hummed one of my cheerful wheelchair-walking songs so that the soul of Alison could home in. I felt Alison's move-less body leaning against me begin to animate again.

'Stay like that, Jack! Keep humming, that's good.' Ash administered a mild stimulant to Alison, then turned to the imprisoned vapour, still caught within its gated enclosure. With firm intent and vibrant voice, he commanded, 'Avril Long, you have sought by forbidden means to come into the body of another human being. It is not for me to judge you. The initiatory secrets that you desire can only be gained by returning to your own form. Go to the judgement that you have avoided this long time. The initiation that you sought to steal cannot be yours while you remain in this incarnation.'

Ash stood behind the wheelchair where Avril's body slumped. 'At my command you will return to your body.' He opened the gate of the invisible fence. The vapour burst forth, strove valiantly to come back to Alison's body, but it was unable. Alison's own soul occupied Alison's body, and there was no ingress for the proud but dying woman whose magical scheming had nearly robbed Alison of her life. Nevertheless, I kept my hands firmly and instinctively clasped about Alison's solar plexus until the soul of Avril Long was finally forced to return to her own wasted body.

As the vapour poured over and into Avril's wasted body, her dark eyes snapped open, seeking here and there and fixing upon her opponent. But her fury at Ash's out-manoeuvring her terrible purpose was unable to find any fuel to sustain it. Her body's reserves were entirely spent and all she could do was impotently spit and curse him, 'You tricked me!'

'Just as you were going to trick this innocent girl out of her life.' I'd never seen Ash so uncompromising. The pair of them, so alike and so unalike, shared a kindred power I was glad not to know. If I ever needed a lesson in what black magic looked like, Avril Long had surely supplied it. Intent without compassion is just murderous.

Downstairs the doorbell was urgently sounding over and over. Gillespie knocked on the door, peering in, 'Shall I let Dr. Carr in?'

'Give us exactly one minute and then send him up,' Ash said through the door. 'Stay with Alison, Jack.'

Ash wheeled the chair, with Avril past cursing now, into the next bedroom, which is where Dr. Carr examined his patient, leaving me marvelling how Ash had arranged things, and how this would play out. So intent had we been with the saving of Alison, that I'd had no sense of the upshot of this night's work. The world of legality, professional ethics and consent washed over me. I considered: the body of Avril had been given no medical treatment by us whatever. The realization of relief washed over me. If she was going to complain of what Ash had done, surely no-one would ever believe her?

After a long interval I heard the rumble of Dr. Carr's voice, as he came out to confer with Ash, 'She's sunk into a coma. I've rung for an ambulance. How is it that a woman that near death has gone unmonitored for so long?' he demanded.

Through the door, I couldn't see Ash's face, but I imagined its neutrality, as he replied, 'Dr. Rivers did urge Elaine to call you out sooner, when he saw how bad she was. I gather Miss Long was reluctant to be seen by anyone, however. We only brought her here when it was clear there would be a delay. We have better facilities than down at the cottages.'

The ambulance from the main hospital arrived within twenty minutes of Dr. Carr's examination.

In the meantime, Alison's body had grown very hot and heavy upon my chest and she was resting deeply. I finally extricated myself from behind her and let her sleep on while I watched in the chair. The two lots of sedation we had administered would ensure that she would not wake for a while, so I settled down to ensure nothing more befell her.

Needless to say, I awoke with a stiff neck at about 6 am when Ash looked in with a cup of coffee for me.

'All serene?'

'Perfectly fine,' I smiled.

I followed him out into the corridor, 'What's afoot?'

'Avril Long died on admission at Kingsley General. Cause of death to be determined. I imagine a post mortem will find natural causes of a neglected condition, whereas you and I know that it was mostly likely hastened by aggravated frustration.'

I searched his face, 'And you feel no guilt?'

His response was certain, 'None... Do you?'

I didn't know what to say. Various professional epithets came to mind, but none applicable to the strange events of that night. Finally, I said, 'I don't know, it seems .... Well, very high-handed. I know we are often called upon to make decisions in treatment, but judgements like that...?'

'No, Jack, I am not her judge, nor even her executioner. She would have died within the week, I think you know that. It was the means by which she attempted to continue to live that was the problem. We had the care of Alison. As for judgement, I leave that to a higher authority. But what Avril Long was after was not only Alison's body and a longer life.'

I tried hard to understand, 'But why was she here?'

'I think it certain that she took the Jelley's studio solely in order to be near the Beacon. Avril Long was a magician from a well-known occult lodge in the Peak District who wanted certain secrets from me... that much is evident from your own testimony... she planted a post-hypnotic suggestion in you to fetch certain records and documents to her. She planned her stay to get to me and to obtain a stay on her life by magical means.'

I regarded Ash with awe, 'I don't ask you about your magical activities, but would that be remotely possible?' I was thinking of myths where ancient parchments or symbols bring the dead to life or impart extended life to the sick.

Ash smiled, deprecatingly, 'It is not quite like that but yes, certain formulas and ways can enhance life, if they are faithfully followed.' I could believe it, looking at him, who never looked a day older than when I'd first met him.

'Then why did she draw upon my energies?'

'Apart from needing your vital forces to keep going, she also needed to get a foot in the door here. She knew of my background and she would have set you up to get to me. Unfortunately for her, her remaining term of life was so short, she didn't succeed.'

'And what if she'd come to you openly and asked for healing or your esoteric secrets or whatever?'

'Ah! That would have been an entirely different matter. Genuine seekers I do not send away. She had much skill but little humanity. However she reincarnates, it will be in a body and life that will teach her more compassion, I imagine.'

I suddenly remembered his antipathy to the holiday lets, 'Is that why you were so disturbed by Ted Jelley's plans for the farm-buildings?'

'Perhaps. I only knew that we were on the verge of a difficult time.' He paused. 'You had better get the breakfast you promised to Alison—I can hear her stirring.'

After her orange juice and porridge, both eaten without help and with great relish, Alison got up and, with Wendy's help, dressed herself. That week, she was able to give a full report of her capture. She later gave descriptions of the men who had held her and, with the assistance of a police artist, was able to give useful information to the Indonesian authorities.

Her joy at seeing her brother knew no bounds. I don't know what Ash had told him, but Will Brady himself said he was entirely happy with our treatment of his sister and he would be making no complaints, 'I don't know much about your work, but I daresay you do get some strange things happening.'

After we waved off Alison and Will, I walked down to the post-box with Ash, passing Jelley's farm as we did so. Elaine gave us a tight-lipped nod as we passed but said nothing. The awkwardness about the holiday lets was now compounded by what she doubtless saw as my neglect. But as we came back up past the farmyard from the post-box, she was waiting for us. With diffident formality, she said, 'Dr. Ash, Dr. Rivers, I see I was wrong to blame you for Miss Long's death. I've just been sorting out her things.... And, well.... I don't know,' she shook her head as if casting off insects. 'Please will you come up and see? The police say they can find no next of kin nor any will, and that any of her things are mine to dispose of. But I don't know… I don't want them anywhere near my home.'

She stood in the doorway of the studio, refusing to come in, saying, 'Filthy things, filthy! If I'd known she was a witch, I'd have never had her over my threshold.'

On the bed was a half-unpacked bag—a robe with a twisted cord, a wand with a crystal tip, books about kabbala and magic, a bronze statue of some hermetic looking god with a lion's head and a snake about his body. The things had a horrid mana of their own. I could well see why Elaine didn't want to touch them.

When Ash came out of the studio, he was unfazed, 'You need not worry about these things, Elaine. I'll dispose of them safely.'

Elaine's relief and gratitude as the horrid things were removed, was replaced by curiosity, 'The other day, when that woman woke up and started screaming… you know, it didn't sound like her at all. It may sound daft, but I was thinking about the things she said about being imprisoned…' She stared up at me, 'It was Alison, wasn't it, crying out?'

I accorded her a nod, but wondered how on earth I might answer her.

But Elaine held up her large, capable hand with, 'Doctor, I really don't want to know. There was a lot more going on, I daresay, but it was down to that woman's meddling.'

'It certainly was!' I agreed with her.

She gave Ash a long, considering look, and then back to me, including me in her remark, 'It's not for the likes of us to be meddling, but thank goodness there are those who have the power for good.' Then she thrust a posy of spring flowers into my hand, 'Give those to Alison with our love, and tell her she's welcome to drop in for tea anytime.' And I knew I was forgiven.

As we swung Avril Long's esoteric regalia up the hill between us, taking a handle each, the lorry to take the lambs to the abattoir was backing into the farm entrance. That was a sight Alison would be spared, at least!

Ash caught my expression, 'Some live and some die, Jack. That's life.'

I turned my shoulder on the lorry, 'I wish I'd never heard of the bloody holiday lets!'

Case 8: SINGAPORE SLING

Wedged into an Air Indonesia window seat over the Arafura Sea, somewhere between Northern Australia and Java, I contemplated the map screen on the chair back with growing panic. I had still another 19 hours to endure before I touched down at Gatwick. The young mother in the next seat had been trying to subdue her screaming infant with no notable success since we had taken off, and the distance till the refuelling stop still read another 1272 miles. The distance still to be endured was grim and did nothing to quell my panic.

38,000 feet below us, the peerless, blue-green ocean seemed a tranquil haven of quietness, with only yellow-rimmed islands and almost transparent rainbow atolls flowering like delicate jellyfish beneath the scudding clouds. I wished myself anywhere down there than in my cramped seat.

This was hardly my usual commute. Just a few weeks ago, I had heard that my cousin's mother, Aunt Grace, had passed away in Australia, and that it had been her dearest wish for her ashes to be scattered in the family plot in Kent. So here I sat, with Auntie Grace's urn in my carry-on bag.

Another series of screaming protests issued out of the tired toddler's mouth. The rest of our section was growing mutinous. The minute stewardess who served our aisle made an executive decision and picked up the intercom, asking if any passenger sitting in a bulkhead seat would kindly swop with the young mother, so that the child might be accommodated in a cot, ensuring that the rest of the plane might begin to catch some sleep.

The tall Australian man with a rugged face who volunteered to give up his legroom was given a spontaneous round of applause. Sure enough, within a few minutes of being laid flat, the squalling infant fell utterly silent and we all turned off our reading lights and tried to get some sleep.

We were within twenty miles of our refuelling stop at Singapore when our section was woken by terrible screams, only this time they were not those of the infant. The Australian sitting beside me was clearly in the grip of a nightmare. Whatever was happening in it, he was desperately trying to fend off attack, for his arms were raised over his face and head. Our tiny stewardess hovered uncertainly beside him, obviously not wanting to lay hands on him, but someone had to waken him. I unlocked my seatbelt and stood to lay a firm hand on either arm, 'It's all right now! Just leave it all behind and wake up.'

I stupidly didn't anticipate the result of my action. Opening his eyes blindly, he reacted out of terror and fear, bringing his hands up round my throat in a savage grip. There were some very nasty moments wherein I stopped breathing, while our tiny stewardess proved that she knew more than a little about martial arts. Separated from my assailant, I fell back into the aisle, where I was attended by two very attractive Australian nurses, off on a backpacking holiday of Europe. We'd spoken in the check-in queue earlier and exchanged pleasantries.

Our section was now in uproar and the steward from first class arrived to discover whether the plane was facing an attempted terrorist incident. I tried to assure everyone that I was all right, but my vocal chords didn't seem to work so well. A Chinese businessman from Hong Kong had wrapped his arms around the disturbed dreamer from round the back of the seat and was yelling that he, 'had control of the situation,' in a most magisterial manner.

The sleeper himself had now come out of his nightmare, horrified and bewildered by the uproar, and smarting from the salutary manoeuvre that had freed me. He reasonably struggled against being restrained and the little stewardess peremptorily bade him stay in his seat, in a voice that brooked no refusal. As soon as he saw me being given oxygen on the floor of the aisle, he demanded to know what had happened, but was treated with the silence meted out to a criminal pariah.

Given that we were approaching Singapore and already in descent, the pilot had obviously radioed ahead so that, on landing, our plane was met by airport security and the police, as a precaution. Everyone was instructed to stay in their seats until the airport police conducted my assailant away, with me following on a stretcher, supported by the small stewardess and Jane, the blond nurse.

By this time, I was desperate to assure everyone that the assault had been resultant from a nightmare and not conscious intent, but I was also aware that my throat would need urgent treatment. Under the oxygen mask, my voice was not exactly functional.

The stewardess related the incident to the police while Jane and I were conducted to the emergency unit at the airport.

Having been on the receiving end of those hands, I knew with certainty that the dreamer had been, or maybe still was, engaged in some kind of military service. His was the reaction of someone trained to use deadly force. As a doctor, I also knew that it only took 33 pounds of pressure to close off a trachea: any longer than 4-5 minutes and that's your lot! I had been very lucky that the stewardess intervened when she did—humiliating though it was to be grateful for the physical intervention of someone only half your height and sporting a pink head veil.

During the medical assessment, I kept miming a need for writing materials. Jane swiftly handed me her travel notebook and a pen, on which I wrote, 'Please find out how the guy is doing and tell the police that it was a reaction to nightmare, not intentional assault. I don't want to press charges, make that clear. Also, please don't let me stop your holiday!'

'I'll do my best,' she promised. 'And as for the holiday, Maisy is going on ahead and meeting me in London. We're both on flexible tickets, so no worries.' But she wouldn't go until the doctors ascertained whether I was out of danger. I squeezed her hand. Not having any knowledge of jails in this part of the world, I had no idea what kind of hell they were giving the guy, but I didn't want to prolong his incarceration.

The doctor told me I was lucky to have escaped with minor injuries, but that he wanted me to be admitted to hospital for the next three days for observation, 'In case you develop any complications.' Jane cast a professional eye over my obs and nodded, saying, 'I'll be back.'

She was as good as her word. Having taken a note of which hospital I needed to be transferred to, she kept in touch, visiting every day. As a doctor, you don't often have the opportunity to be tended by so pretty a nurse. While I looked forward to her visits with increasing expectation, I was also impatient to get going. Apparently the authorities wouldn't release my assailant, Philip King, until I'd sworn an affidavit that he was innocent of any premeditated assault, so he would be held at a detention unit until then. On the day of my discharge, Jane came and collected me like a piece of lost luggage, having arranged for me a room at an airport hotel.

It was the most of Singapore that I'd gotten to see, only my main interest was beside me in the cab, and the landscape could go hang. Over the last, painful four days, I'd come to look out eagerly for that neat blonde head and easy, athletic form swinging into the ward to find me. First love had me by the scruff of the neck. Having such a sore throat still, I hardly needed to hide my tongue-tied adoration. I felt at home with her, as I'd not done with any woman since Amy.

'What would you like first?' she asked, sweetly, as we paid off the taxi.

'A Singapore Sling?' I rasped.

Compressing her mouth in a smile that spread to her sparkling brown eyes, 'Let's just find a nice non-alcoholic cocktail for you, shall we?' She firmly steered me into a bar, 'Something to soothe that throat and not react with the pain medication?'

Still under the institutionalization of the last three bed-ridden days, I meekly followed her. Over a pineapple concoction bristling with fruit, I thanked her for all her care, 'I honestly don't know what I'd have done without you. How is Philip?'

'Not a happy bunny! But we'll soon get him out.'

Later, we took the bus to meet Philip's lawyer, where I swore my oath. The formalities were faxed over and then we took a taxi out to the detention centre where the obliging Mr. Feng helped us navigate what might have been a minefield of bureaucracy. The Australian embassy had also been informed and Philip King was finally released from custody, without charge.

He was brought out from the cells to sign for his personal belongings, looking both thinner and sweatier than when we'd last seen him. His shirt was stained and his jaw set firm in defensive wariness.

I extended my hand, 'Welcome back! I'm so sorry that you ended up here because of me.'

He took my hand, 'No, it's me should be sorry, mate! — You just tried to wake me up. — Thanks to you both for cracking me out of here.'

His eyes played about the detention facility and then closed, as if he were trying to expunge the memory. 'Was it really that bad?' I asked in dismay.

He made an attempt at a laugh, 'Hardly! I've seen a lot worse than this, believe me. — Is there somewhere I can get clean again and change my clothes?'

In the taxi back to the airport hotel, we made plans about getting home. Jane had her open ticket, but King and myself needed to make other arrangements. 'If it's all the same, I will go to London via another airline,' King said. 'I somehow think that Air Indonesia isn't going to want me on board again. — Do you mind flying back on Quantas with me, Doctor? I will pay for us both, since I caused you the delay.'

I was reluctant because I didn't want to say goodbye yet to Jane. Torn between my personal desires and my responsibilities, I made the hard call. 'Well, that's very good of you, thank you,' was all I said in the end, as it felt churlish to refuse.

We took King back to our hotel and checked him in for the night into my twin-bedded room, as the hotel was otherwise full for a conference

After he'd gone up to change, I turned my attention to Jane. Heaven knows, I am a lame kind of suitor at the best of times, but I really didn't want to lose the moment, now that the clock was ticking towards departure and separation the next day.

As we sat in the lounge watching streams of delegates of all nationalities from South East Asia flood in for their conference, I felt I was receding, like the tide. I bought coffees for us both and some extravagant little cakes from the display that had made Jane squeak with delight earlier when we checked in. Iced in many colours, they were made in the likeness of cats — sitting, playing and jumping.

I put the plate down in front of her, with, 'As we've both missed lunch....'

She promptly fell hungrily onto a purple jumping cat, eating it tail first. Licking sugar icing off her lips with a pink tongue, she said, 'That was a real treat! — I'll have to play a few rounds of tennis to work these off!'

'You Australians are so much more sporty than us at home!' I observed.

In the silence that followed, Jane ate two more biscuit cats while my eyes drank her in. Being utterly smitten, I became yet more stiff and formal, 'You know, I cannot begin to thank you. You've smoothed the way for us both... and now....' inarticulately choked with the thought of never seeing her again.

She covered my distress with, 'It's been an adventure, hasn't it? — So what next for you?'

I took my courage with both hands, 'Damn the funeral! Damn work! All I've been able to think about is you!'

To her credit, Jane didn't move, her arm still curved about the back of the red banquette. Her silence was so long, that I was sure I'd blown it, but she said, 'And there was I thinking that you Brits were slow movers! — Look, Doc, we don't know each other well enough for this conversation....' she lowered her head to hide a secret smile, '.... so what are you going to do to improve your chances, Jack?'

Flashing her my most hopeful, ardent look, I kissed her hand and swore, 'Let me create as many opportunities as I can to get to know you better.'

We spent the time before dinner exchanging life stories. Jane had been working as a remote area nurse up in Arnheim Land, in the Northern Territory, serving the Aboriginal people. 'Maisy and I have been up there a couple of years. She's the midwife, while I specialize in teaching basic health maintenance, but honestly, we deal with a whole range of things from mental health to diabetes, febrile babies to snakebites. — You just never know what you'll get.'

She showed me some photos of her at work, 'I get to work in the most remote region of Australia. It's a place of extremes — so you get this strange mixture. People who have just the bare essentials or not even that, in this amazing, beautiful place.... poverty in paradise! Except they are richer than we are... their family bonds and culture are so much stronger than ours.'

'How do you manage, being so isolated?' I asked, looking through the photos and syphoning off one that seemed to be a duplicate, showing Jane with an Aboriginal child on her lap. The little boy's head was laid trustfully on her shoulder, while at her feet a tame dingo was looking up expectantly to the titbit held in her fingers. In the brilliant light of the Northern Territory, her easy, relaxed body and happy smile showed that she was right at home.

'Well, we get good support from the flying doctor, but we have to be ready for anything, whether it's crocks crossing the road or dealing with 00 emergency calls in the small hours. It's such a vast terrain, you can't get across it easily, even by plane. You might see an attempted suicide, a woman with kidney failure, or a guy who had a skin-full of beer and burned himself while trying to light a cigarette with a kerosene canister. You name it, we see it all!'

'Well, we don't have so many wild creatures at the Beacon, but the work is pretty various.' I outlined what I did with Ash, beefing it up a little so I might shine in her eyes too. She listened, giggling over my descriptions of Gillespie's antics. I took the chance to give her my card, so she would have *all* my details, 'Can we meet up during your stay? I'd like to take you to a little village nearby. Watercress beds, woodland streams, and a thatched pub which has a very nice restaurant.'

She brought me back to our friend, 'So, Doc, what about Philip, now?'

'You know I'd have much rather come home with you, but I think we both feel he needs a companion.'

In answer, she nodded her head towards the lift, from which King was emerging, and said, 'I agree. That's a big man, but he's vulnerable, and the pair of you will do better together, I reckon.' She added, with a little squeeze of the hand, 'I'm sorry, too!' Which made me feel even worse.

Over a Chinese meal, we heard a little more about Philip. He'd been going to London to interview for a post at the UN offices in Whitehall, 'Though I'm a bit late, they say they'll hold open applications another couple of days for me, since I worked for them before.'

'What did you do?' Jane asked.

He rested his chopsticks, 'I served in UNPROFOR,' he said. I must have looked blank, but Jane was more discerning and expressed concern, 'God, Phil! That must have been bloody awful!'

'I'm sorry, I'm not good at acronyms....' I said, reaching for the hot crispy fish.

Together they chorused to me, 'United Nations Protection Force.'

Only then did I realize where he must have been recently serving, 'Not... in the Balkans?'

Philip nodded, tight-lipped, but wouldn't say more than 'Eastern Bosnia' To the unspoken question hovering in air, he assured us, 'No. It's not a conversation you want to have over the table... I retired from that kind of peacekeeping, you might say.' It certainly explained the nightmares.

I never felt less dutiful in my whole life than when I said goodbye to Jane the next morning. She gave me a huge squeeze and whispered in my ear, 'See you in Blighty, Doc.' kissing me on my ear. And then I had to watch her move away from me down the concourse, her blond pony-tail bobbing over her backpack. I kept her in view until she disappeared into the mass of travellers entering the maw of the customs gate, aware that half of my life was leaving me.

At Heathrow, Philip King and I parted company at the arrivals gate with a swopping of cards. As I made my way back from Whitstable where Aunt Grace's remains had finally come to rest, I considered my trip. It was clear that Philip was not in the most stable frame of mind, at least, not by night. In the single night we'd spent at the hotel in Singapore, he'd violently awoken every few hours with screaming or moaning. On the plane itself, he had tried not to sleep at all, and had asked me to keep him as wakeful as possible, so I rode shotgun on him to the detriment of my own rest. It seemed the least I could do, after his paying for my flight and for the upgrade that he had somehow wrangled with his air miles. I wondered how he'd get on at his interview and whether he would be able to stay awake for it.

§§

I was welcomed back at the Beacon with an affection that made me truly feel they had all missed me. Wendy made all my favourite dishes, while Gillespie donned his kilt, honouring me with a round of airs and reels because I had so unfortunately missed Burn's Night the week previously. I wasn't sorry to have missed the haggis, I'm afraid to say. After supper, Ash gave me one of his deep looks and hauled me off into the sanctuary, 'For the good of your health.'

The sanctuary was accessible only through Ash's room. It formed the heart of the house, which had originally been the local manor in the 13th century, before several alterations and Victorian improvements. It was the only room that revealed the original core of the medieval structure, having undoubtedly once been the manor's private chapel. Traces of medieval wall paintings remained, and had been gently restored when the Tudor whitewash finally flaked off during Melanie's time. An angel, whom Ash identified as Raphael, by the fish under its hand, stood on the southern wall, while opposite was a female saint, insufficiently restored to be unidentifiable — though Ash guessed she was St. Margaret of Antioch, since there was a local legend about a dragon attached to Hartworth Beacon, and a mention in a medieval pipe roll about a St. Margaret's Chapel here. She was surrounded by dark red cinquefoils, which must once have covered the chapel walls. Her dragon — if so it was — had been so subdued by Reformer's whitewash that it could have been a large dog.

Inside the sanctuary, sound fell away entirely. There was little to distract you. One trefoil-headed window let in the only natural light, and the brightest focus was a hanging oil lamp of silver, set with blue glass. Its twinkling light illuminated a horseshoe of upright chairs, and what would have once been the altar, where stood a wooden sculpture, called 'Spiral,' by Mark Edal. Its endless curves opened and closed if you contemplated it for long enough.

Sitting with Ash, shoulder to shoulder, in meditation before the shrine, I felt a quietness come upon me. Although myself and others were welcome here, Ash rarely invited me to meditate with him, so I took it as a special sign of his esteem. To be frank, I was glad to feel that companionship again. With his hands resting upon either knee, he could have been some pharaonic statue, intent but unmoving. I attempted to reach an equivalent stillness, but the image of Jane kept intervening. Still, I made up for my lost sleep that night, so it must have done me some good.

The next morning Ash declared me 'still officially away' and gave me till the end of the week to 'help my soul catch up with the long-haul flight.' There was wisdom in his pronouncement, so I took myself out in the still chilly landscape, doing the rounds of my favourite places, sleeping at odd times until the jet-lag subsided, until I felt back on the planet again. I welcomed the chill of early February after the equatorial heat of Singapore. Underneath, I was still wordlessly missing Jane but unable to talk about her to anyone. Fortunately, any inadvertent moroseness on my part was put down to jet-lag and the recovery of my throat.

When it came, Jane's call was answered by Wendy. I was out washing mud from the recent rains off the car, so Gillespie was dispatched to find me. With a solemn, meaningful voice, he poked his head out of the front door, calling, 'There's a young lassie on the phone for you, if you're minded to step in...' I ran past him, snatching up the receiver where it lay. Fond or foolish though it was, my heart was triumphant that she'd remembered me. Yes, she said, Scotland had been marvellous, but perishing cold, and yes, she was coming south in a fortnight. We made an assignation, with me offering to pick her up from the station at Bedminster. Returning to the scullery for another bucket of water, I thought that both Wendy and Gillespie had gone suspiciously quiet. They gallantly said nothing about my many trips to the telephone in the next few days.

But long before Jane arrived, I received another phone call. I was just finishing a session with a guest when Gillespie appeared on the landing, miming a receiver to his ear. I pushed past him and snatched it from Wendy's hand only to be disappointed. The voice at the other end *was* Australian, but male, not female: 'Jack, is that you?'

'Yes?'

'Philip King.... You know you told me about your boss? Well, I think I need to see him now. It's all gone on long enough. Can I come and see him?'

I took his number and arranged for him to come down to the Beacon, since the Harley St. practice was closed for redecoration. Then I went to fill in Ash about the details, such as I knew.

His questions soon revealed that I knew very little, not even the nature of the nightmares, and only a probable cause, not a definitive origin. 'In cases such as this,' Ash said, 'We need to learn where the epicentre of the trouble lies, and any contributory experiences. Surmising and guess-work won't clarify how we need to work. From your account, it seems that our new guest has more than Post Traumatic Stress on his plate. — We'll know more when we see him.'

Philip arrived the next day, having flown in from Geneva. He had the apprehensive look of a schoolboy sent to his headmaster's office, and was shivering, though it was a pleasantly warm day.

He took tea with us and had the tour, taking it all in silently. 'When do we start?' he asked, as we entered Ash's office.

'Raring to go, then?'

'Hardly, but the fewer nights you have me under your roof, I daresay the better. — How many other people are here?'

'No-one at present... Sleep still bad then?'

He nodded.

'So what happened about the London job?'

'They thought I was better suited to Geneva,' was all he would say.

At the sight of the sanctuary, he showed a marked reluctance to leave it, 'I could spend time here.... It's so old, yet it still feels clean.'

I agreed, marking the reference, and led the way to his room, 'I've put you opposite to mine, so I can be on hand in the night,' I said.

Like a horse urged to ride through fire, Philip summoned himself together and resolutely crossed the threshold of his bedroom. It looked onto the front of the house, with a view of the downs. He threw down his case saying, with a degree of impatience, 'Can't we start tonight? Before it gets dark?' He peered out of the front window where the afternoon sun was sliding towards the west. At the end of the lane, a few autumn leaves not yet claimed by Gillespie for the compost heap were whirling in the strengthening wind.

Now, it wasn't the first time that we'd met this response — Wendy kept a batch of plug-in night-lights for those troubled by night terrors — but this was something far stronger. I'd seen how his hand clutched the doorframe, his knuckles white. I assured him that I would ask Ash's advice.

'Bring him to the sanctuary after dinner,' said Ash, putting away art materials in the studio. 'We won't do any formal interview tonight, but I would like to open the door to peace of mind for him and what he carries. — Are you good for a short vigil tonight, Jack?'

I nodded. 'I think that would be a great idea—he's terrified of going to sleep.'

Philip ate his dinner with us, taking the measure of Gillespie's wit and ably rebutting his gibes about the recent catastrophic loss of the Wallabies to the Scottish team in the Rugby International. Wendy stated to the air that she didn't want a rerun of Scotland versus Australia at the table. Philip just grinned. He'd brought some wine from duty free that we sat around and drank for an hour or so, going through to the living room where the after-light of the sun was staining the west red and gold.

Knowing Ash, he was using this time to look Philip over before we had all the facts. How precisely he saw into people's souls was something I never fully understood until that week. I imagined that it was due to his magical training, about which he spoke seldom. He had intimated that such a training included the facing and purging of many unfortunate traits, as well as a summation and recapitulation of innate qualities, before anyone might call himself an initiate. Watching Ash and Philip together, this statement suddenly became transparent to me.

Philip had borne great, even crushing, responsibility that had resulted in the breakdown of his wellbeing. Ash wore his responsibility lightly but masterfully, yet he somehow had resources to call upon that were not available to Philip, who looked as if he was now running empty. If Ash was a driver in control of a team of horses, then Philip was more like a chariot driver whose horses plunged wildly, threatening to divide the chariot itself. After an hour or so of pleasant chat, Ash invited us both up to the sanctuary, 'Just for a short meditation and a blessing ceremony before bed,' he said.

Philip nodded, 'Sure! I'm in your hands, Doc.... I like your way of therapy already!' he smiled.

I noticed that Ash had placed an unlit glass-sided lantern upon the step leading to the altar, and that the sanctuary was redolent of a gloriously aromatic incense that I'd never smelt before. Philip's nostrils flared to breathe it deeply and gratefully into his lungs and—just as I had found when I returned from Singapore—a quietness came upon him.

Ash asked him to sit directly opposite the altar in front of the Spiral sculpture, while I sat to his left and Ash to his right.

Speaking on a tone perfectly modulated for the space, Ash uttered each phrase slowly so that it had time to ripple out and return in the clear acoustic of the uncluttered chapel, 'Be aware of the space we are in: this is a sanctuary in which all creatures of good will are welcome. The light over the shrine symbolizes the Undying Light. The Spiral upon the shrine itself represents the incoming and outgoing tides of life that are under the care of that light: this is the path by which we come into and go out of life, like a great breathing in and breathing out. When you are ready, you can close your eyes, or keep them open, as you like.'

Under the instruction of this welcome, Philip's shoulder relaxed against mine, his powerful hands lying quietly in his lap. Having reassured himself of his surroundings, he closed his eyes, trustful as a child. Ash led us into a deeper and deeper space of quietness, his voice gradually dropping, tone by tone, until it was hard to tell whether the space was around us, or within us. It became the sanctuary within the heart that we could enter, at any time: a replication of the chapel and what it held, that was ever present. I'm afraid I fell asleep at that point, having had a long day.

I became aware again only when Ash began to raise the tone of his voice, little by little so that, like a man who hears someone calling from afar in another room, I resumed my attention and tried to follow that calling. The voice calling me was a thread of gold in the darkness: warm and compelling — yet with no forceful coercion — only a welcome to something that I felt instinctively had always been my own. Something extraordinary had happened or was happening in that moment. Presences were coming and going. As with Jacob and his dream of the angels, they were coming down and passing up a spiral pathway and I felt their accompaniment. It was as though there was an angel on either side of me, supporting me.

'Angel' is just a word for what I experienced. But these were no vapid, consumptive-looking, night-shirted wimps, such as you see in New Age illustrations, but rather mighty presences in whom you sensed the glorious smelting of metals, or great rushing winds, deep and mighty waters. The promise of paradise was in their touch, conferring true peace upon me.

I never wanted the voice nor the wonderful nourishment of that communion to cease, but stop it did. The presences who had tended upon me, melted back, following the spiral way. Only their gift remained behind. And the voice that seemed to come from everywhere in the chapel became once more the distinct voice of Ash, 'The gift that has been given is yours. Allow it to pass into and around your body. Allow it to flow into any part of you where you feel pain or obstruction: it flows into tissue, muscle, flesh, blood, breath and bone, dissolving and unknotting, cleansing and freeing all that is blocked. In place of any obstruction or pain, the gift brings you peace, clarity, nourishment, wisdom.....'

Without rush, and in perfect time, Ash allowed us to experience that flow. Then he stood up and moved to the altar where he took up a taper. Lighting it from the shrine light, he took the flaming taper to the opened lantern on the step, saying, 'Holy light, treasury of souls and illumination of the just, be with us all this night. May this lantern accompany the sleep of Philip King, our guest. Through every darkness, lead him, shepherds of his soul.'

Silent tears were flowing down Philip's face. In that moment, he resembled a great hero who had suffered much, and who was finally receiving the grace and goodness for which he had fought so long.

Ash beckoned me to stand and drew me beside him. With a nod of his head, and holding the lantern out before him, he indicated that we stand before Philip.

'Stretch out your hands, Philip!'

Eyes still closed, he extended his hands and we each took one in ours.

Ash said, in a soft, resonant tone woven with that same fiery, metallic core that the angels had, 'As guardians of the Beacon, I, Richard Ashington and....' he nodded at me. I added, 'And I, Jack Rivers...' Ash continued, 'Vow to stand with you this night as your companions and friends. We will keep watch over your rest and not leave you alone.'

Philip stood and faced us, his hands still in ours. Muscular next to Ash's slenderness, taller by a head than me, he said in wondering tones, 'I never thought to hear such words, never! I am not worthy. Thank you, thank you for your friendship.'

Ash passed the lantern into Philip's hand with, 'Sleep is a blessing. Whatever the night may bring, this lantern lights your way: hold to the gift you were given: it remains with you.'

That night, Ash and I took turns to watch by Philip's side as he slept, taking three hours on and three hours off all that night. It was exactly as before: whenever he entered REM sleep, Philip would soon be screaming. Not to get caught out as before though, this time I remained seated beside the bed, speaking calmly, 'Philip, you are at the Beacon in the south of England. Wherever you are wandering, come back and be aware of the lantern that guides you.' As we changed watch at 3am, I whispered my findings to Ash at the door. When I came back at 6am, to give Ash a couple of hours rest, I found him standing and holding the lantern over Philip's feet.

'How long have you been standing like that?' I whispered.

'Since 4.15,' he replied. 'Don't worry, you really don't need to stand! Just move your chair to the end of the bed and hold the lantern there. The trouble is coming into him from the north.'

Not having a clue what he meant, I dutifully took up my post. 'Should I do anything?'

With a compassionate look at the sleeping man, he breathed, 'Just pray for him, and for the release of all tormented souls!'

Philip finally opened his eyes at 7.30am. The lantern was brighter than the incipient daylight behind the curtains. He blinked at sight of me and sat up, 'Have you been with me all night?'

'Dr. Ashington was here in the middle of the night: I took the first and last watch.'

'No-one's ever done such a thing for me before! — Thanks.'

'How do you feel?'

'Like I usually do when I wake up — glad to be alive... No, that's not true. Better than usual. Though I was still wrestling with my... demons... they weren't getting the better of it, this time. There was help... I was going into bat with a good team!'

After breakfast, Philip was in a better position to deal with a formal session. We convened in Ash's room where we were able to bank up the fire against the deep chill of that February morning.

'We've both been able to witness your sleeping and the nightmares. How long have these been happening?' Ash asked.

Philip took a few breaths, shuffled in his chair, then stood up, reversed the chair and sat, resting his deep chest against the chair back, 'This is more comfortable, if you don't mind.'

'Please be easy — if you need to stand up and walk about, that's fine too,' Ash said.

'I've been getting these nightmares since I left Eastern Bosnia in 1995.'

Ash said, 'Please, if you can, tell us what was the situation you found yourself in. You need only relate the facts, if you wish, just so that we can understand the context in the fullest way.'

Philip began to relate events, in an almost clinical way, like a soldier debriefing to his commander: 'The Serbs were determined to take Srebrenica; Eastern Bosnia was strategic to their ambitions in creating their Serbian Republic. The Dutch UN peacekeeping contingent was responsible for safeguarding the area around it, but it was an impossible task from the start. Dutchbat — the name of UN troops — was unable to maintain the so-called "safe area." They were just overwhelmed by circumstances.

On the ground it was chaotic. The Serbs had already begun their ethnic cleansing of Bosnian Muslims. They bombed and fired houses, separated men and women and took them away – the men to prison and the women... well, you can imagine. In Spring 1993, the UN High Commissioner for Refugees decided to evacuate as many Bosnian Muslims as possible, even though it was seen by the Bosnian government in Sarajavo as colluding with the Serbs' ethnic cleansing. Then the Serbs gave notice that in two days they would take the city if the Bosnians didn't evacuate. They refused to go. But, all this time, still more refugees came flooding into the city, so they starved. God, how they starved! Despite UN airdrops and the pitiful few who broke out to fetch food for their families, they began to die.'

'The UN forces were ordered to liaise between the Bosnian combatants still within the city and with the Serbians enforcing the siege of Srebrenica to create a "demilitarized zone" – but we came off badly against both. There were violated agreements on either side. Our commanders tried to negotiate a humanitarian corridor to get people out. The Serbs overcame the Dutch positions and that was when I was sent to liaise and observe. My grandmother was from Montenegro, so I had some basic Serbo-Croat. By the time I arrived, it was beyond chaos.'

'The Dutch HQ at Potočari was hosting several thousands of refugees, largely women, children and elderly: it just couldn't hold any more. Outside there was raping, execution, dreadful things happening: babies beheaded, young girls raped in front of their parents, boys and men summarily machine gunned. The space behind the HQ had heaps of bodies lying in it. There was fire, smoke, screaming, dying. The things we witnessed and couldn't prevent!' He covered his eyes.

'Negotiating in those circumstances was horrific. Finally, about 25,000 women were bussed out, supposedly to Bosnian-held territory, but we know that some buses never made it. As for the men – they were systematically rounded up by the Serbs, bussed or marched off and massacred, in different places, as became clear later. We'll probably never know the entire course of events.'

Throughout this recital, Ash remained still, listening intently. Now he asked, 'What about yourself?'

'I remained in Bosnia until the Dayton agreement and then I came home, but the nightmares have never stopped.' He said, bitterly, 'Oh, I've done all the "right things" – attended counselling, PTSS meetings for combat survivors... I even took up my uncle's offer of working on his sheep farm, to be out in the wild, but I only managed a few months of that – it was too like being in the army again.'

Ash asked, 'What do you recall about your nightmares? – Are they various? Or do you dream the same scenes over and over?'

Philip got up and went to the window, looking out on the slanting sleet that was blowing from the northeast. 'Sometimes it's like a montage of scenes that I witnessed, but mostly it's things I have no knowledge or recollection of... it's like dreaming the dreams of other people.' He shivered, 'Terrible things.....! When I wake up from them, I try to defend myself and the people undergoing those atrocities....'

He turned, 'You have no idea what it was like, being a UN representative, a peace-keeper to whom vulnerable people looked for help... and being absolutely unable to help them or prevent the carnage that followed. — The reproach in their eyes will live with me to the end of my days.'

'It is next to impossible to stop tribal conflict once the ancestral compulsions are engaged,' Ash observed.

'You can say that! I've relived those days over and over, trying to find a better way it could have been resolved: after so much loss of life, you'd have thought I would have given up. But it still haunts me... I can't find any resolution for them, or for me.'

I asked, 'Is that why you interviewed for a new post at the UN?'

Philip's slow, lopsided grin was bitter, 'Sure thing... I'm committed to informing and opening up lines of dialogue before such conflicts can take hold, which is why I'm part of the UN education programme. I've became a Quaker, so I'll never lift a weapon again... My dad is impatient with me... He doesn't accept that my military service should end just because of some nightmares. It was once all I wanted to be, a soldier, but I know now that path is not for me.' He slumped back into his chair.

It seemed to me to be a very responsible way of dealing with guilt. I asked him, 'When you arrived, you said something in the sanctuary... that it had a sense being clean, despite being old. Do you normally associate age with dirt?'

While I was talking, a rictus of fear locked his pleasant features into a grimace. I halted, since he clearly wasn't hearing a thing, 'What's happening?

It took him a while to formulate the words, 'Just talking about the dreams brought the fear of them back.'

Ash asked, 'Can you tell us what you experience?'

Philip shook himself, as if to rid himself of something unclean, 'I just have this overwhelming sense of something ancient, almost like a smell that won't leave me... It comes in the dreams... Look, can we go outside? I feel like I don't want to pollute this lovely place...' He stood and paced about the room.

Ash and I looked at each other. Outside, the sleet was now falling more heavily as snow, and Hartworth Beacon was losing its outline as it settled, with very little green showing now. The temperature had plummeted. That Philip wanted to run away from what plagued him into such weather revealed the severity of his distress.

Ash rose and fetched the lantern from Philip's bedroom and lit it, placing it in front of him on a small table. 'Philip, you are at a point of change and of help. The pollution that you experience is not yours—it belongs to others, I believe. Let your words be heard now.'

Looking between us and back at the light, Philip spoke to the lantern in a low monotone, 'The dream that comes again and again starts with men being marched away. I see them go and I can't stop them. There are boys with them, and they turn and look at me. They go trusting.... and they will never come back, I know.' His voice trembled, 'Then there is killing, maiming, terror, slaughter. Their cries are coming to me and the ancient smell begins, deep at the back of my nose, like a memory. There is wailing, women's wailing, that goes right into my belly. My whole middle is open and the men and boys are marching through me, and the killing is still happening....'

To me, it sounded very like what Philip himself had witnessed or experienced, but he hadn't finished.

'Then it stops, and I am in the fields working. It is peaceful, I am glad and with my family and neighbours. Life is good. Then mounted men are coming, soldiers coming down through the mountain passes—hundreds of them. We try to flee, but they are on our heels. They hack down the aged, chopping them into bits. They catch the priest, and hang him up by his wrists and ankles. He is shot full of javelins and arrows.'

I caught Ash raising an eyebrow at this point. Something was happening in the room that was strangely familiar to me. I reached into my memory for it. Back last autumn, when I walked down to his farm to fetch some honey and eggs for Wendy, I'd witnessed Farmer Jelley de-hairing a pig that he'd slaughtered. The massive animal lay starkly-dead on a trestle in the yard and Ted was going over it with a blowtorch, while Micky followed with a scraper. I had the uncanny feeling that here Philip's words were being consumed by the lantern, burned off, just like the hairs on that pig's back.

'The soldiers rape the older women and kill them, but they keep the younger ones and round them up. The smell is overwhelming and every new atrocity is shown to me in detail, over and over......' Philip hunched over his knees, as if he was about to be sick, 'I'm sorry, I can't go on.'

Ash finally took him outside into the snow while I went to get some cocoa with a slug of brandy in it for Philip. I watched as he stood in the driving blizzard of snow that was heaping up around him, standing face into the wind—as if he were 'snow bathing.' He made no attempt to wipe the snow from his face, just exposed himself to its onslaught, as if it might cleanse him of the terror that came in the night.

Ash came in the back door, rubbing his hands and holding them over the Aga where the milk was coming to the boil. He supped the cocoa gratefully.

'Will he be alright out there?' I asked.

'Let him stay as long as he needs – he'll come in when he's ready.... '

'But what about Eastern Bosnia?'

'Ah! You caught the reference?... As far as I know, no-one fought the recent Balkan war with javelins or arrows. No, I think we are looking at something far older.'

'Is it some kind of incarnational memory?' I asked cautiously. I'd seen enough of Ash's work to recognize some of its features here.

'No! In this case, I think we have an intrusion of historical trauma that was activated by Philip's identification with recent events. There may well be an ancestral component to this.'

'What will you do?' I asked.

At that point Wendy came into the kitchen, expostulating harshly with Ash, 'Are you going to let that poor man stand out there much longer? I've just sent Gillespie up to mend the fire upstairs: he said you'd let it virtually burn right down.'

Ash affected a chastened look. Flinging his scarf about his throat, he said, 'Give me that mug and I'll take it out to him, and see if he'll come in now.'

Wendy thrust it into his hands with a massive tutting. I explained to her while Ash was outside, but she was still adamant, 'Well, it's hardly going to help things if the poor man comes down with pneumonia as well!' And she flounced into the scullery to put more food down for Cinnamon as she was weaving and meowing round her feet, in protest at the strange white stuff falling outside.

Philip came back in with Ash, leaning heavily on his arm, 'Sorry about that. I came over strange in all that snow.' It was evident that he could barely keep his eyes open. Peppered with snow like a polar explorer who'd over-gone his strength, he slumped at the kitchen table, and began to lay his head upon his arms.

Ash urged him to his feet, 'Not here, Philip. Wendy needs to work in here.' He nodded at me to help him, 'Let's get you into bed.'

Together we managed, with some difficulty, to get him upstairs and onto his bed. It was like walking a drunken man, for he couldn't coordinate his limbs at all. We got his top coat off and covered him with a blanket. His breathing worried me, for it was becoming stertorous. But even while I felt his pulse, it slowed, becoming the normal breathing of a very heavy sleeper who snores. On no occasion had I witnessed him enter so deep a sleep.

We hardly needed to tiptoe out, for he was utterly asleep. Retiring to Ash's room, we found Wendy had brought us fresh cups of cocoa and left them in front of a roaring fire. Companionably we drank.

'Shouldn't one of us stay with him?'

'Presently, perhaps,' said Ash. 'I'll take the first watch for a little, but I've a feeling his recitation has given him peace for a while—that and the snow. —I've not seen anyone claimed by the snow that speedily before. It should give him some depth of sleep, during which we can work.'

I drained the last thick mouthful of cocoa and wiped my mouth, 'You spoke of some historic trauma—but you don't mean within his experience, do you?'

Ash stood with his hands on the mantle-piece, allowing the fire to thaw his limbs, 'No. My sense is that previous trauma underlies the recent one. Bosnia was overrun by the Ottomans in the 15th century—it's one of the reasons that so many of the population were Muslim in the last conflict: Christians converted to reap the benefits of the regime change—the ones who didn't had it harder. The initial conquest was about as messy then as it was recently, I imagine.' He turned, 'Tell me, Jack, what distinctive feature did you note in his nightmares?'

The room seemed dimmer as the blizzard blotted out the sky. Only the eerie luminance of the snow now covering Hartworth Beacon gave it light. I switched on the lamp, 'The sense of smell that comes with the imagery... as soon as he smells that, he hears women wailing... he spoke about it emanating from the very back of his nose.'

'And?' I had the feeling Ash was leading the witness, but I complied with, 'Well, we know that smell and memory are deeply connected—I seem to remember some recent research about it?'

'Precisely! Smell triggers memory—usually autobiographical memory, like Proust's Madeleine, only instead of lime-flower tea, it is a smell of mortality that lingers. I knew one post-traumatic stress sufferer who fought in Vietnam. He couldn't abide the odour of diesel, as he associated it with death. He would only have to drive behind a vehicle exuding diesel fumes and his symptoms would recur. —There is something in Philip's own recollection that links not only to his terrible experiences in the war, but also to something that happened in the same region hundreds of years earlier—which is a memory he cannot have personally experienced.'

'So you think there's something ancestral that's been triggered?'

'Yes, but there is another common factor that links everything together. I'm not sure even Philip is conscious of that, though.'

I remembered something, 'Last night you said that something was flowing into him from the north — that was why you were holding the lantern between it and him. What was that?'

Ash turned his face full to mine, 'The dead who have no rest, for whom these events are still happening. They are the ones for whom we must work now.'

'But how?' I asked, bewildered, as we now were far out of my known territory of healing. 'I thought we dealt with the living here!'

Ash smiled warmly, 'And so we do, dear friend! But the dead are the ones who need our help today.'

By the time it got dark, Philip was still sleeping and no attempt at waking him was having effect. Having established that he was sleeping the sleep of relief, Ash said to leave him, for as long as was necessary. People talk about 'a healing sleep', but that was a mighty one indeed. Philip continued to sleep all through that night and into the next day. We took turns to monitor him, feeling his pulse and noting his breathing. None of us detected any REM sleep whatever, meaning that he was dream-free and probably enjoying the deepest sleep he had had in years.

Ash came to me after lunch, by which point we were effectively snowed in until the thaw came or until the tractor made it down our lane. It had snowed all night and the utter stillness of the countryside around the Beacon was total. It was as well that we had no other guests staying. It was like being in a folk story only instead of Sleeping Beauty, we had Philip.

'I've made up my mind,' Ash said. "There is no better time than now. We will work while he is still sleep.'

'What do you want me to do?'

'Witness and pray!'

Ash also asked Wendy and Gillespie to join us. He briefed us in his room, 'What I'm going to do is enable what is troubling Philip to finally leave him, but I need your help. Jack is going to assist me, but I need you both to sing, as we need a continuous road of song.'

'Not "Scots Wha Hae," then?' Gillespie asked, hopefully.

'Something like it, but not an exhortation to battle — more of a leading home *after* the battle... for those who've died.'

The McLeans were great folk enthusiasts and both fine singers in their own right. After thinking a bit, Wendy said, 'Something like *Sacred Companions*?' She sang a few bars: it was a song that called upon strong ancestral help, in which the tune flowed like water.

Ash nodded, 'That's perfect: don't worry about the words of it so much. We just need the tune to keep going — sometimes it might need to go slower or quieter, and sometimes louder and more quickly... You'll get the notion of it.' He turned to me, 'Jack, I want you to witness with all your senses... I know you can, but I want to enhance this perception, if you will permit me... It may not be a pretty sight, but I want you to be the full witness for Philip's sake, so you can tell him what happened.'

'I'll do all I can to help,' I said, 'but don't make me sing, or the poor chap will have a terrible shock. What do I need to do?'

'Come into the sanctuary for a moment.'

I followed Ash inside where he lit some of the fragrant incense that we'd had the night we blessed Philip. 'What is that stuff?' I asked, 'It makes my whole head feel somewhere else.'

'"Byzantium"', said Ash, giving me a thorough incensing with the thurible, as practiced as any deacon. 'It comes from a Greek Orthodox Monastery that mixes it for me. Now, just breathe it in.'

Soon I was clad in a cloud of fragrant smoke that was making me feel quite inebriated, but not in an uncontrolled way. Rather, I experienced an uplifted spirit of clarity. 'Now Jack, I want you to crouch on your haunches for a moment.'

I obligingly hunkered down, rather too fast, for I felt suddenly giddy. Ash leant over me, putting one hand upon the top of my head and the other under my lifted heels. Saying some words in a language I couldn't fathom, he pressed firmly for a moment, releasing me with, 'You can stand up now.'

As I stood up, something odd had happened to me. Just watching Ash hang the thurible on its hook, I was suddenly aware of trails of light—it was like watching the slowed down frames of a video or a vapour trail forming in the sky. At first I thought these trails seemed to be made by movement, but I then realised that, when he was still, Ash was indeed hung with a kind of starry cape that floated around him in a golden mass. I was aware also of something that stood behind him, overshadowing him and realized that it had the same signature as the angel that was depicted upon the wall behind him, only this was a living presence that was resonant with him. Although I knew nothing of these things, I guessed that I was seeing Ash's aura.

He peered into my eyes with a knowing smile, 'I think that is working, yes?'

I nodded wordlessly, as he invited the McLeans into the sanctuary.

We stood together as Ash faced the shrine, holding up his hands to pray, 'Wise Ones and Holy Ones, help us to stand in a place of support for our friend. Philip. In the stillness of eternity may we work together to loose the spell of the ancient story in which he is entangled. May the Soul-Shepherd lead all who are frozen in pain, caught in the shackles of time and place, to a place of freedom, that they may rest in peace.

Gillespie gave a loud, 'Amen,' to the prayer. But I was still too stunned by the witness of my senses, which seemed to have acquired the attributes of a souped-up engine. The colours, impressions, and deepening of my five senses were overwhelming, and I was in awe. Everyone had their own cloak of stars about their body, it seemed. Wendy's was arrayed like many-petalled flowers in an envelope of spring green. Gillespie's was more tightly furled but with the dark sheen of holly. People were like plants in a garden, I remembered thinking.

We went into Philip's room, where Ash and Gillespie pulled the bed away from the wall, so that I could sit beside it. The room received its own censing and the lantern was placed over the bed-head on the windowsill. Taking up the post to the North at the bed's foot, with the McLeans to the other side of the room, Ash began to ward the room, turning about it and leaving a doorway in the North. As he did so, the presence that overshadowed him seemed to float wider, encompassing the whole room, so that I forgot about it until later. Then Ash made long sweeping passes over Philip's sleeping body: his own star cape was tighter to his body, and very thin, threaded with an angry red in places, as if someone had scribbled upon it. As Ash's hands swept to and fro, I was aware of the breach in Philip's star-cape over his torso, stretching between diaphragm and abdomen. It gaped raggedly like a cavernous hole that had been blown open by explosion. I could sense how it ached, hollow and consuming at the same time.

Adjusting my newly acquired vision, I was aware of a succession of movement passing from the North, just as Ash had said, and coming down into and through Philip in an unending procession. It was a sorry crowd of what looked like refugees, running away from what followed them: children, men and women, the old, the young—despairing and half-mad with terror, they kept coming.

Ash signalled to the McLeans and Wendy began to sing softly, the words barely audible:

'You are gathering from the times before,
Companions of the brave,
Assembling on the plains of history.
And the spirits gleam within your eyes
To show us all the way,
Your feet in shoes of bronze
From oceans far.'

Gillespie's beautiful tenor joined in, weaving in and out of Wendy's refrain. It seemed even the music had shape and pattern that were visible to me, as they sang:

Sacred companions,
Shoal on this shore.
Bring us the beauty,
That we still adore.
Dance for the daylight
Sing for the shore,
Keep bright the loving
And we'll dance once more.'

The words were so at odds with what was happening, but I began to be aware that they were forming another kind of scene at the other end of that long, sorry procession. At the top of the bed, near the lantern, different kinds of what I guessed were ancestors were gathering: this lot, however, were calm, imperturbable, efficient, resourceful and compassionate. Immensely ancient and wise, they stood waiting, hospitably. Philip's sleeping body seemed to become more solid as the music unfolded.

Ash signalled to the McLeans to sing more softly. Addressing the procession of refugees, he said in a deep resonant tone, 'Wanderers and travellers, attend and hear! The pain you have known came from the past and has ended now. Time has become eternity. From all sights and sounds, from all smells and tastes, from all sensations you are set free. Discover the strength of your innermost soul, which is free to pass on. Your soul is inviolate. Your soul is set free from your soul-shrine.'

The procession seemed to halt and rest for a moment. Some among them began to rise from out of Philip's body, just as diving birds do from out of the sea, flying up easily and sweetly towards the lantern, where the calm ancestors awaited and received them. But others did not and continued their flight from terror straight into Philip's body. Wendy sang on, with Gillespie joining the refrain,

'Your sea-washed bodies come to praise
The ancient memories' store,
Hidden deep within the sands beyond the bay.
You're still shining out the story,
Blessings of the Ever-Young,

Wine for all to drink,
For we who follow on.

Sacred companions,
Gathering here.
Show us horizons
Where we shall not fear.
Unfurl the sail now,
Chart us the star,
Give us a way now
That we can sail far.'

Philip began to surface within his sleep: I could tell from his star cape which grew more intense in hue — the parts that were light grew lighter and the angry red threading it through throbbed even redder still. I could sense the need for vengeance, restitution and the need to punish coming off the procession that remained hell-bent on passing into the cavern that gaped in his middle. But Ash was also aware of it, and spoke once again, making a gesture that seemed to open the light of the lantern into a wider pathway. 'All you wanderers who still behold what was, behold the Shepherd of Souls: follow and find a place of rest, passing on towards the road that leads to your home. Your soul is set free from your soul-shrine. The nightmare ends and the dawn arises.'

Coming down from the light was an awesome, mighty presence that looked like a tree giant to my vision, taller than the mightiest Cedars of Lebanon, noble and kind at the same time, striding down to meet them. With him, coming out like hosts to meet their guests were other presences, lesser in stature than the Shepherd of Souls, but no less in love than the welcoming ancestors who stood waiting. These presences, whose forms were loosely formed — more densenesses of coloured light than people — flowed towards the ones in the procession of refugees still hovering between going down into the cavern or towards the lantern.

Without any coercion, but with infinite patience, these loving presences accompanied the fleeing ones who still havered about which way to go. This left only those who were unable to see anything but vengeance and anger, guilt and the extremity of pain. In an awful sequence that I will not set down here, I also perceived the cause of their aggression and mental turmoil knowing that, had I or any of mine suffered as these people had suffered, I too would have succumbed to the thought of the terrible retributions that they planned.

With these determined, vengeful ones, the Shepherd of Souls simply reached down and set them in his mighty branches. They looked surprised as the giant tree-being bore them away in his arms, placing them into the cleansing waters that were nearby, where the pain, fear and need for vengeance was washed away

Looking back to the north, I could see no more wanderers approaching. The way was clear as Wendy sang,

'Through the tides of time the waters flow,
Seasons dance their yearly round,
Ancient stories blend with new ones every day;
But the sacred inspirations
From the heart of all we've known,
Guide the paths our children tread
When we are gone.

Sacred companions,
Loved from before,
Welcome you show us
When we learn your lore:
Make bright our hearts now,
Teach us the song,
Play for our dancing,
That souls may be strong.'

Ash was working over Philip directly, like a surgeon, only his hands were his instruments. About him, I was aware again of the one who had overshadowed him earlier, aware that the presence was working through Ash, using his hands and voice. With great wafts of incense Ash cleansed the gaping cavern that was still open in the star-cape. The incense was clearing and erasing the angry red threads and the light of the star-cape itself was beginning to colour, just as the earth is touched by the dawn. Ash seemed to be combing through Philip's star cape with his fingers and flinging away the uncleanness that he found there. Then he began closing up the cavern and sealed it with an anointing whose sigil I could clearly see, as if it had been surgical sutures made of electric light. I had never witnessed such a thing before.

Philip's breathing rate increased as he drew nearer to waking. Wendy continued to quietly sing the tune over and over, with Gillespie joining the refrain, but wordlessly now. It was clear that the work was almost over. The lantern burned on and Ash finally stood still.

The four of us came together naturally around the bed, to clasp hands briefly, our work done. As I extended my hands, I was aware that I too had a cloak of stars—a green shimmer that had sparkles of gold within it. Wonderingly, I looked into the eyes of my friends: Wendy's shimmering with tears, Gillespie's solemn as a judge, Ash's calm and clear. To me they were kindred, closer than my blood family in that moment.

Ash unsealed the room and the presence that had overshadowed it drew back towards and behind him again. 'Please stay here for a bit, will you,' he said to the McLeans. He drew me back in the sanctuary, and reversed the procedure he had done earlier. As the pressure of his hands withdrew, this time my senses were diminished. From being a sports engine with the ability to rove at speed, I was reduced to being an ordinary roadster again.

'All right?' he asked, as the vision fled.

'I cannot begin to say....' I said, in wonder. 'Ash, is that what *you* see all the time?' My respect for him had risen considerably that afternoon.

'Only when I need to... fortunately. But I do have friends who can never rest from such sights... They are gifted with a *an dha shealladh*—"the two seeing at once," as the Gaelic second-sight is called. It's a challenge. —No, I am glad not to have my vision open all the time.'

'I can well believe that's what would send some people mad!—No, I'm really alright. I just feel kind of... stupidly diminished.'

'Never that, Jack!'

I did not ask him about what had stood and worked through him. I did not have the words to ask. Whatever it was, clearly it was part of some greater presence that claimed him in service, though I know now that it was what made the Beacon so special, what welcomed everyone who came for healing and sanctuary.

Back in the bedroom, Wendy and Gillespie had moved the bed back into position against the wall. Philip stirred properly now and was opening his eyes, coming up out of the deepest sleep, stretching. He obviously had momentarily forgotten where he was, but at the sight of the lantern over his bed and the four of us gathered in his room, he knew.

His normally rugged face was innocent as a child's, looking to us for enlightenment, 'Is everything alright?'

I came and sat beside him, 'Everything's fine, Philip. We just came to welcome you back.'

He sat up, puzzled, and then saw the clock. 'How long have I been asleep?'

Wendy said, 'About 26 hours.'

Philip looked stunned, 'How is that possible?... Ah, now I remember! I was out in the snow, wasn't I?... I came over so sleepy.'

'It was the snow that helped you sleep,' said Ash. 'How do you feel?

'Starving!'

Wendy went to get coffee and belated breakfast for him while Gillespie shook Philip's hand, 'Always good to sing for an appreciate audience!' and stomped off without another word, to Philip's puzzlement. We explained what had passed that afternoon.

The next day, I related to Philip what I'd experienced with my temporary vision, to which he listened with growing amazement.

'But why did I get the historical memory as well? I can well understand why I got the scenes from the recent war,' he appealed to Ash.

'You were stationed there over the most intense period when ancestral memory was stimulated by the fresh resonance of conflict,' Ash said. 'You had your own ancestral connection with that part of the world, of course. The only thing that we didn't know was the trigger that joined it all together. Tell me, what about the smell that you reported? What was the smell of?'

Philip's smile vanished, 'Burning flesh.' He looked nauseous again. 'The smell of burning bodies is one you don't ever forget.'

Ash gave Philip one of his side-ways over the head looks and asked, 'Tell me... when you were young, did you ever smell anything like it?'

That this was the most pertinent question yet was evident from Philip's stillness, 'Well, it's not exactly in my own recollection, but something happened when I was a toddler – my mother's related it so often, it's like my own memory, but it cannot really be, I was too young.'

'Was it something at which you were present?' Ash asked, steepling his fingers to his chest.

'Yes, I suppose I was. My mother and sister and I were caught up in a bush fire where we lived in Queensland. It swept in at night and we only just escaped.'

'Did anyone die in the fire?'

'No, it was miraculous really, mother said. She got us into the truck and drove us away, while the staff rode the horses to safety.'

'But someone else died?' Ash persisted.

Philip searched his recollection, 'She said only Bingo died. The dog.... oh my God! It was the dog!' He rushed up to throw open the window, taking great gulps of cold air into his lungs.

He stuttered out the words, 'The dog was chained up and no-one could get to him. I remember the wailing and crying....' And he wept for the dog he had forgotten, howling like a child.

I sat beside him on the ground as he cried, until he fell quiet. He looked up at Ash with tear-streaked face, 'How did you know?'

'I only knew that the sound and smell were somehow connected, that they were the trigger. The chaos in Eastern Bosnia and the ancestral memory of what happened before were linked by the smell. That was what triggered memory and helped other memories replay.'

'So was I remembering something that ancestors of mine experienced?'

'I believe so.'

Philip rose unsteadily with my help. He clutched my arm, 'You cannot know what a gift you've given to me today. To have your support when I was so locked in with this.'

To Ash he said, 'Dr. Ashington, I think you've exorcised me — yesterday and today! The dead can rest and now I can work with a will, without fear.'

For the rest of his short stay, Philip slept normally, without any nightmares.

We said goodbye to two Australians that week. First, Philip, who left on the day that I brought Jane to the Beacon, and then Jane herself who went home a few days later, to my great sorrow, returning to the job she loved. The snow had thawed in all places but the north-facing slopes of the downs, and the grass was shining in the brisk, February sunlight.

'I've been before, but I never get over how very green it is in England,' Jane said, looking out on the incomparable view, as I loaded her backpack into the car. 'It's a shade of colour we don't see so often in the Arnheim Land — well at least, not in the summer.' She turned, saying, 'Why don't you come and see where I work, Jack?'

I took her in my arms, 'When I think of the miles between us, I can't imagine how to be without you.' I kissed her and promised to visit when I next got leave. On returning from Gatwick, I went to check in with Ash on our new intake of guests, to distract myself from the increasing distance between myself and Jane.

As we discussed their needs, we caught the clear tenor of Gillespie coming up from the garden. Ash, pen poised over his notes, suddenly smiled as he identified it, 'Scots Wha Hae, I think?'

Sure enough, coming up from the woodshed, I could hear the words,

'By oppression's woes and pains!
By your sons in servile chains!
We will drain our dearest veins,
    But they shall be free!'

Scots, wha hae wi' Wallace bled,
Scots, wham Bruce has aften led;
Welcome to your gory bed,
    Or to victory!'

And Wendy's voice answering from the kitchen door, 'Oh, put a sock in it, you old battle-axe, you! Wallace and Bruce have been in their long beds these many years! Did nobody tell you?'

Ash nodded, 'A case of letting the dead bury the dead, clearly!'

Case 9: The Earth Djinn

In the world according to Ash, there were more beings than humans and animals in it, for he recognized many different otherworldly beings as well — and I don't just mean angels. Now, he was not what you would strictly call a visiting soul-doctor, usually keeping his practice between Harley Street and the Beacon; he would rarely step out of this routine unless a case proved challenging. The call that he took that day was one of those cases.

It was a rainy Autumn day when Ash thrust his head out of his consulting room just as I was going off to the local deli for sandwiches, saying, 'Please can you get the car ready? We're going to Birmingham this afternoon.'

'What about the client we were seeing at 2pm?' I protested.

'She cancelled today as her child was sick, so we've moved her to Thursday.'

'Can't this new client come in, then?'

Ash looked gravely at the framed surah from the Qur'an on his desk, 'This is one where the mountain has to go to Mohammed.'

He would say no more until we were stuck in a queue in the Great North Road to get onto the Marylebone Road and ultimately to the M40, 'His name is Adnan Jalbani. He's a Pakistani legal student at the Birmingham Law School, or he was until the present trouble stopped him moving about.'

'Has he had some injury, then?' fully expecting to hear that we were heading for a hospital.

'No, he's completely unable to move more than a mile from his home.'

'Agoraphobia, then?'

'No, I think it's more likely he's probably had an earth djinn cast at him.'

I removed the beef and tomato sandwich from my lips. 'A what?'

'An earth djinn. But I need to see the state of affairs for myself.'

'Do you mean *djinn* as in "genie of the lamp?"' I enquired, in tones bordering on ridicule.

'Precisely, although without the Arabian Nights overtones!' Ash grinned. 'Think of the djinn as elementals — the beings that live in the earth, water, fire and air. — He's a Muslim, of course, but a very rational young man who's keen to keep up his Western veneer, despite his fear.'

'What's there to be frightened of? What are his symptoms?'

'He's been unable to travel further than a mile from his home since about one and half months ago.'

I struggled to digest or comprehend this assertion, 'And what happens if he tries?'

Caitlín Matthews

'Well, that's the trouble. He begins to gag as if he's been strangled. His limbs become heavy, and he's unable to move.'

'Still sounds like a traumatic agoraphobia to me...' I resumed my lunch.

'That *would* be easier to treat, it's true! Unfortunately, the symptoms point to other causation. Last week, he tried to get on a bus leaving the area and in desperation even took a taxi, but he was so violently ill that the driver had to stop and try to revive him at the roadside.'

We finally made it onto West Way, squeezing ourselves into the line stretching as far as the eye could see.

I asked, 'What are his home circumstances?'

'Ah-ha! A very good question indeed! Just what I want to learn.'

I sat and contemplated the arterial regions of West London as we jerked between one set of traffic lights and the next.

'You say that someone *cast* an earth djinn on him. It sounds like something from that M.R. James story, the *Casting of the Runes*.' I had rather enjoyed the black and white film of the same name where a black magician passes some runes on a slip of paper to his victims who subsequently die horribly, pursued by some monstrous spirit. The film had stayed in my mind largely due to the sound effects, though I had recently learned, to my chagrin, that these had been made by dint of someone twisting a cotton reel on some twine. I added, 'Sometimes things are less impressive when you see them for what they are.'

Ash leant back waiting as he hit the handbrake yet again, 'I would agree, but, it is almost certainly some kind of spell, and fear is a terrible thing.'

Despite the number of cases I had seen through Ash's eyes, I still had my doubts: 'You don't seriously believe in such things, surely?'

'Just because we live in the innocent and uncomprehending West, doesn't mean to say that the magical practices of most of the world can't affect us here. In many countries, envy and ill-will result in the aggrieved party going to a sorcerer to pay for a spell or curse to be cast upon the unfortunate victim.'

I made a disgusted sound, 'People *pay* to have spells cast? — I can't believe such a thing.'

Ash compressed his lips and overtook a heavily laden vehicle, 'Humour me, Jack. Can you not recall a person who once made your life seem hellish?'

Immediately, Miles Knighton, administrative head of department at Leeds Infirmary, came to mind without much bidding: an obnoxious fellow with a fine conceit of himself who made everyone leap about, change shift and do every inconvenient thing that can make life or work impossible.

'I can indeed!' I told Ash all about the time Knighton cancelled all Christmas leave after it had been agreed upon and booked in. 'Most of us would have liked to make a wax effigy of him and melt it over a slow fire, I can tell you.'

'You see!' said Ash, turning up his open hand, 'A perfect example of human nature at work... Now, transfer that feeling to a culture where there are experts who have the wax, the pins and the fire, who can be hired at will, and you have precisely the kind of situation that poor Jalbani is suffering.'

I masticated the rest of my sandwich in chastened silence.

Finally, as we reached Acton, Ash asked me, 'So, what ran through your head at the time when you were suffering from the influence of Miles Knighton?'

'I wished he would drop dead — we all did! He was an insufferable fellow.'

As Ash shot me a glance, I backed off, 'Well, of course I didn't *really* want him to drop dead, just for him to get off my case.'

'And what effect do you think those thoughts might have had?' Ash inquired, ever so politely.

Scornfully, I considered it, 'Well, Knighton's hide was as impervious as a water buffalo's. Not much, I'd have guessed. Are you going to tell me I should have been praying for Miles, the pain in the arse?'

'Perhaps not. In any case, your uncoordinated, group resentment probably had very little effect, beyond boosting his own sense of power and helping to further relish your victimization, but what if your whole department had gone in a body and paid for his demise or suffering? What effect might that have had?'

'God knows! I wouldn't even know where to go to get such a thing done in Leeds, which is where the hospital was.'

'Indeed! I dare say there is more goes on there than people know, as most services are available if you look hard enough — a disaffected Wiccan or cash-strapped Chaos Magician perhaps — but if you were in Caracas, New Orleans, Singapore, Lagos or Akrotiri, you probably could just walk in and pay someone over the counter.'

'And then what? Plagues of boils, demons popping out of cupboards, loss of erectile function?'

'Possibly all three, depending on what you ordered, and who was doing the spell. However, it does take sustained malice to throw a spell or a curse and maintain it, which is why we are looking at a causation nearer the victim, rather than further away. Neighbourly disputes, partners in business, manipulative family members... that sort of thing. Those we see and live with, those whom we resent daily, can work themselves up into quite a spiral of malice.'

Rendered speechless in the face of his certainty, I spent the rest of the journey peering through the encroaching mizzle in a bemused stupor.

You reach Birmingham by a series of long arterial roads, through multiple red brick suburbs or their leafier conurbations. The city wasn't looking its very best as finally we reached Balsall Heath and parked: the mizzle had turned to dirty rain. We were to meet our client in a local Wimpy Bar, as that was the only convenient public place near him that he could reach, and he didn't want us visiting him at his house.

Since they banned smoking, Wimpy hasn't really been the same. At least the smoke used to mask the grease of that much frying. The place was nearly empty except for a couple of elderly men marking up the racing papers and some students playing a game of portable chess. Over in the darkest corner of the place, near the toilet door, under an intermittently faulty light, a solitary young man huddled.

Jalbani sat, head towards the wall, with his jacket pulled tight about him, though it was a fuggy day for October. His body language reminded me of many a poor youth who had landed in the lock-up for the night after experimenting with alcohol or more damaging substances that sent behaviour hay-wire. The difference was only in the demeanour and cleanliness of the young man, but I noted a much deeper withdrawal, as if his eyes looked out of a prison.

When he stood up to greet us, you could see how pathetically thin he was. Asian skin tone is like café au lait, but his was more like Wimpy coffee, ashen pale and insipid, 'Dr. Ashington? Dr. Rivers? Thank you so very much for coming. Please sit down. Can I get you some coffee?' His toneless voice was a mere fragment of leaf torn from its branch.

Over two pale, bitter coffees, Ash interviewed him. 'To what do you contribute your condition, Mr. Jalbani? What do you feel is going on?'

His eyes dropped evasively and, even to my ears, what he said sounded like pure rationalization, 'I have many inconveniences arising. I am a student of law and I want to be worthy of my father's trust. He has paid for me to be here, but I am unable to attend college due to this trouble. I am a man of science, you understand. I support Western values and clarity of mind. Never have such things happened to me. I refute them utterly!' He pushed both hands away from him, in a show of resistance. 'I have been studying very hard... and my mind has lost its equity,' he ended, pathetically.

Ash nodded encouragingly, 'We are also men of science, Mr. Jalbani, but we also meet things that Western science does not take into account... You told me on the phone that you are unable to move further than a mile's radius of your home? Now, much study doesn't make such things happen. Do you know the expression, "no smoke without fire?" Such things have a cause somewhere. Dr.

Rivers and myself look at these happenings forensically in order to understand and cure them.'

Jalbani's pallid face opened a crack at the word 'cure' but then he shook his head, eyes closed, 'It is hopeless.'

Ash persisted, pitching his voice smoothly to that tone that invites confidence, 'So what do *you* think is going on? — If you were at home in Lahore right now, what would you immediately think of?'

This line of questioning normally elicits interesting results, since the patient is rarely ever asked such a thing by the expert practitioner, who thinks he should know, believing the patient to be entirely ignorant about his condition. But Ash's way, which I have since adopted with great success, reassures the patient that his own experience is indeed valued.

Finally, after a lot more rationalization, Jalbani admitted, 'If I were home, I would think that one of my father's enemies has been to an *amil* who has cast a spell on me.'

Ash was clearly delighted with this answer, though I had no idea what an *amil* was. It was only as he went on, that I got a notion. Ash posed the empirical question, 'Tell us about the things you've been experiencing, apart from the inability to travel far.'

The dry words pattered out of him in one shameful rush, 'A smoky kind of thing started appearing in my room and touching me... I was shaken while I was asleep... then the thing opened my door and went away. It made me very frightened to lie down again.' He rolled his eyes with fear, 'When I went to go into the front room, I often see strings with knots in the doorway and in other places in the house. I would swear that sometimes it looks like the knots were put into the bricks of the house outside the porch. I tried pulling out as much of it as I could. I recited the holy *Qu'ran* and burned the strings.' By now he was shaking, so I laid a hand upon his arm. He put his hand upon mine and closed his eyes, drawing comfort from me.

Ash nodded, sagely, 'I understand! — Have any of your personal things been tampered with as well?'

Jalbani looked mulish. Reluctantly he admitted, 'Yes, in my indoors shoes — little strips of paper started to appear under the insole.'

'What was on them?'

'Writings that made no sense.' He said quickly and dismissively.

'Have you kept any of them at all?'

'I destroyed them.' Which was a shame, I thought, as I would have liked to have seen these. The situation was becoming more and more like the *Casting of the Runes*, to my mind.

We all drank some more truly dreadful coffee. I then asked, 'Who else lives in your house? Is it student accommodation?'

'No, it belongs to my uncle. He allows me to be there. He owns three houses in England. His daughter, Rameen and her husband, Karim, live there with their four children, with Karim's mother.'

The thought of sharing one of the houses round here with eight people gave me another idea, 'And are relations between you all cordial?'

Jalbani's reluctance to speak grew more marked, making my antennae go up.

'It is very kind of my uncle to give me a place while I study. I am beholden to him....' This dutiful admission sat at odds with the tone of his voice, which told us that things were far from fine.

'Tell us how it is for you at your uncle's house,' Ash suggested. 'Do you share your room?'

'It is a small house, sir. I have no room of my own. I sleep on the divan in the front room at night.'

I think we were both thunderstruck by this. Even the most modest student household affords you a room of your own, albeit everything in one bedsit. I couldn't help asking, 'But where do you study? Where do you keep your things?'

'I have been sitting out in the yard, but now it is cold, my cousin allows me to study in the back kitchen where I have a small cupboard for my books and things, so I can be warm.'

Shades of post-industrial Birmingham life! Mrs. Gaskell could have woven a novel about the housing conditions of such students.

'Would you be willing to walk with us beside you for about a mile?' Ash asked him.

Jalbani's face grew further ashen at the prospect.

'We are both medical practitioners and would ensure you are supported. We will not leave you with this, we promise,' I added. I felt rather than saw Ash's veto, as he is not a man for false promises.

Jalbani rose unsteadily, 'I will show you,' he said, but with all the hope of a soldier about to be sent over the top.

Together we left the Wimpy and struck out down one long residential street, lined with sycamores, heading for the centre of Birmingham. Just as we were about to cross the road, about three quarters of a mile further on, Jalbani suddenly faltered. His body sort of folded up, as if his bones had been removed, and he started to choke. Ash immediately pulled him back and lowered him to the ground before he could accidentally step further. I helped take his weight and I can tell you that it was as though his body had turned to stone: his muscles were rigid and his weight more than the dead weight of an unconscious person, despite his thin frame. Had I not seen it, I wouldn't have believed it. It was as though something else was pulling upon his body. The law student's face was now red and his eyes were rolling up, showing the whites of his eyes, while his hands clutched at his throat. We pulled him back even further and sat him against a brick wall, where his muscles began to unknot and relax.

To clear his airway, Ash pulled back the neck of Jalbani's shirt, only to reveal clear marks of ligature. No-one had been near him, save us. No-one at all. We had been walking either side of him, like bodyguards. If I hadn't seen it with my own eyes, I would not have believed it.

'Take his pulse,' said Ash.

It was febrile, leaping about all over the place, like someone having a seizure.

A passing woman with a baby in a pram stopped to ask if she could help, 'My house is nearby, he could rest while you call an ambulance.'

We thanked her, assuring her that we didn't need one, that we were both doctors, and that our friend would be fine soon. She walked off doubtfully, with many a backward glance in our direction. Having dismissed her so readily, I now wasn't so sure.

Jalbani sat up, breathing heavily but evenly. The marks around his neck were still visible, but were slowly fading. He gratefully swigged from the water bottle I offered. 'It is like this, always now, for some weeks. —I fear I will be thrown out of my course and my father will disown me.' Pride and tears mixed in his voice.

Ash crouched beside him, 'Adnan, do you trust me? Will you allow me and Dr. Rivers to help you?'

Jalbani looked between us, the merest glimmer of hope fighting with the desperation that was engulfing him, 'I don't know, sir. I feel you are a good man, but I don't know what power you have over this. You do not know how terrible it is.'

'Would you like to have power over it?' Ash demanded.

'If I were strong, I might, but I am but a poor, ignorant student and I have no power to help myself over something like this.'

'When we are weak, we need some bigger help.' Ash observed. 'Would you say these words after me? *A'oodhu bi kalimaat-illaah il-taammati min sharri ma khalaqa.*'

Jalbani repeated them in wonder, while Ash translated for me, 'I seek refuge in the perfect words of Allāh from the evil of that which He has created.'

He spoke again: *'A'oodhu bi kalimaat-illaah il-taammati min ghadabihi wa 'iqaabihi, wa min sharri 'ibaadihi wa min hamazaat al-shayaateeni wa an yahduroon.'* Again Jalbani repeated the words, phrase by phrase.

I frowned down at Ash, 'What *is* that?'

'It is a formula that people use when they encounter evil: "I seek refuge in the perfect words of Allāh from His wrath and punishment, from the evil of His slaves and from the evil promptings of the devils and from their presence."'

Jalbani stood up, straightening his spine, 'These are words of hope... Though I am a man of science, I also acknowledge Allāh.'

'Good! Then we can begin to find help,' said Ash. 'Tell me, is your local imam a man of wisdom, someone you can trust?'

'I've not been to mosque for weeks. It is... too far...'

'Beyond the limit, then?'

He nodded.

Ash asked, 'Please can you write down your imam's details. I would like to visit him on your behalf and see how we can bring this sorcery to an end. Can you phone him and warn him we are coming?'

We walked slowly to a working phone box where Jalbani spoke into its receiver, covering his mouth with his hand as he did so, while Ash and I stared into the nearby park.

'He is out at present but will be back at 2pm, if you can stay that long?' Jalbani looked a little calmer.

'Then let us walk you home and ensure that you are alright.'

Jalbani seemed remarkably resistant to such a prospect, and it became clear to me that his troubles were very much to do with the family household. He promised to go to the library which, fortunately, was near his lodgings, 'There at least I can continue my studies until it closes....'

'We will be back long before that, I assure you!' Ash said to him.

We had walked him to the library, and were back at the car, where I was still struggling with the thought of poor Jalbani's attack. 'What is causing all of this, Ash? — I once saw a hysteric produce similar phenomena, faint lines upon her own skin, but that was nothing to those ligature marks....' I was speechless. 'If I'd been working in an Accident and Emergency ward and he'd been brought in with that, I'd have said someone tried to strangle him.'

Ash looked grave, 'Almost certainly the slips of paper in his slippers are surahs from the *Qu'ran* that have been written backwards — it's something that black *amils* specialize in.'

I spread my hands, questioningly, 'Black *amils*?'

'Magicians and healers. People go to ordinary *amils* when they feel the presence of something supernatural in their lives — rather as people come to us with their problems. *Amils* are devout practitioners, Islamic healers, who pray with people and give them treatments and prayers. In Muslim society people will go most often to an *amil* if they have marital misunderstandings, or health conditions that seem unrelated to normal causation, or a sense of oppression. Often people with issues of depression or blockage, will go to an *amil* for relief. But I suspect that the one responsible for this has gone to a black *amil* — what you would call a sorcerer, Jack. — Someone who has no compunction about how he manipulates the universe in return for money.'

I listened solemnly, 'Well, whoever arranges such things, I bet that there is someone in that household who is helping along these happenings and putting them where Jalbani is finding them!'

'I'm sure you are right, for this is indeed a serious enchantment. But it is assuredly an earth djinn that is causing his choking and inability to move out of its radius, and that is more serious.'

'What do you mean? What is a djinn?'

'The djinn are what we would call in the West "elementals" — the creatures that live in the air, fire, water and earth. In Islamic lore, they are one of three sapient creations made by God.'

'So they don't live in bottles, then?' I enquired.

He smiled, 'The geni in the bottle is just one example of their kind. In Islamic lore, they are very like the faeries — creatures of free will that can take many different forms, but who often act in what seem to us amoral ways — being sometimes neutral, benevolent or malefic, according to the circumstances. King Solomon was said to have had djinn in his service for the building of the Temple and other things. Most Muslims are careful of the djinn, rather like people here used to be respectful to the faeries. If a Muslim yawns or sneezes, he will cover his mouth and nose, lest the djinn stray in. If a woman turns on a tap, she will pray, so that nothing bad comes through the faucet. — Those would be examples of the air and water djinn, you see?'

'You explain things very well. I think I get it. But what will get the earth djinn off Jalbani's back? I mean we're not on our own patch here... how will we do it?' I said 'we', but of course I meant Ash, as I didn't have a clue how we might proceed.

'As you've seen he is so completely without resources or support, and in the grip of terrible fear. No, unfortunately we cannot spirit him away to the Beacon, where he might have relief from this spell.'

'What help will it be to contact the imam?'

'Well, for one thing, it will enable us to set foot into his cousin's house, for an imam is probably one of the only people who could get us inside. — If we manage that, I would appreciate your good offices to help him.'

'In what way?' I asked, bewildered.

He patted me on the back, as we got back to the car, 'By being your good, ordinary self and using your considerable instinct for honing in on the dynamic of the household.'

We drove to the mosque office and were received there by the elderly receptionist who seemed to be everyone's uncle. Many small children and their mothers kept passing the office door and every one of them would look in — some shyly, some much bolder — and all were given a sweet from the jar on his desk. He brought us small cups of hibiscus tea with very sweet biscuits while we waited.

Imam Mohammed Uddin finally showed up at 2.10pm with profuse apologies. He was a short man with a little pot belly set before him, barely constrained by his tunic. 'It was the traffic, I fear.' He unwound a cotton scarf from his neck, and picked up his messages from the old receptionist who indicated to us, 'Now, how can I help you, Mr., sorry, Dr. Ashington?'

Wringing the rain from his felt hat, he ushered us into his office. He was a good listener, asking astute and practical questions, some of which we couldn't answer, of course.

'Poor Mr. Jalbani!.... I have come across some unpleasant things in my time, but nothing so evil.... The question is, who has initiated these doings?'

'That is where we hope you may help us. It is clear that Adnan is never going to finish his studies if he stays in that household. If we can get him rehoused, then he will have enough stability for us to help him. He currently has no room of his own or even a shared space that he can work in and, of course, there is the matter of his being unable to go to college....'

'You say he is under obligation to his uncle?'

Ash nodded, 'There may be matters between his father and brother that we cannot know about, of course....'

The Imam raised an astute eyebrow, 'Or, it could be a simple matter of envy?' He was already flicking through a directory on his desk, looking at the possibilities. He excused himself and made a couple of quick calls. Turning back to us, he said, 'There is an elderly widow and her son who is unable to work due to sickness: they have space at their home and, in return for some errands, he could stay there — a whole room to himself.'

Ash thanked him, 'The problem began when Adnan entered his uncle's family house, occupied by his cousin and her family. I would appreciate going to visit there, so we can see for ourselves, but I am hoping you would enable us to understand the situation from a quick visit.'

The Imam consulted his watch. 'I know the family slightly. The mother, Rameen, is probably collecting the children from school at present. We can pick up Adnan on the way and call in with the good news about the room... and we can, as you say, see for ourselves.'

I thought the Imam was taking all this very well, beyond a level that would have had most Vicars probably reaching for the whiskey. As we gathered ourselves to leave, the Imam looked right into Ash, saying, 'Amilah Safia said that you were a good man. I am glad that Adnan found you first and not some rogue *raqi*....'

Ash caught my uncomprehending look over the short Iman's head, and whispered to me, 'Safia is a Muslim scholar who works with me in the Guild of Ecumenical Psychology. And the good Imam is glad that Adnan didn't find some cut-price exorcist!'

'Muslim exorcists?' I mouthed to him as we unlocked the car, now thoroughly out of my depth.

We called in at the library and picked up Adnan who was very pleased to hear the news about a room of his own, but simultaneously cast down about the possible cost of this, 'I am beholden to my uncle. My father would surely be unhappy to have to pay for me to live elsewhere, though....'

The Imam assured him, 'It is arranged that you will live at the new house free of cost: the elderly widow, Khashifa, only asks that you perform some errands for her, so she can look after her son, Azfar. He is severely crippled and she hasn't the strength to do all she would like for him. She opens her home to you as a brother and as an act of *zakat*.'

I learned afterwards that *zakat* isn't charity, but an obligation. But it would explain the mutinous expression that now appeared on Adnan's face. I could see that he was going to protest again, from pride this time, but the Imam was firm, 'I am sure that your father would be very unhappy to learn how you have been prevented from studying the law. He has been paying your tuition fees and your first duty is to him. — It is part of *zakat* to look after those who have been slaves or captives.' And Adnan fell silent.

It was now 3.40pm and we had been in Birmingham all day. As we drew up in Highgrove Avenue, opposite the Jalbani house, a short, veiled, determined-looking woman, with her three girls all in their school uniform were coming up the road. A much older woman came to the door as Rameen's youngest daughter ran ahead to knock on the glass, calling inside to be admitted, 'Daadi!'

'That is Ermina, Rameen's mother,' Jalbani said, from the back of the car. The older woman had a face like one of the three witches from *Macbeth*.

'And the youth by her side?' Ash asked, as a teenager with a disturbing squint in his eye joined her at the door.

'That is Badran, my nephew. He has been tested by Allāh.' Even as we watched, Ermina pulled Badran by the arm, trying to coax him inside. He resisted, staring over at the car and refusing to shift. Adnan ducked down lower in his seat. It was clear that Badran had some form of mental illness, but the girls very sweetly persuaded their brother back into the house.

We waited a few moments before we approached. Ash steadied a very shaky Jalbani, 'Remember, we are coming in as your friends to help move your things to your new lodgings.'

Jalbani and the Imam went ahead, while Ash and I followed up the rear. A pall of trepidation seemed to fall upon young Adnan.

Mohammed Uddin knocked at the door, smiling every one of his gold-capped teeth. Rameen glared suspiciously at Adnan and the Imam, peering over his head at us, but was obliged to let us in, as Ash had said. The Imam introduced us as his friends and colleagues. We exchanged restrained greetings and were conducted into the sparsely-furnished front room. A tapestry of Mecca hung over the settee, which was the only seating, if you didn't count the cushions on the floor. This, then, was Adnan's bed. The kitchen had obviously gone into hospitality mode, as one of the older girls came in shyly with a tray of decorated glasses in holders and a tall tea pot from which she expertly dispensed neat tea. The youngest came round with a tray of biscuits. I lowered myself onto the settee with the Imam, but Ash curled himself onto the floor on a cushion like a cat. Adnan settled down next to him, taking protective camouflage. The disturbed youth, Badran, peered into the room, loitering at the door. Ermina appeared at his side and cast what can only be described as an evil look over the company. We all began to feel as if we were held captive in a fish-tank. I now had a very good notion of what Adnan had been experiencing.

As promised, I was on watch for the possible instigators in this case. Rameen was one tough lady, but her mother in law, Ermina struck me as being a much more likely candidate. Not only was she older, but her hostility seemed chiefly focused upon young Jalbani — as well it might, since her son, Karim, had fathered a gaggle of daughters, but only one defective son. Healthy, intelligent Adnan must have come as a supreme reproach to her family, I supposed. Badran came to sit next to Adnan, taking his hand in his, and peering round at Ash who flashed a friendly smile. The youth was evidently delighted to have some interesting company: I imagined that the family didn't take him out that often.

But he was the only one enjoying himself today.

After a short, polite interval, Rameen got down to business. I don't speak any Urdu, but it was evident that she was quizzing the Imam as to the cause of his visit. He answered very mildly, but within a few minutes, the room was in uproar, as the proposal to move Adnan out of the house into a more convenient place was mooted. It was too fast and furious for me to follow, so I asked Adnan to show me where his things were kept.

He led me through to the back kitchen, a miserable little scullery where his meagre student possessions sat ranged on a shelf, over the washing machine, while the large backpack that constituted his wardrobe, hung from a rusty hook behind the scullery door.

'Is there a back way out of here?' I whispered as we shovelled the law books hastily into a carrier bag. But Adnan didn't answer me. He was staring past my head. Blocking the way behind was Ermina. With the veil slipping over one side of her face, she had stationed herself like a withered tree in the hallway. She had one arm raised, one eye closed and was clearly about to lay some imprecation upon us. Transfixed with terror, Adnan cowered back into the scullery's recess.

The Imam descended upon her as the words began to spill from her throat, as he said in a loud commanding voice, speaking over hers, 'A'oodhu bi kalimaat Allāh al-taammah min kulli shaytaanin wa haammah wa min kulli 'aynin laammah.' I recognized this verse from what Ash had said earlier. But Ermina didn't stop, continuing her vituperative cursing as before.

Rameen took in the situation and shouted something at the girls who all ran to Adnan in the back kitchen, and began to try and prevent him from leaving, hanging onto his clothes and crying in an affecting manner. To add to the proceedings, the disturbed youth, Badran, gaped at their antics with wide eyes, before himself bursting into tears and rocking to and fro. When he began to bash his head on the wall, Ash intervened, preventing him from hurting himself. I could see his lips pronouncing some formula of his own, as he held the teenager back.

'It is time we left,' announced the Imam, conclusively, despite the mayhem going on around us. Ash nodded to me to get out.

Given a task I understood, I physically lifted Adnan out of the girl's desperate grasp, pulling him backwards through the back door which gave onto a weed-filled yard. Their pleading fingers finally loosened once we were through the back gate. We ran the length of the dirty narrow path that connected the backs of the terraced houses until we came into the alleyway leading to the road. The hue and cry of the girls' screaming was so loud that several neighbours looked out in amazement to see what the fracas was about.

It was becoming like an episode of *City Search and Rescue,* only I wasn't in a police uniform, and my charge wasn't a trafficked person. Back on the street, we made swiftly for the car and piled into it, Adnan folding himself small in the back. Ash and the Imam were already waiting with the engine revving. With a turn of speed I had never previously seen from Ash, the car sped out of Highgrove Avenue, now filled with bemused neighbours, and across the main road, into a quiet, leafy street, where he pulled over. It was hard to equate what I had just witnessed with this inoffensive part of Birmingham.

'We cannot return to the mosque—it is simply too far,' Ash said to Mohammed Uddin. 'I think you are clear about the kind of work we need to do, now. The question is, where can we do it?'

'We will need to perform a *ruqyah,*' said the Imam, nodding.

'What is that?' I asked.

Ash turned round, 'An exorcism. —Do you know somewhere we can go?'

The Imam sunk in thought for a moment, then rootled in his copious pockets, and triumphantly holding them up, exclaimed, 'I have the keys to a community hall where I am speaking tomorrow. Let's check if it's free now.'

While he directed Ash, I kept my eye on Adnan, hoping to goodness that the place we were bound wouldn't be too far for him. I didn't want to have to pull him out of the car and revive him as we'd had to do earlier that day. He seemed very subdued. Good angels were smiling on us, it would seem, as we pulled into Balsall Community Hall's car park without any trouble. The place seemed locked up.

The Imam went and unlocked the side-door and was greeted by the caretaker who was round the back sweeping up the leaves. In a broad Brummy accent, the man told us, pointing with his broom handle, 'The back meeting room is free until 6.30pm. You can use that one, gov. Just don't leave any valuables there—we got the alcoholics and druggies in later.'

The institutional smell of disinfectant, cleaning fluid and sweaty feet hit us, but the room had a lockable door and that was all we needed. Shelves stacked with pamphlets about the Boy Scout Organization spilled onto the floor in the corner, while the notice board advised us of the times of yoga classes and Alcoholics Anonymous Meetings. The only windows were at ceiling level to admit some light, which also suited us for our purposes. Ash shinned up on a chair under one of the windows and prised one open by the merest crack. He had also brought a car-blanket and two bottles of water which lay on the table, while the Imam arranged some chairs, positioning one in the centre of three others. I stood apart with Adnan who was now mostly leaning upon me after his ordeal at the family house.

'My uncle will kill me for leaving them without any rent...' he said. 'They rely on me...'

'Not anymore they're not!' I assured him. Sounding like an aggrieved parent myself, I insisted, 'That's not your problem now. If your father had the least idea what was going on in that house, he would have done just what we have done — get you out of danger!'

I made him sit down, as he was becoming heavier on my arm. As I settled him, I was moved at how very thin he was under his clothes, nothing more than a starveling sparrow.

Both Ash and the Imam were so intent on their preparations that neither of them were attending to Adnan who had acquired an air of extreme fragility. It seemed to me that he, or perhaps something in him, did not want to stay for what followed. Whatever was upon or with him was beginning to make itself apparent even to me, as Ash went about the room weaving his golden trail of overtones, just as if we had been in his study at the Beacon. Like the superimposed ghost of a photo taken on a wind-on camera, the djinn was becoming palpable as a double exposure over Adnan's sad features. A kind of bulbous, gargoyle like mass, smearing over him and boiling up to the surface. The extreme peril the young law student had been living in was finally clear to me, and my scornful scepticism died at that moment.

Ash noticed how quiet he had become, 'Is there something you want to say, Adnan?'

Making a supreme effort, Adnan nodded, diving into his huge backpack. He pulled out a jacket, saying, 'You asked me about the slips of paper. I forgot that I found this in my jacket last week.' He tendered Ash a used business envelope from which a slip of paper protruded.

I regarded this strip with some trepidation. It was as though the *Casting of the Runes* was playing out under my gaze, though this strip had Arabic characters on it, not runes.

Ash drew it out, gave it cursory investigation and showed it to the Imam, holding the strip with the very edge of the envelope. Mohammed Uddin gingerly took it and read, turning white, then red with anger. Feeling in his top pocket, he produced a lighter and set the strip of paper on fire, dropping it into the metal waste paper basket.

As the paper fell into ash, he spoke gravely, 'It is not permitted to have anything to do with the djinn, to invoke them or call upon them in any way.'

'Yet someone has done so,' said Ash, in a calm voice.

The Imam quoted, translating hesitantly, '"Those are the ones who have purchased error in exchange for guidance, so their transaction has brought no profit, nor were they guided."'

Inviting Adnan to sit in the central chair, the Imam began to pray, '"Bismillaahi arqeeka min kulli shay'in yu'dheeka, min sharri kulli nafsin aw 'aynin haasid Allaahu yashfeek, bismillaahi arqeek."'

Adnan opened his tightly clenched eyes and, seeing my puzzlement, asked, 'Sir, can you please pray the prayers in English too?'

Mohammed Uddin nodded, and said loudly,' "In the name of Allāh, I perform *ruqyah* for you, from everything that is harming you, from the evil of every soul or envious eye, may Allāh heal you. In the name of Allāh, I perform *ruqyah* for you."' He spoke in a hasty and determined tone.

Holding his hands before his eyes, and then his ears, the Imam prayed some more in Arabic and then in English, '"Allah – there is no god except Him, the Ever-Living, the Sustainer of all existence. Neither drowsiness overcomes Him nor sleep. To Him belongs whatever is in the heavens and whatever is on the earth. Who is it that can intercede with Him, except by His permission? He knows what is before them and what will be after them, and no-one can encompass any of His knowledge, except for what He wills. His throne extends over the heavens and the earth, and their preservation tires Him not. And He is the Most High, the Most Great."'

Adnan was trying to relax but his body began to jerk and shudder, just as if he was about to be felled to the ground again. I badly wanted to support him but one glance from Ash made me stay tight in my seat.

Mohammed Uddin was perturbed by the convulsions beginning to take place, and I understood then that this was not his usual area of expertise. He turned to Ash, 'You are not a believer, Doctor, but Amilah Safia says that you are a holy man who lives under the hand of Allāh,' said the Imam, sweating profusely. 'Will you pray with me?'

Ash had been waiting for this invitation, I think, and stepped forward fearlessly, placing his hands lightly upon Adnan's head, saying, 'In the name of Allāh, the compassionate and merciful, may the djinn that holds in thrall this young man, Adnan Jalbani, depart far from his body.' He seemed to gather himself, and with great energy, said loudly, 'Depart and be gone!' As he spoke the latter part of this, he suddenly lifted both hands from Jalbani's head and flung something towards the crack in the open window. I could have sworn it was a small stone, as it hit the window with the smart tap of a pebble, but it left a bullet-like hole in the lower pane of glass.

The Imam blenched at the sight of this, but I wasn't so sure that some sleight of hand had taken place, as I couldn't reconcile the sound and hole with whatever had been in Adnan. Then Ash took up one of the water bottles and, clamping one thumb over the open top, liberally sprinkled water over Adnan's head and upper body, then all about him.

Continuing to sprinkle the water over Adnan, he said in a commanding voice, 'In the name of Allāh, depart, all you djinn, from the body of Adnan Jalbani! Leave him cleanly and do not return! May Adnan Jalbani freely pass to walk the ways of Allāh, under his will.'

Young Jalbani suddenly ceased his jerking and convulsing. His lids fluttered and he opened both eyes with wonder, as if he had discovered a great treasure. Then he discovered that he was rather wet. Taking a handkerchief from his pocket, he began to mop his face and hands, saying devoutly, 'Allah-u-akbar. Rab-bana walak hamd!'

'Praise is due to our Lord!' breathed the Imam, giving thanks.

Seeing that the main business was done, I leapt up and wrapped the car blanket about Adnan's shoulders, as he was beginning to shiver. Ash sat down abruptly, breathing heavily. The Imam began to fuss over him and made him drink from the unopened bottle of water.

Leaving the Balsall Heath Community Hall a little wetter than we had found it, we headed towards Birmingham central, Ash driving very slowly as the odometer reached the mile's extent. I was monitoring Adnan, one hand on his pulse as we edged forward, urging Ash to caution until it was clear that Adnan was alright. When the odometer told us we had done a mile and a half, Adnan was still breathing and unaffected. We all agreed that the earth djinn was gone. The sense of relief and exaltation in the car was profound.

But I could see that Ash was spent and made him swop over with me, as I took charge of the car, saying to the Imam, 'I think we all need a square meal and something to drink. Will you join us?'

Adnan's voice piped up from the backseat, 'Can we please go to the Khyber Pass? I ate there once with my friends… it is very good.' The total release in his voice was one of the best things I have ever heard. Whatever had been upon him was now removed and he was tearingly hungry, as were we all.

We accordingly made our way to this esteemed Indian restaurant where we feasted on a variety of curries and peshwari naans, all washed down with lassi and mango juice. Adnan ate enough for two young men, I thought. It was a fine young man we had rescued from enchantment. He laughed uproariously at the old jokes that I dropped into the meal, but Ash was more silent, as if he was still coming back from a long way off. At my quizzical glance, he shook his head, 'It just took a lot of energy. A good night's sleep and I'll be fine.' But I think we had pushed the boat out a little too far on that long day, myself. When we had finally reached the stage of trying to find room for what remained in the serving dishes, it was more than time to take Adnan to his new digs.

We fetched up at the home of the widow, Khashifa, who greeted us kindly, making us all come in to her warm kitchen where her son, the crippled Azfar, lay near the fire on a couch. He was in his forties and clearly unable to work, for his whole body was twisted to one side, but his hands were busy whittling wooden ornaments for a local charity, which Khashifa then painted and assembled. The long-suffering widow's beauty had once been great, I would guess, but now it resided in her graceful hands as she smoothed the blanket over her son's crippled body.

Our welcome was in marked contrast to our entry into Rameen's house earlier. This was a proper home, with a welcoming hearth. We all trooped upstairs to admire the wonder of Adnan's 'room of his own,' which had a desk and shelves for his books. It was clean, comfortable and warm but, more importantly, it had its own door as well as its own bed. It was still hard not to let outrage mount at the thought of the arrangements at his cousin's house. Ash and I were content that he had fallen on his feet.

After helping Azfar upstairs to his bedroom, Adnan came down to see us out. Pulling the door behind him to keep out the cold night air, he grasped both our hands tightly, 'I cannot express my gratitude to you both. You and the Imam have saved my life. I can now return to my studies and be a credit to my father. Thank you. If I can serve you in any way, when I am qualified, then I will represent you at my expense!' He struck his chest with a mighty gesture of magnanimity.

'Should we ever stray off the path and need your counsel, we will come straight to you,' Ash promised him, with a solemn twinkle.

We bade Adnan farewell and drove the Imam back to his own house. On the way, I asked him, 'Have you had much dealings with the djinn?'

Mohammed Uddin raised his brows, "No, indeed! It is not permitted. And I pray to the prophet, may peace be upon him, that I never come so close again!' He wiped his brow another time.

'Ash said that they were like elementals, but I wondered how they came about?'

He replied, 'Men were created from the black mud but the djinn were made from the flame of fire — we have different natures. In *Sūrat l-dhāriyāt* , it is written, "We have created djinn and human beings only that they might worship Me." — The Qur'an was sent for both men and djinn that they might worship Allāh.'

I struggled to translate this belief into Christian terms, making a similar connection between human beings and faeries, 'It seems a much more liberal idea than in the Bible, in that respect. I think only people get to read and understand that... in our way of thinking. Most people here have forgotten all about the faeries, and hardly bear them in mind...' I mused.

The Imam obviously thought my words frivolous, and risposted, 'In Cyangugu, in the terrible troubles in Rwanda, many arsonists ran away rather than attack a mosque because they believed it to be protected by the djinn you know!'

I looked doubtful at this assertion, but the Imam nodded, 'Truly!'

Then, looking back at Ash dozing in the back of the car, Mohammed Uddin said, 'It was an extraordinary thing he did today. Without his knowledge and the support of Allāh, poor Mr. Jalbani would never have experienced his freedom again, I think?'

I nodded, 'Your prayers helped too, don't forget? — I've worked with Ash for a few years now, but he still surprises me. I don't know how he operates most of the time, but today was a whole new chapter. — I think this is your street?' I pulled over, but Ash seemed deeply asleep, so we didn't disturb him.

The Imam shook my hand, turned and waved from his doorstep and was received by his wife and family. As the light from that doorway fled and the thick Birmingham night descended, I felt the strange tug for a home of my own, and an unfamiliar loneliness claimed me as I drove south into the tangle of motorways. I ran the day's events, trying to understand them, but my arrant mind kept returning to Jane. I hit the radio to relieve my loneliness, turning it low so as not to disturb Ash. It made it no better that the local radio was playing the song that I would ever associate with her, 'Golden Hair, Lovely Face,' as I switched on. I may have shed a tear or two, in sheer longing for her to be beside me now as I drove. She was so far away — half a world away — maybe just setting out on her day's rounds in the Northern Territory, as I was battling sleep.

This maudlin mood might have claimed me utterly, but the traffic was dense due to some road-closures and I had to concentrate in the rainy darkness. Resolutely, I changed the channel to listen to the news. Soon I was reconsidering the day again. It had so many surprises, not least a revisiting of the themes that thronged the *Casting of the Runes*, which I had never aimed to experience, outside a cinema.

As the car left behind the densely populated cities and suburbs, and we came finally in sight of the South Downs, a voice said sleepily from the back seat, 'Damn! We didn't leave any money to mend the window!'

Case 10: THE LAST OF BRIDES

I never discovered which gods Ash worshipped. There was the statue of the Tibetan Manjusri in his Harley Street rooms and a tangka of Avalokiteshvara on the stairs at the Beacon, but he was not a Buddhist. He kept a little iron-stone statue of Our Lady of Monserrat, dark amid her plum-coloured draperies, on the shrine to Melanie Rydale, yet he was no Christian. Although he remarked, like Leonardo Da Vinci, that he could not abide a crucifix; in his eyes 'it crucified the Lord again' — a remark that only the devout might make, you would think — yet he never went to church. And his was not the creed-lessness of a secular man, for I knew him to be deeply reverent and observant of the higher moralities, though I could never quite pin him down. It seemed to me that he held some spiritual ambassador's passport admitting him into crypt or synagogue, mosque or temple — for he knew the customs and usages of such places — but he was either of all, or of none of them. He somehow passed their portals, to be recognized as a pilgrim, but as for his own secret shrine, that was never revealed to me.

Now that I look back, I see more clearly that his creedal homelessness enabled him to receive the hospitality of the whole world, and that tribal boundaries had no hold upon him. He could walk through them all because he could take their colouration when necessary, while no hint of their colour adhered to him. To be recognised everywhere is a remarkable talent.

For myself, I have been a sort of ashamed and expedient Anglican when necessity arose while, at the same time, deeply drawn to the Northern myths. I like a touch of ritual, but as you can't get to meet a Norse *godi* or experience a good old-fashioned Anglo-Saxon *blot* too often these days, so the Anglicans tend to win out when the fancy takes me to pray. But I suppose a cross or a Thor's hammer would have served for me, had I needed an emblem of my religious proclamation. For the meantime, I suppose I affected my own kind of creedless 20st century mufti to camouflage my leanings. Ash once said that the Russians have a name for what I am: a man of *dvoeverie* or 'double-belonging.' Yet I am still sensitive to the spiritual needs of my patients. Whatever the textbooks say, a person's faith or spiritual practice drives their life and is a resource in times of trouble, as Ash often said, 'It is much easier to work with someone in whom the wheel is already turning,' than to push the thing to move at all.

That year, we had under our wing a man shattered by the wars in Iraq. Duncan MacKenzie was the last scion of the MacKenzies of Gilliebhridhe, the only survivor of a party of Scots Guards, killed by a booby-trapped tank outside Basra. His grandfather, Grahaeme MacKenzie, the MacKenzie of Gilliebridhe, brought his grandson down from the Highlands himself, with the help of a nurse.

The MacKenzie addressed Ash with a trusting confidence, making me think that they might have known each other from before, 'Duncan's been with us since he was discharged from hospital, but the Highlands are, well... too open for him. The gentler southern lands would be better, we all feel.' The laird was a long, gaunt man with a walrus moustache. Age sat nobly upon him, etched in the deep lines either side of his long nose. Once a Scots Guard himself, having served in Cyprus and Suez, the MacKenzie had already lost a son, Duncan's father, at Tumbledown Hill in the Falklands in 1982. It was rare to see such loyal, generational devotion to duty in this day and age, but then few families held to such a firm military tradition as the MacKenzies. Now it looked as if the thin red line had finally come to its close with Duncan.

Then a man of 28, Duncan, the Laird's grandson, was sandy haired, his body robust and disciplined in its lean, military frame. They had reconstructed his body, and grafted skin over his burns, but his blue eyes held the innocent bafflement of a child exposed to the reality of life too early. There was not a trace of adult awareness to be seen, and none of a boy's street-cunning either. Whether you diagnosed it as Post-Traumic Stress or Combat Fatigue, he had become effectively and completely regressed as a result of it. To my eyes, we had taken delivery of an eight-year old boy trapped in an adult man's body. As we soon found, he didn't speak except when he wanted to, though he was certainly not dumb. If he wanted to do something, he would do it, but if he didn't, wild horses couldn't make him.

I could only guess how the MacKenzie had known of Ash and his work, for he said, 'I'm entrusting my grandson to you, Doctor, for you know more of the hidden things of this world and have the ministry of unhoused souls as my grandson.' And he gave into Ash's keeping a strange wooden box, set with a huge clasp. It was bound with a dull metal of some ancient manufacture, and had two battered metal roundels by which it must have been displayed hundreds of years ago: 'Give him this when he is able to take it up. You'll ken when that will be.'

Ash didn't ask what was in it, though I was curious to know. He received this trust with a bow of the head and shoulders, with a priestly gravity that seemed all out of keeping with the situation, 'I will keep it safe until the time.'

As he gripped my hand before leaving, I knew that the MacKenzie himself was then a very sick man. Or so I judged professionally from the tell-tale nodes upon his neck and the febrile pallor that hung about his gaunt face.

'That man has a cancer growing in him,' I breathed to Ash as the tall laird departed.

'Indeed,'Ash said softly. 'That's why he entrusts his grandson to us. He will not see Duncan again and knows it. He will not be able to impart what his grandson must assuredly carry forward.' This was gnomic, even for him, but I was inured to such sibylline utterances.

Duncan MacKenzie was little trouble to us. He sat and read in the library willingly, although the newspapers gave him the horrors and had to be speedily removed from the hall when they arrived, lest he read about more assaults, bombs or deaths in the headlines. We all conspired to maintain a safe environment for him, with Wendy going to the most extreme lengths, I thought. With her, the gentlemanly Duncan sometimes emerged, with him politely opening the door for her; but on his worst days, she became like Peter Pan's Wendy, caring for one of the lost boys. Duncan would only go out on dullish, over-cast days, when he would walk, companioned, up the Beacon with compliance, if little vigour. On sunny, cloudless days that reminded him of the desert, he hid inside and fiddled with some old radio set that Gillespie was trying to mend, his fingers busy with cogs and circuits like any boy with a hobby. Loud calls, or unkind words — even if overheard from a radio drama — would send him sobbing into the settee, as if he himself had been rebuked.

He was really at his best helping in the garden, where he had a genuine feeling for the soil. It wasn't the best time of year for gardening, being October, but at least he could help Gillespie tidy up the beds, and rake and prune when the weather allowed.

As usual, Ash's policy of 'wait and see' was employed: he told me that he didn't expect Duncan to show any signs of change for a while, and that we were likely in for the long haul. Just how long, we didn't know. Whatever guests liked to do best, whatever gave them the pleasure of engagement, Ash let them pursue it. It was not until the bonfire was being built for Guy Fawkes Night that Duncan showed a genuine and indeed almost professional interest in the proper laying of a fire. I began to fear that we had an incipient pyromaniac at hand, such was his enthusiasm, but Ash said to let him help.

Bonfire Night was crisp and cold, with a clear sky, the earlier rain having taken itself off. We had planned to have a bonfire for about a week and had gathered the fuel, which had been sat in the wood-store. Given Duncan's condition, we planned to have just a few sparklers, but no Guy, as Ash didn't approve of burning anyone, even in effigy. 'Besides,' he remarked, 'the MacKenzies are Catholic and it wouldn't do to stir up old strife. Guy Fawkes was a martyr to his people, even if a misguided one.'

To watch Duncan light that fire was more than intriguing. With adult solemnity and reverence, he circulated the bonfire, checking it first before setting to work with knife and flint, with which our soil is gratuitously littered. I had never seen anyone do such a thing before, and he showed me the way of it. I couldn't believe that Gillespie hadn't previously dowsed the wood in petrol, it sprang up so fast into the November night. The flames stood nearly as tall as myself, while the sparks melted upwards into the pin-prick stars above our heads.

The archaic enjoyment of a winter fire in the chill darkness seized upon us all, but Duncan seemed particularly enraptured. It was going well until some fool set off a series of deafening rockets from just above us on Hartsworth Beacon. Duncan immediately flung himself to the muddy ground, covering his head as if from mortar attack, which he assuredly thought they were. The rockets flared swiftly up, bursting in a crackerjack volume of popping sparks and whistles. Their light was so piercingly fierce that the whole line of the Downs was illuminated for several seconds.

Sparklers forgotten, we spent the remaining evening settling Duncan down, and so it wasn't till after midnight that I sank into one of Ash's deep armchairs to enjoy a whiskey — it usually has the effect of sobering me up if I'm drunk, confused or exhausted.

Ash regarded the fire through his glass, 'Tell me, Jack. Do you think the old gods die and fade when their votaries are no more?'

'Didn't some Greek chap hear something of the kind?' I was too tired to remember whom.

'Ah, that was the pilot, Thamus. Over a windless sea came the words asking, was Great Pan dead? "And there was a cry of lamentation, as of many disbelieving people".... No, such rumours are in vain,' Ash answered his own question. 'The Gods may withdraw, but they do not depart. When someone has returned to rekindle the flame upon the altar, it may be that the gods also return to help him.'

'What do you mean? Are you speaking of Duncan?'

'Indeed, I am. Something is nearer than it was. But it is not yet accomplished.'

'What gods do you mean?' I objected, 'Duncan is a Catholic, surely?' At the beginning I had tried to take Duncan over to the church in Christminster, as the MacKenzie had requested, but he was not really able to cope with a city yet with noises and crowds. So Father Nicholas Dougherty from the Carmelites over at Buckden Priory accordingly brought the sacrament out to Duncan every week, sitting with him and making light conversation, though his communicant made little response.

Ash had picked up one of his smooth pebbles from the bowl on his desk, turning it over and over in his hands, 'There are older gods, Jack, and they are still served, I think, along with the saints.'

Exasperated, I exclaimed, 'I do wish you'd let me in on your musings. You cannot imagine how annoying it is to be treated like the dog in the corner.'

Ash shook himself, 'I'm sorry, Jack. I was talking more to myself, and had no thought of you.' He sat up straighter in the armchair, 'Would you really like to help Duncan?'

'I thought we already were?'

He considered me, 'I mean… beyond your professional capacity…'

I realized that he was asking me to venture into his more esoteric territory, 'More hypnotism, or will it be incantation this time?' I asked, pleasantly.

'Just gaze into the fire, if you would, and think of Duncan.'

To humour him I complied, sitting forward to stare into the hearth. A log stirred, broke, and fell down into the grate, exposing a vast glowing cave of brightness. In the embers, I could imagine a great open altar with such a flame at its heart. There was nothing much more than that. Just me and the fire — me watching the fire — the fire receiving my attention. But as I fell silent and began to look into the glowing coals in earnest, a strange fancy grew upon me, and a single phrase began echoing round and round my head.

'He is the Last of Brides,' the words came from my lips, but I had no idea whence they came or what they meant.

Ash, who had been watching me as I gazed into the fire, sat back and smiled, nodding, listening to my account.

'But, how can a man be the last bride?' I asked, resuming my normal rationality. 'It doesn't make sense!'

Ash demurred, 'Not "the last bride", but "the Last of Bride's" wasn't that what you said?'

I shook myself thoroughly and went to put on the kettle. As I stalked down the corridor that led to the kitchen, I felt a slight shiver, remembering Ash's saying about the undying gods and their votaries, I couldn't get the image of Duncan's rapt, fire-watching face from my mind. The whiskey had woken me up too much and I had to make myself a mug of cocoa to counteract its effect, with which milky comfort, I stumped off to bed.

I slept deeply and dreamed of Duncan. He and I were friends in my dreams, and I considered myself honoured to be his comrade. The dream-Duncan was much as he must have been before his detachment caught it. He was an inspiration to be with, resourceful, courageous and insightful. If he had been head boy at my school, he would have been hero-worshipped by the younger boys as their champion. I could understand how his men would have trusted him, and to what extent he would have felt responsible for them. In the dream, we were on some long journey, a quest for something important. In the final scene we had just arrived at the place.

'Now the Last of Brides is come,' was said by some solemn, unseen voice that made my whole being thrill with expectancy. Some mighty revelation was nigh. As in a ritual, the scene unfurled. I remember a ruined building with a curious window in silhouette, very dramatic, back lit by the setting sun. Then a singing began that tore at my heart as Duncan went forward alone to do something heroic. I only knew that he alone must do it and that, if he failed, I should have to continue, or at least try, but before I could work out what, the wretched alarm exploded into insistent beeping and the dream doors slammed firmly shut. Cursing, I hurled the clock against the wall. I had been at the point of some admirable, even holy task – the achievement of the Grail or something like it – and now I was stranded on the shore of the waking world by some infernal Chinese plastic clock. I could have wept, ignoble Perceval that I was.

I went to look in on my dream friend, but Duncan was still groggy with the medication we'd finally had to pump into him the night before, as Wendy had reported when she handed me my tea. I let him sleep on. The postman delivered the mail and I carefully tugged out the tell-tale airmail letter from the heap as surely mine. It was from Jane, letting me know that she wouldn't be able to take my weekly phone call as she would be upcountry seeing to an outbreak of fever. It had been posted last Friday. The immense distances involved in her work were too much to imagine. This was now Thursday morning and our only precious time together was always scheduled for Friday mornings, before breakfast, so I was doubly incensed.

I made an ill-tempered, hasty breakfast that gave me indigestion. Then I saw to our two other guests who were fit to be discharged. When they'd gone off to be reunited with their families, Ash remarked, sweetly, 'Do I detect a distinct lack of enthusiasm for our successful work?'

I rounded on him, for the last thing I needed was Ash's irony. 'What? – No, it's not *them*,' I growled.

'Come and tell me about it, Doctor Rivers,' he said, with quiet formality.

It was as well he hadn't put a hand upon my arm, for I think I would have hit him, such a well of savagery opened in my middle. The loss of my dream and now the loss of Jane for another whole week. Not to hear her voice... I struggled to respond politely, taking refuge in clipped informative phrases.

'I'm sorry. My dream last night – the alarm shattered it to blazes. I've been trying to catch its shirt tails all morning – I can't get more than the last few lines.'

'Tell me.' He was treating me like a client, but I didn't care anymore.

We went to sit in the library where Wendy, helped by Duncan, had set a roaring fire. She discreetly and very sweetly brought us coffee the way I like it and slunk away as Ash began to catechize me. But that morning, he had drawn the world's most uncooperative client, and even he finally gave up on me and let me brood it out.

We had many more bonfires through the winter as Gillespie cut back branches and removed some rotten wood to make space for a new fence he had planned. Duncan laid each fire, showing me how to obtain a steady draw. The manner of it was very peculiar. He would not make a fire at all unless the site were first completely clean. The area had to be raked and levelled first. When he was satisfied, Duncan made three trilithons of logs, like a mini Stonehenge in the fire-pit, angled to make a circle, on which the rest of the wood rested. 'These are the three doors,' he would say, and then he'd mutter something in Gaelic that I couldn't understand as he set the fire alight. Then he'd watch the flame with a grave attention. I would often get impatient at first. But if I tried to return to the house to do some paperwork, Duncan would very firmly catch me back and make me watch with him. At first it felt like being sentry duty, but as time went on, I realized that Duncan was as intent and serious as a child at play. Once I had slowed myself down enough to join the game, I began to see more of his world. I learned to stay still and gaze into the fire in earnest, watching the goblin-caves and dragons' breath flames engulfing the sticks, discovering the nature and temperature of the fire from its colour. Sometimes, it was as we had been in Ash's room, looking into the fireplace: scenes, names and songs, threads of story or myth would present themselves to me, weave themselves into me and then pass out of memory.

In some manner, I become closer to Duncan as a playmate or confrère, rather than his doctor. He now looked to me as his companion to walk him up Hartworth Beacon when it was exercise time. Gillespie privately called him my dog, so willingly did he come to my side when I called, though he was careful not to say so in front of Duncan himself. Ash kept his own council, beyond his official weekly check-up to test how he was doing, but he nodded sagely when he saw us ready to go forth with staves, scarfed up to the nines against the colder weather.

I began to wonder whether he would ever recover. I said to Ash that it looked as if his family would be supporting him all his life at this rate.

Ash wasn't perturbed, 'You have his trust, Jack. And that's worth a lot more.'

It was true that Duncan had become like the younger brother I'd never had.

§§

That November, I asked leave to attend a conference on mental health to which I'd been invited. Ash looked at the programme on the leaflet, asking, 'Are you going to present a paper?'

'Well, I saw that there was an afternoon on health and spirituality, so I thought I'd talk about care of the soul – though, of course, they would probably much rather hear it from you than from me.'

Ash demurred, turning his piercing grey eyes with their faint dark line about them upon me, 'Don't you think that you have something valuable to contribute to that debate?' And he sent me off with his blessing.

The conference was housed in a rather dull, sixties style campus in Bedford, with the usual prickly academic and professional rivalries that always surface at these events. Listening to the papers and the debates following, I found myself occupying a very different place from when I'd last attended such a gathering a few years back. It is hard to explain, but I began to realize that, when I'd first come to the Beacon, it felt as if I'd always been racing to catch up with Ash and his strange ways of dealing with our guests. I'd once been like the men and women here at the conference, sunk in rationality so far that I couldn't exercise an iota of freedom of spirit.

Listening that day, I had the sensation that the delegates were much like I had been back then: clumsy in expression, slow in understanding, missing the whole point of the truth. They were practitioners who had a fixed idea of mental health, with a regime of talking therapies and other prescriptions at their command; but they missed 'the many-splendoured thing' – the soul – in all their debates, relegating it to a religious arena, as if the soul only belonged to the religious. Their language and expression of the soul's subtlety was gauche and inappropriate, striving for a technical vocabulary that they just didn't possess.

If I'd learned nothing else from Ash, I knew that, unless you took into account the nature of the soul and how it must be respected, that no healing could come. The lucidity of mind that I now possessed was entirely due to Ash's tuition, and my exposure to his methods: he had shown me how to shepherd the soul, not by force of command, but by following where the soul led. It had become my profound belief that the soul goes towards what feeds and heals it; that the patient himself diagnoses the cause of what is wrong, and expresses this through simple metaphor; that when causation is witnessed and addressed, the soul is able to move onwards healthily. These, my colleagues, were still more intent on their own understanding of what was wrong, sometimes using methods that prolonged the client's suffering, by re-exhuming the body of their problems, enumerating the bones and burying it until the next session. With Ash I had learned in a different school, where solution could be discovered simply, with insight and discernment, helping the stray fragments of soul to swing back into their accustomed place.

Some of these things I spoke about in my paper, carrying all before me. Afterwards, several eminent practitioners approached me, seeking to draw out what it was that I had, or whether I was prepared to address their department, university or association. Even Katherine Merchison, editor of one of the biggest holistic publishing firms, made overtures for a book on the same topic as my paper. I had never before experienced such praise and adulation.

Over dinner, I watched the dining delegates with an air of abstraction. I experienced a strange floating sense of difference which was not fuelled by any ego-fuelled vaunting from my success that day, but rather more from what brought me closer to the art that we all professed: the healing of minds and souls, the restoring of fragmented lives.

The babel of voices bellowed up suddenly as dessert was served. I ate my apple tart slowly, nodding to fellow diners as they made points across the table, like a cow chewing the cud, content to be forgotten, not as the man of the moment. Instead of a coffee, I took myself outside to look up at the stars that hung low over my head, shimmering the sky with pathways of light. Orion had begun to stride across the heavens, Betelgeuse and Rigal studding his belt with brightness. Now I too had resources under my belt, given to me by Ash: resources that I could never relinquish, for knowledge had brought me into a new territory. I wondered how they would shape the pathway that lay before me.

Rabbi Ariel Klein, who was also one of the speakers, came out to smoke a cigarette under the stars. His eyes twinkled behind the heavy black frames on his nose, as he looked me over consideringly, 'Now what do they call it in Ireland? – Ah, yes! You have become the white-haired boy, no?'

I tried to look modest, 'If I said anything of moment, it's entirely down to the mentoring of Ash, I do assure you!'

The Rabbi, who knew Ash very well indeed, smoked in silence for a while, admiring heaven's handiwork. Then, narrowing his eyes, he looked me over for a second time, 'Had you been one of my people, I'd have said it was time for you to be ordained and made Rebbe of your own schul.' He stubbed out his cigarette, 'But, as it is, I daresay Dr. Ashington has it in hand?'

Turning on his heel, ignoring my baffled expression, he left me to my contemplation of the stars.

§§

And so the days ticked off the calendar towards Christmas. Having not lived in a family home for some years since I broke up with Amy, I had been at the mercy of whatever celebrations the medical establishment of the time had provided. Forced jollity under mental strain makes for a stressful Christmas, and I had often chosen to work over the holidays, rather than getting myself maudlin over a ready-to-heat turkey meal and a bottle of claret in some miserable boarding house, while watching the seasonal comedy repeats. Some institutions can become the dumping ground for relatives who are too maladjusted to handle social gatherings, in any case, and the magic of Christmas was often disappointingly in short supply for those incarcerated at the time. For me, Christmas had become a statutory alcohol binge at the staff party and little else.

But Christmas at the Beacon had proved to be a wholly other experience. As soon as Advent arrived, so did the Advent wreath, with its candles — with one lit each Sunday throughout December. Wendy placed it in the central hall, where it felt as if they were calling Christmas home from wherever it had been. Decorations made from the greenery that surrounded us — ivy, fat-berried holly and yew branches, woven into wreathes and swags with ribbons — began to appear about the old house. The brass knocker of the door was ingeniously adorned with sprays of woven ribbons, and on the porch, near to Melanie's shrine, a large bunch of mistletoe was hung — it felt secretly, as if it had been hung for me and Jane.

Everyone seemed to enter into a state of preparation, and I was no different. That year, there was the promise of a very special gift, since Jane had rearranged her plans to come over from Australia and join me: I admit I had paid for her ticket, but she didn't object, so... Things between us had proceeded to the point where only each other's company would now serve. While our weekly conversations and occasional letters, which I kept writing almost like a diary until they were long enough to send, could convey the warmth and longing, the unsaid words still stood between us.

On this point alone was my high excitement held in check. When I had first taken up the post of warden at the Beacon, I had had no partner. Ash himself had very particularly quizzed me on this front and I had assured him that there was nothing to prevent my taking the wardenship. At the time this had seemed to me like something from another era, more like the qualification for a religious vocation. But I was not made to be celibate all of my life, I knew now. And so I worried about how I would break the news to Ash, if Jane said yes to my unspoken question, and what that would mean. Ash had been happy to invite her to stay over Christmas, since our case-load had lightened and we would have no other guests, but I had not been entirely honest about my own intentions, either. Would our coming together require me to leave the Beacon? Hopeful and worried by turns, with so many imponderables weighing upon me, I became noticeably grouchy.

Both the McLeans were well aware of our exchange of letters, and the way I would never read one in front of them, savouring Jane's words to myself in private. Both discreetly kept well out of my way when I used the guest phone to speak to her once a week. Each in their way tiptoed round my gloom, but I was in no mood for their silent sympathy, preferring instead to spend my time with Duncan.

Duncan's own excitement helped precipitate my own longing for Jane's arrival. His usually dull eyes lit up at the sight of the beauty that the house put on as the winter deepened. He must have been brought up in an old house, I think — I later discovered that it was a baronial castle — for he kept stroking the walls of the house and stopping to gaze in wonder at the new decorations that the McLeans devised. The kitchen was full of delightful preparations in which he was most interested: orange peel, brandy, marzipan and clove permeated the house like incense. Wendy always put by a little plate of what she had made for Duncan to enjoy. The Christmas cards began to arrive in daily flocks, and were dealt with smartly by Gillespie who affixed them to the exposed beams of the house using Wendy's patent method of tapes over which the cards were folded, so that they stayed tidy and didn't overwhelm us.

Ash's contributions to the preparations began with music, which flowed out of the piano unceasingly — Bach's Christmas Oratorio and medleys of carols, as well as some special piece that he was devising that he carefully made sure we never heard the whole of at one time. Then he brought down a dusty box from the storeroom, containing some ancient German glass ornaments that were to be hung on the tree. Duncan handled the twisted glass cascades with such delicacy that Ash said he could put them up, but the box itself also held some deep attraction for him, for he snuffed and sniffed at its ancient smell of its soft wrappings like a dog searching for truffles.

By tradition, on Midwinter's day, the fir tree was brought in from the Wilderness where it normally lived the rest of the year. Myself, Ash and Gillespie manoeuvred it into the living room, setting it up with no end of trouble, since the tree had grown a few inches since the previous year and now scraped the ceiling, so it required a little judicious trimming. Ash stood on a chair and gave it a hair-cut while Gillespie and I positioned it in its pot. Wendy and our last remaining guests who were going home for the holidays helped dress the tree, with Duncan allowed to attach the blown glass ornaments. Gillespie then extinguished the main lights so that the Christmas tree lights could be switched on. I moved swiftly to be beside him, lest the darkness upset him, but Duncan stood swaying in front of the twinkling tree with the glass ornament box pressed to his nose in wonder, making appreciative sounds. He suddenly turned, saw me watching him, and there was the very briefest flash of a grown-up Duncan – but so suddenly gone that I thought I must have imagined it.

As he drank a large mug of tea that Wendy brought, I thought that Duncan looked a good deal improved and said so to Ash when we returned to his study to look over the monthly reports.

He nodded, 'Soon, now, I think. It is a pity that his grandfather cannot see him.'

It is always piquant how the rich depths of Christmas coincide so often with the starkness of necessity. News had arrived earlier that week that the old laird had taken to his bed and wasn't expected to last more than a few days. The family seat of the MacKenzies at Druimnoit was too long a journey for Duncan, we agreed. It was a death that would change his life irrevocably, since his grandfather was like the North Star to both extended family and clan. I secretly wondered what effect this inevitable news would have upon Duncan, not least how his clan would handle the news that their new laird was utterly unable to attend to his duties and responsibilities.

That night, having said goodbye to all our guests except Duncan, we were visited by the Women's Institute carol-singers who bravely trooped up the lane over the ice with their lanterns to serenade us with Good King Wenceslas and Silent Night. We stood in the porch to listen, and then had the whole gaggle of them in for spiced negus and mince-pies. Duncan was rather overwhelmed by so many people at one time and retired to shelter near to the tree as the women sat and chattered or peered at the painting and drawings in the living room. They kindly didn't bother him, as he sat holding onto one of the glass ornaments and sucking his thumb. He didn't come out again until they went away, heavier with funds for the church roof and a hot spiced apple in hand to warm their wanderings.

Now that Jane's arrival was imminent, I had mixed feelings about meeting her again in the company of others. I felt both shy and possessive: while I wanted her to enjoy a traditional Christmas with us, I also wanted to have her all to myself. I had to give myself a good talking to, that some company would help us find how to be together.

The next morning was bright but icy. I took the call from Jane, that she had arrived at Gatwick. She was to take the train to Christminster where I was to collect her from the station, so I set off in a high state of anticipation, allowing far too long to make the journey in my haste to be with her. Amid the parcel-clutching passengers on the station, rising like Venus Anodyomene, with one small case and a backpack, Jane emerged from the bustling throng, pulling her scarf closer about her throat. I took her in my arms and kissed her, knowing in that moment how my unspoken question might be answered, though I still had no idea how things might work out. She nestled into my arms, as I smelt the distinct tea tree and rose perfume of her hair. She shivered, 'I've not been here in the winter before. It doesn't get much colder than this, does it?'

'You'll need a hat,' I said, kissing her on the top of her head, glad that she wasn't wearing one now, so that I could rejoice in the fall of her beautiful hair about her face.

Such was the Christmas traffic, we found ourselves blocked in inside the carpark until an ambulance and police car cleared the station entrance, where there'd been an incident.

'Is it alright?' she asked.

'It is more than alright, now,' I assured her.

She laughed, 'I obviously don't read English expressions at all well, then!' lightly mocking me and smoothing my mouth wider into a smile, before kissing me again. Then in an outrageous Australian parody of her own accent, 'Cheer up, cobber, it might never happen!'

As we drove back at the end of the day, it was clear that the north-facing slopes of the downs would remain white for many days yet, and that the fall of dark would bring an even more severe frost. The temperature gauge in the car read -1C already, and it was only 3.30pm. Sure enough, we woke the next day to frozen pipes in the East Wing and the prospect of an enforced period of rest.

I could not have anticipated the effect of Jane's arrival upon Duncan. He was much put out that I was so often in Jane's company and not his exclusive property. At first, like a jealous toddler, he tried to get in between us, elbowing in. Jane was very good with him, allowing him to sit between us and include him in what we were doing. In a way, it made it easier for us to be together. Wendy had ever so discreetly made up a room for Jane in the nearest of the West

Wing range of guest rooms. But there was no way that I would be visiting her under that roof with everyone speculating whether we were or weren't. Jane had brought her own contribution to the decorations: a set of nesting Russian dolls which she'd picked up at her refuelling stop in Vladivostock. Duncan found them enchanting, particularly liking the second largest doll, stroking its face and then stroking Jane's cheek, holding it up beside her, as if making comparison. There was nothing at all offensive about his behaviour, but I had to check myself to stop him touching her.

The Russian dolls began to unlock something in Duncan, for he began to talk aloud as he played with them, 'Baby doll in the little doll, little doll in the flower doll, flower doll in the rose doll, rose doll in the Jane doll, Jane doll in the mummy doll.' He had never uttered such joined up phrases in our hearing before. Ash and I exchanged looks over his head: it was like watching one of those developmental stages in childhood unfolding.

That night, Ash treated us to a concert on the piano, playing the whole of his new piece, which was a medley of local folk songs, as well as other Christmas music. Duncan usually avoided the room when Ash was playing as he found the piano a rather disturbing beast, but that night he sat with his hand stroking the varnished wood, feeling the vibration with a new attention, I thought. He kept taking his hand away and touching it to his own cheek, 'Bees?' he asked. Placing my own hand on the piano, I experienced what he had been feeling, in the vibration, 'Just like bees,' I said, 'We call it 'music.''

On Christmas Eve morning, I tried to interest Duncan in a game of football on the frosty lawn, but he was more interested in the frost itself, so I left him stroking the box hedges and poking at the iced-over pond in the Wilderness with a stick. He didn't seem to mind the bitter weather. Jane insisted on taking photos of everything for her fellow nurses at home, so we all had to line up and be snapped before the best of the light went from that side of the house. Duncan couldn't be persuaded to pose, so we didn't try and make him. But Ash took a picture of myself and Jane standing in the porch, which I still have on my desk today, catching that extraordinary day for all time.

After soup and a hearty ploughman's lunch, Jane and I walked up to the Iron-Age hill fort together, while Duncan stayed helping Wendy in the kitchen to finish the mince pies. It was really the first time we had had to be together without Duncan intervening. What we said to each other, I cannot now report, but our relationship deepened from that day forward, as we felt our way towards a stronger intimacy. I spoke my fears and uncertainties aloud and she listened with understanding. Yet still I didn't ask her, for that declaration would change everything, and I still didn't know what it was I could offer her if I left the Beacon.

The first stars were coming out by the time we came down again, thoroughly chilled by now. We found Gillespie shining his flashlight up the path for us, standing waiting at the stile as we descended, 'I ken it's frosty enough for you slide down. Are you coming in for your tea?'

'What's happened?' I asked, when I saw his face.

'It's the lad. When he couldnae find you, we had a hard time with him. He had a tantrum and threw things.'

We quickened our steps. Duncan was with Ash, sitting staring into the fire. The atmosphere was tense.

'How are you doing, my friend?' I asked him, throwing off my coat.

The look he flashed me had all the resentment of a cat left to its own devices for a week. He even pointedly curved his shoulder away from me. Meanwhile Jane sat on a low stool and picked up the poker to raise the fire, but he snatched it from her grasp and put it back in the stand. It was clear he had the hump with us both and our best efforts would be of no avail, so he sat like a malevolent imp at the hearth.

Wendy peered into the living room with relief, 'I'll fetch the tea.'

As one household, we attempted to do the regular, familiar things that usually settled Duncan down. Wendy set down a plate with marzipan cakes near to him but he bolted two at once, chewing with his mouth open in a clearly provocative way. I was cursing myself for having left him, but I couldn't see what was different—I had left him for a whole weekend when I'd gone to the conference, after all, and he'd been very glad to see me back without all this palaver.

Ash set down his teacup and went to the piano, nodding at Wendy. This was the signal to bring down the crib which always sat on the round table by the hearth. It was a traditional Austrian crib, with beautifully hand-carved statues. Kneeling down in front of the table, Wendy began to set it up, with the camel, ox and ass, the shepherds and wise-men, while Ash played the piano, giving us a medley on *Es Ist Ein Ros Entsprungen*, 'A spotless Rose is blooming...' Duncan began to calm down, and he crouched down beside Wendy as she placed the Holy Family, unable to be left out of these intriguing proceedings. The crib and the baby were carved of two different pieces and she gave the baby into his hands to place in the crib.

Instead of doing so, he stared at the Christ child in his palm in the strangest way, as if reminding him of something. It lay there with its arms outspread, the counterpart to its mother's clasped hands, as if saving the world at the very moment of the Incarnation. Duncan stroked it all over and then, looking up alarmed, placed his right palm over it, as if sheltering it from danger. We all became very still, as it was obvious that a chain of logical thought was flowing within him. Suddenly, he was on his feet and with a determination that was completely at odds with his usual shuffling gait, he took up the Russian dolls from the sideboard, bringing them back to the fireside.

With intent concentration, he began to dis-case one doll after another, uncaring of where they fell until he reached the smallest one. Picking up the Christ child carefully, he lifted the smallest Russian doll, attempting to open it as the others had done—of course, it would not, as the last enclosed piece wasn't made to open. He wrenched at it with all his strength and still it wouldn't open. I was preparing to stop him becoming violent, since his agitation was growing stronger, but he amazed us all by exclaiming in a clear adult voice, 'It won't open. It *must* open!'

Picking up the Christ child again, his conscious mind struggling to come to terms with the physical impossibility, he tried to insert the baby with its far-flung arms into the smallest Russian doll, 'We must hide it! Quick!' he looked at us, as if we were fools for not understanding.

It was Jane who picked up the two halves of what Duncan called the Jane doll, and extended them, saying, 'I think the baby will go inside the Jane doll. Shall we try it?'

He looked into it, and indeed, the Jane doll was big enough to take the infant with its outstretched arms. Duncan checked that the baby was alright inside and then screwed the two halves of the Russian doll together with great satisfaction. He then stood up abruptly, dropping the Jane doll into Jane's grasp, making towards the door as the marzipan cakes began to force their way back up. Gillespie and I managed to get him to the bathroom in time to vomit up the whole lot.

Suddenly he was shivering and shuddering as if he had emerged from a deep freeze, only he was also sweating profusely. His pulse was pulling and leaping like a cart-horse, as Gillespie drew off his cardigan and wrapped it round Duncan's shoulders. He lurched forward, throwing both of us off and staggered back to the living room. Feeling the walls as he had done when the Christmas decorations were first put up, and rubbing the thick exposed beams in the walls, he burst into the room with its shining Christmas tree and golden fire, looking around it with the eyes of a man coming off a long flight into the arrivals lounge of an airport.

On cue, Ash came forward, with outstretched hand, 'Duncan MacKenzie? I am Dr. Richard Ashington, but you can call me Ash.'

Duncan took his hand, asking, 'Where am I?'

'You are at the Beacon, which is my home on the South Downs, in England. These people are my friends and companions.' Ash retained his hand, which was as well as Duncan swayed uneasily. Ash took his full weight and, with Wendy's help, manoeuvred him to an armchair. Surveying us with surmise and wonder, he asked, 'So I'm not in Basra, then?' His voice and demeanour were those of an adult.

'No indeed!' Ash smiled. 'You are in a safe place, and it's Christmas Eve.'

Duncan looked down at his own, obviously unfamiliar, clothes and back into Ash's face, 'How long have I been back?' He felt the patchwork marks of the skin-grafts on his skin. 'I think I must have been very ill...?'

Ash made a judgement call and said, 'It's been several months since you and your unit were attacked. You survived it...'

Duncan digested this swiftly, '...but they didn't?'

Ash never flinched, 'No. Your grandfather brought you to us, so you could recover and find yourself again.'

It was a lot to process, and we didn't want to go too fast. Within a half hour, Duncan was apprised of what had taken place and what had subsequently happened to him. He looked round at us all, speculatively and a little sheepishly, 'I think you have all been very patient with me?'

We smiled at him, but Gillespie said, 'Ye've been nae bother to us, laddie, but the MacKenzie now....'

Realization opened in him and he pleaded, 'Where can I speak to my grandfather?'

I led him to the phone, lurking nearby in case he had a relapse, and with my fingers crossed that the MacKenzie was *compos mentis* enough to speak with his grandson. It was gift enough for a dying man that Christmas, I thought.

Christmas Day or not, after the pleasantries of waking up with Jane delightfully perched on my bed with a gift in one hand and a cup of tea in the other, Ash and I had our first formal interview with Duncan, to fill in the gaps. He was happy enough to remain under our care for a week to ensure that he was in working order, but he was keen to return home to Driumnoit and see his grandfather and the rest of the family.

I remember that Christmas as a blessed time, not only that Jane was with me, but that we had welcomed back a wanderer from exile. Duncan joined in the fun and even pulled a cracker. Just a split second before, realizing that even such a small explosion might trigger a larger reaction, I was signalling to Ash as Duncan pulled a cracker with Wendy. At sight of my anxiety, Duncan fell back in exaggeration, as if the cracker had indeed been a landmine, then winked. And so a potentially nasty moment passed.

After an immense spread, as we were all lying around the roaring fire that was half-way up the chimney, Duncan told us that it was the smells, the sounds and tastes of Christmas that had begun to unlock things for him. I remembered him snuffling at the box of glass ornaments, redolent of the pine resin paper they'd been wrapped in. 'Even the winter cold helped. — They don't have much ice or frost in Iraq,' he observed. 'I think it reminded me of home.'

Later, peering out at the twilight sky, as he drew the curtains, Gillespie solemnly informed us, in the tones of an ancient Highland seer, 'If yon sky's anything to tell us, it'll be a gae long round of turkey dinners we'll be having the week.'

'Wendy's bought enough food to feed an army,' I pointed out. But, sure enough, the snow started in the small hours and Boxing Day morning saw us thoroughly snowed in. We all went out to clear, with brooms and shovels, so that there was at least the beginning of a path between us and the end of the lane — which would clearly remain blocked for some time. Jane was so entranced by the excessive drifts of snow that she couldn't be made to be useful at all, 'If this comes only once a year, I'm going to enjoy while I can,' she determined, even climbing to the top of a bank and rolling down it until her clothes were saturated with snow, and she had to be shooed inside to change, 'It's so utterly lovely,' she sighed, in contentment, her cheeks red as one of the Russian dolls, her skin reflecting the cherry jacket that she wore. With her breath coming in great clouds, framed by the flint-faced walls and white, silent downs, she earned a long kiss as I sent her in.

When I turned back to the shovelling, Ash was standing very quietly, his eyes following as Jane went inside and then, markedly, back to me. The grey streaks that had come into his temples over the last years, made a startling contrast with the darkness of his hair against the pristine snow. In that still moment, it was as if I, too, was seeing him for the first time, just as I knew Jane and I had been seen. A sudden anxiety sprang up in me, which I covered by throwing a snowball at Wendy, only to have Gillespie pour a shovelful of snow over my head, so that it went down my neck in a chill shower, and the moment passed.

On the 30th December word came that Grahaeme MacKenzie was dead and our Duncan had become the MacKenzie of Gilliebhride.

'How had we best tell him?' I mused.

Ash said, 'Go and get Duncan, tell him to come to the sanctuary.'

In the formal setting of the sanctuary, he took it well, all considered, for he'd known how things stood at home.

Leading Duncan before the eternal flame, Ash took from the side table the box that the MacKenzie had left for him. The spotlight flamed suddenly upon its metal bands as he turned, so I knew that they were of ancient silver, 'Your grandfather asked me to deliver this to you. I think he knew that you and he would not meet again, for he was very ill when he brought you. His forethought means that it falls to me to pass it from his hands to yours, if you will take it.'

Duncan squared up as he would have done on parade. His eyes flicked between the box and Ash, 'I will take it.'

'Do you remember the formula?' Ash demanded.

He nodded, saying in more formal tones, the words of an old ritual, 'As the MacKenzie of Ardnafinn, as the Gilliebhride, I request my inheritance.' He held out both his hands.

Ash responded, his voice shining as steel, 'As the approved tanaiste, you have the right, but I am authorized to give these holy things only into the hands of the one who will swear the oath.'

'I will swear it.'

'Place your right hand upon the shrine.'

It was then that I realized the nature of the box, for I had seen its like in an exhibition: a saint's *cathach*, I think they called it, a reliquary that was borne into battle or carried in procession before its people. That was why it had two such huge metal rounds — to attach to a pole that would have borne horizontally between the shoulders of two men.

Duncan placed his hand upon the shrine, 'I swear upon the relics of St. Bride, that I will be a faithful Gillie Bhridhe from this day forward until the ending of my life. I vow to kindle the fire and smoor it as my forefathers and mothers have done, in the way that I have been taught. And before the ending of my life, I swear to teach the way of the fire to the one who will succeed me as tanaiste. In the name of the Three who were and are and will be, I so swear!'

Ash put the shrine into his hands, and then blessing him, said, 'Into your hands I deliver the shrine! May the blessing of St. Bride rest upon you and upon your successors forever!'

Over coffee afterwards, Duncan explained, 'The MacKenzies were the hereditary coarbs or successors, of St. Brighid's monastery at Ardnafinn from early times. Of course, that institution came to an end at the Reformation, there's only ruins there now, but the title fell to the Ardnafinn MacKenzies and it's from them that I descend.'

'And the name "Gillie Bhride?"'

'It means "the Servant of Bride," the saint of the perpetual fires of Kildare, whose nuns came to Scotland in the wake of Columba. It is we who kindle the fire before any major event—as you've seen, for I think I showed you?'

So that was why the bonfires of that autumn had been so professionally laid!

We saw Duncan off later that day, since Farmer Jelley had finally responded to our pleas to bring his snow-plough up our lane. It had been a wicked week for beasts lost in the drifts, and he had enough to do, God knows. Duncan had been one of our longest staying guests and his absence was soon overtaken by new cases, but we did not forget him. The thaw came quickly after that, and when more green than white painted the Downs, it was time for Jane to also go homeward.

I dithered like a fool right up until the night before and then, in the Wilderness where we'd gone out to look up at a fine half-moon and the circumpolar magnificence of the stars, I finally asked her the long-awaited question, presenting her with the facetted diamond ring that I had been keeping for this moment, 'I don't know how things will work out, I don't even know what I'm offering you, as I'm not a prophet like Ash, but I know I love you and will forever.'

She took the ring and put it on her finger, 'It's like a star itself,' and hugged me. 'The practical bits will take care of themselves, Jack. We just have to decide whether it'll be lived at my end or at yours?'

I stared into her eyes, 'I don't know. We both have skills that will travel. Can you wait a little while while we work something out?'

We kissed.

'As long as it's not for too long, Jack!'

The winter lengthened into a testing February, the shortest month made longer by the absence of Jane who'd gone back to her beloved Northern Territory. Ash's work-load seemed to suddenly increase and he was more often up in Harley St. than he was at the Beacon, so much of the work was falling upon me. I had the sense that he was more withdrawn or preoccupied with something. A series of long embossed envelopes arrived from a firm of solicitors in Christminster. He was so much occupied that it fell to me to deal with the night-staff and relief rotas, and to interview a couple of auxiliary staff for a difficult case that had arrived, 'I trust your judgement, Jack. Do what you think is best for our guest,' he'd said.

T.S. Eliot called April the 'cruellest month,' but it is assuredly February that should bear that title. In that bleak time, several people known to me, both friends and distant relations died—these were expected deaths, from extreme age and illness, but no less mourned for all that. February is a departure month for many, with the hope of the New Year over and the first proofs of spring still to come, many slip away then. So it was with the greatest possible pain that we heard of the sudden death of Duncan.

He had gone home, attended his grandfather's funeral, and set about the business of withdrawing from the army, having decided that he would turn his hand to estate management as the best way to support his clan and the inheritance he had entered into. However, the Scots Guards required him to go out to the Middle East one more time, to be part of diplomatic meetings that were taking place. Within a day of his arrival, he was hit by a sniper and died instantly.

It was not the first time that one of our guests had died, of course, but this death, following so many others, struck me hard. Ash and I spoke on the phone about it, but a sense of unreality remained with me. Ash's perspective on this death was, as ever, a much longer one than mine: 'He found himself again, and that is good. When he comes again, it will be as a whole man and a great leader.' It was little consolation to hear his prophecies. I could only think about the amount of care and healing we had given, and the terrible waste of a young life.

By mid-February, with all the promise of St. Valentines but none of its joys, I was waiting anxiously for Ash to come back to the Beacon. Jane and I had finally started to talk about how things might be after we were married, but I could give her no satisfactory answers, and her irritation at my procrastination had resulted in a long silence that ached between us.

Finally, on a day of clear blue sky and icy wind, Ash drew up outside and I went out to help him in with his luggage. He was tired beyond measure, but would only say, to my anxious enquiry, 'Just London, Jack, that's all!' He turned to regard the line of the Downs. 'This makes everything better.'

He sat down to dinner with us all, hearing the minutiae of the household, and asking about two new guests who had joined us but, as usual, saying little about himself. I tried to learn what had kept him up in town so long, but he would only say, 'Tomorrow, I think.' And I sensed a reluctance in him to broach things with me.

I spent most of the night fearing that I had offended in some particular way from his procedures, but could locate nothing wrong on my part. So that when, after breakfast, he asked me to his study, I experienced a mixture of trepidation and anticipation.

When I came into the room, he was sunk contemplatively in his chair, swathed round with a white cashmere wrap against the cold. As his face flashed open to greet me, I dismissed all my fears and uncertainties, determined to grasp the nettle, but he surprised me first.

'I have decided to make a long retreat,' he informed me.

I must have looked bemused, I suppose, 'What? — Where? For how long?'

He chuckled, 'You never disappoint, Jack. Straight to the point, as always! It's a silent retreat in a hermitage in the mountains of Nepal. I shall be alone in a cave, though the monks of the local Buddhist monastery will be supporting me. I will be gone at least three years.'

I was rendered speechless by this revelation and had to sit down. It seemed to me such an appalling prospect — isolation, silence and exile all at the same time! Then I woke up to the reality, 'But what will happen to this place?'

'You will run it with your wife and whoever you deem suitable.'

I was aghast at the thought, 'But, I'm not you. Everyone wants *you*. I'm just your... understudy. Anyway, how do you know I'll marry Jane?' I asked.

'Oh, I think I know,' he smiled his impossible smile.

As the ground was disappearing from under my feet, he said, 'There's another thing. It was forwarded by the executors of Duncan's will.' Ash got up and took something from his desk. He handed me a thin, sealed envelope with my name written upon it. It contained one sheet in Duncan's handwriting. I took it to the window to read:

'My dear friend and brother,

I trust I can call you so. In you, I have seen and recognized a nobility of soul that no-one of the remaining MacKenzies possesses. Rather than that the sacred task fall into neglect or dishonour, I am leaving you the tools of the Gillie Bhríde, for I am the Last of Bride's servants and have no heir to follow me. Use it as I have shown you and pass it only to one who is worthy. Although I cannot appoint you officially as my tanaiste, yet I can appoint you as my successor, for I have shown you the way.'

I passed the letter to Ash, swallowing hard on the mixture of tears and pride that welled inside me. The honour that he had done me was past speaking of. With the letter came a communication from the secretary of the Clan of the Ardnafinn MacKenzies, with a request that I fulfil the annual requirement for the kindling of fire upon the altar stone of Ardnafinn every 31 January. Apparently, this flame was kept alight all year in the ancestral house at

Druimnoit, being also borne in procession at the Highland Games in August. The relic box, the secretary explained, had to remain at Druimnoit Caslte for insurance purposes.

'But they sent this too!' Ash passed to me a small wooden box. It was a miniature version of the reliquary, with a tinderbox with its flint, knife and a little shammy bag full of dry shavings.

Ash gleamed up at me, 'Now you'll have to get married. Duncan was the last of Bride's servants, but you are the first of another line — the Flame Keepers — and with this flint and knife, you'll summon the fires back and watch them, and teach your child to do the same.'

'Now hang on, Jane and I haven't even discussed having children.'

With his usual gnomic prophecy, he said, 'I daresay they will come, nonetheless.'

I was being pulled in two, 'But how.....?'

Ash put one hand on my shoulder, 'I've seen how you struggled to work things out for the best between Jane and your work at the Beacon... My dear friend, you belong here, and you can make this your home with Jane here for as long as you like.'

'But you engaged me precisely because I had no relationship!' I cried, recalling the day vividly, and how non-politically correct it had sounded to my ears.

He nodded, 'That was then. I needed to train you up, without distractions, and you've given your love and care to all who've come here. Everyone you've treated warmly remembers you. You are like an uncle or a father or a brother to them all.'

I let the unshed tears fall and clutched his shoulders, with both hands, half shaking him, 'But how will we manage without you? I don't have the magical skills or charms or the second sight, for God's sake. However will we manage?'

'You'll manage exactly the same you always did, only now you'll have to listen harder to your very fine instincts and be guided by your oversight.' He continued, 'I'm relying on you to keep the Beacon aflame, and with Duncan's gift you'll do it well.' He let go of me gently and turned to gaze up at the bare eminence of Hartworth Beacon, stark now in this leafless month, 'When Melanie took this house, she swore an oath on Hartwell Beacon that it would be a sanctuary for those who need a deeper healing. Now you will be its continuance...'

Inexorably, Ash outlined how it would be, though I barely heeded his words. I kept stopping him to ask, 'But you will be coming back?' havering between, 'How can you go?' and 'What will become of me?' Finally, he wore me down until I asked, 'But *why* do you have to go? I didn't think you were a Buddhist!'

He stopped me with, 'My soul needs me to go.... It is a dedication that I owe.'

A suspicion gripped me, 'You're not ill are you?'

He shook his head, 'No, just tired. I need time to refuel and return to myself.'

And he would say nothing more about it, nor about his return.

I see now that I must have entered into a kind of pre-bereavement—the kind you see in people who know they are going to die of their condition, or lose their spouse to illness, or have a limb amputated; they start to bid farewell to all that they have held dear even before the event happens. The weight of the thought of his passing, the burden of running the Beacon, and a sense of my own worthless incompetence were keeping me wakeful most nights. I somehow believed that Ash wouldn't—couldn't—go away without making sure that I was on a more even keel than at present. But the dreaded day was speeding ever closer. As my being grew heavier with fear, so Ash himself grew lighter. His warm baritone could be heard singing all over the Beacon as he went about his preparations. He was more like a man going on holiday than on a long spiritual retreat, unburdening himself even as the weight fell heavier upon me.

Wendy and Gillespie had taken the whole thing a lot better than I. They were content to remain, to support me and, though they were sad about the impending departure, they had always known that Ash would go one day. After a particularly gruelling afternoon in which he signed over the deeds to the Beacon to me, witnessed by Wendy and Gillespie and the solicitor from Christminster, the reality of the change became too much. The realization of my predicament, the fact that Ash was really going away, that I would be alone, were like horrible overlays on my mind that now fused together.

'Why are you leaving it to me? Don't you mean to ever come back?' I pleaded for the hundredth time.

'It is a long period that I shall be away. If there are any matters arising, you will have to bear the responsibility. Besides, I am like Duncan, I have no heirs or others to whom I would care to leave the Beacon. Melanie was clear about that—she left it to me, who was no son to her, just I leave it to you. You know how we do things here, the nature of the welcome we offer... You will keep faith with our work.' His certainty did not feel deserved.

Gillespie was the one who found me in the back snug of the White Hart over at Borhunt, well-laced with spirits and sodden with melancholy. Apparently, he had exhausted every other pub in the region before discovering me, and his ire was well roused. He somehow walked me through the streets and, when I fell down near the Roman well, he was the one who pushed my face deeper into the cold waters, dried me off with his scarf and hauled me back to the van.

'Sorry for yourself, are ye? — Well, I tell you, laddie, *yeou...*' he stuck his hairy forefinger into my chest... 'are going to be the backbone of the Beacon, just as Ash was, and just as Melanie was before him, God bless her!' Through my mazy stupor, I remember he treated me to his most dreich and disgusted look, usually reserved for daft politicians, his pom-pom on his tartan tammy shaking, 'But for tonight, you're going to spend the night in the summer house, winter night or not. You're not fit for a bed. I've seen dogs in better fettle...'

I vaguely remember tottering down to the Wilderness, hoisted under Gillespie's oxter, and being laid down on the bench, with my head carefully positioned over a bucket. Which is where I awoke very early the next morning, nearly frozen stiff, to find a very insistent Cinnamon pawing my eyelids open. From that day, till several years later, Ash's cat attached herself to me and me alone. Whether Ash had stage-managed this by some strange esoteric means or whether her feline brain had worked out who was now the main provider of service, I don't know. But from that moment, I became her person.

Jane was coming to stay for a few weeks, before Ash's departure, to help cover the gap that was opening in my life. Like a man under sentence of death, I received her from the station.

'Where's the funeral, Jack?' her cheery Australian greeting echoed down the platform as the train sailed to a standstill.

I attempted a haggard smile at the vision of loveliness she presented, stepping down from the carriage with a swing, in a coral coloured tunic, entirely at odds with the bitter season, and standing out against in the dourly dressed crowds of winter, like a technicolour woman in a black and white film, 'You look like the Great Barrier Reef in person, my love!'

'Then I better watch out for barracudas!' She looked into my face with a knowing expression, shaking her head, 'No, don't try that smile anymore, Jack, — it's not working!' she advised with her usual frankness, sliding her arm through mine and hugging it hard.

Having Jane with me should have helped: her solid support and funny turns of phrase, her simple cheerfulness and imperturbability in the face of all odds, gave me the courage to keep my spine straight and solider on. As it was, all was not well with me.

The week that Ash was due to leave, the equinoctial winds blew steadily from the west sou' west, lambasting the Beacon. Yet the old house withstood it, until one night. I was awakened that night by an urgent Cinnamon, who had moved from pressing a paw under my chin to hooking open my eyelid with a gentle claw, finally needling my scalp with a less gentle call to awake when I tried to ignore her. Cursing her, I flung out of bed, only to hear the tinkle of glass. Immediately alert, I padded cautiously downstairs, lest we were being visited by burglars but I could detect no intruder. Throughout the house, a shimmering atmosphere hung still. It was rather that the wind was heaving at every entry, making the hallway into a wind tunnel. More glass splintered, and I immediately located its source as the porch.

I had to physically hold the inner door back by my bodyweight, for it was if some immense force was trying to gain entry to the house. There, behind Melanie's shrine, the casement had been forced open by the insistent wind. A fierce, uncaring tendril of creeper had pushed Melanie's picture forward, and now lay in the porch amid a soggy shower of shards, since the bowl of snowdrops had also gone over. Fortunately, the sanctum light itsef had gone out when it had fallen.

It felt like the last straw.

I tramped off to the kitchen to get the dustpan and brush to sweep it up, superstitiously lamenting that the shrine should be so damaged on my hand-over watch. I gently brushed the remaining glass out of the frame with the side of my thumb, only to catch a long shard in the quick of my nail. A bead of blood welled up and, before I could stop it, fell upon the unprotected photo. I cursed again.

Dealing clumsily and one-handedly with my injury, I drew out the shard and wrapped a sticking plaster around my thumb to stem the flow. The photo looked beyond redemption to me, as I used a piece of cotton wool to remove my blood from Melanie's image. Her constant, calm gaze continued to regard me. Feeling ashamed, I realized that the least I could do would be to close up the casement, which I finally did with a twist of insulating wire from Gillespie's shed, and to rekindle the light. I was about to search for matches when I remembered Duncan's gift, becoming suddenly gripped with the idea of kindling the flame in a more traditional fashion.

Placing the sanctum light on the hall table, I cleaned the wick, making it stand tall again, and fetched the steel platter from the dresser, on which I spread my tools. I also fetched a long taper from the hearth, which was used to light the fire. Using the kindling, the knife and flint, I raised a flame on the platter, and set the taper into it before the flame died. I was about to light the sanctum light, when I knew I must follow Duncan's example, and so I prayed aloud, 'I'm lighting this flame in the name of the Three who were and are and will be. I'm lighting this flame in the name of Bride...' remembering the image upon the sanctuary walls upstairs, I added, 'and in the name of Raphael, that the healing may continue and the welcome be true...'

The most extraordinary sense of being supported came upon me, as the house shook and protested under the assault of the winds. Many, whose hands had done just what I was doing, kindling the flame, stood behind me and held me in the warmth of their regard. The help that I had so vehemently fought against, in my attempt to deal with Ash's departure, was suddenly present, flowing into me. My mind flashed open with the revelation that all I had to do was not struggle to be in control, but to hold the situation lightly, merging back into the spirit of this blessed house as my chief support. Behind Melanie, behind the painted angel Raphael, behind even the spirit of the house, or the Beacon itself, stood a long line of those who knew what I knew now, and I was a part of them, as well as of something much greater. Strength and certainty returned to me.

I lifted the sanctum light high, illuminating the hallway and the stairs, 'May the welcome of this sanctuary be perpetual...' I found myself saying.

'So be it!' Ash answered from the stairs where he stood watching me.

I jumped, 'Goodness, Ash! You move like a cat.'

He came out of the shadows into the pool of light, 'Sorry, but I heard someone moving around and I came down to see if one of our guests needed help.' His eye fell upon the photo, so I showed him the damage that the wind and my clumsiness had wrought, 'I can't get the blood off the photo, Ash. I'm so sorry.'

He took it from me, and what he said was odd, 'You can have another made, don't worry. The negatives are upstairs in my desk—you'll find them.'

He examined my thumb with a professional eye, 'No going back now, Jack, not now you've committed yourself with blood!' His eyes caressed the photo, and its steadfast gaze looked back trustfully at us both, 'I was wondering when Melanie would touch you....' he said wonderingly.

'She nearly left it a bit late,' I said.

He looked into and around me with one of his assessing glances, 'But not too late...?' he enquired.

'No...I'm ready now.' The certainty in my voice surprised me, but it was truly so.

Then I saw that Ash was fully dressed and that there was a backpack on the stairs, and I realized, 'You're going *now*? Now, in the dark? Without saying goodbye....'

'You and the McLains have been saying goodbye to me so much these last weeks, that part of me has already gone, Jack. The time has come for the rest of me to depart.'

'You won't write?'

His grey eyes widened in amusement, 'You know that I won't. The postal service doesn't run to hermetic Nepalese caves, you know.'

I gripped his hand, saying, 'You are the lowest, most despicable coward I ever knew, and I love you like a brother, you infuriating man! You didn't even know that I would step up... My God — you were ready to go without knowing that for certain...' And his audacity just took my breath away.

'Oh, I was certain,' he assured me.

I helped him out to the car with his meagre belongings in the pre-dawn chill of that early March morning, and waved as he drove off. My chest and shoulders kept still the clasp of his embrace, even as my heart was breaking.

The wind had dropped, finally. The line of the Downs stretched silently as the fore-light of dawn silhouetted them with a greenish-blue glow, and Cinnamon came out to weave around my feet, begging for breakfast.

'We haven't forgotten you,' I said.

About the Author:

Caitlín Matthews is the author of *Celtic Love: Ten Enchanting Tales*, *Psychic Protection Handbook* (*Psychic Shield* in US) and *Singing the Soul Back Home*, as well as many other titles. She has an international reputation in the metaphysical field as a writer, teacher and shamanic practitioner. She lives in Oxford, with her partner, the writer, John Matthews.

www.hallowquest.org.uk

About the Publisher:

Starseed Books is an imprint of Lorian Press LLC. Starseed Books specializes in fiction but also publishes biographies, books for the Ancient Order of Druids in America and other material.

Starseed Books
Attn: Jeremy Berg
6592 Peninsula Dr
Traverse City, MI 49686

www.lorianpress.com

[handwritten notes]

Title Number.
LT 199178
8 A1. application.
10 Sept deed.
AS1 probate
copy fee.

Lightning Source UK Ltd.
Milton Keynes UK
UKOW04f045020218
317246UK00001B/58/P

9 781939 790161